A VERY DEADLY SIN

Denis Brookes

A Justin Parkes Thriller

FOREWORD

I should like to thank all those who made the writing of this book possible. To my wife, Jane, for her unceasing encouragement. To the panel of volunteer readers who gave me favourable reviews of the manuscript. Also my thanks to my daughter, Nicola, for her technical advice on police matters. I must also give a blanket thank you to everyone who has played a part in my life experience and training and a similar apology to all those who I have offended whether intentionally or unintentionally.

Last, but in no way least, may I express my gratitude to my good friend, John Galloway, for the art work of the paperback cover and for his generosity in giving me a replacement computer when mine developed a terminal illness.

CHAPTER 1

The digging was fairly easy. The soil around Pontesbury in Shropshire appeared to be from an ancient seabed, as there were accretions of shells and the occasional fossils, which fortunately broke easily under the blows of a pickaxe, and could be shovelled out along with the soil onto the spoil heap which lay to one side. Justin Parkes had been a self-employed grave digger for over a year and liked the freedom it gave him after many years of taking orders in other jobs - although there were times in the winter when icy winds blew and rain lashed down when he wanted to be somewhere warm and dry. Anyway, today was a warm and sunny day in early August with the birds singing in the trees around the burial ground and he felt at ease with the world.

He knew from grisly familiarity when reopening double graves, when he was getting near to the coffin which had been lowered in place many years ago when, without warning, his feet broke through the rotten, crumbling lid exposing the putrefying remains inside and releasing the cloying stench of death and decay. Despite his past experience, he gave a start as he saw, staring at him, out of the rotted flesh of a skull with its rictus of white teeth, one bright blue eye in startling contrast to the dark adjacent empty socket, surrounded by pieces of mummified skin and tendrils of grey hair. He was used to bodies in all stages of decomposition but this was the first time he had came across someone with a false eye. Recovering himself, he stamped the top of the rotten coffin as flat as he could, climbed out of the grave, shovelled soil back in from the spoil heap until he had enough to cover the remains, then eased himself back into the hole to level the floor and make it presentable for the next coffin.

Justin possessed a cheerful and outgoing personality which made him easy company and popular with his peers. Standing six feet tall with broad shoulders and well-honed muscles he felt that for a 42 year-old he was wearing well. His clean-shaven face and wide mouth, which portrayed an easy innocence, along with his fair hair and blue eyes, was one that attracted women. Justin, it has to be said, was equally attracted to women and had enjoyed many girlfriends over the years, but he had difficulty in maintaining a relationship and, shamefully, would break hearts as easily as he courted them. It wasn't that he was unkind to his conquests in his everyday conduct. In fact quite the opposite, as in many ways he was a caring friend and accomplished lover. It was just that once he saw signs that his girlfriends were getting serious and wanted to settle down he dropped them like a stone. He didn't feel good about it at the time but managed to balance it against the great sense of relief he felt upon regaining his freedom. Justin sometimes wondered whether his father deserting the family home when he was nine years old had a bearing on his inability to trust and stopped him committing to a relationship.

Justin had been born into a comfortably well-off middle class family who were able to send him to a private preparatory school in his home town of Shrewsbury, which prepared young gentlemen for the entrance exam for Shrewsbury Public School. But despite the best endeavours of long-suffering masters, Justin resisted all their efforts to impart knowledge and determinedly maintained this mindset until taken away at the age of ten as a result of his parents' marriage break down and eventual divorce. Occasionally Justin would cast his mind back to his time at school but generally didn't dwell on what was for him an unsavoury and unnecessary waste of time. Despite his stalled academic progress, Justin did possess a keen and intelligent mind and later, as a mature student at a Shrewsbury college of further education, he decided to apply himself to his studies and managed to obtain six good GCSE passes.

But as well as breaking hearts, Justin had another flaw. He skipped through life trying to avoid any responsibility. Treating life in a superficial manner, he was unable to settle in a job for any length of time. Something made him seek other pastures, new experiences, fresh challenges. He would start a new job with great enthusiasm but after a time become bored with the stifling routine and would leave. Or perhaps it was someone else's fault that he couldn't settle. Sometimes he wondered what he actually wanted to do in life but was never able to find an answer. He smiled inwardly at the wit who wrote that, whilst a rolling stone gathers no moss, it can achieve a certain polish. Justin liked that as he considered that his past experiences in life had given him a definite sheen.

He broke off from his labour to drink thirstily from a bottle of water he had placed at the side of the grave, when he became aware that he was being watched. He lowered the bottle and turned to see a stocky boy of about ten years of age had quietly walked up behind him. The boy was silent and Justin noticed he his face had a sorrowful look. He didn't speak, so Justin felt he had better break the silence.

"Hello, young man," he offered "what are you up to then?"

The boy was silent for a moment. "My Granddad's in there," he said, pointing at the open grave. "He died when I was two. I can't remember much about him." He hesitated for a moment before continuing. "He had a glass eye. Nan said he used to take it out at night after he'd turned out the light and put it on a saucer."

Justin decided that he wouldn't add his recent experience to the glass eye information, and after being asked who the grave was for, told the boy that he was preparing the grave for Elsie Jones with her funeral being at 10.30 the next day. The boy took a deep breath.

"I thought it was," he told Justin with a catch in his breath, "it's for my Nan." He paused. "I didn't think she was going to die. The doctor said it was her heart."

"I'm very sorry," said Justin with true feeling. Having lost his mother some years before, he had an understanding of the pain caused by bereavement.

There was a pause, then the boy asked.

"Will the coffin hurt my Nan?"

Justin was puzzled by the question but studying the youngster's face, and realising he was sincere, told him that she would feel no pain in her coffin and gently asked what he meant.

"Well," said the youngster, "yesterday my Dad and my Uncle Norman were looking at the bill from the undertaker and my Dad said: *'blimey, Norm, just look at that coffin, they don't half sting you!'*"

Justin managed to keep a smile from his face as he explained what the expression meant and, after a few more exchanges, a visibly relieved boy said goodbye and wandered off and out of sight.

Justin's thoughts went back to the time when he was digging another double at Leighton just outside Shrewsbury. A youngster appeared at the side of the grave and, after a few heartfelt sighs, informed Justin with great sincerity that he had always wanted to stand in a grave. Wanting to assist the boy in one of his life's ambition, Justin propped a ladder in place against the head of the grave. The boy clambered down, looked around in awe and finally departed hopefully, thought Justin, having become a more rounded character after his uplifting experience.

What was it, mused Justin that made people of all ages want to look into holes in the ground – especially graves? Possibly, aware of their mortality, they wanted to see what was in store for them? He didn't know what they expected to see. Perhaps a mouldering corpse. He recalled on two other occasions at burial grounds at Montgomery and Adderley he had dug where instructed and in each place uncovered in the dry sandy earth skeletal remains wrapped only in a rotting shroud. He assumed that they were pauper burials from long ago, without the money for coffins and headstones, and therefore not entered in the parish register. He decided not to tell the church wardens of the unexpected finds as it would involve filling in and digging another grave. Removing the bones and pieces of shroud, he dug another small hole in the floor of each of the graves, placed the sorry remains in them, and covered them so nothing could be seen. He wasn't sure of the legality of his actions, but felt he had made the best of a difficult situation.

As Justin continued working on the grave he was digging, he mused on the events which led him to his current occupation. After leaving the Army having completed six years' service as a vehicle mechanic, he had drifted in and out of various unskilled jobs until he had seen a

Shrewsbury firm of undertakers were advertising for driver/bearers. He applied, was called in and, his interview being successful and his driving skills tested in a limousine and found acceptable, was told to start the following day. His boss, William Percival of Percival and Son, who was himself the son of the founder of the firm, presented a well-rounded, pin-striped, avuncular presence with the ability to glide silently around – all necessary attributes when dealing with the bereaved. He had a highly-coloured florid face, which was an indication of the blood pressure problem that medication could control but not cure and which, eventually, would ensure that whilst in his early fifties, after succumbing to a heart attack, he made the smooth transition from proprietor to client.

But all that was in the future. Justin found the work at the undertakers varied and his workmates easy company. He was expected along with his driving and bearer duties to deal with the corpses, dress them ready for viewing and, on occasions, help the embalmer with his macabre tasks. Justin liked Tom Gollins the embalmer. Tom was a tiny, desiccated man of some seventy years whose waxy, tightly drawn skin over his facial bones and claw-like hands gave the impression he had tried embalming himself before practising it on the cadavers. But what Justin liked about him was his nonchalant approach to these somewhat unpleasant tasks, happily chatting away as he pumped the blood out of veins and injected embalming fluid to preserve the tissues. Justin would watch with admiration when Tom had to close a gaping mouth before a body was presentable for viewing. Taking a large curved suture needle with strong thread, he would pass it through the frenum behind the top and bottom lips, pull it tight and knot it. The result was nicely closed lips which Tom would then massage into a gentle upward curve, thus giving the deceased a slightly self-satisfied look.

Other tasks involved moving bodies around and Justin recalled with horror a spectacular mistake on his part which should have earned him immediate dismissal. One cold November day he had been told by Mr. Percival to take a coffin with deceased to their Telford branch which was dealing with the funeral. He drove over alone that afternoon and, owing to lack of space in the yard, he parked the hearse on the road at the rear of the premises.

Going inside Justin found that there was nobody available to assist in unloading the coffin but decided he would manage alone. Although forbidden to do so, he felt comfortable with the procedure as he had managed a solo unload on numerous occasions. This time it went catastrophically wrong. He placed the wheeled bier at the back of the hearse and drew the coffin down onto it. As he did so the end of the bier nearest the hearse deck rose up, as expected, with the weight of the coffin at the other end. Normally this posed no problem, but this time, unbeknown to Justin, a wheel dropped out of the raised end. When he drew the coffin fully onto the bier it tipped to one side and, despite his best efforts to keep the bier upright, saw in slow motion horror the coffin and its occupant crashing onto the road.

Even worse was to follow. The lid tore free from the coffin and the body of this unfortunate elderly female rolled onto the road on her side and, as the shroud only covered the front of the body, she lay there face down with her naked nether regions on flagrant display. Knowing from past experience he would be unable to put the body back, Justin ran into the funeral directors office and in a low urgent voice said,

"EMERGENCY! Don't ask questions, just come with me."

The director, knowing a state of raw panic when he saw it, immediately cut the phone call he was on and they ran to the scene of the catastrophe just as a school girl was passing, who either appeared not to notice, or was in a state of such profound shock she had blanked the image from her consciousness. With some difficulty they rolled the lifeless form into the coffin and, after replacing the lid as best they could, together picked up the coffin and scuttled awkwardly across the yard and into the building. Fortunately there was a workshop there with a carpenter who was able to expertly repair the damage to the lid. It was greatly in Justin's favour that he and the director had forged a friendly working relationship. Even so, he had to rightly take on the chin a strongly worded dressing down with the merciful conclusion that nothing more would be said about the matter. Justin realised that had he been reported to Mr. Percival he would have been beating a path to the job centre. Not that it would have been a great problem, but just that he wasn't ready to move at at that time. What Justin didn't know was that the horror of this incident was soon to be eclipsed by an evil which he was unable to resist and which would remove him from his carefree existence and take him down into a dark pit of terror and pain.

Justin recalled the circumstances which did eventually lead him to leave the employ of Mr. Percival. Although his appearance was avuncular, Mr. Percival was quite irascible underneath this cool professional exterior and on occasions, when things were not to his satisfaction, give the very real impression of a controlled explosion. On this occasion Justin had been instructed to drive to Glasgow and pick up a body from a Greenock undertaker. He had taken the firm's Ford Transit van containing a fibreglass coffin, called a shell, with a shroud to cover it all, and departed in high spirits expecting to be there and back within the day.

But the journey was anything but straightforward. After an uneventful hour into the journey the traffic started to back up until, just north of Warrington, all three lanes ground to a halt with traffic nose to tail as far as he could see. As Justin waited, the sound of emergency sirens, the flashing of blue light and the procession of emergency vehicles speeding up the hard shoulder, indicated a serious accident ahead. It was no surprise to him that it took four hours for the wreckage to be cleared before the police opened just one of the lanes. Before the traffic started to move Justin was able to text Mr. Percival to inform him of the long delay.

Fortunately the remainder of the journey passed without incident and finally, when Justin arrived at the funeral parlour the undertaker's wife gave him the unwelcome news that as Justin was late her husband had been called out and would be back when he had finished dealing with a bereaved family. As the undertaker was the only person who could release the body, Justin had to wait until he arrived back some two hours later, just in time to hit the evening rush hour. Fed up after crawling his way out of Glasgow, Justin decided to drive as far as Carlisle and book into a B&B for the night. He phoned the office to tell them that he was too tired to drive any further that evening. He was unable to talk with Mr. Percival as he was out on business, but spoke with the General Manager who told Justin he thought should be all right by him but wasn't sure what Mr. Percival would say.

The following morning, fully refreshed after a fortifying full English breakfast, he motored back to Shrewsbury and upon reporting in to the office was met with an incandescent Mr. Percival who asked where the bloody hell he had been and why he had left a body unattended all night in the van. Initially, somewhat taken aback, Justin soon recovered and very quickly a furious barrage of claim, counter-claim and a few personal remarks erupted into a shouting match which only stopped when the General Manager, upon hearing the row, emerged from his office and managed to bring about a sort of truce. As neither party was prepared to admit unconditional surrender Justin decided that, although not fired, his position was untenable and resolved to move on as soon as possible. Then a stroke of luck came his way.

The self-employed grave digger who Mr. Percival used, along with other undertakers, had decided to retire. Justin heard of this and went to see him to get tips on how to go about things. After meeting and being taken to a dig and shown the procedures, he decided that it would be a convenient way out of a strained situation and spoke with the General Manager to see whether he would use his services as a self-employed grave digger. After discussing the matter with Mr. Percival it was agreed that they would, and a relieved Mr. Percival was able to kill two birds with one stone by getting rid of an employee who had the temerity to answer back and at the same time having someone to dig his clients' graves.

As these reminiscences went through Justin's mind he patted down the last of the loose soil he had spread over the floor of the grave and looked with quiet satisfaction at the smooth-sided coffin-shaped double grave he had dug. He placed the shovel and pickaxe at the side out and climbed out using the short ladder he had left at the grave side. Continuing with his work he started to dress the grave ready for the interment later that day.

The spoil heap was covered with green matting and further matting was draped over the sides of the open grave. Then two scaffolding planks were laid either side of the grave, with two beams placed across which would eventually take the weight of the coffin. Finally the two long webbing straps, which the bearers used to lower the coffin, were placed alongside the beams and neatly folded either side on the planks. After checking everything was in order, Justin placed the tools in his wheelbarrow, made a final check to see everything was correctly in place, before putting the barrow out of sight behind a low hedge which divided the old and the new burial grounds.

With the internment being a couple of hours hence there was no point in going back home, so Justin settled down in his Vauxhall Astra van to eat his sandwiches and drink tea hot from his Thermos flask as he read his newspaper. Later, after the internment and once the last of the mourners had departed, he filled the grave leaving a smooth domed finish to allow for settling and placed the turf he had cut earlier over the bare soil. After barrowing the spare soil to a dumping place behind some trees at the edge of the graveyard, he loaded all the trapping of his trade into the van, securely tied the planks to the ladder racks on the roof, and set off back to Shrewsbury to his flat on Abbey Foregate and a welcome shower, a change of clothes and a can or two of his favourite lager. Life is good, thought a carefree Justin.

A few days later it was Friday. Friday night was pub night and it all happened at The Castle. The Castle, situated off Coleham Head, was a bit of a spit and sawdust place but it had a good cellar, a friendly landlord named Len and was the spiritual home of the Shrewsbury Folk Club. Justin liked folk music and the down-to-earthiness of the club followers and, showered and changed after his day's work, walked in to a hubbub of music, song and laughter along with the cries of triumph and anguish of the darts players. He shouldered his way to the bar through the throng giving and returning greetings as he went.

He grinned at Len as he saw a pint of lager was on the bar before he could order it. Len, the landlord, had a habit of turning his profits into liquid intake on a fairly regular basis, but Justin was relieved to see he was looking reasonably sober and exchanged a few pleasantries as he paid for his drink. Len was a real character and never tired of telling anyone who would listen landlord related stories, especially how he sorted out the phantom crapper. He would describe with glee, how every

Sunday, he would open at noon as usual but became dismayed when his regulars would report that someone had filled and splattered the gents toilet cubicle with very smelly diarrhoea and had not pulled the chain. Len, though normally easy-going, became annoyed and finally incensed at this betrayal of his facilities and good nature and was determined to catch the culprit.

After some clever detective work he narrowed it down to a regular named Arthur who would turn up at opening time on Sunday, order a pint, and after taking a refreshing mouthful, scuttle off to the gents with considerable urgency and there leave his unflushed deposit. Realising Arthur was at the limit of his ability to contain himself when he had to visit the gents, Len made sure one Sunday the toilet door was locked. Arthur appeared as usual, ordered his pint, took his first, and as it happened his only swallow and, rushing down the corridor to the Gents with clenched buttocks found his way barred. Len and the regulars in the bar obtained much enjoyment as they observed, through a crack in the door, Arthur 's bowel contents exploding into his trousers and with sides aching with laughter, watched as left through the back entrance and squelched up the road back home. Unsurprisingly, Arthur never drank at the Castle again.

Justin took a well-earned pull at his pint and turned round to look for Caesar and Lynn. He saw them at the other side of the room and they waved him over pointing to a seat they had kept for him. Good old Caesar and Lynn, thought Justin. Always there to help, good company and with a great sense of humour and really the only true friends he had. He worked his way through the press of bodies and settled down with them for an evening of chat and laughter.

Caesar and Lynn Hall were like chalk and cheese. She was a tall, willowy ex-police constable who had served with West Mercia Police and was currently employed by them as a civilian scene of crime investigator. With her chestnut bobbed hair and model good looks she looked anything but what she was, a very efficient ex-officer as many a villain had found out in the past when the handcuff had gone on and, behind her attractive appearance was a shrewd, intelligent and brave woman. If the truth must be told, Justin was strongly attracted to her but out of respect for his friends behaved in an entirely appropriate way.

Caesar, on the other hand, whose real name was Vincent and had earned his nickname after appearing at a fancy dress party attired as a Roman emperor, was short and dark with a shaggy mane of hair over a full beard. His large head was supported by a thick neck above wide shoulders and a great barrel of a chest. But when he stood up it could be seen that all this powerful upper body was carried on narrow hips and short thin legs. Someone once remarked that he looked a miniature version of Pavarotti the opera singer but, with his spade-like hands, Justin thought he looked like a mole. He was a skilled self-employed joiner and worked from a lock-up unit at the Monkmoor Trading Estate not far from where he and Lynn lived in the Highfields district of Shrewsbury.

They had all met through the Shrewsbury Folk Club and Justin, on leave at the time, had been intrigued one evening to see Caesar perform a solo on a Jew's harp, managing at the same time to vocalise with some rather strange and unidentifiable noises. He was very impressed that anyone could play in front of an audience solo on an accompanying instrument without a hint of embarrassment and, when the entertainment was over, started chatting and discovered as serving soldiers they had a lot in common. By a remarkable coincidence they had both been stationed at different times at Allenbrook Barracks in Paderborn, West Germany, with Justin in the R.E.M.E. vehicle workshop and Caesar a sapper in the Royal Engineers, and were further intrigued to discover that they both were Shrewsbury born and bred. From that day a strong bond of friendship was formed which continued after they were both demobilised after their military service. When Lynn came to the folk evenings some time later and she and Caesar eventually became an item, and later husband and wife, a warm three way friendship developed. As they chatted away over their drinks, Justin told them of the sad little boy and Grandma's stinging coffin. Caesar leaned forward.

"I can go one better," he said in his deep voice, taking a long satisfying pull at his pint, "and I swear it's true. You remember I told you I went to work in the Isle of Man and that I had a sideline as a grave digger."

Justin nodded. "Yes, I remember. Wasn't that when the local police had a warrant out for your arrest and you had to go underground?"

Caesar pulled a face of mock disgust. "No it wasn't, you big tart. It was actually when the Mafia had a contract out on me! But getting back to the tale," continued Caesar ponderously, as he took another manly swallow and wiped the froth off his whiskers. "One day I had to re-open a grave at Laxey. As you know the stone mason removes the headstone before opening up, so I didn't know who had been buried there. Well, I had only got down a little way when I just felt someone was staring at me. So I looked up and saw a boy of about eleven or so leaning against a headstone nearby eating an apple. We looked at each other for a bit and I suddenly noticed that his clothing seemed odd. He had knee stockings, shorts and tweedy jacket like they used to wear in the 1950s. And then," Caesar snapped his fingers, "he vanished just like that."

Caesar took another long pull at his pint. "What's interesting is I asked the undertaker who had been buried in the grave and he told me it was the 12 year old son of the old lady who had just been planted."

"Incredible," said a clearly impressed Justin, "I'll bet it shook you up a bit."

"No, not really, I just carried on. But I wouldn't have minded a bite of his apple!"

And so, amid much laughter the evening progressed until the call of 'Time, Ladies and Gentlemen, please' came from behind the bar. Justin said his farewells to Caesar and Lynn and noticed that Len had, as usual, left the bar to be run by a regular and was slumped in a corner fast asleep. It was like that most evenings with Len sparked out and the regulars clearing the tables, along with the slow drinkers, and posting the keys through the door after locking up. It was no secret Len had a drink problem and two years later yet another trip to hospital to dry out proved to be his last. His funeral service at the Shrewsbury crematorium was well attended by regulars who joked that there was so much alcohol in him that the fire brigade was put on standby for the occasion. As expected the wake at The Castle was happy and boozy, just as Len would have wanted it. But that day lay far in the future.

After leaving The Castle, Justin walked under the railway bridge and over the Old Potts Way to his flat on Abbey Foregate, barely five minutes away, and opposite the supermarket. He was in a cheerful mood after his evening out, but had made sure he had limited his intake as an early start the next morning with a clear head was essential as a Whitchurch undertaker had booked him for a single at an eco-burial site with the interment at one in the afternoon. Justin had drunk sensibly that evening as he wasn't going to commit the same mistake he once made after a particularly heavy Friday night at The Castle.

He recalled how he had woken the following day with a foul mouth and a painful hangover with the task before him of digging a double grave at Dorrington for an 11 o'clock funeral. Despite his pounding head he arrived at the cemetery just after eight o'clock and, after carefully measuring the outer dimension of the grave as supplied by the undertaker, he cut the turf and laid it aside for later. After manfully digging for some twenty minutes he heard a *Good Morning* from the direction of the church. Looking up, he was surprised to see the vicar leading a donkey with a length of rope attached to its halter. Justin returned his greeting.

The vicar looked puzzled. “Can I ask who the grave is for,” he asked and listened politely as Justin gave him the name of the deceased and of the undertaker and the time of the funeral.

“That's odd,” said the decidedly nonplussed cleric, “I haven't been informed of any of this. Are you sure the service is here?”

“Yes, absolutely sure,” replied Justin with confidence. He scrabbled in his pocket and produced a piece of paper on which he had written his instructions.

“See here it says...Oh! Bloody hell – beg pardon vicar – it's at Alberbury at 11. I'm really sorry,” he stammered, “but I don't have time to fill in. I promise I'll come back this afternoon and leave everything neat and tidy.”

Without waiting for a response, Justin threw his tools into the wheelbarrow and, under the disapproving eyes of the vicar and the donkey drove like a demon from Dorrington south of Shrewsbury to the west near the Welsh border, arriving at 9.30 am at at Alberbury church. By great good fortune the ground there was compacted sand and, with his hangover now a thing of the past, he power-dug a double grave, unbelievably, in a fraction under one hour. He had just finished dressing the grave when the funeral director came to inspect his efforts and, after finding everything satisfactory, went to the church to await the arrival of the hearse and funeral cars. Justin's blood ran cold as he thought of the horrific scenario of the coffin being carried after the service to a non-existent grave. He vowed it would never make the same mistake again and later, when he returned to Dorrington, was relieved that the vicar and his donkey were nowhere to be seen as he reinstated the ground to its original condition.

But none of this troubled Justin as he woke to a sunny Saturday morning with a clear head. He had his usual breakfast of two mugs of filter coffee and slices of toast made from his favourite multigrain bread which he spread thickly, one with honey and the other with peanut butter. Once finished, he made his way to the bathroom to clean his teeth. He always made a point of cleaning his teeth after breakfast as he felt it made sense after all the sugar he had eaten. After some vigorous scrubbing he rinsed his toothbrush and inspected his even white teeth in the mirror. Satisfied with the result, he returned to the kitchen, filled his flask with tea and, taking his filled lunch box from the refrigerator, left the flat after locking the front door behind him. Descending the steps at the front of the building, he walked across the road to his van in the car park opposite, unlocked the doors and settled into the driving seat for his journey to his next job at Church Stretton.

At peace with the world and in good humour, Justin sang as he drove south along the A49. It was a rather suggestive song about a plump landlord's daughter of Yarmouth Town who entertained sailors on an industrial scale after they pulled on a string she had dangled from her bedroom window. Singing the final chorus, he approached the traffic lights at Church Stretton and turned right up the hill and past the shops towards the graveyard at the church of St. Laurence. Parking his van by the covered lych-gate he walked through it and along the path between the graves to find where he had to dig. As it was a new grave, not a re-open, he reasoned it had to be near the latest burials and sure enough, right at the end of the line of newish headstones, he saw a peg in the ground with the correct name written on a piece of paper pinned to it. After fetching his tools from the van, he carefully measured the outlines of the grave and set to work, knowing from past experience that after the easy layer of top soil the ground was compacted interposed with a shale-like rock which needed determined pickaxe blows to break it up.

As he dug deeper with his head down he hear someone say *Good Morning*. Straightening, Justin observed firstly a pair of highly polished black lace-up shoes, followed by dark pinstripe trousers with a sharp crease and, moving his gaze upwards, noted a matching well cut jacket and waistcoat, white shirt and light blue tie. As he took his gaze past the man to the lych-gate he saw over the low churchyard wall a dark blue car with privacy glass windows which he recognised as a BMW 5 Series. At the other side of the graveyard he also noted what appeared to be a young woman, with her back to him, tending to some flowers on a grave.

Justin wondered if the smartly dressed man was an undertaker and had need of a grave digger but, looking at the man's clean-shaven face, realised with a slight sense of unease it was unlikely. His features were of Arab or Mediterranean appearance, but hard and immobile with thin lips and cold dark eyes which looked unblinkingly at Justin. When he spoke his voice was without an accent and surprisingly quiet.

Despite his misgivings, and not to be outdone in courtesy, Justin returned the man's greeting and waited for him to speak.

"Justin," said the man, "it's nice to talk at last."

Justin wondered what he meant by *at last,* and why it was *nice*, but decided it would be prudent to let him continue.

The man paused for a second then, with a cold smile which failed to reach his eyes, went on. "I've been finding out about you and want to make you a business offer. It's my belief, Justin, it'll be one I know you won't want to turn down."

The mention of a business offer interested Justin as it had the smell of money about it, but he was initially wary. Although he currently led a law-abiding life, it was not always the case as there had been several brushes with the law in the past resulting in court appearances. Further, there were many other transgressions when he was not brought to book and even after joining the army he was frequently on a charge and several occasions was held in detention until he could be dealt with. It was only after his concerned training officer had pointed out to Justin that if he carried on in an insubordinate manner he was set for discharge, so he had better sort himself out. He was then posted to Arborfield in Berkshire where he decided it was time to buckle down and six months' later, passed out as Class 2 vehicle mechanic. Shortly after, his posting came through to Paderborn in Germany and there he settled down and conducted himself well until his demobilisation as a corporal six years later.

But Justin was interested in what this mystery man had to say and wanted to know more about this business offer. Feeling at a disadvantage at the bottom of his grave, he climbed out and drew himself up before the him.

"It appears you know my name," he said, "but I don't know yours. Difficult to do business without an introduction."

The man put out his hand and as they shook said, "The name's John." He smiled as he spoke but again the eyes were cold. "Before you ask, Justin, that's the only name you need to know."

Justin felt a slight feeling of unease as he found John's attitude somewhat menacing and was not sure he wanted to continue. However, despite his reservations, there was a bit of Justin which wanted to know more about the financial side of things. After all, he reasoned, if he didn't like what he heard he could always say thanks but no thanks.

"Well if that's what you want, no problem. John it is. Perhaps you'd like to tell me what this irresistible business proposition is. But a word of warning, if it's iffy I'll have nothing to do with it. Okay?"

Justin, old son," said John, raising his hands as if in horror, "as if I'd do something like that to you. No. What I'm going to put to you is completely above board and doesn't involve you in anything shady."

Justin usual flippancy was put on hold as there was something about the man that made him feel it wouldn't be welcome. Hardly the life and soul of a party, he mused, but let's hear him out.

"It's like this," continued John, his unblinking eyes fixed on Justin, "All I want you to do is to tell me when you dig a new single or re-open a double grave. I need to know where it is being dug and the date you dig it out. I also need to know the name of the deceased. You have to be able to give me at least two days' notice of the grave being dug. What's most important is that the grave has to be left finished and open for a burial the following day. Not difficult, is it?"

"Not put like that, it isn't," said a decidedly nonplussed Justin. "but it sounds bloody odd to me. You just want to know when I dig a single grave, or re-open a double, where it is and it has to be left open overnight. Come on pull the other one."

"Justin my friend, trust me. I swear on my Mother's life everything is above board. Truly that's all I want to know. Just those few details. You don't have to know any more and you can take the money that goes with this business deal with a clear conscience."

With the mention again of financial gain some of Justin's misgivings took a back seat as he realised there could be profit in this strange arrangement. He looked again into those cold black eyes and decided he wasn't going to look like a pushover.

"Although this is the most bizarre thing I've heard of in all my life, and believe me I've come across a good few in my time, there's just one thing I want to know. You mentioned money for information. What are you offering?"

"Five hundred pounds for each grave you tell me about which conforms to our requirements. Paid in cash, used notes, by post to your home address."

Despite his misgivings, Justin's greed drove him on. "Have you any idea how much that would be?" He met again those cold eyes. "Look, mainly I dig for Percivals the undertakers of Shrewsbury, but also being self-employed for many other funeral directors in Shropshire and over the border into Wales and, occasionally, Cheshire. Off the top of my head I guess I dig four singles or re-opens a week and two or three are left open overnight. You're telling me you are prepared to pay one to one and a half grand each week just to have the information you want?"

John nodded his head without breaking his unblinking gaze. "Got it in one, Justin. You catch on quickly."

"Listen mate," replied Justin, "I find it impossible to believe that what you want from me is for innocent purposes. No one pays that sort of money, or indeed any amount of money, to look at an empty grave. What's your game? Are you going to put your victims in and cover them up before a coffin is dropped on them? If you want me on side you'd better tell me straight what you're up to."

John shook his head as though in sorrow. "Justin. I promise you that I'm not going to put bodies in your graves. But that's all I can tell you." His lips smiled but there was no reflection in John's cold dark eyes. They continued to bore into Justin's. "Trust me that's all I want from you. All you have to do is send the details to me by e-mail and in return, once the grave is dug, you'll get five hundred quid in cash each time. What's not to like about that?"

Whilst Justin pondered over this latest information, a sudden thought came to John and he asked, "I take it that there will be a headstone on the grave with a name corresponding to the one we will be given by you?"

"Yes, there will be," replied Justin with a raise of his eyebrows. "But probably not for a month or even longer. That's because the stone mason has to let the ground settle before it'll take the weight of the stone. In fact, possibly even never, if the relatives can't afford a headstone. Take it you hadn't thought of that?"

John, indeed hadn't thought of that and mentally kicked himself. He prided himself, with much justification, that he never overlooked even the smallest detail and now he had stumbled at the first hurdle. He thought quickly. "Not a problem, Justin. I would want you to give me the details on the headstones of the two graves either side of the one you have dug. Or, if it's at the end of a line, the details on the headstone at the one side. Do you think you can manage that?"

Whilst Justin made a living from his grave digging, he wasn't making a great deal either, so the extra cash for him amounted to a small fortune. He was unsure of the legitimacy of this deal but slowly he was being won over by the thought of earning large sums of extra income without having to make any great effort. Slowly but surely Justin's greed started to overcome his natural caution, but even so he wasn't quite ready to commit himself. He turned away to think for a moment as John stood motionless and waited. Turning back he met those unnerving eyes, hopefully he thought, for the last time.

"Tell you what I'll do. What you've told me is very odd but I can't make up my mind just now. I need to think it over and see if I want to go ahead. How can I get in touch with you?"

He looked carefully at John to see how he was going to react. He was relieved to see no change in his expression. The thin, humourless smile appeared briefly as he replied to Justin.

"That's all right, my friend, you think about my offer." He proffered a piece of paper which Justin took. Printed on it was an e-mail address. "This is my contact address. Once you've made a decision let me know. If you want to go ahead then the arrangement stands, but either way let me know by tonight at the latest. There's no problem if you want out and, if you do, you'll not hear from me again."

"Yes, that's no problem," agreed Justin, despite his misgivings. "I'll do that for you."

"Just one thing more." John reached into his jacket pocket and drew out a white envelope which he passed to Justin. "I don't want you to tell anyone of this conversation, understand? What's in that envelope is yours whatever you decide to do. Just tell me that you keep your mouth shut about all this."

Justin had the distinct feeling that it would be very much in his best interests to remain silent about his dealings with the sinister John, and assured him he would say nothing to anyone. They shook hands and Justin watched him walk back to his car and drive away towards the main street and out of sight. He became aware that his hands were wet with sweat and, as he wiped them dry on his trousers, realised that John had penetrated his carefree outer shell and found his uncertain core. He didn't like the sensation one bit he decided as he continued with his excavations. Suddenly he remembered the envelope he had been given. Resting his foot on the spade he was using, he took it out of his back pocket. I was quite thick and he wasn't sure what to expect. But once he had opened it taken out the contents he was staggered to count twenty £50 notes. He recounted them and, yes, it came to one thousand pounds. Staggered at this unexpected largess, Justin decided it would be better if he concentrated on the job in hand and try to work out what was happening once he was back in the security of his flat. He bent to his task with his thoughts whirling around in his head at this strange turn of events.

Later that day, after his work was finished

and he had showered and put on clean casual clothes, he prepared his evening meal. He had recently bought himself a halogen oven after Caesar and Lynn had recommended one and found that, despite its small size, it could almost replace his conventional oven. For his evening meal he decided on fish and chips with garden peas which he would put on the electric hob when the food was almost cooked. As the oven did its work Justin buttered two slices of bread and pondered over the strange events which he had experienced. He could be certain of only two things. Firstly, he now possessed one thousand pounds in cash and, secondly, he hadn't the faintest idea what John was up to. As he pondered the timer on the cooker pinged and Justin put his now cooked meal along with the peas on a plate and carried it over to the table which was placed against the sitting room wall where he tucked into his meal.

Whilst he ate, he tried to explore all the possible reasons why anyone would want the sort of information he had been asked for. He wondered if this John was an undertaker but discounted this idea almost immediately, as no reputable undertaker would refuse to give his full name and, he reasoned, could not gain any benefit from knowing when a grave was being dug for another undertaker. Further, no undertaker would give a strange grave digger a grand in notes before any deal had been done. After consideration, Justin was unable to see how the information requested could have any commercial advantage. He thought about criminal activities, but for the life of him he couldn't imagine any illegal activity which could benefit from an open grave. Obviously, something could be secreted in the bottom of a finished grave and covered over but the problem would be to recover whatever had been hidden there, as the work involved in digging down to a coffin, removing it before retrieving the concealed items and then having to replace the coffin and reinstating the grave. Justin knew that it wouldn't be feasible. Apart from the effort involved there was the problem of carrying out all this intense labour without being seen by someone even if it were carried out at night. No, he decided, totally impossible.

By the time he had finished eating, Justin had to admit that he was no nearer to an answer than when he had started, and he came to the inescapable conclusion that it was unlikely he ever would. He walked over to the fridge and took out a can of lager, snapped open the ring pull and, after carefully pouring it into a tankard, settled into an armchair to decide what he should do next. Justin didn't like to do too much thinking. His was a carefree life where he skipped lightly over events, ensuring he didn't penetrate too deeply, and trying not to leave any waves. He had arranged his life so that he could enjoy himself without the burden of responsibility. He thought of Caesar and Lynn and how it would help if he could put the matter in their hands and they could decide for him. But he remembered that he had promised John he would say nothing to anyone. Despite his many shortcomings, Justin was a person who would keep his promises and, for that reason alone, he would keep the matter to himself. But he also suspected with a chill that John was not a person to be trifled with and felt that it was very much in his favour, and possibly physical well being, that he said nothing to his two friends.

As Justin washed his the dishes after his meal he came to the conviction he was in this on his own, and had only a short time in which to make up his mind as to what he was going to do. He left the dishes to dry on the drainer and, still undecided, walked into the sitting room to turn on his computer. He went through all the arguments again and, although he felt that the arrangement with John were suspect, he was unable to imagine any particular activity on this John's part, either legal or not, which could benefit from the information he had been asked for. On balance, he reasoned, there can't be any harm in giving John the details he wants and, anyway, the sums of money involved were so large they were not only very tempting but potentially life changing for him. And in this manner, with greed overcoming caution, Justin sat down in front of his keyboard and logged onto his e-mail account. Clicking on *Write* he carefully put in the address John had given him, put INFO into the subject line, tabbed down and wrote *'John. Thought about your offer and will accept. Details to follow soon. Regards. Justin'.* After hesitating for a moment, he took a deep breath and hit *Send.*

Well, that's it, mused Justin, the die is cast and born of long practice he was able to banish his worries to a hidden corner of his mind and recover his easy-going attitude to life. With the warm thought of the considerable wealth which was going to come his way, he walked into the kitchen for another lager. Snapping the ring pull on the can he walked back just as his mobile ringtone sounded. He connected with the caller and was surprised to hear John's voice at the other end.

"Justin, my boy, very pleased with your decision." The voice was smooth, with no inflection of triumph.

"Thought you might be," replied Justin

cheerfully, although somewhat taken aback at the speed of John's response. “I've given it some thought and I'll pass on the details you want. And thanks for the grand. Unexpected, but much appreciated. But one thing, will you promise me that there'll never be any come-back from whatever it is you are up to?”

“Yes, I promise you Justin that you'll be like teflon. Nothing can stick to you. All you have to do is send the details, dig the graves, keep your mouth shut, don't ask questions and for each grave dug to our specification you will receive by post five hundred in cash, just as I told you. Just one thing,” he continued, “ if you do as I instruct you won't have any further dealings with me until I tell you it's all finished by the end of the year. Is that clear?”

Justin noted that John's voice had a hard edge to it and that where previously he had asked Justin to do things, he now was giving him orders. Still, he reasoned, he was effectively working for him and, anyway, as he had just been told he would have no further contact with him he decided it wasn't a problem. He assured him that everything was crystal clear and was surprised when John hung up without another word. He checked his mobile to find John's number and found it withheld. Odd bugger, thought Justin as he returned to his beer, and good bloody riddance!

After an untroubled night's sleep and an unhurried breakfast Justin received his first telephone call of the day from a Welshpool undertaker who wanted a single grave at the splendidly named church of St. Michael and All Angels at Criggion three days' hence. Justin wrote down the the details of deceased's name, coffin size and timings and, after giving assurances that all would be in order on the day, went to look up Criggion on his road map. He discovered it to be a small village some twelve miles from Shrewsbury on the banks of the River Severn, or Afon Hafron as the Welsh call it, and some two miles north of the Breidden Hills. Keeping to the arrangements agreed with John, he turned on his computer and sent an e-mail to the address he had been given with all the details he had asked for and added a *read receipt* request. Within a few seconds to his surprise his e-mail account pinged with an acknowledgement of receipt but nothing else. Well, thought Justin with a sense of relief, not bad for a grand down and £500 to come - providing, of course, this John keeps to his side of the bargain and the promised cash actually arrives.

The following day dawned slowly as the light struggled through dark clouds with the almost certain promise of rain later. Rain was the downside to Justin's work as it was not always possible to take shelter in his van when there was tight timing for completion of a grave, but it was just one of those things he tolerated for the freedom of self-employment. After breakfast, Justin gathered his things together and left the building to cross to his van which he parked at the supermarket opposite his flat. He gave a wry smile at the macabre thought which came to him out of nowhere, that when you bury your principles money makes an effective shroud, and hoped it wouldn't apply to him. Approaching his van, he keyed open on the remote fob and saw that that the doors didn't unlock. He pressed the lock button and the locks clicked shut and then unlocked when he pressed the unlock again. Strange, he reflected, as he was certain that he locked the van yesterday. He shrugged as he reasoned he must have forgotten and, putting the matter from his mind, eased into the driving seat to start his day's work for Percivals at Longnor. But Justin had driven only a few miles when the threatening clouds decided to stop threatening and released a steady downpour that gave the impression of being set in for the day. This, in fact, proved to be the case as the rain continued unabated for the duration of the time he spent digging and despite his waterproof clothing, a very damp Justin eventually loaded up his van and headed off to his next dig with the heater fan on full speed trying to clear the fogged windscreen.

But the misted windscreen was the least of Justin's problems. What he didn't know was that the arrangement he had naively made with John would have far reaching and horrific consequences.

CHAPTER 2

A few days later it was time to dig the single grave at Criggon which a Welshpool funeral director had booked. The day was cool as the wind had turned to the east and with it came a light overcast. But at least it wasn't raining and, as the forecast was for it to remain dry all day, Justin felt the dig should be an easy one. He did have one reservation, as having never previously dug a grave at Criggion, he was unsure what type of soil he would encounter. From past experience of burial grounds up in the hills Justin knew them to be usually rocky and difficult but from what he saw on the map, Criggon sat midway between the floodplain of the River Severn and the Breiddens and hopefully he would find there a fine compacted silt.

As usual, Justin carefree nature had reasserted itself and he had managed to put his misgivings about his arrangement with this John out of his mind especially now that the promised £500 had arrived. That morning he had taken a brown envelope out of his letter box fixed to the wall in the entrance hall and walked over to his van before opening it. Inside were ten used £50 notes which had been placed inside a folded sheet of plain white paper. Justin looked at the postmark which was not very clear but appeared to be Cheshire and was dated the previous day with a first class stamp. He examined the envelope closely, even sniffing inside as well, but finding nothing unusual put it and the cash in his glove box, started up and pulled out of the car park heading into the town centre. Continuing with his journey he took the A458 Welshpool road out of Shrewsbury then, after a few miles, turned north west onto the B4393 and eventually arrived at the burial ground at Criggion parish church around 9.30am. The graveyard was surrounded on three sides with tall elms from which there came the harsh cries of the rooks from their untidy nests in the tree tops. There were many old yew trees which spread their ancient branches widely and created areas of gloom over the graves. Justin was sensitive to atmosphere and found that all burial grounds had their own character. Some were pleasant, open and light. Others uncomfortable and some heavy with a hidden menace. Criggion, he discovered, had an atmosphere which made him feel uneasy and, with a shiver down his spine, Justin determined to press on and finish as quickly as possible.

However, to Justin's delight, the going was relatively easy and after a leisurely two hour dig the grave was finished and dressed with all the webbing and planks left in their correct places. After a careful look round to check all was neat and tidy, Justin returned to his van, loaded up and, having no further work that day, set off back home to a welcome early finish.

Back at the flat, Justin knew there were tasks which he couldn't put off any longer. In short, the whole place needed a thorough clean and there was a mountain of laundry which was growing larger by the day and, if he didn't do something about it immediately, there would be nothing clean for him to wear. He went to the laundry basket in his bedroom and stripping the sheets and pillow cases from his bed, gathered everything together and carried the huge bundle into the kitchen. He dropped it in front of the washing machine and, realising there was too much for one load, crammed as much as he could into the drum, before throwing in a soap pod. He was about to close door, hesitated, then put in a second pod and set the programme to a hot wash. Next he turned to a tall cupboard and brought out an upright vacuum cleaner and raised his eyebrows as he saw the dust cylinder was filled to the brim. Now he knew why it wasn't picking up very well, he told himself, as he emptied its contents into the waste bin in the kitchen creating a cloud of dust in the process.

As he hoovered the carpets, Justin pondered about the bizarre circumstances of his agreement with John and just why he would want details of the graves he dug. What earthly use could such information be and what legitimate purpose, if any, could it be used for. He was aware that this John had effectively warned him not to ask questions and Justin felt that it was very much in his interests to stay silent and keep his head down. But a part of him wanted to know what was going on and, as he pushed the vacuum cleaner across the carpets, decided he was going to find out more about this odd arrangement and determined he would go to Criggion once it was dark and check on the grave he had dug.

After putting away the vacuum cleaner and finding the washing machine had finished its cycle Justin emptied the load into a plastic basket, and after cramming in the second load and setting it to wash, took the basket out through the back door of the building into the neglected garden where he had his own washing line. As he pegged the items onto the line he thought of the mammoth ironing session ironing he would have to look forward to. Although, after six years serving in the ranks of the British Army Justin was proficient with a steam iron, it didn't mean that he liked the task, especially when he had left the laundry to build up into a Herculean labour. He wasn't sure how many times he had promised himself that he would launder more frequently, but this time he thought forcefully he really meant it. After pegging out the last load onto a sagging line and hoisting it to a safe height with a clothes prop, Justin went back into the flat to wait until dusk. Later in the afternoon after he had received two e-mails from undertakers, both booking him for re-openings of existing graves, Justin acknowledged receipt and printed them off.

Much later, once the light had started to fade, Justin set off in his van for the hour's drive to the burial ground at Criggion. Arriving in the tiny hamlet in the dark he decided to exercise caution, and parked his van out of sight of the church on the grass verge opposite a large house with a Bed and Breakfast sign in the front garden. After a quick rummage around behind the passenger seat he found the torch he was looking for. He quickly flashed it on to check the batteries and satisfied with the beam left the van to walk the short distance to the burial ground. Being a small hamlet, Criggion had few street lights and Justin made use of the shadowed areas to make his approach to the low wall at the edge of the cemetery where he looked around carefully to check the coast was clear. Although it was dark there was a half moon in a clear sky giving him enough light to be able to make out details in the cemetery. He didn't expect to see anyone there at this time of night and, with the street empty of people, Justin decided it was safe to continue with his inspection.

Climbing easily over the low stone wall which surrounded three sides of the cemetery, Justin walked carefully on the grass at the side of the path to where his grave lay, very much aware of the heavy, unpleasant feeling which he had experienced earlier in the day. Once at the plot he stooped to peer down into the open hole and, after again checking he was alone knelt on one of the planks he had laid along the side. Clicking on his torch with his hand shielding the top of the beam, he lifted the matting he had dressed the grave with, and closely inspected the sides and floor of the grave. But there was nothing he could see that was untoward and, even after lowering himself in and carefully checking the floor more closely, found the soil to be compacted and undisturbed, he was convinced that nothing had been interfered with there. Next he turned his attention to the spoil heap. After lifting the grass matting realised that any search he might make would be futile as anything secreted in the loose soil would be exposed when he filled in the grave the following day. Replacing the matting, Justin reasoned that nobody would be so idiotic as to hide something in a spoil heap besides a grave in the dark for someone to come that same night and retrieve it and, having ruled out any interference in the grave itself, Justin came to the sure conclusion that he really didn't have a clue as to what this John was up to. Deciding that there was no point in looking further, he left the burial ground the way he came in and arrived back at the van without seeing a single soul in the short walk through the sleepy hamlet. Turning the van around, he set off back to Shrewsbury with the thought of a welcome can of lager once he had settled down for what remained of the evening.

Back at the flat Justin decided he would prepare his sandwiches for the next day before his drink and was taking the loaf out of the bread bin when his mobile ringtone trilled urgently. Bit late for business, he thought, must be Caesar, the old dog! But when he connected the call the voice on the other end made his blood run cold. It was John and he got straight to the point.

"Justin, my boy we need to have a serious talk." His voice was low and icy. "A little bird tells me that you have been back to Criggion. What are you playing at?"

Justin was staggered. How the bloody hell did John know he'd been back that evening. Surely he couldn't have been followed. He steadied his voice and, trying his best to sound confident, decided that the truth was the best option.

"Hello, John. Yes, I did go back as I'm still wondering what I've got myself into. Anyway, the good news is that I couldn't find anything amiss – so no harm done. Tell me, how on earth did you know I'd gone back. Are you having me followed?"

John was silent whilst Justin spoke but when he replied, Justin felt his the thin veneer of his bravado vanish.

"Now you listen, and you listed good, you stupid bastard" his words were hissed, laden with menace. "You're dead right I'm keeping an eye on you and I'm telling you in a way that'll penetrate even your thick skull that if you break the agreement in any way you'll be finished. You say no harm done, well let me tell you," he continued with a voice heavy with suppressed violence, "put one foot wrong again and a great deal of harm will be done – to you. Understand?"

Despite his strong outward appearance and

brash attitude to life, Justin sadly lacked moral and physical courage and throughout his life had always made the effort to avoid confrontation or unpleasantness. This time, although still bristling at the offensive way he had been addressed, he knew he couldn't prevail against what was a decidedly chilling encounter with a strong and very frightening person. With an unsteady voice now that his faux courage had evaporated he decided that a touch of subservience would be best.

"Look John, I'm really sorry I went back. I give you my word that nothing like this will happen again and I'll keep exactly to the arrangement we agreed on. On the other hand, I could give you your money back and we could forget the whole thing. Is that okay?

"Dear me, Justin," John hissed, "this is one arrangement you will not wriggle out of. I've made sure you'll never stray again. Now listen carefully. We've infected your computer with a Trojan Horse. Placed on your system is a locked file. It's so configured that you can neither open nor delete it. Justin, you've been a naughty little pervert as it contains hundreds of pictures of children in pornographic action. Should you try to interfere with the file, or if you step out of line again it will immediately be opened and a little bird will send everything to the West Mercia Police Child Exploitation Unit with full details of the disgusting man who has downloaded them."

"What, you mean, actual ....." started Justin.

"Don't interrupt me Justin, I haven't finished. I want you think carefully about the proceeds of this nasty trade in human misery and how you think you'll manage to explain to the police how you are actually as clean as driven snow." And in a low chilling voice that boded ill added, "and one last thing, Justin, keep your bloody gob shut, or you are history. Understand?"

But before Justin could reply the line went dead. If at the start of the conversation with John he was frightened, by the time he rang off he was sick with terror knowing he was mixed up in something which was at least seriously suspect and, at worst, most certainly illegal and most definitely very dangerous. He though he had better check whether his system had been tampered with. He sat down at his computer and opening his documents folder was horrified, though not surprised, to see a file he had no knowledge of labelled *Tinkerbells*. With John's warning still ringing in his ear, he left it alone and closed the application with now the certain knowledge that he was involved with a monster he was unable to control.

Justin then did what he usually did when

problems arose, he went to the fridge, took out a can of lager and pouring it into his tankard sat down to lament at the passing of a happy and carefree past into a horribly uncertain future. After a while he told himself to get a grip, calm down and think things through. Without having to give it much thought, he knew he was unwittingly involved in something big which was beyond his comprehension but also, he reasoned, if he did exactly as this John told him then he should be safe.

As he pondered he suddenly remembered something significant John had said about the e-mails - *we've infected your system!* Until then he had always spoken in the first person, how *I* would do this or that. Justin wondered whether John had slipped up by inferring he was part of a group but still couldn't make any sense out of any of it. He wanted to talk things over with Caesar and Lynn as he valued their common-sense approach to life's difficulties but, as Lynn worked for West Mercia Police, she could hardly keep quiet about Justin's highly suspect arrangements, and he knew he couldn't involve her. Then there was the worrying problem that John knew his every move and his warning not to speak to anyone and, even more disagreeable, the implied threat that should he step out of line again he would be killed. My God, thought Justin in despair, I'm up shit street without a paddle. I'm on my sodding own. Then, keeping to his usual method of dealing with a problem, a sorely troubled Justin drank two more cans of lager and eventually took himself off to bed and a fitful night's sleep.

Justin woke the following morning feeling distinctly below par and decided that after he had finished work he'd drop in on Caesar at his workshop. He always felt better after seeing Caesar and even though he couldn't talk about the big problem he had with John, knew he'd give his spirits a boost after some manly verbal knock-about with his friend. But Justin had another reason for visiting the unit. Kept there under a dust cover was his pride and joy – a classic Norton 650SS motorbike. Made in 1966 with the famous slimline featherbed frame with roadholder forks and resplendent in silver and black. It was Justin's one indulgence which he would take it out in good weather for a ride out on a Sunday all over North Wales, often covering over 200 miles in a morning. The thought of seeing his bike, or his surrogate wife as Caesar called it, and his friend later that day lifted Justin's spirits and, as he set off to Waters Upton to dig a double grave for Percivals, he began to regain a little of his cheerful high spirits.

The grave he dug that morning was for an

afternoon burial and so Justin remained there until he could fill in and make good before driving back to Shrewsbury. Instead of parking at the supermarket, he drove straight to Caesar's workshop on the Monkmoor Industrial Park and parked in one of the empty bays in front of the unit. He was pleased to see that Caesar's big Volvo estate was there and walked in to the comforting smell of wood, sawdust and glue. Caesar hadn't heard Justin come in as he was noisily running a piece of timber through a band saw and had his back to the door, but a minute later he had finished and turned to see Justin. What could be seen of his face through his great shaggy beard, broke into a broad grin as he greeted Justin.

"Justin, you old dog, what brings you here," he boomed, "am I graced with your presence because you wanted to tap into my superior intellect or have you come to pay homage to that two-wheeled, steam-driven wreck over there?"

Justin grinned happily. He loved the cheek and gave as good as he got. "Listen, you hairy moron, my bike's got more intelligence in its spark plugs than you've got in your entire ravaged body. Anyway, if you can stop insulting me, I want to tell you I have plans for my lovely machine."

"Scrap man coming, is he? All right." He

held up his hand in mock surrender. "I'll be sensible. Tell me what you've got planned."

"Well, you remember that I told you the front brake on the Norton is a single leading shoe and, frankly, it's not up to the job of stopping safely in modern traffic. So I decided some time back to price a twin leading shoe and the cost of having the front wheel re-spoked when it's fitted."

"Yea, I do recall you banging on about it a bit back and you're dead right the original brake left a bit to be desired even when it was new." Although no longer owning a motorbike, Caesar had been a keen rider some years back and was genuinely interested in Justin's Norton. "Going to be a bit pricey, isn't it?"

"Just a tad but well worth it. I've found an old retired mechanic bloke in Whitchurch who does bike work as a hobby. He tells me can supply a new eight inch twin leader for three hundred and seventy pounds and will fit and re-spoke the original wheel for eighty and with no VAT. I've shopped around and no one can get close to him."

"Justin, me old mucker, nice to know you're in the money. What are you doing, running a night shift? Anyway, now you're so flush you can buy some shares in my business." Despite the banter, Caesar was looking keenly at his friend.

“Seriously though, is everything all right with you?”

What do you mean,” asked Justin, slightly startled by the enquiry, “ I'm just fine and dandy. Don't know why you asked.”

“Just basic concern, old fruit. It's just that you look tense and your face is a bit drawn. Is anything troubling you or are you not feeling too good?”

“No, honestly, Caesar, I really am fine. I had a bad night's sleep last night and I feel a bit jaded, that's all.” Seeing that Caesar look relieved at his answer and wasn't going to press the matter, he changed the subject by talking about the job on his motorbike.

The two friends chatted away as they got on with their respective tasks. Caesar turned back to the tall boy he was repairing whilst Justin took the dust cover off the Norton. Despite its protection, fine sawdust had penetrated from underneath and, as he expected, there was a thin covering all over the machine which he would have to wash off before he took it out for a run. Bringing his tool kit in from the van, Justin started to remove the front wheel. First he slackened off the brake cable at the adjuster and, once slack was able to take out the split pin and free the clevis from the operating arm on the brake drum. Next, he slackened the two pinch bolts at the bottom of the forks and using a brass rod drifted out the hub spindle. Now with the wheel free but held by the front mudguard he called Caesar over and together they lifted the front of the motorcycle to enable it drop out completely.

After teasing Caesar that he wasn't aware of any help from him on the other side of the forks, Justin set about finishing the job by deflating the TT100 tyre, and taking the tyre and inner tube off along with the balance weights fitted to the spokes. Finally, using the special spanner he had brought with him, he took out all the spokes so that the rim was ready to taken over to Whitchurch to have the new brake and spokes fitted. Just as he finished returning the tools to his tool box he heard a cheery greeting from the doorway and looking up was pleased to see Lynn. She walked over to Caesar gave him a kiss and tugged his beard playfully before skipping over to Justin and giving him a very agreeable peck on the cheek.

"Well, I never did! I leave you two alone for ten minutes and you destroy a perfectly good motorcycle. You're nothing but a couple of hooligans," she said with mock severity. "Right, you've had enough warnings – you're both grounded!"

Justin and Caesar grinned happily at Lynn's telling-off and, after making them promise never to misbehave again, she went over to the kettle on a table at the back of the workshop to make them a mug of tea.

“Didn't expect to see you at this time, Lynn” said Caesar, “haven't got the sack have you?”

“No chance – I'm too good at my job for that. You remember the building society robbery I was on last week which took me into four hours into overtime? Well, with the spending constraints West Mercia have to cope with, instead of paying overtime we're given time off instead. Once I'd done my bit this morning the inspector told me to scoot. So here I am brightening up your drab and uneventful lives.”

As she uttered those words, Justin wished that his life was uneventful and drab and that he could go back to those carefree and easy days before the nightmare of John had come into his life. Again, he was sorely tempted to unload the whole sorry business onto the understanding shoulders of his friends but held back once more out of fear for the consequences. Over the course of his life Justin had dug a deep pit inside himself into which he buried all the unpleasantness which came his way and which he was unable, or unwilling, to deal with. But however hard he tried to stamp down on the soil of forgetfulness, these painful events were like the undead and every so often would dig their way to the surface to torment him – usually in the small hours when he would awaken with painful recollections which boiled and churned through his inner being.

With an inward sigh Justin attempted to sent the thought of John and his predicament into the tomb of oblivion and tried not to think about the mess his greed had got him into.

"Penny for your thoughts," said a familiar voice. Justin awoke from his reverie to see Lynn standing in front of him holding out a steaming mug of tea. "Justin, you look like a man with the worries of the world on your shoulders."

"I know what the problem is," interrupted Caesar, shaking his great head in sorrow, "he's got too much money and doesn't know what to do with it." He turned to Lynn. "I think it's our duty to help him spend it."

"Great idea. That's what friends are for. Anyway, have you two forgotten that it's the Bromyard Folk Festival at the end of September - and there's a great line up. I looked online and saw our favourites – Flos and Friends; Keith Donnelly; the Baker's Dozen and about thirty more as well. Tickets have gone up a bit and it's £108 which includes camping. So to help Justin out of his predicament," she teased,

"I say he pays for us including all food and lots of drinks!"

Justin laughed. "All right you two, I'm not that flush. I'll book my ticket when I get back to the flat. What say we get there early on the Friday and get our money's worth. Can we all go in your very old and wheezy – thought surprisingly comfortable – Volvo as usual?"

Caesar nodded his bear-like head in agreement and, as they began to discuss the details of their impending trip, Justin was able to push his troubles below the surface of his everyday consciousness and begin to regain his usual superficial cheery self once more. The three of them chatted on for a while until Justin said he had to be off and, picking up his motorcycle wheel ready for his trip to Whitchurch, he took his leave amidst the usual insults from Caesar and the promise to meet up with them at The Castle on Friday.

After driving back to his flat, Justin decided that he had better stock up on groceries as the cupboard was looking a bit bare. He parked at the supermarket opposite the flat and taking a shopping bag which he kept in the van, walked in to the disco music which the large supermarket chains seem to think is part of a comfortable shopping experience. A while back Justin had written to one supermarket head office to point out that it had been proved that soft, relaxing music and songs encouraged shoppers to slow down, with a feel-good factor led them to spend more. He received a polite response which said that they had not had any complaints about the tapes they played in store. Justin was going to write back and say that he hadn't complained but was just making a constructive point based on fact, but decided he couldn't be bothered – anyway, there was always Lidl and Aldi which had no music of any kind. He did shop there if he was passing on his way back home but the store opposite his flat usually won as it was the most convenient.

He picked up a basket and sauntered along the aisles picking up the essentials he knew he needed and looking for some impulse buys. He did want bacon but having become unimpressed with the white gunk and water which oozed out of most of the rashers he fried, looked out for a free-range pack. He couldn't find any and was just about to ask an assistant when he saw an organic British brand brand which stated on the packaging *No white bits!* Should be free of white goo, he thought, and put it with the other purchases. Picking up what he needed from the vegetable display he wandered down to the drinks section and, after selecting two six packs of his favourite lager, took his purchases to the till where he could see the best looking female operative. Although he had never actually managed to secure a date he did enjoy the opportunity for a bit of light flirting and was gratified on those occasions when he found a favourable response. This time, however, his winning smile and cheery chat received a cool reaction and, as he put his debit card in the machine and punched in his pin number, decided he wouldn't use her checkout again.

Leaving the store he crossed the road, now busy with early evening traffic, and let himself in through the front door and up the stairs to his flat. After putting his purchases away he set about preparing his evening meal of haddock in breadcrumbs with broccoli and new potatoes. After putting the potatoes to boil on the gas stove, he put the fish into the halogen oven and set the temperature to 175°C and the timer to 15 minutes. He found the oven easy to work and impressed that it used about a quarter of the electricity used by a conventional electric oven. After ten minutes he put the broccoli in with the potatoes stem down to cook and sat down with a tankard of lager whilst he waited for his food to be ready. A ping from the oven told him time was up and he put out his meal on a plate which had been heated by being placed over the saucepan in which the potatoes had been boiled. Adding a dollop of tartare sauce from the jar he kept in the fridge he took his meal over to the dining table and set to.

Once he had finished and washed up he poured himself another lager and settling into an armchair in his sitting room, Justin did what he did best when faced with difficulties, and tried his best to avoid thinking about the problems which had entered into his outwardly well-ordered life. But however hard he tried he was unable to stop the goad of his predicament rising up and prodding him from the depths of his sub-conscious. What Justin couldn't understand was how this John was able to track his movements with such precision. How on earth did he know that he had gone back to the Criggion grave? He was sure he hadn't been followed as he drove there, as there had been no headlights visible in his rear view mirrors after he had turned onto the B road leading to the village. He wondered whether John, or more likely one of his henchmen, had been keeping a look-out near the graveyard and then dismissed that idea as ludicrous knowing that in a tiny place like Criggion a stranger would have stood out like a sore thumb - and not only that but the grave would have to be observed all night. No, thought Justin, that's not the answer.

Then he had a sudden idea. Could his van

have had a tracking device fitted? Justin had scant knowledge of these things but felt sure that they were sophisticated and could pinpoint someone's whereabouts precisely. He then had a revelation as he remembered the morning when he went to open his van and found it unlocked and was convinced he had locked it the day before. Could that be significant, he wondered. Well, he thought, there's one way to find out and picking up his keys left the flat to give his van a close inspection. Once in the car park, Justin started to look over all the exterior panels of the van and, after finding nothing untoward as he expected, began a search under the wheel arches and as far as he was able under the front and rear and along the sills. Unable to find anything that shouldn't be there, he turned his attention to the interior reasoning that if a tracking device could send a signal when placed under a vehicle, then it was likely that they were powerful enough to send a signal from inside as well.

The search of the interior took some twenty minutes, and included removal of the door panels using the tool kit he kept in the van, to make sure nothing had been inserted behind them. With his mechanic's knowledge, Justin was sure that no device had been placed anywhere inside the van. Finally, he opened the bonnet and began a thorough inspection of the engine bay. Although he had no precise knowledge of tracking devices, Justin reasoned that they were like to be relatively small and therefore easy to hide. But also, he deduced, they could be made to look like a legitimate component such as a part of the electronic systems and as such would fool anything other than an experienced eye. With this in mind Justin gave the engine bay a detailed search which after ten minutes revealed nothing that wasn't meant to be there.

As he walked back to the flat after carefully locking the van, Justin was puzzled. Although he could be reasonable sure there was no tracker fitted to his van and, as far as he was able to tell, he was not being followed he reasoned that as John knew of his actions and movements he must have an extremely effective covert surveillance system at his disposal. He came to the conclusion that he was in a living nightmare from which he had no means of escape. He toyed with the idea of running away, somewhere, anywhere, but realised that it was unlikely he could escape from the prison of John's dominance, and his blood ran cold as he was now forced to the inescapable conclusion that any attempt to free himself from this contract would very likely mean he would have to be eliminated - he couldn't bring himself to say the word killed -

as he knew too much. With this disagreeable thought in mind, and knowing that he was unable to turn to anyone for help, Justin decided that he would have to bury his fears and stamp firmly on the grave if he was to retain his sanity. From, now on, he reasoned, if I just do as I'm told, keep my mouth shut and enjoy the money then all will be well. This John will at some stage have completed whatever it is he has to do and I'll be of no further use to him. I'll be off the hook and can enjoy my wealth and forget all about that bastard.

After coming to his decision, Justin felt, once again, some of his cheery nature return and decided to enjoy himself as before. But what Justin would not admit to himself was that his life had changed and already would never be the same as before. What he was not to know was that his ability to push problems down and dance irresponsibly over them was soon to end, and that he would be faced, not just with appalling events, but would be forced to face his inner weaknesses. To overcome them he would have to battle with the demons of cowardly irresponsibility, greed and selfishness which he had allowed over the years to exert their malign and subtle influences over his thoughts and actions.

For Justin's life was soon to become far worse that he could ever imagine and had he known of John's background he would have been very frightened indeed.

CHAPTER 3

John had a decision to make. Could he rely on Justin to fall into line or had he outlived his usefulness. The operation he had been tasked with had a fixed timetable and he had to make a decision quickly because, if it became necessary to make alternative arrangements, Justin had to be neutralised. He was a good judge of character and thought Justin would be totally compliant, and it had come as a surprise that he had gone back to check on a grave. However, after some serious deliberation, John felt confident after his recent conversation with Justin that he was frightened enough to do as he was told, and therefore the operation would continue as planned.

John was an important man. He was also very intelligent, highly educated and utterly ruthless in his pursuit of his goals. Born Bahadur Najafi in 1983 in Iran, an only child to his father Daichi and mother Nasrin, into a comfortable existence in part of District Eight of Tehran called Narmak, which lies to the east of the city on the gentle slopes of the Alborz Mountains and is notable for its many pomegranate orchards.

His was a difficult and protracted birth and it was feared that both mother and child would not survive the experience. But, with the expertise of the maternity hospital, first his mother pulled back from the brink and, some five days' later, their weakened infant began to make his voice heard and could be taken from the incubator and into his mother's arms. His parents decided that the only name for him must be Bahadur which means *Fighter* in Farsi and after his early struggle with life, little Bahadur grew into a sturdy and determined child and, as the problems of his birth meant his mother was unable to bear any more children, became their only child and the recipient of his parents' undivided love and protection.

John's father was a highly-placed officer in the Iranian Ministry of Intelligence and Internal Security (MOIS) also known as VEVAK in Farsi. He had started his career in intelligence with the Shah's SAVAK secret police which had been formed in 1957 to prevent dissent. They proved to be highly effective and were renowned for the use of the most horrific forms of torture which often led to the maiming and deaths of those men, women and children unfortunate enough to be the subject of their attentions. With the overthrow of the Shah in 1979 the SAVAK organisation was ostensibly disbanded and soon after replaced with a new security apparatus called SAVAMA. This proved to be only marginally less brutal than its SAVAK predecessor, mainly because members of the Shah's secret police were given the opportunity to effectively remain in post under the new SAVAMA heading. As the alternative to joining was to be liquidated, it came as no surprise that the majority transferred their allegiance to their new master, the Ayatollah Khomeini. There were, of course, those whose past meant that they were not given any choice and many of the upper echelon, such as the head of SAVAK, General Nassiri and most of the board of Directors were tried and executed. Whilst the rule of the Ayatollah Khomeini ended some of the worst atrocities committed by SAVAK, the introduction of Sharia law meant any improvement in human rights for the Iranians was, at best, marginal.

Although John's father was a skilled interrogator, he did not personally administer torture – that he left to the soulless sadists who gained pleasure from applying appalling torments to their victims – but made full use of their talents and frequently sent victims to the interrogation rooms in the knowledge that once they had been broken he could more easily extract the confessions he needed. He was not troubled by his actions, merely seeing them as a necessary means to an end and, such was his success as an interrogator, he was soon promoted to Head of the Department of Domestic Security. It was shortly after his promotion that he was approached by an operative from MOIS and told that he was to be transferred to their section which dealt with counter espionage and disinformation. Daichi Najafi was under no illusion that this was an offer he could consider in his own time - in post-revolution Iran you did as you were told – but was in fact pleased to move across to an organisation which gave him more freedom to operate. Unlike SAVAMA which was placed in a clear and accountable national command structure, MOIS was directly, and solely, answerable to the Supreme Leader and enjoyed its own secret budget which was not open to public scrutiny. In total MOIS employed some 30,000 officers and support personnel and was able to offer, by Iranian standards, attractive salaries and fringe benefits such as subsidised housing in pleasant neighbourhoods on the outskirts of Tehran and specialist schooling for the sons of operatives. John's father found his new employment suited his talents and whilst there he decided on the path his son would follow and, as in all patriarchal societies, John would be duty bound to do as his father instructed.

Now that the family was financially secure and with bonus of assisted fees, it was possible to send John to to the best schools that the capital could offer. They were, of course, subject to strict adherence to the teachings of Holy Koran, but they also set great store on the tradition subjects such as the sciences and languages. After three years in primary school, John moved up to the MOIS approved Middle School where he excelled as a student and also as a keen and accomplished sportsman. It was of significance that John's preference was not for team events but for individual sports such as field and track events and especially wrestling, at which he gained a fearsome reputation as a relentless and skilled opponent. It was at the Middle School that he started his language lessons and, despite the Western nations, especially the USA and Great Britain, being called the *Great Satan,* the Ayatollah knew the value of the English language as an effective tool in any espionage organisation and made its teaching compulsory for all pupils after primary school.

After leaving Middle School and being marked as a model pupil, John was enrolled as a first year student at the MOIS High School in central Tehran. There he showed an aptitude for chemistry and biology as well as a flair for English, all achievements which not only made his parents proud of their only child but, in his father's plans for his son's future, John was succeeding in all the disciplines which he would need for his eventual employment with MOIS. For this was a future not just at the desire of John's parents but, in the way of totalitarian regimes, their inflexible will would identified children with special abilities, groom and encourage them with, or without, the collusion of their parents, into occupations of direct benefit to the apparatus of the State.

By the time John had entered High School his father had made it plain to him the direction his development and future employment would take and, as a dutiful son, John had been pleased to be told about his career plan. It was stressed that he had to excel at chemistry and biology and master the English language until he was fluent. So important was the necessity of speaking fluent English that MOIS arranged for John along with other selected students to be given an evening class once a week at the University where a British born Muslim lecturer of foreign languages would teach his charges idiom, slang expressions, irony and regional accents. He also explained how the English are self-deprecation and how important it was to think like them in order to be able to apply the language they were being taught. In short, John was being taught to be able to pass himself off as British born national as, unbeknown to him, a future had been planned for him which would come to fruition many years hence.

In 1980 Saddam Hussain's Iraq decided to take advantage of the previous year's revolution and mount a land grab whilst Iran was in a state of turmoil. Unfortunately, the Iranians were more strongly organised that the Iraqi's realised and they were soon repulsed effectively back to their starting point but, instead of suing for peace the Iraqis dug in and there began the longest conventional war of the 20th century. For eight long years the two sides slugged themselves to a costly and bloody stalemate as the front line wavered back and forth without either side gaining any significant advantage. The conflict took a terrible toll on the two countries with around one million soldiers and civilians being killed in total before hostilities ceased with the United Nation's Security Council Resolution 598 being reluctantly accepted by both sides in 1988 – though it was not until 1993 that the last of the prisoners of war were repatriated.

John was fortunate in that he was too young to be enlisted into the conflict and fortunately never joined the thousands of boy soldiers who from the age of twelve were put into combat in the front line in order to replace the horrific losses of the regular Iranian troops and, tragically, incurring the same level of losses. But all that was in the past when John was enrolled at the prestigious Rostam High School in Tehran which the state had created to take the high academic achievers and, more pertinently, those who had been singled out to serve the glorious revolutionary cause. As is the way with Moslem countries, with the sexes separated in the education system, Rostam High School was for boys only.

Just as with his record at Middle School, John soon proved himself to be well above average as a pupil and soon came to his teachers' attention as someone who merited a move into the elite grade which took only the most brilliant students and, equally importantly, the sons of those highly placed in government departments dealing with internal and external security, such as his father. The regime at Rostam was severe with a high level of discipline exercised by the tutors and a rigorous routine of prayer imposed by the religious imams. Similarly, all academic subjects were subject to the same level of pressure and this was raised even further for those pupils in the elite grade. It is of interest to note that very few students failed to live up to the intellectually high standards expected of them and John was no exception. In fact, he very quickly rose to the top of his peer group both religiously, academically and in sport and was marked by the school as a person who was to be assisted at all levels. On a personal level, John exulted in his high abilities and revelled in his new status and the kudos his abilities engendered amongst his peers. There were, of course, those who were envious of his success and some were inclined to try to bring him down to size physically. But the bullies were in for a sharp, painful shock when they realised that John was able to use his wrestling expertise to teach them a lesson they would never forget – usually without any difficulty- and including those who were several years older and physically much larger than him. On the odd occasion when he was beaten he would ask for a return match and would persist until he had finally won. It was apparent to his tutors that John possessed a ruthless side to his nature and that he would not rest until he had crushed all opposition. This was not to say that he was unpopular amongst the other students, as he had friends he spent time with, but he never let himself become close to anyone, except his parents with whom he had a warm and loving relationship.

And so the years of study passed at the

Rostam High School until it was time to take his diploma which was an essential requirement before applying for permission to sit the university entrance examination. All university applicants are required to pass, amongst other disciplines, an examination in Islamic theology, which limits the access of most religious minorities to higher education. In John's case there was no problem with this requirement as he was well versed in Shia theology and able to quote verbatim all the required tracts of the Koran a true believer must be able to recite. As expected, his proud parents saw him pass the entrance examination with distinction but it was at this point that events took an unexpected turn when, instead of a letter offering a place at Tehran's central university to study chemistry and genetic biology, John's father received a phone call from his Head of Operations who told him to attend a meeting the following day with his son at the Parsian Azadi Hotel, situated just off the Chamram highway in central Tehran. They were to be there at 10.30 in the morning, he instructed, and were told not to report to reception but to go straight up to room 315 where they would be expected.

The summons was unforseen and Daichi Najafi felt uneasy at what it may have in store for them both. In Iran the application of the law could be subjective, punishment arbitrary, so an ability not to offend in any way those in positions of authority was essential, as the wrong word or an attitude which was considered, with or without justification, to be disrespectful could end in arbitrary dismissal from one's job. All such decisions were absolute in their consequences as there existed in Iran no means of redress - no mediation, no possibility of grievances being heard and certainly no Industrial Tribunals to appeal to. Although John's father was unable to think of any action he had taken in the past which could have given offence, he was still feeling nervous the following morning as he and John arrived at the entrance of the Parsian Azadi Hotel and ascended the steps through the revolving doors into the impressive marble lined entrance foyer.

Daichi Najafi's experience in subversive techniques enabled him to quickly note that the concierge behind the long reception desk looked up as he crossed the foyer and nodded to a swarthy, stocky man who was sitting in an easy chair on the opposite side of the foyer. Just as it should be with MOIS, he thought, as he and John headed to the twin lifts to take them to their appointment in room 315. He caught a glimpse through the closing door of the stocky man walking towards the lifts.

No prizes for guessing where you're going he mused with a grim smile.

The lift stopped at the third floor and the doors hissed open to reveal a sign on the corridor wall directing them to the right for room 315. Once outside the room Daichi Najafi carefully looked over his son and, seeing everything in order, knocked firmly on the door. A voice bade him enter and with the hiss of the lift doors opening behind them, father and son entered a room laid out for meetings. At the head of the table was a man known to Daichi Najafi as *Sarhang* – the Colonel - whose name, known only to a few close associates was Mahmoud Taqi-Pessain, and who headed a secretive department within MOIS which specialised in placing agents and sleepers in countries around the world.

The slim, neatly dressed man wearing western clothes, rose from his chair and walked round the table and extended his hand.

"Salaam, Daichi Najafi," his eyes looked keenly at Najafi, "I see you know who I am."

"Salaam Alaykum, Sarhang," said John's father, shaking the proffered hand. "Indeed I do recognise you, Sir. Your reputation for excellence goes before you and you are held in great esteem."

The Colonel's lips twitched briefly at the

expected compliments and turned toward John as his father introduced him. John waited politely until he was greeted by the Colonel.

"Salaam alaykum, Sarhang Agha – Colonel Sir," said John as they shook hands. "It is a great honour to meet you."

With the greetings over the Colonel waved John and his father over to the table and without preamble told them why they were there. He opened a folder which John, cleverly reading the inverted lettering, had observed his name on the outer cover.

The colonel had noted John had seen his name on the front. "I'm pleased that you have noted your name on the folder, Bahadur, and I had expected nothing less than the keenest powers of observation. In this folder are the reports from your High School tutors and they say without exception that you have proved yourself a model student of high intellectual ability with a strong and determined personality. It is for this reason that I have summoned you to this meeting and, as you are still a minor, it is desirable that your father gives his approval for the offer I shall put before you."

The Colonel shuffled through the papers in the open folder until he found the sheet he was looking for and after a few seconds study looked up at John.

"Bahadur, you have been noted as exceptional across a whole range of disciplines and in your personal attributes, and in light of these excellent accomplishments I am now putting a career path before you. We have reserved a place for you at the Intelligence department of Imam Mohammad Bagher University. The course commences in two months' time just after your eighteenth birthday and last for one academic year - approximately nine months. In view of your excellence in your science disciplines we want you to transfer to an intensive three year course with the Department for Molecular and Cell Biology. After, for another year, you will attend a postgraduate course at the Biological and Genetic research centre at Leicester University in the United Kingdom."

The Colonel fixed John with a firm gaze as he leaned forward to emphasise the point he was to make. "However, I must stress that these arrangements can be altered at any time should changing circumstances necessitate, and you will have to adapt accordingly." After John gave him the assurance that he understood, the Colonel continued.

"The time we have planned for you to spend in England is of the utmost importance for the path we have chosen for you, when you must be able to speak English as a native. You must be able to understand their warped sense of humour, etiquette, idiom – in short in that year you have to become English. You will have to put aside your loathing for their degenerate life style, the immodesty of their women and their lack of belief not only in their own religion, but in the only true religion of the Prophet Mohammed. It is also envisaged that after finishing your research at Leicester university you will be returning to England for a month each year as a tourist so that you can be aware of any developments and to maintain your linguistic skills. However, I must repeat that these plans may, of necessity, have to be altered and an entirely different path could be placed before you."

The Colonel leaned back in his chair and fixed John with a steady gaze. "We have total confidence in you and I can confirm that my department will fund all your tuition fees here and in England and, of course, all expenses for travel and accommodation abroad. You will, in addition, receive a generous allowance throughout this time. Upon satisfactory completion of your studies you will be taken on as an operative in my department in MOIS."

The Colonel waved his hand in dismissal as John started to thank him. "There is just one more matter which has to be brought to your notice." The Colonel paused for a moment in order to choose his words. “I cannot divulge precise details at this stage, but can say you have been selected as the right person for an operation planned for the future which will alter the course of world history and bring nearer the time when Islam will rule the world.”

The colonel fixed father and son with a stern look. “I am sure that it is unnecessary to remind you that not one word of this conversation, or any disclosure about this meeting, must be relayed to any living person or written down in any communication or personal record. Have I made myself clear?”

The Colonel watched closely as father and son bowed their heads in agreement and gave him their sincere assurances they would do as instructed. John turned to his father for approval and, after seeing his smile and nod of assent, turned to The Colonel and gravely told him he would be honoured to accept and that all his efforts would be at the service of his country and its goals. That John, with his father's blessing, would accept the offer was never in doubt in the Colonel's mind, but he was gratified to note that John remained collected and controlled throughout. Yes, he thought, we have chosen wisely.

But it was to be many years before the destinies of John and Justin were to intertwine dangerously and frighteningly in the green and peaceful rural county of Shropshire.

CHAPTER 4

Justin slowly came to after a difficult night's sleep. Unusually for him he had been troubled by a vivid dream. In it he had been walking in the countryside and enjoying the pleasant surroundings when he became aware that he was being followed. At first he couldn't see what it was and decided to walk faster. But however fast he walked the presence was gaining on him and when he looked back he saw a dark shape with the face of John. Then he tried to break into a run, but it was as though he was wading through treacle, whilst John was able to run at full speed. Just as John was about to engulf him, Justin awoke with his heart racing and consumed with a feeling of dread. The dream disturbed him and he lay awake for an hour until the alarm went off at seven o'clock when he dragged himself out of his bed.

He realised that the business arrangement with John was getting to him and decided to make a great effort to put it into the grave where he habitually put problems which he was unable, or unwilling, to deal with. As he went to the bathroom he thought of the sad task he had to perform that morning having been booked to dig a grave for a child. Despite his shallow outlook on life, Justin did possess some finer feelings, and found the death of a young person distressing as it seemed unfair that someone just setting out on the path of their destiny should have their life cut short so tragically. The girl's grave was to be dug at Leighton and he recalled from a previous visit that the church clock, which rang out every quarter, had a cracked bell whose off-key sound somehow added to the melancholy of the burial ground. On a practical level, Justin knew how difficult it was to dig a grave for a small casket as it was awkward to work in a confined space which, for the sake of neatness, had to reflect the size of the coffin.

After he had eaten his breakfast, he drove through town to Coton Hill and took the road to Leighton Church. Once there, with some difficulty as expected, he completed the grave, dressed it and went back to his van to wait until the interment was completed. Comfortably settled in his van he turned his thoughts to the forthcoming Bromyard Folk Festival with pleasant anticipation – not least that he would be with his friends Caesar and Lynn – as a chance to put all his worries behind him and just enjoy himself. In the past they all would travel down to Bromyard in Caesar's Volvo estate and would camp in their large frame tent. Caesar and Lynn would take one bedroom and Justin, either alone or with his latest girlfriend, would sleep in the other. The Bromyard weekend was a whirl of laughter, dancing, music and song, as well as the large quantities of beer which were drunk, and a chance to let one's hair down.

Justin had a sudden thought. By now the money he had been getting from John had become a substantial sum in his bank account and he decided he would treat the three of them to a stay in a hotel rather than camping. He made up his mind he would book hotel rooms for them once he got back to the flat and surprise them when he told them what he'd done when they met at the Castle that coming Friday.

But first he had to complete the filling-in now the last of the mourners had departed. He walked over to the graveside and looked down at the coffin. It was a tragically small all white coffin and Justin read the brass plaque on the lid to see the little girl was called Sally Gwilliam and was just eight years old. Poor little thing, mused Justin as he shovelled the earth into the open grave and stamped it down around the edges of the coffin. He wondered what killed her, how she had died – accident, illness? He shook his head at the cutting short of such a young life and carried on in a sombre mood until he had neatly completed his work for the little girl he never knew.

Whilst not immune to serious thoughts, they never lasted for long and by the time Justin had loaded up and set off to Shrewsbury, he had regained his usually buoyant self. Once back inside the flat he went to his computer and looked up hotels in and around Bromyard. He decided that it would be prudent to use a Trip Advisor and check on the reviews posted there. The first hotel he looked at had mainly negative reviews from guests who had been subjected to appalling rudeness by the owners. Reading through them with amusement, Justin determined that he was not going to risk booking rooms at a venue which appeared to be Herefordshire's very own version of Fawlty Towers.

Trawling on he found positive reviews for the Royal Victoria which was situated in the town centre and made up his mind to book them in there. Phoning through he was told by the friendly receptionist that he was only just in time to reserve two double rooms as they were near capacity with bookings for the Folk Festival. Worked out well, thought Justin, as he gave his debit card details and his e-mail address which was asked for in order to confirmation the booking. He then went on the website for the Folk Festival and was just about to book three tickets when he had a sudden thought. Although he didn't currently have a girlfriend, it was possible he might cultivate something meaningful before then and, as tickets sold out quickly, he decided to pay for four. Keying in his card details and name and address he pressed send and was relieved to see that the transaction had gone through followed by a message that the tickets would be posted to him within five days. Justin looked forward to the surprise he would see on Caesar and Lynn's faces when he gave them the news and began to feel that perhaps life wasn't so bad after all.

Friday came and the Castle filled with the noise of the Folk Club and its followers as Justin sat with Caesar and Lynn enjoying their regular weekly meeting. Justin waited until he thought the moment was right before breaking the news.

“Now, dear friends,” he said meaningfully as he held up his hand for silence, “I've got something really important to tell you.”

“Bloody Hell!” Caesar widened his eyes in mock surprise. “Don't tell me you're getting hitched. I've got it, you’re having a vasectomy.

No, you're taking holy orders. Oh, don't tell me you're going to undergo ....."

He stopped as a laughing Lynn dug him in the ribs with her elbow. " Shut up, you man-child. Pay no attention to him Justin, you can be assured that there is one sensible person here and I'm all ears."

"It's all right, Lynn," grinned Justin, "I'm immune to his insults. He reminds me of Pinocchio - one day I know this puppet made of wood will become human. I'm a patient man and don't mind waiting for a couple of decades."

Caesar chuckled. "Go on then, me old mucker. I'll be serious. What's this piece of stupendous news?"

"Well, you guys, I want to treat you to a bit of luxury which you don't expect when we go to Bromyard." Justin eyed his two friends as he built up the suspense. "You, that is we, are going to be waited on hand and foot for three days. I've booked us into the Crown and Sceptre and, dear friends, the treat is on me. Everything, bed, breakfast and evening meals as well. Furthermore, dear friends, I have bought tickets for us as well. Well, what do you say."

Lynn spoke first as Caesar sat there with an open mouth showing through his generous whiskers. "I take it this isn't a joke, so I say thank you lots and I accept here and now. It's unexpected and very generous of you." She turned to Caesar. "Go on you big dummy, don't just sit there with your mouth open, say something."

Caesar managed to lose his surprised look. "I knew it," he exclaimed, "You've won the pools, premium bonds, lottery or better still all three! Seriously, though, it's a terrific offer and, yes, I accept with pleasure. Now then, is it extra to have breakfast in bed?"

And so the evening passed in a cheery and boozy fashion until the *time ladies and gentlemen* was called by Len and the pub started to empty. The three friends walked together until they reached Justin's flat on Abbey Foregate, parting with fond good nights with Caesar and Lynn continuing on the short walk to Highfields.

But Caesar had a niggle at the back of his mind. "Lynn, I'm a bit concerned," he said with furrowed brow as they strolled towards the Lord Hill column. "I know it's none of my business, and I don't want to detract from Justin's generosity, but don't you think its a bit over the top. I mean, we both know that whilst he's not skint his grave digging hasn't made him rich and booking us into a hotel for three nights plus dinners must have cost him hundreds of pounds."

"Well," said Lynn thoughtfully, "I did wonder myself but, in fairness, although we have a rough idea, we don't know exactly how much he earns or what his savings are. If you're worried he is up to something a bit iffy on the side, I think it unlikely. Justin's a bit of a lad but we have always known him to be on the level. I'm sure it's just his way of showing his appreciation of our friendship."

Caesar was silent for a moment. "Yes," he agreed reluctantly, "I'm sure you're right, Love. I'm worrying about nothing."

But even as he said those words, there still remained a nagging doubt in his mind that possibly all was not as it seemed. Unbeknown to him, so also did Lynn, but she had decided to kept her thoughts to herself.

The following morning, after saying goodbye to Lynn as she left for another day investigating a crime scene, Caesar set off for the twenty minute walk to his unit. He would normally take his Volvo estate back home but if the weather was fine he would leave it at his workplace which was big enough to park it inside. Today was fine with a bright blue sky wearing a few scattered white clouds and a sun which was already promising another hot late summer's day. Against expectations and the gloomy predictions of the weather men, September started out to be a fine stable month and Caesar was pleased to have the exercise the walk gave him. After about fifteen minutes, at the top of Monkmoor Road, he passed the angular and uninspiring block of Shrewsbury police station and shortly after arrived at his unit.

He was surprised to see a courier van parked outside and then remembered that Justin had told him that his refurbished wheel for his Norton was being delivered that day and he had completely forgotten. Fortunately the driver had only just arrived and was in the back lifting out a well wrapped package which he gave to Caesar after he had signed for it and, with a cheery farewell, slammed shut the doors and drove off in a cloud of diesel smoke. Need your injectors seeing to, old son, thought Caesar as he unlocked the door and walked inside to start his day's work. Carefully putting down the wheel by the Norton he took out his mobile and sent a text to Justin informing him his wheel had arrived and that he would be in the unit all day. Within seconds he had a text back saying *see you later.* Caesar smiled as he had expected a swift response knowing that the Norton was Justin's pride and joy and he often joked that it was a wife or baby substitute for him – a charge which Justin cheerily agreed with, adding that it probably cost more to maintain than a wife and child.

Meanwhile, after leaving the house, Lynn walked to the garage and took her Volkswagen Polo out onto the drive before getting out to pull down the up-and-over door. Back in the car, she was just about to drive off when her mobile rang with a text. She looked at the screen and saw it was from work telling her to come into the office and acknowledge receipt. She quickly sent *on my way* and set off on the short drive to the police headquarters thinking that had she been told a bit earlier she could have given Caesar a lift to work. She wondered what was happening as she was scheduled to go directly to a crime scene at Whitchurch, but was not unduly surprised at the change as her job involved a high degree of flexibility.

After parking in the staff car park she made her way to the side entrance and punched in the security code. She gave an exasperated sigh as it refused to work and, after trying twice more, realised that the code had been changed and, as often happened, no one had bothered to let her know. She traipsed round to the main reception and, after showing them her ID, was allowed in and, after getting the new entry code from the receptionist, made her way upstairs to her manager's office eager to find out what was the unexpected summons was all about.

In front of the door marked Inspector C.W. Fischer Lynn paused, knocked and, upon being bade enter, walked in to see the familiar face of her departmental head. Lynn liked her manager whose manner was polite and restrained, along with a real feel for the needs of his staff, and a puckish sense of humour. It was joked that he was well named for someone who had to find clues and bore the nickname *Fishpots,* used behind his back, with good humour. As they greeted each other Lynn was aware that there was someone else in the room who was seated in one of the chairs in front of Inspector Fischer's desk and with her experienced eye noted a woman of some thirty years of age with brunette hair drawn back into a pony tail, who was wearing a smart two piece trouser suit in light grey with a white blouse set off with a red bead necklace. She was also aware that she was very attractive with model good looks as she sat with long legs elegantly crossed exuding an air of relaxed confidence.

They both looked across at Inspector Fischer as he spoke. “Lynn, thanks for coming in so promptly, much appreciated. I'd like to introduce you to Maggie Challinor,” he waved his hand towards Lynn, “ Maggie this is Lynn Hall.”

After the greetings were over, Fischer

cleared his throat and looked at Lynn.

"You're probably wondering what this is all about, Lynn, but before I start I have to remind you that even as a civilian you are still subject to the Official Secrets Act and that everything that is spoken of in this room must not, under any circumstances, be relayed to any unauthorised person." He gave an apologetic shrug as he saw the look on Lynn's face.

"I'm aware that there was no need to remind you, but I have to follow the instructions under which I'm currently operating."

"That's all right, Boss," said Lynn, "I know how these things work. Have to say, though, I'm becoming more intrigued than when I came in."

"Be assured that you'll be more than intrigued as we go on. In a moment I'll explain Maggie's role, but first I have to point out that you are going to be asked to take on a specific security assignment which, although there will be little in the way of personal risk, will involve what may be a difficult conflict of loyalties. With this in mind I have to ask at this stage whether you want to take part. I'm sorry, but I am unable to give you more precise details until I have your agreement that you will take part. However, I must also say that if you decide you cannot, then there will be no record of this meeting and you have my word that there'll be nothing which will impact upon your position within the department. If you do agree you will, to all intents and purposes, be continuing with your current duties as a scene of crime investigator. But I do need you to decide now."

Fischer looked expectantly at Lynn as she tried to marshal her thoughts. The matter of danger, she calculated, was neither here nor there as she had faced it every day of her career as a police officer. But the mention of a conflict of loyalties did cause her some concern. Although nothing had been said directly she felt it was likely mean on a personal level, not within the department. She looked again at Fischer, whose face gave nothing away, and made up her mind, reasoning that her boss would not be a party to asking her to do something unacceptable.

"Okay, Boss," she said, "you're dead right I'm more than intrigued. I'll accept the brief. What can you tell me?"

"I'll tell you as much as I am allowed," answered a visibly relieved Inspector, "but even I can't be told everything owing to the high security level of this exercise. Let me first inform you of Maggie's role. She is an undercover surveillance operative with MI5, and has been seconded to West Mercia Police until this operation is wound up for whatever reason. I may add that Maggie has served with distinction with the Metropolitan Police Anti-terrorist unit for several years before transferring to MI5. She's relocated to Shrewsbury and has moved into one of our safe houses in town and, would have me believe is doing her homework in order to pass herself off as a Salopian." With a smile Fischer turned to Maggie. "But better that you brief Lynn as it's your baby."

"Thank you, Sir," she answered as she turned to face Lynn directly. "As Inspector Fischer has pointed out this operation is on a need-to-know basis and, like him, I cannot give you all you would wish to know. But this much I am allowed to say, that this operation has national and we believe international ramifications, and has been put in place to ensure domestic safety from a serious threat to our security."

Lynn nodded in acknowledgement but kept silent as Maggie continued.

"We know of your friendship with Justin Parkes. What I would appreciate is for you to give me an assessment of him – his character, behaviour, life style and so on."

Lynn was slowly beginning to understand why her boss had mentioned a conflict of loyalties and hoped she had not agreed to something she would later regret. She thought carefully before she spoke.

"I've known Justin for as long as I've known my husband as we all came together through the Shrewsbury Folk Club many years back. I liked Justin from the start as he's cheerful, outgoing and, I have to confess, a terrible flirt. He has no trouble attracting the ladies and nearly always had a girl friend in tow. But I had reservations about him as it became apparent that his carefree attitude was a cover for his insecurity. Caesar and I noticed over the years how he would be all over his latest girl friend and then for some reason drop them in a what can only be called a callous way. It was for that reason I resisted his charms, which he tried on with me, until it was clear Caesar and I had become an item and he backed off."

"Don't get me wrong," she paused in order to qualify her statement. "I don't want to paint a dark picture of him. He has many good points and has been a true and dependable friend to Caesar and me. He can be generous in giving his time helping out and has always been reliable. He's clean and neat about his person. Doesn't smoke. Hard working. Likes his pop but is rarely drunk, and even then is funny and easy-going. And as far as I know, using my ex-copper's nose, he is not up to anything illegal. Is that what you want to know?"

"Yes, that's helpful," said Maggie nodding her head, "but I need to know about his financial situation, Lynn. What can you tell me about that?"

"Well, although we've been friends for many years we haven't discussed out finances with each other." Lynn thought for a moment. "Obviously, over time we have had a rough idea of Justin's income and I would say that whilst he's solvent he doesn't have a lot of spare cash floating around. His van is about six years old, I think, and he hasn't talked about replacing it. He lives in a nice flat – not top of the market but spacious and well maintained – which must take a chunk out of his income in rental charges. But I have no idea how much money he has in his bank account, though I can say that he is not one for splashing it around even if he were able to. Oh, just remembered. He does have one indulgence. He has an old motor bike, a classic Norton which Caesar lets him keep in a corner of his unit. I recall Justin had the front wheel rebuilt, or upgraded or something, which Caesar told me would have set him back about £400 or so."

"What about Bromyard." Maggie asked pointedly, "I understand that Justin has paid for you and Caesar to stay at the Crown and Sceptre for three nights."

"Sorry, Maggie." Lynn raised her hands in apology. "I wasn't keeping it from you I genuinely forgot about it. Yes, that's quite true.

Caesar and I were somewhat surprised as we didn't think Justin had that sort of money. But in fairness, as I've said, we really don't know what he is worth, we just have a rough idea what we can see he spends his money on."

Maggie spoke seriously. "Lynn, thanks for the information. I'm now going to tell you how you can be of use to this operation. As Inspector Fischer has stated, it is not possible to divulge full details but if there is to be any hope of success it is essential that I'm able to cultivate a friendship – to be more precise – a very close friendship with your friend Justin. I brought up Bromyard as you are aware we know of your plans to go there in September for the Folk Festival. I also shall be there but, before that, what I want you to do is to introduce me to Justin as a friend from the past. As you know," she went on checking some note on a pad she held, "the Shrewsbury folk Festival is next month and I want us to come across each other as though by chance when you are with Justin."

Maggie checked her notes again. "I understand," she continued, "that events are all over the town but mainly at the show ground on Berwick Road, perhaps we can arrange to meet up there?"

"Got a better idea," said Lynn brightly, "there are regular jam sessions at the Castle over the weekend and we all go there." She grinned at Maggie, "But I'm sure you know that already. Anyway, we can be certain Justin will be there as it's just round the corner from his flat. Another thing, we don't go to many of the events as we have the Bromyard Folk Festival only two weeks later and we save ourselves for that."

"Good idea," agreed Maggie, "All you need to do is text me when you know the three of you will be there and I'll be with you within fifteen minutes. I'll be alone and all you have to do is greet me as an old acquaintance from police days and invite me sit at your table. I'll be there as I'm interested in the folk scene. It'll be up to me to ensure that Justin finds me attractive enough to want to start a relationship and in order for this to work you and I will have to put together a past – which as we both served with the police shouldn't be difficult- a past which includes incidents and personalities from our past police career, our likes and dislikes and very importantly time lines."

She suddenly remembered something. "I should add that I will claim to be currently self-employed as a proof reader for some of the smaller publishing houses. This cover will enable me to work from home and mean I can keep a close eye on Justin's comings and goings."

"Also, equally importantly," added Maggie, looking slightly uncomfortable, "because of the highly classified nature of this operation, you must not divulge anything about your role to your husband. I'm sorry to stress this to a professional like yourself but, if it's any consolation, we've chosen you because we have every confidence you can fulfil the task we've asked you to undertake. Lastly, let me add, that there is nothing more we require from you. You'll carry on with your crime scene work, as Inspector Fischer has confirmed, and go about your life as usual but with the addition of me as a long-lost friend. Do you have any problems with what you have to do?"

Lynn thought for some moments before replying. "No, no problems. I can do as you ask. When do we get together to work out matching stories?"

"I can answer that," interposed Inspector Fischer, as he stood up from behind his desk. "I've other duties so you can have my office for the remainder of the day. I'll arrange for the canteen to send in drinks and something to eat for your lunch. I'll be back around four thirty." He turned to Lynn. "By the way, as you should have been out today you can say I called you in to discuss the unexplained death at Cross Houses last month. I got the file out this morning, it's here on my desk." He tapped the open file, took his cap from the top of the filing cabinet and, after wishing them good luck, left the office.

After Inspector Fischer had departed, Lynn and Maggie started to put together bullet points to create a template for their relationship which would hold up to scrutiny. Maggie explained that they would need to keep in contact in order to refine any any of the narrative which needed clarification but would try to phone rather than run the risk of meeting as their story would be that, after retiring from the police, Maggie moved away for a whilst and contact was lost between them. Their first meeting would be when, ostensibly, they come across each other by chance at the Shrewsbury Folk Festival event at the Castle pub which would give them the opportunity to meet as old friends from their police force days. Maggie, as she previously stated, would claim to be a self-employed proof reader for some of the smaller publishing houses, and had decided to return to live in Shrewsbury as she lived there until she was ten years of age.

It was of no surprised to Lynn to discover that Maggie had booked herself into the Crown and Sceptre for the weekend of the Festival and by middle afternoon, after some intense brainstorming, felt that together they had put together a scenario which would stand up to close scrutiny and, because they could not take away any written notes, they spent some time memorising their cover story until they were able to repeat it without hesitation.

Although their relationship was professional, Lynn found herself liking Maggie. She was impressed with her efficiency in putting together their story. Also she found her to have a warm outgoing personality with a well-developed and well-placed sense of humour and these, coupled with her attractive good looks, meant she was confident that Maggie would not find it difficult to develop a relationship with Justin. Lynn wondered how things would work out if Justin found himself a girl friend before their planned meeting at the Castle, then, knowing Justin, she came to the conclusion that it was likely he would consider Maggie to be the better catch and do what he was good at, and dump his current fancy piece. When she mentioned her misgivings, Maggie told her that that scenario had been worked through by her department and she can be assured that Justin would be foot loose and fancy free when they were introduced. Lynn wondered just how that could be arranged but decided it was better not to ask. She was still troubled about one aspect of this deception.

"Maggie," she asked hesitantly, "I know you

can't tell me everything, but I would like you to open up a little if you can. You see, I am genuinely fond of Justin and, whilst I'm aware of his shortcomings, I do know him to be essentially a decent person at heart. Can you tell me if he's in trouble and why he is subjected to this level of surveillance?"

Maggie looked thoughtfully at Lynn for some moments in silence. She took a deep breath and chose her words with great care before answering.

"All right, Lynn, I'll give you the most I'm able to. I can't say whether Justin is in trouble but I can say that it is possible he is caught up in something as an unwitting pawn – a patsy or fall guy as our American cousins put it. I have no doubt you realise that he has been under covert observation for some time and, in that time, has been seen with a person that we suspect is a serious threat to national security. The problem we have now is that this suspect has gone to ground and to our great frustration we've been unable to locate him. We feel sure that Justin is the only possible link to him we have and possibly the only chance of finding this person. I'm sorry but that's all I can tell you, except to emphasise once again that Justin could be crucial in uncovering what is being planned against this country, and possible elsewhere across the globe. But I stress, he must not in any way become aware that he is being used by us."

"Maggie, there's something else I don't understand," Lynn clasped her hands together, "instead of all this intrigue, why don't you go to Justin and let him report back to you directly. Surely that would be the easiest way forward?"

"We had thought of that, but soon discounted it as a viable method of obtaining the information we wanted. Justin, I'm sorry to say, does not have the strength of character to be able to handle the responsibility. As you have already told me, he can be frivolous and doesn't take life seriously. We have given it much thought but decided putting him in the know would seriously compromise the operation. I'm sure you understand that his part in this has to be kept from him."

Lynn did understand about Justin and was grateful for the added information, although, as she ruefully admitted, she was not much further forward in making any sense of the whole thing. However, she did understand her role and was confident she would be able to do as she was asked and threw herself in to the task of completing the cover story. Later that afternoon, after they had finished their intense session, Inspector Fischer bustled back into the office and after a few pleasantries, they took their leave of each other, with Lynn making her way back home.

Once back at the house, she made herself a cup of tea and sat down to think things over before Caesar finished work. After some consideration, Lynn decided she had no problem with the task she was to undertake. During her years in the police, and currently as a crime scene investigator, she was able to put her life into compartments. What constituted work was put firmly away when she was at home, remaining there until she was back at work, and she knew that she would give nothing away to either Caesar or Justin.

What intrigued her was what it was all about. Despite Justin's shallow hold on life and his lack of responsibility, she did have a genuine affection for him – in fact, when she first went to the Folk club where she met Caesar and Justin, she initially found herself strongly attracted to Justin until she realised that she couldn't see herself putting up with his jack-the-lad attitude to life. She came to the conclusion that a friendship would be preferable as he seemed incapable of forming any meaningful and sustained relationship with women. She was still fond of Justin and was glad that their friendship had endured over the years. She just hope that he was not in trouble, but her gut feeling was that he must be involved in something serious as MI5 would hardly be likely to send a field officer to Shropshire on undercover duties specifically to befriend him for some trivial reason and, anyway, Maggie had said that she wasn't sure herself. But, she concluded as she sipped her tea, she had a task to carry out which involves national security and, with all personal considerations set aside, she would carry it out as instructed to the best of her abilities.

As she waited for Caesar to come back from work, she thought back on the path her life had taken to bring her to this point. She had been born in Nantwich, a well-ordered market town in south Cheshire which in was listed in the Domesday Book During the English civil war, Parliamentarian Sir William Brereton had a stronghold there which, in 1642, was attacked by Sir Thomas Aston in the King's name, but who was eventually forced to retreat. Later that year the Royalists ousted Brereton, and garrisoned the town for the King. To this day, and for over 40 years, the faithful troops of The Sealed Knot Society have gathered in the historic town to re-enact the bloody battle that took place almost 400 years ago and marked the end of the town's long and painful siege.

Lynn smiled to herself as she recalled the excitement as a child of seeing the actors in their Civil War costumes. The bearded Royalists in flowing cloaks with wide-brimmed hats sporting long feathers, and the clean-shaven jowls of the Parliamentarians with their steel helmets and breastplates all holding muskets and pikes and, all made the more surprising, by seeing many of them taking a break in the coffee shop near St. Mary's church in the town centre.

Hers was a happy childhood. She was an only child and, although indulged, was never spoiled by her loving parents. He mother was a primary school teacher and her father in middle management with a company which extracted silica sand at Arclid for the glass industry. Maggie remembered the holidays they took each year in the Lake District and the fun they had boating on Coniston and Windermere. She recalled some of the walks they took and, as she became older and stronger, the difficult climbs up the various peaks. She would never forget the time when aged fifteen her father took her to climb Helvelyn along Striding Edge and the effort she had to make to overcome her fear of the narrow path along the arête with its sheer drops either side, before eventually making her way to the summit feeling a great sense of achievement. She was grateful that her father left it until later to tell her of the solo mountaineer who, some years before, had slipped on Striding Edge and tumbled some forty feet onto a small ledge breaking his leg in the process. The ledge was out of sight, but fortunately it did have a rivulet of water running across it which saved his life. He remained there for five days, resigned to death, before someone heard his weak cried for help and he was rescued.

Lynn thought back to the time when she decided on the police as her career. Academically she was average and managed to obtain seven GCSE's but where she did excel was at sport and she became captain of the under 16 hockey team in her last year at school. Despite her parents' disapproval, she decided that academia was not for her and persuaded her parents that she needed to find her way in the world and look for a job until she had decided on what she wanted to do. Realising that Lynn had made up her mind to follow her own path, her parents gave her all the support she needed and were pleased, in a way, when she found a position nearby waiting on at the upmarket Rookery Hall Hotel. With no previous experience she was trained in all aspects of service before she was considered able to wait on table alone and soon came to the notice of management as a quick learner with a cheerful disposition and respectful attitude towards the guests. Little did she realise at the time that the experience she gained waiting on was to stand her in good stead when she joined the police – the ability to take down precise details of the orders, to resolve problems and to deal with difficult customers with real and imaginary complaints. Above all she strengthened her natural ability to remain calm and in control under pressure and sometimes severe provocation from the occasional troublemakers.

She remained at Rookery Hall for two years before deciding she would like a change and experience something different. Her mother suggested that her school was looking for classroom assistants and thought she might like to apply. The idea appealed to Lynn as she imagined it to be a complete change from her present job and after filling in the application form which her mother brought from the school, was pleased some weeks later to receive a letter asking her in for an interview. She was even more pleased when a week later she was told her application had been successful and, subject to a satisfactory Enhanced Disclosure search as she would be working with children, she could start once her certificate had been received by the Head Teacher.

As expected, there was no problem with her obtaining the Disclosure Certificate, although it did take three weeks for her to hear that all was in order, before she was told could start the following Monday morning when all the necessary paperwork would be completed before her training commenced. The following day, with all the paperwork signed and in order, she was introduced to the teacher she would support and set to work with enthusiasm to learn her new duties. Although experienced in methods of dealing with adults, Lynn found that children were a very different proposition. Her school's catchment area was at the rougher end of Nantwich and some of children exhibited difficult and challenging behaviour, which made realise that she had a great deal to learn if she was to be able to exert control. Difficult though it was initially, but with the help of the teachers, she soon found from within herself the means to resolve the problems of anti-social behaviour which some of the children exhibited and obtain a rapport with them. Again, although she could not know it at the time, this experience would prove invaluable when she became a police officer.

After two years as a classroom assistant, and now aged twenty, Lynn felt it was time she found herself a career and after researching several possibilities decided that she would find a rewarding future as police officer. Initially she applied to the Cheshire Constabulary only to be told that they were not recruiting for one, possibly, two years but she was welcome to apply next year on the off chance that their recruitment had recommenced. Finding this check on her career path unacceptable, Lynn looked over the nearby county border into Shropshire and made an application to West Mercia Police which, to her great joy, and that of her parents who were delighted she had made a sound choice, resulted in an initial interview followed five weeks later with the offer of a place on their assessment course.

The assessment course was held at the West Mercia Police headquarters at Hindlip Hall in Worcestershire and was an intensive week of tests of initiative, physical fitness, general knowledge, role play and interviews. Lynn loved every minute of her time there and excelled at every test. At the end she knew with certainty that a career with the police was for her and waited impatiently for confirmation that she had a place on a cadets' training course. In due course a letter of acceptance arrived and confirmation that she was to join the next available training course at Hindlip Hall.

As she finished the last of her cup of tea Lynn smiled to herself as she recalled the good times she had on her six week course and how she was stretched physically and mentally to reach a level of competence she never realised she possessed. After the passing out parade, when each trainee became a fully fledged constable, she was told that she was to be posted to Shrewsbury and took up her post at the main police station on Monkmoor Road for a further four week induction training where she soon realised that she still had a lot to learn. But learn she did and was soon marked as above average by her line manager and as a result was often tasked, with considerable success, with resolving difficult crimes.

But all was not plain sailing. After eight years as a constable Lynn decided she would try for her Sergeant's exam which she sat and passed both written and interview parts. However, of the eighteen who sat the exam, eleven passed only to discover that there were only six sergeant vacancies and, as Lynn was not amongst the top six she was not offered a position. Unfortunately, the system in place with West Mercia Police meant that there was no waiting list for the next vacancy and she would have to go through the entire application and testing process the following year if she wanted to reapply. The next year she had the disappointment of a pass which was not high enough for her to be offered one of the few vacancies. Lynn made the reluctant decision that her destiny must lie elsewhere, and when she discovered that the force was looking for civilian scene of crimes investigators, made the decision to apply and, if successful, resign her position as a constable. She was pleased to be accepted and found that, although the pay was less the hours were considerably more civilised and her new duties varied and fulfilling and, as a civilian employee, far less formal.

She brought herself back to earth from her reverie with a sigh, as she recalled the strange turn of events which faced her at the present time, and decided to use the time constructively before Caesar returned from work and go once again through the cover story which she and Maggie had put together. She was confident of her ability to carry of the deception, but it was as well that she was unaware of the terrible blow that fate had in store for her.

CHAPTER 5

Back at his workshop Caesar was putting the finishing touches to an antique bobbin-turned side table he had in for repair as he waited for Justin to turn up. I know what he's like, thought Caesar with a smile, he come in frothing with excitement, slap on the new wheel and go off for a blast down country lanes. But first Caesar decided to deliver the finished table as the owner lived in town and also he wanted to be paid for the renovation he'd carried out. He wasn't worried about Justin turning up as he had been given a key to the unit when he had stored his Norton there so that he was able to access it over the weekends and evenings and, after loading the table into his Volvo, set off for the delivery address in the up-market Kingsland area to the west of the town.

Forty minutes later, minus table but with the payment in cash in his pocket, Caesar drew up outside his unit to note that Justin's van was parked there and was not surprised to find

Justin inside surrounded by paper and bubble wrap carefully examining his pride and joy, the newly refurbished wheel.

"What ho! Justin me old mate," Caesar greeted Justin with a smile, "surprised to see you here so soon, thought you might leave it a couple of weeks before unwrapping that tatty old bit of tinware."

Justin laughed at the friendly insult. "Just try and keep me away from my lovely little girlfriend who never answers back. Anyway, what do you mean, tinware? This is quality stuff and as I like you I'll give you a two hour lecture on twin leading shoe front brakes with the thrilling addition of the advantages of stainless steel spokes."

Caesar gave a deep groan. "Suddenly I've lost the will to live. Tell you what, if you promise not to bore me with motorbike trivia, I'll make you a brew. Deal?"

Justin nodded in agreement as he finished removing the remainder of the protective wrapping from the wheel and, after tidily putting everything in the waste bin, proceeded to proudly cast his eye over the new brake assembly. Firstly he removed the drum and examined the brake linings. Running his fingers over them he decided that they needed to be smoothed and with some fine emery paper which he took from the tool box by his side, gently ran it over the linings until he was satisfied they had all trace of roughness removed. Next he checked the operation of the cam linkage to check that it were adjusted so that both shoes came on at the same time. He was pleased to see that the set-up was spot on and replaced the drum. Next he had the task of replacing the inner tube and tyre which took some time as the tyre was reluctant to be levered back over the wheel rim. Finally it was done, and using a foot pump which he had brought from the van, the tyre was inflated to the correct pressure before the complete wheel was offered up into the forks. Once secured, Justin attached the brake cable and wound back the adjuster until he had left a small amount of movement on the handlebar brake lever before the brakes came on. Satisfied with his work, Justin stood back and called to Caesar to have a look

Breaking off from his work, Caesar ambled over over to inspect the finished result. Despite the banter Caesar did admire the old Norton and, after squeezing the handbrake lever a couple of times, agreed that it did look the part. It was whilst looking over the machine that Caesar glanced at the motorcycle protective clothing that Justin kept on pegs on the wall. He saw with surprise that the old rather tatty Belstaff waxed cotton jacket that normally hung there had gone and in its place was a brand new padded leather biker's jacket and next to it a new full-face flip-up visor helmet. Looking further, he saw with astonishment a pair of new full-length, leather zip-up motorcycle boots which had a pair of padded leather gloves draped over the top. Whilst Caesar had no precise knowledge of the price of motorcycle protective gear he made a quick calculation of their cost and at a conservative estimate came up with a total of at least £600. He thought of Justin's generosity with the hotel booking for Bromyard which, along with the cost of the refurbished wheel and the bikers clothing, came to total which made him wonder how he was able to afford such largess. But Caesar decided to keep his thoughts to himself as it really was none of his business to question Justin's spending – especially as he and Lynn were recipients of his generosity.

"Well, I have to admit it does look impressive," he said easily, "and now I have a distinct feeling that you will be taking your pride and joy out onto the open road wearing the new gear which my beady eye has observed."

At the mention of his new clothing, a slightly defensive look came over Justin's features but he spoke normally as he replied. "Oh, that. I thought I'd treat myself as the old waxed cotton jacket was getting distinctively past it's sell-by date and I needed a new helmet as well. But you are indeed correct, Caesar, me old mucker. I will be going out for a run as the new linings need bedding in. I'll give it a twenty mile run which should do the trick and then if it's all right with you I'll come back here and take the drum off and clean out all the dust."

"Not a problem," said Caesar, "but you won't find me here when you return as I've arranged to see an antiques dealer in Whitchurch who has just bought himself furniture from a sale at a stately home which has filled a removals lorry. He wants me to go over the stock and quote for any refurbishment and repairs. If it comes off I'll have work for several months. I'll be going back afterwards to my long-suffering wife straight after, so lock up once you've finished here, will you?"

With Justin's assurances that the unit would be left secure, Caesar departed with a cheery farewell leaving Justin to get into his new new leathers. What Caesar didn't know, when he tried to calculate the cost of the new clothing, was that Justin had bought at the top of the range and he had seriously underestimated the total cost. In fact, it came to over £800, but Justin now had so much money in his bank account, and in cash in the flat, that he was now wondering just what he was going to do with it all. After Justin finished putting on his gear, he pushed the Norton off its centre stand and wheeled it outside. He put it back on its stand whilst he went back to collect his helmet and, after lowering the roller shutter door and padlocked from the inside, left the unit through the side door which he also locked and checked the handle to make doubly sure it was secure.

As he pulled the helmet over his head a thought suddenly came to him as to how he could make use of the large sums of money now at his disposal and decided he would develop the idea once he had given it more thought. But now his thoughts turned entirely to the pleasure of the ride he was about to undertake. He swung his leg over the Norton and pushed it forward to take it off its stand. Next, he turned on the petrol tap under the tank and, as he did so, remembered that he hadn't checked how much fuel there was in it. Being an old bike the Norton had no fuel gauge and the intrepid riders of the day would simply remove the fuel cap and look inside whilst rocking the bike from side to side which helped them to see the level and estimate how much was inside the tank. With experience it was possible to leave the cap in place and accurately predict how much fuel was there by the feel of the liquid sloshing around as the bike was rocked. Justin listened carefully and thought he had at least two gallon remaining in the tank – more than enough for his jaunt as the Norton if ridden carefully would do over fifty miles per gallon - and ample for the twenty or so miles he planned on.

He bent down and pressed the tickler studs on the top of each carburettor to flood the float chambers for starting. Then he moved the choke lever to full on and pressed his full weight down on the kick-start lever. The Norton had been fitted with electronic ignition by its previous owner and, although purists might shake their heads at such vandalism, Justin found that just one kick was enough to fire her up. As he expected, the twin cylinders burst into life with a rough sound until Justin eased the choke lever back to half-way when the engine settled into a steady rhythm. Easing the gear lever up into first and releasing the clutch lever, he left the industrial estate and set off along Monkmoor Road with the intention of taking a run out along country A roads which would give his new front brake a good opportunity to bed in.

Leaving Shrewsbury on the A488, and with the Norton now up to running temperature and the choke off, Justin opened the throttle and was rewarded with the typical flat bark of the bikes of that era as he laid the machine through the bends on the country road through Hanwood on his way to Minsterley where he intended to turn north to Westbury and thence back to Shrewsbury, thus keeping to his original intention of a twenty mile run. Unsurprisingly, once he got the wind in his face, and knowing he had enough fuel, Justin's original plan was swept away as he gave in to the exhilaration of heeling the big machine over through the sweeping bends of the Shropshire roads and instead of turning north at Minsterley he carried on south to Lydham, just north of Bishop's Castle and turned east onto the A489 which crosses the rolling southern foothills of the Long Mynd, and which was made for motorcycling with its ten miles of sweeping bends and easy gradients, before it levels out when it joins the A49 two miles north of Craven Arms.

Heading back towards Shrewsbury, some twenty miles north, along the wide well-surfaced road he soon passed Church Stretton with the dark outline of Caer Caradoc to the east, and decided to open up the Norton along one of the many straights with which the road possessed. Justin was a mature rider and seldom used excessive speed or acceleration in deference to the age and value of the machine but once soon after he had bought the Norton he decided to unleash its full potential along a temptingly deserted and straight section of road. He soon discovered the Norton's weakness – vibration. He knew from his mechanical experience that most twin cylinder engines had a crankshaft with the pistons at 180°. This meant that when one piston was at the top of its stroke the other was at the bottom, thus enabling the moving parts to be balanced and so achieve smooth running. But the Norton had retained an old engine design where the two pistons moved up the bores together. This was not a problem when the original engine was designed as a 500cc but over the decades it was enlarged to 600cc, then 650cc and, finally with the Atlas, to 750cc, the vibration was so severe that when the Commando version was marketed, Norton isolated the entire engine and gearbox with rubber mountings in the frame which allowed the engine to vibrate but isolated the rider from the worst of the discomfort.

When on that occasion Justin had taken the Norton over the ton the vibration coming through the seat was such that he wondered if it would affect his ability to father children and he soon throttled back to a more comfortable speed. With this in mind, he kept his speed down as he swept past the sparse traffic on his way back to Caesar's workshop. He was pleased with the new twin-leading shoe front brake. Initially there was a spongy feel when he squeezed the lever on the handlebars, but as the miles rolled by and the brake was used more, he found it became firmer and proved to give, as expected, considerably more stopping power for far less effort. There was now excessive travel on the brake lever now that the linings had bedded in, which he expected, and he decided to take the drum off when he got back in order to remove the brake dust which had built up as the linings bedded in with use.

Back at the workshop Justin wheeled the Norton back to its designated corner and pulled it back onto its stand after remembering to turn off the petrol tap under the tank. Taking off his helmet he saw that it was splattered with the remains of July's insects and went over to the sink to wash off their remains before they set hard and, after checking his expensive leather jacket ran a damp cloth over the front to remove the squashed mess. Justin then quickly dropped the wheel out and after taking off the drum carefully tipped out the brake dust and wiped round the drum using his handkerchief. Once finished, he replaced the dust cover over his machine and well pleased with how things had gone left the workshop with the intention of treating himself to a Chinese takeaway round the corner on Monkmoor Road.

As he drove back to his flat Caesar, at the other side of town, having finished his business in Whitchurch was just then pulling up at their house in Highfields.

Lynn was at the stove when Caesar let himself in through the front door and didn't hear him over the noise of the extractor fan above the hob. The first thing she knew of his return was when a pair of brawny arms encircled her and a bushy beard tickled her neck.

"Ummm! What a lovely aroma," said Caesar sniffing appreciatively as he looked over her shoulder, "and the food smells pretty good as well."

Lynn laughed. "Saucy monkey. How about saying hello when you come in instead of attacking me from the rear like something from the swamp."

"Suppose I could. But hang on a minute now," said Caesar, pretending outrage. "How come you didn't fight back when a pair of foreign arms grabbed you? It could have been the milkman or window cleaner wanting a specific kind of payment. I'm getting worried about you. Explain yourself at once, young lady!"

"The explanation is simple, you big gorilla, we get our milk from the supermarket and the window cleaner doesn't smell of wood and glue and is clean-shaven. Anyway if we could try and develop a sensible conversation, perhaps you could tell me how your Whitchurch trip went."

"Very well," said a now serious Caesar, running his fingers through his beard. "I found the place no problem and met this guy Eric Lawley at the warehouse as arranged. He got this big set-up and as well as being open to the public, has a website for on-line sales and also deals with the trade. A bloke does all his renovation in-house but he's retiring next month and Eric decided he didn't want the hassle of employing someone else and thought he'd try me as, naturally, I came highly recommended."

"No doubt this Eric had heard of your innate modesty as well." Lynn grinned. "Seriously, sounds good so far. So how's it been left?"

"First things first. I'm as parched as Death Valley. I'll make us a wet." he said as he checked the kettle's contents and switched it on. He neatly sidestepped Lynn as he placed everything next to the kettle to make a drink of tea. "Eric told me he'd managed through a contact to get first bite at a stately house which was being emptied and has filled, not one as I thought, but two small removal lorries with stock. Some of it ready for sale but about a third of it needing work."

"What he's done is to try me out with a couple of pieces which I have in the estate as we speak, and if satisfied with the turn round, cost and finish on those two, he'll use me from then on," said Caesar as he poured the boiling water over the tea bags in the mugs. "As everyone knows, everything I do is first class and,

all being well, we should have a steady income from him. Anyway, enough of me, how did your day go"

"Caesar, I'm really pleased for you," said Lynn, "but my day was not as expected. I wasn't out and about as Fishpots called me in to try and tidy up some unresolved matters relating to the unexplained death at Cross Houses last month. It took up the whole day and I'm not sure we made much progress." Lynn decided to move the conversation onto safer ground and quickly changed the subject. "Anything else happened?"

"Nearly forgot. I arrived at the unit this morning to find a carrier there delivering Justin's fancy new wheel. I sent him a text and he said he'd be with me soonest. No surprise then when he turned up a short while later visibly drooling with excitement and set about tearing off the wrapping to finally exposing this thing which, for Justin, is of indescribable beauty!"

"Know what you mean," laughed Lynn, "it's no wonder he can't keep a relationship going whilst he's in love with his motorbike."

"True. But there is something troubling me," went Caesar as he blew noisily on his tea before taking an enjoyable sip. "You know how we wondered where Justin's spare cash came from now he's started to splash it around. Remember how he hangs up his riding kit on the wall by his bike, well, I didn't say anything at the time, but I noticed that he's bought a load of expensive biker gear – boots, jacket, helmet and so on. I'm not well up on cost but I do know anything leather is pricey and at a minimum it has to have set him back by my estimate at least £600. In fact, on reflection, I think it would be considerably more. We've know Justin for many years and although never exactly on his uppers he's never had much spare cash to indulge himself."

Lynn realised she would have to choose her words with care. "That's right, we've both noticed he's splashing it around but we really don't know how much he earns or how much he saves. He might have put his gratuity aside when he left the army and not touched it until now. He could be prudent and put small sums aside over along period. Could have had a lottery or premium bond win. Let's be honest, Caesar, we are probably making a mountain out of a molehill and that there's nothing untoward. Let's forget it, shall we?"

Caesar nodded his great shaggy head.

"You're probably right," he admitted reluctantly, "and, of course, it's none of our business really. It's just that if he's getting himself into a fix I want to help him out of it. As you know we've always be able to talk about our problems to each other. So shall I leave it until he decides to open up to me."

Although Lynn agreed with him she was uncomfortable knowing with certainty what Caesar only suspected. Justin was into something and, whatever it was, she knew that for the intelligence authorities to be involved it couldn't be something trivial. But she kept her thoughts and feelings to herself as she busied herself with the evening meal. Professional that she was, she still felt uncomfortable maintaining her role in this operation a secret from Justin and her husband. It was just as well that the events which would unfold were kept from her, for if she knew the ordeals that she, Caesar and Justin would have to endure, the knowledge would have tested her loyalty and courage to the very limits.

Back at his flat, Justin showered and changed into clean casual clothes. September that year was exceptionally hot so he put on a pair of light cotton chinos and a blue check, short-sleeved shirt and, after carefully examining the take-away's menu, decided on sweet and sour pork in batter, chicken chow mein and egg fried rice. Then he phoned to place his order for collection in twenty minutes time. Just right, he thought, for a refreshing drink of lager before I have to go and pick it up.

After pouring his drink, Justin settled down in an armchair and took stock of things as they currently stood. He had to admit that he had got himself tangled up in something he couldn't understand and, to be honest, he really didn't want to know. He felt with great certainty that too much knowledge would be a bad thing, especially as this John character had an uncanny knack of knowing exactly what he was doing. After the chilling telephone call from John following the late night visit to the grave at Criggion, he decided he would do exactly as asked and from then on had carried out the agreement to the letter. When he had been booked to dig a single grave, or reopen an existing one which had to be left open overnight, he dutifully e-mailed the details to the designated address and, two or three days' later, he would receive a letter containing used bank notes. He had noted that the post marks on each envelope were stamped either Shropshire, Staffordshire and Cheshire. Justin wasn't sure why they had been posted from three different counties, but reasoned that this John character was trying to make it difficult to know where he was located. Anyway, he made up his mind, it doesn't matter so long as the cash-stuffed envelopes kept coming.

He broke off his reverie to look at his watch and saw that his twenty minutes had almost elapsed and left the flat to walk briskly round the corner onto Monkmoor Road and the Chinese takeaway. He paid the smiling assistant and took the bag back to the flat to begin his keenly anticipated meal and, after laying the containers out on the table, set to with a hearty appetite. As he ate he returned to the train of thoughts he had begun. Justin would be the first to admit that he was not, by nature, a profound thinker. He preferred to skim gently through life always looking to find gratification and never wanting to accept responsibility for his actions, but his present situation was one that had the effect of pulling him reluctantly back to earth and, try as he might, he was never able to completely shift the dead weight of consequence from his shoulders. As he spooned more food onto his plate he thought that if he kept his nose clean, did exactly what he had to, then he would have no further contact with this sinister John cove and would eventually be free of him once the arrangement ended. Anyway, he thought with satisfaction, the multiples of £500 were building up nicely in his bank account and he now had a sizeable balance with the knowledge that it would be hugely increased by the time the arrangement with John had finished.

The thought of all that money enabled the care-free Justin to overcome, in small degree, the frightening reality of his predicament and he returned to the idea he had whilst on his ride out on the Norton. Although easy-going, Justin was not a spend-thrift and he had sensibly put aside his gratuity when he left the army and, as he had always been able to live within his means, was able to add to it the small pension he was entitled to after his term of service. This savings account had increased slowly over the years and was now a considerable sum and, with the money from his business arrangement with John added to it, Justin felt sure that he would be able to raise the deposit for a mortgage and realise his dream of owning his own place. He wasn't sure at this stage whether he wanted a house or a flat but realised that although he now was in a position to start looking for property, he had to try and arrange a mortgage to see how much he was able to borrow taking into account the sum he had available as a deposit. He was also aware that being self-employed he would have to supply proof of earnings which he thought might be for two or three years of trading and felt pleased that he would be able to do that. For Justin, despite his many shortcomings, did show considerable maturity where financial matters were concerned. He had always lived within his means whether employed or self-employed and exercised considerable constraint over his spending so that he was always in credit. He had no credit cards – just a debit card for his bank account which was always in the black with a safety net of an interest-free overdraft facility of £200 which he had never had to use. His one indulgence was his Norton. His van had been purchased with cash and he thought with satisfaction, he owed not a penny to anyone. Furthermore, he had an accountant who reconciled his books and prepared them for the Inland Revenue and Justin made sure he paid his dues to them in good time. Time, he thought with eager anticipation, to put thought into action and see my bank about a mortgage and then have a wander around the estate agents.

As Justin cleared away the remains of his takeaway and took his dirty plate and containers over to the sink to wash, he thought he would like to share his exciting plans with his friends and resolved to ask Caesar and Lynn to his place for drinks one evening soon. In the morning he would telephone the bank before he went to his first job to arrange an appointment with the mortgage advisor to see what they would advance and, once he had some spare time, see what properties were available within his budget.

Justin's spirits had bounced back at the possibilities which lay before him in the property market and he was once again able to push the corpse of his dilemma back into the oblivion of the grave which held all the disagreeable things in his life which he found difficult to face. What Justin had no way of knowing was that this particular corpse would join the ranks of those who refuse to die and rise from the ground and destroy the comfort zone which he had built up around himself. He was soon to find out that he was far from being in control of his life. But all that was to come and, in good spirits, Justin sent a text to Caesar asking him and Lynn over to his place the following evening for drinks and nibbles. Half an hour later he received a reply from Caesar to say he though it was a terrible idea, he wasn't looking forward to it one bit, and provided that nothing more interesting cropped up like clearing road kill from the M54, he would drag himself there under duress. Justin laughed when he read the response – he had expected nothing less! He decided to buy the bits he needed tomorrow afternoon after he'd finished his last job and drive round to Iceland on Brixton Way as he knew they had really nice party ideas like mini pizzas, spring rolls and the spicy things that they all liked. He remembered that they sold wine and he thought he'd pick up some of the Pinot Grigio that was Lynn's favourite tipple. He hadn't forgotten that Lynn had to have her wine ice-cold and last time she came to his place for drinks he had put her glass in the freezer beforehand. It was so cold that he was afraid that her fingers would stick to the glass and give her a frost burn. But Lynn, after taking a careful sip, announced that it was just right and asked Justin to put another wine glass in the freezer for her next drink. He thought she was joking, but she wasn't! Then having decided on his plans for the following day, Justin took himself off to bed feeling contented that he was getting everything in his life back on track.

The following day promised to be another scorcher. A deep blue sky with small pompoms of fair weather cumulus greeted Justin as he looked out of the window through which a sun shone hot with promise and prepared himself for another day's toil. In fact he only had one grave to dig that day and looked forward to being back at the flat for a late lunch. The grave was a re-open at the chapel graveyard at the wonderfully named Preston Gubbals which straddles the Wem road a few miles north of Shrewsbury. Justin had dug there once before and found it a nightmare as the entire burial ground was so woefully overgrown that the kerb stones around the plots were almost impossible to see and, as the paths were similarly covered, it was difficult to take a wheelbarrow to and from the grave to get rid of the excess soil. The entire dereliction was compounded by the fact that the digging was heavy clay and a high water table which slowly flooded the bottom of the grave, but the plus side was that it was for 11.30 the following morning so he could wait in his van and fill in later. Justin had looked around at the scene of dereliction and neglect the previous time he had been there, and judging by the spiders' webs across the chapel's windows, the locked door with the porch strewn with leaves from the previous autumn and the mummified remains of what looked like a blue tit, he came to the conclusion that it had been a long time since a service of any kind had been celebrated there.

There was one other thing that Justin didn't like about the burial ground. He didn't consider himself to be a person with an over-active imagination and had dug graves in many cemeteries which had been dark and sometimes forbidding. He had even, when the pressure of work dictated it had to be so, dug graves in darkness during the winter months using a lantern or the van's headlights if the graveyard layout allowed it, and in all the years he had been a gravedigger he had never seen or felt anything untoward. But Preston Gubbals was different. Justin was aware of a heavy, oppressive atmosphere as soon as he entered through the crumbling gate and along the weed-strewn path under the dark overhanging yews which led directly to the front of the chapel. The entire area was enclosed under a thick canopy of trees in which no birds sang, and even when the sun shone a gloomy quality hung heavily over the toppled headstones wrapped around with thorny dog rose, wild elder and brambles which had over-run the last resting places of the deceased.

It was a re-open on the first occasion and after he had set up and started digging he became aware of being watched. He took a look around the graveyard but, unable to see anyone, continued with his task. But the feeling of being watched persisted and now he began to feel uncomfortable as whatever it was emitted an aura of malevolence. The sensation made the hairs on Justin's scalp and arms stand on end and, as he felt the gaze to come from behind him, turned suddenly to see what could be there. There was nothing to see but, disturbingly, the presence's malevolent aura was now boring into him and, how ever many times he turned, it felt as though its gaze drilled into him from behind. Determined not to be scared off by something he couldn't see, Justin quickly finished opening up the grave, loaded his tools into his van and greatly relieved drove back to Shrewsbury.

The following day, although the dark and gloomy atmosphere lay all around him, he was not assailed by any feelings of being observed and was able to carry out his tasks without any uncomfortable sensation. He finished dressing the grave an hour before the committal service and was pleased that everyone departed quickly. Justin wasn't surprised, as the graveyard was not a place where anyone wanted to linger and, after filling in and replacing the matted masses that passed for turf, he loaded his van with relief and drove back to Shrewsbury and his preparations for the evening get-together.

After arriving back at the flat, Justin threw together a light meal of soup with cheese and biscuits with green olives followed by a banana. Justin liked his bananas when the skin had started to turn – he called it leopard spotted – as he found the fruit to be much sweeter. He was aware that the down side was that if he had bought a big hand he had to eat them up quickly before they went off. This problem was resolved when he discovered that Lidl sold organic bananas which were smaller in size than the ones that he usually bought from the supermarket opposite, and consequently he was able to finish them off before he had to throw any away.

After eating Justin showered and changed into his casual clothes before tidying the flat ready for the evening. He put the wine and the cans of lager in the fridge, remembering to put two wine glasses in the freezer ready for Lynn, and took the party food out at the same time. Although the instructions on the packet advised heating from frozen, Justin found that the heating time was too long and always defrosted first.

Earlier, Justin's telephone call to his bank's mortgage advisor had resulted in being offered an appointment at four o'clock that afternoon owing to a cancellation. After leaving everything in order for the evening's entertainment, he walked over the English Bridge and up Wyle Cop to the Halifax in the High Street which occupied a handsome building opposite the pedestal in the Square bearing the statue of Robert Clive of India. Once inside he made himself known at the reception desk and shortly after was shown into an office and introduced to the advisor. Justin was greeted by a pleasant matronly woman in her early fifties who quickly and efficiently took Justin through a series of questions to discover how much the Halifax could advance him.

After his appointment was completed, Justin was pleasantly surprised how much the bank had provisionally offered him. He decided, before he went back to the flat, to have a quick look in some estate agents' window displays to see what was available in his price range and, after some scrutiny of the properties on display, felt that he would be able to find what he wanted. Reassured, Justin set off weaving his way through the streets crowded with people who had just finished work all intermingled with the large numbers of visitors who throng the ancient town of Shrewsbury in the summer months. By the time he had crossed the English Bridge, the crowds had thinned and on an impulse he decided to have fish and chips for an early evening meal and bore left down the back of the Abbey to the chip shop. He was served straight away as there were no other customers waiting and took the well-wrapped package the short distance to his flat with his mouth watering with anticipation. Justin wondered what it was about the smell of fried food, especially bacon and chips, that, however close it was to when he had eaten, always tempted him to eat more.

Back at the flat he made short work of his meal and, knowing that he would be soon drinking with Caesar and Lynn, decided not to have a lager after he had eaten but wait until they arrived. Before he settled down to read the Express he had bought that morning, he felt the smell of fried food was a bit powerful and lit an incense stick which he knew would neutralise any strong smells. And so, with everything ready for the arrival of his friends, Justin relaxed to read his paper with a pleasant feeling of inner contentment.

Just before eight o'clock there were steps heard from the stairs, followed by a thunderous knocking on his front door which Justin knew heralded the arrival of Caesar and Lynn. When he opened the door Caesar started to barrel his way in only to be restrained by Lynn.

"Manners, big boy," she said primly, "didn't your parents tell you to allow a lady to enter first?"

"A thousand apologies," said Caesar taking a step back and bowing low, "after you, M'Lady,."

The gallantry of the gesture was somewhat spoiled as Lynn gave a squeal when Caesar pinched her bottom and so with the evening off to a good start the three friends made themselves comfortable in anticipation of an enjoyable time. Justin busied himself getting the drinks and amused Lynn when he brought in her super-cooled wine wearing a pair of oven gloves for protection.

"This is nice," said Justin as he took a swig of his beer, "I've got some nibbles for later which will be heated in my new sophisticated halogen oven. Then I've got some news I want to share with you later."

My more mystery and intrigue," said Caesar with his eyes twinkling from under his bushy black eyebrows, "anyway what about telling us how you got on with that barn find heap of rusting scrap you call a motorbike. Did the new brake system flip you over the handlebars when you tried to stop?"

Justin laughed at his friend's sarcasm – he was well used to it and gave as good as he got. "Thanks for asking, you horrible cynic. It was money well spent and, in fact, as a special friend I want you to experience the joy I felt when I applied the brake lever. I was going to insure the Norton to cover you but realised that I'd have to fit stabilisers before you cocked your leg over my two-wheeled girl friend and tried to wobble off."

"Right," interposed Lynn silencing Caesar just as he was about to unleash a riposte, "can you two over-excitable alpha males belt up for a minute and stop slagging each other off. Why don't we talk about what we're going to go to when the Shrewsbury Folk Festival is on next month?"

"You're right, Lynn," said Justin, pretending to look contrite, "it's time we grew up and I've started right now – don't know about that Neanderthal husband of yours though."

He and Caesar laughed as Lynn rolled her eyes and shook her head in sorrow as Justin went on.

"Now, we need to get organised. I find that the Shrewsbury and Bromyard festivals are too close together for me. We all love the folk scene but you can have too much of a good thing. I'm not going to the main event at the show ground, good though it is, but I thought we could go to one or two of the events held at various venues around town. That way we won't have burned ourselves out before Bromyard which is about two weeks later. What do you both think?"

"Funnily enough" said Caesar, "Lynn and I were talking about that earlier today and thinking along the same lines. We thought we could go to the Castle on Saturday for the first part of the evening and listen to the singers and then later go to the ceilidh in the community hall across the road at Coleham Head. And after that, if we still had enough energy, we could go to the Castle on Sunday lunchtime, down a couple of sherbets, and watch the Shropshire Lasses do their stuff. Remember last year when they finished one dance by lifting their skirts and flashing their knickers?"

"I do, I do," agreed Justin, with a dreamy expression on his face. "Do you remember the one with the best legs was called Susan and she wore those lovely frilly bloomers. And I also recall that she ...."

"Down boys," interrupted Lynn, well used to this laddish nonsense, part of which was to get a reaction from her. "Firstly, if you can be sensible for a minute can we come to an agreement and, secondly, my glass is empty."

Caesar examined his tankard with an outraged expression. "Bloody hell, Parkes," he roared, "my pot's a dry as one of your graveyard bones and it's been that way for all of twenty seconds. Call yourself a host?"

"Rectified in a twinkling," smiled Justin as he went over to the fridge to get fresh drinks and take them back into the sitting room. He felt it was time to put the party food into the oven and busied himself placing everything onto trays and arranging them in the glass bowl in order to allow the heat to circulate freely. Once satisfied he set the correct temperature and timer for fifteen minutes and went back to join his friends.

"To come back to what you suggested," he continued, "it sounds okay with me so, Saturday, Castle and ceilidh and, if our strength holds up, the naughty Shropshire Lasses Sunday lunchtime. Just one thing, though. My work pattern can be unpredictable. If I get chocker with work I sometimes have to dig over a weekend. It's unlikely, but I thought I'd better warn you just in case."

Despite Justin's reservations, Lynn felt a sensation of relief that a firm arrangement for the festival weekend had been achieved and she now was able to inform Maggie and arrange to bring her and Justin together at the Castle that Saturday evening. As these thoughts crossed her mind, she looked across at Justin's cheerful face as from deep within her rose a desire to protect him from any harmful consequences of his predicament. Despite her professionalism, she could not prevent a feeling of guilt knowing that she was, in some measure, deceiving two people she thought the world of. She realized with a start that she was being spoken to.

"Penny for your thoughts," said Caesar, "or are they worth more than that?"

Lynn recovered herself with a smile. "They are priceless, as you well know and always deeply profound." She sniffed appreciatively. "My, that food smells good and I'm ready when it is. But, Justin, you said you had something of momentous importance to tell Caesar and me.

We're all agog. What is it?"

"Thought you'd never ask, but give me a second and I'll get the nibbles out before Lynn faints from lack of nourishment." He went into the kitchen and carefully put the food out on a large serving dish before bringing it through to the sitting room. Once he had made sure his guests had charged their plates, he turned back to where he left off.

"Well, I also thought it high time that I matured – don't laugh Caesar – and join my two best pals and become a home owner." He paused for a moment as he looked at his friends to check their reaction to the news before continuing.

"I went to the Halifax today and they worked out a provisional sum for a mortgage and, as I've enough saved to put down the necessary deposit, I'm able to afford a modest terrace house or possibly a flat. What do you think of that?"

Not wanting to give anything away in her expression, Lynn made a point of not looking at Caesar as she replied to Justin's news.

"Wow, great. Got anything lined up yet – or is it a bit soon?"

Justin laughed. "Yes, it is a bit. I only got provisional approval this morning and I still have to submit the last three years' accounts for forensic scrutiny! Although, I have to admit that I did cast a critical eye over the window display at the estate agents in Barker Street. What I'd do is get myself round the others and see what they have whilst I wait for the Halifax to come back to me with hopefully a firm offer."

Caesar had heard this unexpected announcement with some surprise as he wondered how Justin could possible have enough to put down a deposit. He glanced over at Lynn but was unable to make eye contact and, in fairness, he decided, he wasn't going to do anything that would detract from his friend's obvious delight at an impending home ownership.

"Great new, Justin my lad. It's about time you reached man's estate and I'm glad you've finally taken my fine and upstanding life as the foundation for your long overdue launch into adulthood. In fact, I was saying to Lynn only yesterday that I thought you voice had deepened and only good can come of it." He ducked as Lynn threw a cushion at him and they all laughed before starting to discuss what sort of place Justin should have.

And so the evening progressed with much laughter and warm recollections, interspersed with the occasional serious topic, until it was time for Justin's friends to depart with endless verbal sparring still continuing between Caesar and Justin. After seeing them off, Justin went back to his armchair to finish off his drink and feel that, despite all the problems life had brought him, he was at last getting things back on track. With a warm glow, which was in truth partly alcohol induced, Justin took himself off to bed where he slept soundly the night through.

The following morning he had the luxury of a lie-in as he had only one job booked that day with an eleven o'clock start at a remote cemetery at a place called Stoke-on-Tern near Hodnet. It was a single grave he had to dig, and he had done as arranged with John and e-mailed through all the details several days before. He stretched as he considered whether to get up and have some breakfast or stay for a while longer. He ran his tongue round his mouth and tried to ignore the thick head he had woken with. That's the problem, he thought, when Caesar comes round I always have a couple more cans that I really should have, but a strong coffee should sort me out.

Justin threw back the bedclothes and swung his legs over the side of the bed, but before he could stand up his mobile on the bedside locker sounded its ring tone. Yawning, he picked it up and pressed the receive button.

“Good morning, Justin Parkes speaking.”

"Good morning, Justin," answered a voice which produced a knot of fear in Justin's stomach, "we need to talk because something has come to my attention which we have to deal with."

Justin tried to put an an act of cheery bonhomie. "Hello, John. Don't tell me that another little bird has trilled in your ear. What's it this time?"

"You can cut the brave man act, Justin, it doesn't fool me." John's level voice was icy with menace. "I've told you before and I'm telling you again, and for the last time, don't do anything outside your usual routine. Didn't I make it plain to you at the outset not to do anything which might draw attention to yourself. And you've done just that."

"You've lost me. I don't know what you are talking about," said Justin with an unsteady voice now his initial bravado had evaporated, " how have I drawn attention to myself? I haven't done anything out of the ordinary."

"Think, Justin my son. This little bird you mentioned has told me that you are planning to buy a house. This would lead some people to believe that you have come into some sort of windfall and then they might start to wonder where all your money came from. Now we wouldn't want that to happen would we, so when you next see Caesar and Lynn you make sure you tell them that the bank has turned you down."

Justin felt a shiver of fear run down his spine. How had John known of his plan to buy a house he puzzled as John went on.

"Don't get worried, Justin," John continued, but now with a hint of compromise in his voice, "we're not going to make a big deal of it. We want you to act as you have done in the past. Don't change your routines or habits. Go to the Castle on a Friday, get your Norton out for a blast - but don't spend any more on brakes and expensive leather gear – and have fun at Bromyard in September when you treat your friends to a hotel stay, but don't make any more unusual purchases until I tell you the business arrangement is finished. It's not long now, Justin, just hold tight until the end of December and then it will be all over and you'll never hear from me again. And, Justin, there will be a big end of contract bonus for you. How does five grand sound?"

Justin thought that five grand sounded very good, though he didn't like the sound of everything else John had said. He pulled himself together before replying with a voice that had the rasp of fear in it.

"Okay, okay, I've got it, John. Same old routine, nothing out of the ordinary and then you promise that I'm free by December?"

"Justin, my boy, you learn fast. You have my word."

As usual the line went dead without the courtesy of a goodbye and Justin was left looking with despair at a blank screen on his phone. He placed the mobile on the bedside table and put his head in his hands as he tried to make sense of the troubled thoughts which tumbled around in his brain. He was scared and he didn't mind admitting it. How on earth had John known he was planning to get a mortgage. Even if he had been followed to the bank by one of his people, how could he know what his business was once he was inside. Mind you, he reasoned, if he had been followed, then his tail would have seen him go to the estate agents in Barker Street so, putting two and two together, that could be how John knew.

More troubling for Justin was how John knew of his Norton's front brake up-grade and the purchases of leather gear. He had bought the clothing on line and, after some thought, he deduced that his computer had been compromised by John to the extent he could track every input he made. He didn't know a lot about computers, but he did know that a trojan horse had been sent which had put the child pornography file into his system, so possibly it was able to report back every command Justin made.

So that was another worry he could just about square, but what he couldn't reconcile was how John knew of the brake purchase. Justin had made all the arrangements for the up-grade on his phone. The carrier was arranged and paid for on his phone using his debit card and he paid the mechanic in cash when he dropped of the wheel at his house in Whitchurch. As he continued his ablutions and dressed, he racked his brains over these worrying thoughts. After a while he realised that all the arrangements carried out using his phone had been made in his flat and, just as he suspected previously that his van had been fitted with a tracker, he wondered if his flat had been bugged.

Part of him thought it was unlikely he would be able find it as he was unable to discover a tracker when he examined his van and wondered now, as he thought then, whether he was being paranoid. Paranoid or not, he determined to give the flat a thorough search before he went to work. Just before he started, he speculated on what he would do if he found a listening device. He could hardly remove it, or them, as this would alert John and Justin knew that he would be in big trouble, if not danger of some physical retribution, but if he did discover something then he would know not to say anything which he didn't want to be overheard.

With this in mind, Justin commenced a meticulous search. He carefully examined the places where a bug could have been placed using knowledge gleaned from the various spy film he had viewed in the past. Chairs were up-turned; the back of pictures and mirrors exposed; his bed was pulled apart; light fittings closely examined and every bit of furniture minutely scrutinized until Justin was sure that everything was clear and that he was only the victim of his fertile imagination. But the downside was, that if he hadn't been bugged, it still left the question of how John had such precise knowledge of his plans and movements. Then a thought suddenly came to him. The only people he had told of his house purchase plans were Caesar and Lynn the evening before. Both Lynn and Caesar had known of the Norton's brake purchase and Caesar had commented on the leather gear and it was likely he had told Lynn about it.

But even as these thought went through his head, Justin reasoned that it was unlikely his friends would be passing on this knowledge. And even if they did pass it on to someone else, how in the name of sanity could John have been a party to it. Justin felt he was clutching at straws but in the absence of any other rational explanation decided he would bring up the matter when he saw them at the Castle on Friday.

All the comforting feeling of being back in control that previously had coursed through Justin's soul was cruelly destroyed by John's disturbing call that morning, and it was with a heavy heart that Justin took himself off to his lonely toil at Stoke-on-Tern, wishing with all his being that his greed had not landed himself in this predicament. Later, as he drove along the A59 to where he turned off at Hodnet, he thought ruefully of the corpse he thought he had thought securely laid to rest in the repository for his difficulties and which had now, like the undead of voodoo tradition, risen from the grave to haunt him. Self-pity coursed through him as he wondered if his life would ever be the same again. It was as well that he didn't know it was going to become a lot worse.

Eventually, Friday night arrived and with it the keenly awaited meeting with Caesar and Lynn. They were used to seeing Justin with a girlfriend, even thought they did change with alarming regularity as he found another more to his taste and inclinations, and had been surprised that he had been without any arm candy, as he put it, for such a long time. Justin, it's true, did miss female company, especially the physical aspect of a relationship, but he found it difficult to start chatting up women whilst he was consumed with the heavy burden of trouble he found himself in. Nevertheless, he was determined to enjoy himself and, by the time he arrived at the pub he had managed to regain some of his care-free personality.

He spied Caesar and Lynn who, as usual, had arrived early and taken their favourite seats in corner. Justin, noticing their glasses were nearly empty ordered three drinks at the bar and being served by one of the regulars looked around for Len. Unsurprisingly, he saw him sitting at a table with his chin down on his chest snoring loudly and deduced that he must have had another of his intensive lunch time sessions. He knew from past experience that by closing time he would have made a dramatic recovery and joined in with the hardened drinkers who carried on for some hours with the doors locked in flagrant disregard of the licensing laws. Carrying the drinks carefully through the happy throng he took his seat with his friends and, trying to forget the dire predicament he was in, started chatting about the forthcoming ceilidh. But try as he might he was unable to recover his usual carefree self and it was not long before he noticed Caesar giving him a searching look.

Lynn, on the other hand, who knew that

Justin was in some sort of trouble, was not surprised and said nothing, but Caesar who was more direct asked Justin if everything was all right or was there something troubling him. Again Justin told him that everything was in order and he had no worries, but Caesar knew his friend was not all right and that he was hiding something from him. Despite his rough banter Caesar had a caring nature and would do anything to help his friend, but he knew when to hold back, and decided to leave it until either Justin felt able to open up to him, or there would come a time when he could sit him down with him and have a heart to heart.

He and Lynn listened as Justin told them both that he had a problem with his mortgage application and had decided to leave off house hunting until next year when he'd probably try a different mortgage lender. If Caesar previously only suspected that Justin had some troubles in his life he was now certain, since he knew Justin couldn't have been rejected by the Halifax in just two days since being asked to submit certified accounts. Now he knew with conviction that Justin was in a mess, but held his tongue until he could talk over his concerns with Lynn.

And so the evening progressed until Len awoke from his stupor, surprisingly alert and vocal, and joined in with the serious drinkers.

The three friends knew from experience that it was time to leave before Len locked the doors when they would be trapped in the pub until Len once again descended into his second episode of oblivion. And so, with a lightness induced by alcohol, the three of them walked them back to Justin's flat where he parted from them to take himself to bed and a troubled night's sleep. There would be many more such nights as his problems were compounded and he was drawn deeper into an uncontrollable and dangerous intrigue.

CHAPTER 6

The last week of September was wet and cold. A strong wind blew from the north-east bringing an unseasonal late summer chill and flurries of rain from the dark grey clouds which the gusting wind drove overhead. All of this made Justin's work heavy going and was invariably the moment when he questioned whether there was a better way of making money. Usually September was a quiet month for him and he used to wonder whether those fading away decided they would hang on as Christmas approached and delay their final journey until the New Year. Whatever the truth of the matter, as the month progressed he became busier until he often had to work well into the evenings and, on one occasion, finished so late on a Friday night that he was unable to make his weekly trip to the Castle. The high volume of work coupled with the difficult digging conditions meant that Justin often returned to the flat so tired that it was all he could do to clean himself up and cook a meal. Difficult though this time was, the hard physical labour had the blessing of taking his mind off the trouble he was in and he also had the pleasing knowledge that his bank balance was increasing rapidly.

Eventually, the work load eased and the weather decided that perhaps after all it was still just late summer and, as everyone had suffered enough, allowed the sun could shine and raise the temperature along with everyone's feel-good factor. This came as a great relief to Justin as he was looking forward to the Shrewsbury folk festival ceilidh and feared that he would be too tired to go or, at the very least, be too tired to enjoy it. Perhaps someone else would have turned work down but Justin, despite his faults, never let anyone down. If he made a promise he kept it and was known by all the undertakers as someone who could be relied upon completely.

On the Saturday of the ceilidh he had finished filling in a double grave just after lunch and once back at the flat, unusually for him, had fallen asleep in his armchair. Justin was pleased at this departure from his normal pattern as he awoke feeling greatly refreshed and for the first time since his run-in with John, more like his old self. Looking at his watch he saw with surprise that it was nearly five o'clock and that he had slept for over two hours. He decided to spend some time with his accounts bringing them up to date before he got himself ready for the evening's entertainment and sitting at his computer desk, logged on and brought up his accounting spread sheet and entered his income and outgoings for the month. After half an hour he was finished and then opened up his e-mail account to check his in-box. There was only one which read – *Justin. Don't forget our conversation.* Justin hadn't forgotten but the relentless pressure from John was starting to erode his feeling of security and, although he was not aware of it, the stress was starting to show in his features and had resulted in a loss of body weight. With a sick sensation in the pit of his stomach he closed everything down and logged off. He had planned on having a good meal before going out for the evening but now had lost his appetite and instead made a peanut butter sandwich which he ate slowly, washed down with a glass of milk.

Seven o'clock came as Justin left the flat for the short walk to the Castle. There were low clouds in the distance, but a setting sun shone through the gaps as he walked in front of the Abbey and crossed the road into the car park opposite, over the Old Potts Way, and under the railway bridge to the Castle's rear entrance. The pub was fairly quiet this early in the evening and Justin had no problem seeing his friends in their usual corner giving him a cheery wave. He noted with interest when he entered that with them was an attractive dark-haired woman wearing faded denim jeans and a floral blouse seated next to Lynn and he was pleased to see that the spare seat was next to her. Justin called over to ask if they wanted a drink but Caesar pointed to their full glasses with a shake of the head and, after paying Len for his pint he walked over to their table. As usual it was Caesar's banter which opened the conversation.

"Here you are, Maggie," he boomed, "this is the terrible man we told you about. He's broken more hearts than you've had hot dinners and is on the black list of all Shropshire mothers with daughters older than sixteen!"

"Caesar, you'll be hearing from my lawyers in the morning," grinned Justin as he turned to the stranger. "As you probably know by now Caesar suffers from paranoid delusions so pay no attention to him. He has the most appalling manners, a bizarre sense of humour, some of the most anti-social whiskers ever known and supposes that he thinks he has actually made an introduction." Maggie smiled at Justin as Lynn took over.

"Maggie, let me once again bring some female sanity to the proceedings. May I introduce Justin, and Justin this is Maggie." Justin and Maggie shook hands warmly with Justin keeping hold for a moment longer than was necessary to see what sort of reaction he would get. He found to his pleasure that the pressure was reciprocated as Lynn went on.

"Maggie and I have just met up again after some years – more than I want to remember if the truth must be told – after we went our separate ways. We both joined the force together and were on the same training course at Hindlip Hall. Then we were both posted to Malinsgate in Telford for about five years before I went to Shrewsbury and Maggie, shortly after, to somewhere else. At that point we lost touch with each other, as you do, until now."

"Nice to meet you, Justin" said Maggie in a soft voice, "and don't worry, I quickly got the measure of Caesar and don't believe a word he says. I'm told you are a full-time grave digger. It sounds a bit gruesome - not to mention like hard work."

"It is and, before Caesar gets in his usual gag, it isn't a dead end job. Anyway," he joked, "I prefer the up-market description of self-employed sexton."

Caesar gave a hoot of laughter. "Hark at him. The boy has pretensions of grandeur. Sexton indeed! Next he'll be telling you he's a champion folk dancer. I warn you Maggie, don't get within a country mile of him when the music starts. The UN has designated his feet weapons of mass destruction!”

They all laughed at Caesar's nonsense and as usual Justin forgot his troubles as he threw himself into mood of the moment and, having sized up Maggie, decided that he would most definitely throw his hat into the ring and see whether his charms would entice her into his arms. They spent an hour at the Castle before drinking up and walking the short distance to the hall at Coleham Head where the ceilidh was being held. As they arrived the band had finished warming up and the caller had taken the microphone to greet everyone and get sets assembled for the first reel. They decided to sit out the first couple of dances and taking their drinks from the bar settled down at a free table to watch the fun. The first dances were the easy ones for those who were new to folk dancing but even so there was always plenty of amusement as some dancers forgot the moves after the caller had walked them through and destroyed the set they were in, accompanied by much laughter as they tried in vain to recover their places.

The nice thing about folk dancing was the progression where as the set advanced through their moves each participant had a turn with all the others and from it an experienced dancer would be able to deduce whether the girl or boy fancied was giving the other a squeeze or look of encouragement. It was a continuation from the times when courtship had a formal but innocent form of etiquette and, as far as Justin was concerned, held great relevance for the evening and his desire for success with Maggie.

When the four of them eventually joined a set on the dance floor, Justin was impressed to observe that Maggie was comfortable with the caller's walk-through and, as the band struck up and the action started, proved herself to be a competent dancer, with only a few quickly corrected mistakes with stripping the willow where the dancers progress down the line interweaving with all the other dancers in the set. They stayed on the floor for a further two dances and hot and flushed returned to their table and the welcome refreshment which awaited them. Justin made sure he was sitting close to Maggie and chatted away to her as best he could over the noise of the band. He found that his interest was reciprocated by her and he noted that without being too forward she would lean close enough when they spoke for her hair to brush his cheek and he was able to smell the perfume she was wearing.

Part way through the evening the band took a break and took themselves off the bar to replenish their drinks, whilst Justin used the period of relative quiet to pursue what he desired be his latest conquest and hopefully bring an end to a long girlfriend-free period in his life. The four of them chatted freely before taking to the floor for some of the more complicated dances which the caller reserved for later, and which would tax even the most experienced dancers. This proved to be the case with all of them at different times managing to forget their moves. Although this gave them much cause for merriment, it didn't go down to well with the serious dancers and so they decided to sit out the rest of the evening with a drink. And so an enjoyable evening drew to a close with the time-honoured tradition dance of the Circassian Circle which, mercifully, was simple to perform. This was just as well as a fair number of the participants had by this time imbibed sufficient alcohol to make them unsteady on their feet.

Feeling the glow of a pleasant evening, the four of them walked back the short distance to the Castle where Maggie had parked her car. As they all said goodnight, Justin thought he would test the water, so to speak, and try a quick peck on her cheek. He felt a quick thrill of pleasure when Maggie put her arms round him and gave him a quick kiss on the cheek as well. They stood and waved as she drove off in her car, before walked together through the cool autumn evening the short distance to Justin's flat where, still in high spirits, they parted company.

Unlike the other three, Maggie after a half of bitter in the Castle, had been drinking only soft drinks as she was driving back to the police safe house she had been allocated in Frankwell on the wonderfully named Drink Water Street. It amused Maggie that directly opposite the street sign there was an advertising hoarding exhorting people to drink a well-known brand of whisky. It made her recall with amusement an advertisement for an American deodorant which used the unforgettable strap line - *Turn your armpits into charmpits!* She wondered whether it had helped or hindered sales and decided, with a chuckle, that it was probably the latter.

As reversing her car neatly into a nearby parking space in front of the terraced house and letting herself in through the front door, she ran through the events of the evening. Although outwardly one of pleasure, she knew that being on an assignment meant that she could not let her guard down for a moment in her dealings with Justin. She looked back over the time she had spent with him to assess whether she had made any slips in the cover story she had concocted with Lynn and, after some deliberation, decided that it was water tight. She reviewed how she had interacted with Justin on a personal level, knowing that the success of her task rested entirely on whether she could make herself attractive enough for him to want to start a relationship. She knew from her background research that he was a flirt and, in truth, was attractive to women. He also had a robust sexual appetite and from what her research team had uncovered, was very good at seduction with the inevitable results which were immensely gratifying for both parties.

Maggie decided that she had on balance managed to show interest in Justin without appearing too easy but she knew that the most difficult part lay ahead where she had to ensure that they started an intimate relationship. She was all too aware that if she failed then the whole operation would be compromised and she determined to carefully pursue Justin, with the assistance of Lynn, to ensure that he invited her to go with him to the Bromyard Folk Festival. She was also well aware that it would involve sharing his hotel room but knew exactly what was involved in this type of covert surveillance work and, as a professional, was fully prepared to enter into a physical relationship if that was the only way to achieve a positive result. Anyway, she mused, as she climbed the stairs to bed he's not bad looking and he's easy, amusing company and, very importantly, he smells nice and clean. She yawned as she walked into the bathroom feeling pleased that today had gone to plan and she would be able to give a satisfactory report to her field manager in the morning. As she changed into her pyjamas and climbed into bed, she resolved to phone Lynn to make an arrangement to meet at the Castle the following Friday, but on reflection thought that as there was little time before Bromyard it might be as well if she made the first move and phoned Justin. She wasn't going to spoil things by being too forward but reasoned that as Justin obviously found her attractive she was unlikely to frighten him off by getting in touch first. She would get Justin's mobile from Lynn tomorrow she decided as she turned off the bedside light and settled down to sleep.

After leaving Justin at his front door, Caesar and Lynn continued along the Foregate towards the Column when their conversation turned from the enjoyment of the ceilidh to concern about their friend.

"Y'know what, Lynn, old girl," said Caesar apologetically, "I don't want to be a bore but I can't help noticing that Justin is a worried man."

"You think so. What makes you think that?" Lynn replied guardedly. She knew she was on delicate ground and frankly as the position she found herself in was a new experience for her and so didn't really want to be drawn on the matter. "He seem in good spirits this evening – especially after he got the obvious hots for Maggie."

Caesar laughed. "Too true, Love. A testosterone charged Justin could never be mistaken for a Benedictine monk! But seriously, I've know him for a long time and he's always been the same – a bit laddish, a bit of a joker, great company but always untroubled. Now something has happened to him. He has lost some of his, how would you say, his sparkle. His face is just that little bit drawn and I know he has lost some weight. I feel it in my bones that Justin has got a problem of some kind and a problem which he can't open up to us about."

Lynn realised that it would look odd if she strongly denied that there had been a change in Justin's demeanour, because it was quite obvious that there had been.

"Do you think it's because he was turned down for a mortgage and it hit him hard?"

Caesar shook his head. "No, Lynn, I don't. Although that seemed an odd business to me when he had been turned down before his books could be properly checked out. I'd noticed that something was amiss about a month ago. You remember don't you, when he was spending money we thought he didn't have on his Norton and all the expensive clothing, not to mention the hotel at Bromyard – and I asked him then if anything was troubling him. He said there wasn't, just that he'd been sleeping badly."

"Yes," agreed Lynn, "I have to admit that he's carrying a weight of something on his broad shoulders. But what can we do about it if he won't or can't share the problem with us?"

"What do you think if I sat him down and got him to open up," suggested Caesar as they walked past the law courts at the back of the Shirehall and up the hill into Highfields, "perhaps I could pop round to his flat one evening with a few cans and get him relaxed enough to talk about what's troubling him."

Lynn though this a very bad idea but being unable to explain and not wanting to appear suspicious by saying so directly, chose her words with caution. "That's a possibility, Caesar, but can I suggest that it may not be quite the right time. Why don't you leave it until after Bromyard and see how things are then. Perhaps if he has a problem he may be able to resolve it without our help and also, if I know our Justin, come Bromyard – if not before – he'll have his hands full with Maggie."

"All right," Caesar agreed reluctantly after some thought, "as usual your common sense has reigned in the impetuous Caesar. I'll leave it 'till after Bromyard and we can talk it about it then". He gave a huge yawn as they turned into their driveway. "And now I'm ready for bed."

After parting from his friends, Justin climbed the stairs to his flat and let himself in. Still buzzing from the evening's dancing, he decided to have a lager and wind down before going to bed. He took the filled tankard over to his armchair and thought about his meeting with Maggie. True to form, Justin was now back to his normal good humour at the thought of the amorous chase which lay enticingly ahead. With his troubles weighing him down he had just about given up on trying to find himself another girlfriend but was much heartened after finding that Maggie had shown some interest in him. Not a lot, to be sure he thought, but enough to make him confident that he could make the running and win her over. Justin gave a contented sigh as he saw a rosier future and once again he pushed the metaphorical corpse back under ground and with much of his good humour recovered, patted the earth flat once again in his thoughts as he drained the last drops of his ale and took himself off to bed.

As he settled down to what he hoped would be dreamless slumber, he would have been surprised to know that he had come across Maggie once before but, not having seen her face at the time, he could not have known. At the meeting with John at Church Stretton, Justin had noticed a young woman in the near distance with her back to him arranging flowers at a headstone. Had he been able to see her face at the time it was quite likely that he would have recognised her as the same person he was introduced to at the Castle that evening. That day Maggie had made sure that her features were shielded from both Justin and John for, had either of them seen her face, her surveillance role in the operation would have been fatally compromised and she would have been replaced by another operative. Blissfully unaware of this, Justin settled down under his duvet and, aided in no small measure by the large volume of beer he had consumed that evening, soon fell into a deep sleep which, mercifully, was free of disturbing dreams.

The next morning Justin woke to lowering clouds and a steady downpour which had made an unwelcome return, dampening the expectations of all those who had made plans for a Sunday of outdoor endeavours. Justin's plan for the morning was to take himself off for a long ride through the Welsh hills before lunch but, having woken later than usual owing to the excesses of the preceding evening and noting the rain, Justin decided that he would give the Norton an over-due service that morning and hope that the weather would improve by the afternoon. He remembered his grandmother reciting the couplet born of country wisdom: *rain before seven, fine after* and had found it to be to be invariably correct.

Hoping that today would not be the exception, he finished a leisurely breakfast and drove the short distance to Caesar's unit where he let himself in through the side door. Earlier that week he had bought oil for the oil change and carried the can in along with the greases and cleaning rags needed for the servicing. First he removed the dust cover from the machine and, after carefully folding it up and placing it on top of a nearby locker, took a spanner from the tool box which he had brought in from the van, slackened the drain plug under the sump and slid a drip tray underneath before removing the plug completely and allowing the oil to drain out. As soon as he had done it he realised that he should have run up the engine first to heat the oil and allow it to thin and drain more easily but he noted that the colour of the waste oil was still a clean golden colour and shrugged as he knew that there would be no problem if some of the old sump oil remained. Anyway he was in no hurry and could give it plenty of time to slowly drain whilst he carried on with other tasks.

Slackening off the adjusters on the twin throttle cables, Justin gained enough free movement to pull the outers back from their seats and slowly dripped a light oil down the inner wires. As it was slow work waiting for the oil to gravitate down, he slackened off the clutch cable and repeated the process, alternating between the them until he was satisfied the entire length of the cables had been lubricated, before resetting the adjusters. Next he removed the primary chain cover. Originally the primary chain ran in an oil bath along with the clutch plates but, as was usual with British motorbikes of that era, it was almost impossible to prevent oil leaking from around the cover despite the rubber seal. With his mechanical knowledge Justin thought that the clutch should be effective without the oil and that the chain could be coated in a heavy graphite grease with out any harmful effects. He had been correct in his assumptions and was pleased to find that all that was necessary was to adjust the clutch springs a half turn in order to retain a smooth clutch take-up. He looked closely at the primary chain and decided that he would apply fresh grease and after working it carefully into the links removed the excess with one of the rags he had brought with him.

Wiping his greasy hands clean on a fresh piece of rag, Justin felt that a strong drink of tea would help to dispel the remnants of his hangover and walked over to the small kitchen area where the kettle and mugs were kept. He checked that there were tea bags in the packet and that Saturday's milk in the tiny fridge was usable and, finding everything in order, filled the kettle and switched it on. Once it had boiled he poured the water over the tea bag and, as he waited for it to brew, was surprised to hear the ringtones of his mobile sound from his pocket. Quickly wiping his hands on a piece of rag, he checked the screen and saw a number he didn't recognise. He pressed the receive button and was both amazed and pleased to hear the soft voice of Maggie replying to his greeting.

"Justin, it's Maggie. You may remember me," she teased, "you gave me a strenuous lesson in folk dancing last night!"

"Yes, I do remember dancing with a mysterious dark-haired maiden. That wasn't you, was it?"

"Oh!" said Maggie pretending outrage, "is that the slight impression I gave. I'll obviously have to work a bit harder at my image." She was pleased with Justin's positive reaction to her phone call and felt vindicated in her decision to initiate contact.

"Maggie, you don't need to change anything," Justin laughed as he turned on the charm. "Of course I remember you and don't be modest about your dancing, it was very competent. I hope you had a great time – you certainly seemed to enjoy yourself."

"Certainly did, Justin. I hope you don't think me too pushy in contacting you so soon but I wanted to get to know you better. There, I've said it – now you'll think me a trollop."

Justin laughed again. "Course I don't. In fact, you beat me to it as I'd made up my mind to get your mobile number from Lynn and subject you to my tried and tested wooing technique, guaranteed to induce an attack of the vapours in innocent damsels, and one which I hope you are susceptible to."

"Oh, Lah, Sir," said Maggie, entering into the spirit of the exchange, "Me heart's all of a flutter at the thought of your woo. But once it's stopped fluttering how about telling me what you are up to today?"

"Caesar has a workshop near me," Justin continued, "and he lets me keep my motorbike here. At this very moment I'm toiling mightily with grease up to my elbows giving it a service."

Maggie was well aware of the existence of

Justin's Norton and had decided that it would be used to help her gain his trust and interest.

"I didn't know you had a bike. My last boy friend had a huge bike called a Honda Fireguard or something. I used to go pillion on it and I really liked the two-wheeled experience until I discovered he had found someone else to warm his seat!"

Justin was unable to stifle his laughter. "Sorry for the mirth, Maggie, but I think you mean a Honda Fireblade, and is warming his seat a euphemism for something else? Anyway, enough of that. Sorry to hear of your break-up. Hope it wasn't too painful."

"Well it was for him when I found out he was married. But moving on, I was wondering what you were up to today? I've got a free day, and as we got on well at the ceilidh I thought I'd make use of the modern woman's prerogative and make the first move. From what you say, I've just beaten you to it."

"Indeed you have," said a very pleased Justin hardly able to believe his good fortune. "I've got a suggestion. Why don't you come to the unit to have a look at my pride and joy whilst I finish the service, and then if the weather dries up we could ride out to a country pub for lunch. How does that grab you?"

But before Maggie could answer, Justin had

a sudden thought. “I forgot to ask, have you got any biking gear. I've got a spare jacket and gloves but no helmet for you.”

“No problem there, Justin, I've kept my helmet and leathers from my last time on a bike. I'll put them in the car come over now and, yes, I'd love to have lunch with you. If the weather stays wet we can go in my car. You'd better tell me where this unit is,” she remembered to ask.

Justin gave her directions to the Monkmoor trading estate then continued with the servicing. He replaced the sump plug after wiping the metal particles from the magnetic tip, and refilled the sump with fresh oil. The last job was to check the tension on the chain to the rear sprocket and, finding it needed the slack taking up, he loosened the wheel nuts. He was just about to jack the wheel back on the adjusters, when he heard the sound of a car outside followed soon after by the side door opening and a *cooee* from Maggie. Justin walked over to greet her and gave her a kiss on the cheek whilst holding his hands in the air.

“Sorry, can't use my hands as they are covered in grease - no doubt to your great relief,” he teased. “I'm almost finished. Just got to adjust the chain and tighten everything, wipe off the oily smudges, and that's it. What's the weather doing?”

“The clouds are starting to break and I

reckon it'll start to dry up shortly." Maggie looked over at the Norton. "Gosh, what's that. I just assumed that you'd have a modern bike but that looks great. What is it? I take it you don't like to take it out in the wet."

"It's a 1966 Norton 650ss. It was a bike well ahead of its time and, should you grace its pillion seat, dear Maggie, you'll find that its road holding matches modern bikes. Just bear with me whilst I finish off. By the way you look a million dollars this morning," he added belatedly.

"About time too," Maggie said with faux hurt expression on her attractive features, "I don't think much of your chatting up technique so far. You'll really have to lay on the woo if you are going to get anywhere with me."

Justin promised he would make a great effort in that respect and bent to his task of adjusting the chain tension. He was surprised and gratified at how easy Maggie was in his company and how she seemed keen to develop a friendship with him. That she liked bikes was an added bonus and as well as an outgoing personality he found it impossible not to notice she possessed a gorgeous figure and a very pretty face. All in all, Justin decided that he had fallen lucky. But something different was stirring deep inside which was a new experience for him. All his previous relationships had been conducted on the basis that Justin's needs and wants came first and consequently his behaviour with his girlfriends, although outwardly caring, had been superficial and selfish.

With Maggie something fundamental had occurred. Instead of just using her as he had in the past with all his girlfriends, he wanted to find out more about her. It was, for Justin, a new feeling and one which he found strangely exciting. He glanced up at Maggie as he worked at the rear wheel and found to his delight that she met his eyes with a gaze that gave him a warm glow inside. He smiled at her then dropped his eyes as he continued with his task. Once satisfied with the tension on the chain he tightened the nuts on the rear wheel, then re-adjusted the rear brake linkage until it had the required free movement. Once finished, he looked up at Maggie.

"There, all done," he said straightening up. "Just bear with me whilst I clean my dirty paws." He walked over to the sink where he kept his hand cleaner and, scooping out a handful, turned on the tap and proceeded to remove all the grease from his hands, using a nail brush to clean under his nails. "I know a good place where we can eat. The Bear at Hodnet does good food and it's only fifteen minutes away– fancy going there?"

"Sounds good to me. Shall we go Dutch?"

"Well, I'm all for equality," said Justin,"but this time it's my treat. Next time we'll do that, if that's okay with you?" Drying his hands, he went to the door and looked out. "Great, the sun's out and the road's beginning to look good. . Should be dry shortly under foot – or should I say under tyre. Let's get our gear on"

After they had put on their motorcycling gear, Justin opened the shutter door and wheeled the Norton out at the front of the unit. Securing the doors after him, he checked that his van was locked and, pulling on his helmet, kicked the powerful bike into life. Pushing it off its stand he flicked down the pillion foot pegs and nodded at Maggie to get on. He was pleased to see her swing her leg easily over the seat and settle down with her feet on the rests. Justin was impressed that she hadn't kept her feet on the ground which was an indication of nervousness and mistrust in the rider. He had once given a ride to one of his girlfriends who, each time he had banked the bike into a bend, had leaned the other way. Needless to say this made cornering rather fraught as they see-sawed round the bends and, unsurprisingly, she wasn't around for long.

Setting off, Justin rode along Telford Way and over the river Severn, then up the Whitchurch Road to the Battlefields roundabout and onto the A49 towards Shawbury. Now out of the speed limit, he opened the throttle and took the Norton up to an easy sixty miles an hour. He was impressed with his pillion passenger. Maggie was relaxed and to his relief leaned with the bike through the corners. On her part, she was relieved to find that Justin was a competent rider and handled the big machine with skill. She had wondered before they had set off whether he would do what she had experienced in the past with some men who thought they had to prove their macho credentials by driving like idiots, thinking they were impressing her.

Soon they were passing the RAF helicopter flying school airfield on their left as they approached Shawbury and with the traffic lights on green, wove their way through the village, then along the straight at Edgebolton and back onto the open road towards the Hodnet bypass where Justin turned left and, shortly after, arrived the Bear Hotel in the centre of the village. On the journey there, Maggie had been carefully thinking how she was going to take things forward. It was essential that she had to be invited to stay with Justin at the Bromyard Festival. It was obvious that by agreeing to join him in a double hotel room the weekend would be on an intimate physical level and, she reasoned, it would be a lot easier if she and Justin became lovers before that. In fairness, the thought of intimacy was anything but repugnant, as she found Justin quite a dish and was grateful for that for it made her task so much easier and meant that she didn't have to act her part. Nevertheless, she would have to move carefully as she didn't want Justin to think she was easy, or at least, she admitted ruefully to herself, not too easy.

With these thoughts in mind, she noted the competent skill with which Justin turned the Norton into the Bear's car park and stopped close to the entrance. They took off their helmets and leather jackets in the entrance foyer, aware that some pubs didn't like bikers, and hung them on a coat stand which stood in one corner. Despite it being just after noon, there were already some ten cars parked up and, when they walked into the bar, they found it filled with the cheerful chatter of people who seemed to know one another. Justin turned to Maggie.

“Looks like it could get crowded quite quickly in here. Why don't you grab a table. There's one for two just over there in the corner by the fireplace. I'll get some drinks – what do you want?”

“Thanks, make mine a small dry white, please. I'll bag the table and fight off all comers.”

Maggie walked over to the seat whilst Justin waited his turn to be served at the bar. He was eventually seen to by an elderly man with a neat goatee beard and a welcoming manner who took his order of a half of lager and a white wine. Any ideas Justin had about how welcome bikers were, were soon dispelled when the friendly man, who happened to be the owner, told him he had seen him arrive and told him of his much loved Velocette Venom from bygone years, before the pressure of custom at the bar put an end to his reminiscences.

"Well , Maggie, we can stop worrying about our reception here," Justin told her as he put the drinks down on the table, "the old guy behind the bar used to have a Velocette in the far distant past and had seen us come in on the bike of his dreams. Sadly, we weren't able to get into one of those hour long conversations about motorbikes," he teased, " where any women on the scene falls into a deep coma."

Maggie laughed. "I know all too well what you mean. My two-timing biker chum used to go on about his Honda Firebasket – or whatever it's called - until I lost the will to live! Anyway, enough of this idle chatter, I'm starving and I espy the waitress coming over with the menus. I know what I'd like without looking – the roast beef."

"Excellent," agreed Justin rubbing his hands

together, “I'll have the same. It's a real treat for me as it's difficult to have a roast meal when you live on your own.”

He turned to the waitress and placed their order with her and declined the offer of more drinks. Maggie was pleased to see that Justin was being sensible and only drinking a half pint of lager. She normally was equally cautious but reasoned that by the time she was back at her car the effects of the small wine she was having with her food would be long gone from her body.

She decided to bring up the matter of the Bromyard Folk Festival. “Lynn tells me that there's a big folk festival shortly that you're all going to. Bromyard, isn't it?”

“Yes, that right. At the end of the month. The three of us have been going for years now. It's a great weekend, lots to do and great acts.”

Maggie seized the opportunity Justin had given her. She gave him a coquettish look. “Um, only three? Lynn told me that it's usually the four of you.”

Justin met her gaze and burst into laughter. “Out of consideration for your delicate feelings I had decided to gloss over the true numbers. But, yes, I am a normal man with normal urges and I have been known to share my impressive charms with a girlfriend. Mind you, not one of them manages to match your allure."

"Stuff and nonsense, you aged lothario," responded Maggie with mock primness, "I bet you say that to all the girls."

It was true that Justin did use that chat-up line, but this time there was a difference. Despite the short time they had known each other, he was finding himself drawn to Maggie in a way he had never experienced before with any of his previous relationships and, this time, genuinely meant it. Maggie saw that her flippant response had not gone down well and reached across the table to Justin hand and gave it a squeeze. Although the surveillance operation took precedence over everything else, and meant that she must not do anything which could compromise her budding relationship with Justin, she also found that despite her professionalism Justin had tugged at her feminine instincts and she found herself becoming more involved than was safe. She was well aware that she had to remain detached from her emotions, for not to do so could jeopardise the entire undertaking, and have a direct bearing on its success or failure but, at the same time, she had to develop a strong relationship with Justin.

"Justin, love, sometimes a joke can go to far. I'm sorry. Thanks for the complement."

He smiled ruefully. “It's okay and you are right. I do use it as a chat-up but with you I meant it. I don't want to embarrass you, but I find you very attractive – and I don't just mean in looks. Anyway, we had better come back down to earth as I see two heavily laden plates approaching our table.”

Two large plates filled with beef and all the trimmings were placed before them and, with an *enjoy your meal,* the waitress left them to enjoy themselves chatting away as they tucked in to their food. The time passed quickly as it always does when two people in close accord are enjoying each other's company and by the time they had ordered and eaten two enormous puddings they were ready to admit defeat and give the coffee a miss. They stayed for another half hour until Maggie said she had some work to do before Monday and would Justin mind if they headed back to Shrewsbury. Justin agreed and went to the bar to settle up for their meals and drinks. The owner was still serving and as he dealt with Justin's card payment told him again how pleased he was to see a classic Norton in such great condition and being used as it should be. After a short exchange with him Justin and Maggie went outside and geared up for the journey back.

Relaxing behind Justin as he took the Norton back through the village to the main road, Maggie gave some thought to the events of the day so far. On balance, she thought, it had gone well. There was a definite interest in her on Justin's part and she knew that it was as close as could be to her becoming his girlfriend and lover. The last part gave her some cause for concern as she had decided it was essential that she and Justin become lovers before the Bromyard weekend. The ultimate goal was to find this man known as John and, as the only known contact with him was Justin, it was crucial that she and Justin became intimate and, as he had done with some of his past girlfriends, hopefully be invited to move into his flat. In this way she would be able to keep him under surveillance without there being any obvious tailing activity. As her field manager had pointed out to her, it was possible to put a tail on Justin and there was a good possibility that he would not be aware of it. But there was always a risk that this John who had gone to earth, or some of his team would notice they were being observed as it is almost impossible, however skilled the operatives are, to mount a twenty-four surveillance operation without some give-away signs.

There had been a small measure of success when one of the operatives initially observing Justin had noticed that he appeared to be followed. Justin's tail had been a male in his late twenties to early thirties, fair skinned and clean shaven with a muscular build. He had been discretely followed to a newsagents where the operative had overheard him buying a newspaper and a soft drink where he noted his accent was British and most likely from the Birmingham area. Maggie's field manager had called off the tail as he considered the risk of being observed too great and had put in place other systems for remote surveillance. He now waited for Maggie to become part of Justin's life, for he believed that it was the only way to discover the whereabouts of the man who called himself John and whom it was believed was a serious threat to the UK's security.

It was with these thought in her mind that she found herself back at Caesar's workshop and eased herself off the pillion seat. She gave Justin a wide smile as she thanked him for the lovely meal and a safe ride. She had, in fact, enjoyed herself. Justin had been good company, making her feel at ease and able to make her laugh at his jokes and witty asides and it made her job so much more easy than if she was forcing herself to establish a rapport with someone whom she found unpleasant. It was important now that Justin made the next move as, having made the running so far, she would look far too pushy if she made arrangements for the next meeting. Her mind was soon put at ease when Justin turned to her after wheeling the Norton back to its reserved corner.

"I've had a great time too," he said as they took off their motorcycle gear, "this isn't a chat up line, Maggie, but I find you very attractive. I haven't felt this way before, but I – how can I put it – I've just clicked with you. Oh, dear. I'm not expressing myself very well, probably because this is new territory for me, but in the short time we've know each other I've become very fond of you." Justin had wanted to say what was truly in his heart and that was that he had begun to fall in love with Maggie, but stopped short fearing that he might frighten her if he said what he truly felt within himself.

Upon hearing his declaration Maggie felt a great sense of relief. "Why, Justin, I don't know what to say." She thought carefully for a moment before replying so that nothing she said could spoil this moment which was pivotal to the success of her mission.

"I didn't want to say anything at this stage which could spoil our friendship," she went on, "but I'm so glad you said what you said as I feel the same as you. There's a lovely warm feeling inside me when I'm with you and I'm so happy you feel the same."

Now confident that she had Justin where

she wanted him, she threw her arms around him and, as she felt his strong grasp encircle her, offered up her lips to meet his in a warm and passionate embrace. For Justin this was a new and exciting experience as previously any kiss would have been the impetus for a sexual encounter. This time he was thrilled to discover that his over-riding emotion was one of respect for Maggie and not one where his lower nature imposed itself for personal gratification. For the first time In his adult life, Justin had found a finer part of his inner self which wanted to protect and respect, and not one where he saw a woman as something to be used to satisfy his basic urges. Eventually he pulled back his head and looked at Maggie with eyes that were soft with this new-found and wonderful feeling of love.

"Maggie..." he began and had to swallow hard before he could continue, "I find it hard to say how I feel at this moment as my emotions are all over the place. But this much I can say, I've never felt like this about any other woman. I think you are the loveliest person I have ever known and I hope you'll let me show you that I can treat a woman with sincere respect."

"Justin, darling," she said as she pulled his head down to give him a slow, gentle kiss, "I think that gives you the answer you are looking for. I want nothing more than we get together as a couple." Now confident that she was safe in making the next move, she went on, "I can't do anything today as I've got work to do before tomorrow. Can we meet up for a meal in on Tuesday? I could come to you or we could go out. Which do you prefer?"

"Tell you what," replied Justin, "you come to my place and I'll show you that I'm a dab hand in the kitchen. I have my mother to thank for that as she showed me how to cook when I was a teenager. What about seven thirty-ish on Tuesday. I'm on Abbey Foregate directly opposite the supermarket near the Abbey. You can park in their car park and you'll see number eleven right in front of you over the road. Go in and up the stairs and you'll find my flat on the first landing – it's got a number two on the door. I'll put a bottle of Chardonnay in the fridge ready. Oh! Just remembered, you'll be driving and you can't drink alcohol."

"Wrong," Maggie responded firmly, "I will be having some of that Chardonnay as I'll come there in a taxi and go back the same way." As she spoke she was hoping that the return taxi trip wouldn't be necessary and that things would progress as she planned and that staying the night would be the inevitable progression of their date.

They stayed for some time in a warm cocoon of shared emotion until Maggie said she had to get back and buckle down to her preparation for the next day. With a last lingering kiss Justin walked her out to her car and watched as she drove off towards town before returning to cover the Norton and lock up the workshop. He found himself in high spirits – a rare feeling after all the disturbing times he was going through – and found himself singing *The Lark in the Morning* as he drove back to his flat feeling certain that things were at long last beginning to look up for him. He started to plan what he would cook on Tuesday.

The day dawned bright and warm on the Tuesday of their date and Justin managed to finish his work at mid-afternoon by making an early start with a re-open at Worthen followed by a twelve mile drive to the church at Montford Bridge where he had to fill in a grave which he had dug the preceding day for the interment late morning that Tuesday. As he worked at finishing his tasks his thoughts were on the dinner he was to serve for Maggie. Since their last meeting his emotions had been in a pleasant whirl as he experienced these new and exciting feelings which his relationship with Maggie had revealed, and he was determined to put on a good show for her with a meal to remember. He started to work out the ingredients for the three courses he had decided to make which would be creative and challenging. Part way through this process he remembered the wise words of his Mother who, from her own past and painful experience when entertaining guests, told Justin to never attempt a dish which he had not tried and successfully made before. Always, she told him, cook something which you are comfortable with, even if it is just good plain fare, which you know you can put on the table without fear of disaster. Good old Mum, thought Justin, as he never ceased to be amazed at how powerfully his late Mother had influenced his life for the better and, with her advice firmly in mind decided on a well tried and straightforward set of dishes. By the time he had put the finishing touches to the final grave he had decided on what he needed and went back to his van where he carefully wrote down what he had to purchase once he was in Shrewsbury, before starting up and heading the few miles back to his flat.

After parking his van at the supermarket as usual, Justin decided that he would do his shopping first before going back to the flat to clean up and change. He locked the van and taking his shopping bag and the list from his pocket, entered the supermarket, picking up a basket once inside. He took his time wandering round the aisles which were pleasingly uncrowded and, apart from the disco-themed piped music which Justin found annoying and unnecessary, relatively quiet. He went first to the vegetable section where he looked for two avocados. He only needed one for the starter he had planned, but remembered his Mother's advice to have one in reserve in case the first had something wrong with it. He also remembered a dinner he had been invited to where the hostess had decided on an avocado starter without knowing anything about them. Unaware that they had to be ripe and softened, she had somehow managed to cut in half the rock-hard avocados and remove the stone without causing herself an injury and then, for some reason, decided they were fit to be served to her guests. Justin remembered that it was impossible to put a spoon into the flesh and the embarrassed assembly had to leave their avocados after scooping from the centre the prawns in a sea food sauce.

Justin resolved that he was not going to have a repeat of that mistake and spent some time gently squeezing the avocados on display trying to find ones which felt soft through their skins. He found most of them were hard and would need several days of ripening before being fit for consumption, and was on the point of giving up and thinking on another starter, when he saw to his delight a small display of ready-to-eat avocados packed in pairs which were gave slightly to the touch and were just what he wanted. In the same section he picked up a pack of button mushrooms, some cherry tomatoes on the vine and, on an impulse as they were not on his list, a pack of asparagus. He had decided on fillet steak for their main course but, as he didn't like the look of the packaged steak on offer in the meat chiller cabinet, he went over to the butcher's counter where he asked to see a complete tenderloin. Once presented, and its meeting his approval, he asked for two pieces from the thick end to be cut and wrapped. All that now remained was to find a nice pudding which took him over to the frozen cabinets where he was face with a mouth-watering choice. He did consider just a fancy ice cream but decided that it wasn't special enough and so picked out a raspberry and kiwi fruit pavlova and, remembering he had missed something, had to go back to the dairy shelves to get a carton of double cream cream to go with it. Lastly, he decided to add another bottle of wine to his basket as he didn't think one bottle would be enough. He had decided not to drink any lager as it could be a bit powerful on ones breath if the other party hadn't drunk any – especially if some serious kissing was on the cards – and was going to stick to wine with Maggie. Also, he hadn't seen how much she would drink when she didn't have to drive afterwards. For all he knew she might be able to match him drink for drink.

With these thoughts in mind Justin looked at his watch and saw it was four thirty. Plenty of time, he thought, as he made his way to the tills where his purchases were put through by an attentive young man with a badge stating that he was Thomas, Assistant Manager, who politely and efficiently dealt with him and, with his cheery farewell sounding in his ears, Justin left the store and made his way across the road to his front entrance. Once inside he checked his box for post and took the three letters he found inside with him as he went upstairs to his flat. But before he could mount the stairs to safety the door to the bottom flat opened and eighty-four year old Mrs. Williams tottered out. Justin felt sorry for her as she appeared to be without any friends or relatives and spent her time alone sitting in an armchair in her front bay window watching the passers-by and, for her most importantly, observing who was coming in through the front door. She would then make her way unsteadily into the hallway out to grab them and hold them in passive conversation until they could find a way of extricating themselves from her surprisingly steely grip.

Justin always tried to make time for her, but even he found her slightly overpowering and tried to run into through the front door and up the stairs before Mrs. Williams could get to him. He rarely succeeded and resigned himself on this occasion, as he had on countless others, to spending ten long minutes hearing all about how she ran a big car sales business and how she was the one who nobody crossed as she always got her own way. Justin had no doubt where the long since deceased Mr. Williams once stood in the pecking order, and would have had no option but to succumb to a superior force and adopt a subservient role in the marriage and business. But, fortunately, after a few minutes and to Justin's great relief, Mrs. Williams released her vice-like grip on Justin's arm and weaved her way back to her flat saying that she was tired and was going to have a nap.

Back in the sanctuary of his flat, Justin put his purchases down on the kitchen worktop and looked at his letters. The first one he opened was from the Halifax asking if he still wanted to go ahead with his mortgage application and listing the things he would need to supply if he did. The second was from his local Vauxhall dealer with some unrepeatable offers on vans, which Justin knew would be repeated every year and be presented on each occasion as unrepeatable. The third was another payment for his last single grave containing the usual £500 in used notes. He checked the postmark on the envelope which, like some the others, bore an indistinct Shropshire post mark. Justin shrugged his shoulders at the reminder of his dubious arrangement with this John character, but with the thought that it wouldn't be for much longer, put the matter out of his mind as he began working out the timing for the evening.

Looking at his watch, he saw that he had two hours before Maggie would arrive and decided that he had plenty of time to organise the meal as it was one which needed little preparation. For starters he had decided that he would thinly slice half an avocado for each of them and arrange it in a circle around the edge of a side plate. In the centre there would be the small sandwich prawns, which he preferred as he felt they had a superior texture and taste compared with the king-sized ones, and over them he would drizzle a seafood dressing which he would make from a mixture of mayonnaise, tomato ketchup, lemon juice and a splash of worcestershire sauce and, just before serving, paprika would be sprinkled over the sauce as a finishing touch. However, he knew it had to be left to the last minute as avocados discoloured if left out after being prepared, but he was able to prepare the sea-food dressing which he put away in the fridge for later. He also remembered to put the avocados in as well knowing that they would be easier to take out of their skins and slice when chilled. Lastly placed the bottle of wine alongside the other in the fridge door.

Deciding that he had done all that was necessary for the time being, Justin took himself off the bathroom where he stripped off his work clothes and luxuriated under a hot shower as it washed away the dust from his last job. Just before finishing he turned the shower on to cold and stood there for a minute until his skin was tingling before drying himself and returning to the bedroom to dress. Opening his wardrobe he rummaged through until he found the a pale blue cotton, short-sleeved shirt and a pair of cream trousers which he had given a sharp crease to the legs before they had be put away. After dressing, Justin looked at himself in the full-length mirror on the wardrobe door and, satisfied with his appearance, took a comb and arranged his hair with his usual side parting. As he pulled on a pair of dark blue socks and a well-polished pair of black loafers he ran his hands over his face pondered as to whether he should shave again. Deciding that it was necessary he pushed an electric razor over his stubble until he was satisfied that his skin was smooth. Justin thought ruefully it would be just his luck if Maggie was a lover of the modern trend of two-day stubble, especially as he wasn't, preferring the smooth clean look. But he was sure that his charm would win the day.

By now the time was six thirty and with an hour before Maggie's arrival, Justin contemplated having a warm-up drink to get himself in the mood as he put it. Strangely, this time he decided against it and put back the bottle of wine he had taken from the fridge. He had rather surprised himself by this decision but realised with a sure feeling that he wanted to be himself for his guest tonight, and not supported by alcohol as he normally would have been. He wondered what had come over him to act so out of character and came to the conclusion that with Maggie he had found in her something that simply brought out the best in him. He wanted to impress her and, for perhaps the first time in his care-free life, he had thought less of what he selfishly wanted and more of someone else. It was a sensation that warmed him and he held onto it as he laid out the items for the meal and then turned to laying the table which, in the absence of a separate dining room, had been placed along one side of the sitting room. Once this had been done to his satisfaction, Justin hunted through a cupboard and unearthed a candle holder and, after some more rummaging, found a tall red candle with a pleasing spiral design which he inserted into the holder and placed in the centre of the laid table. Finally, in another drawer in the kitchen, he unearthed two linen serviettes which he folded and placed neatly by each place setting.

Standing back he passed a critical eye over the arrangements and, finding them satisfactory, returned to the kitchen and took some thick cut chips out of the freezer and left them to thaw on an oven dish - he believed they cooked better thawed than frozen as advised on the packet – then settled down in his armchair to relax before Maggie's arrival. He had barely seated himself when there was a knock at his door and upon opening it saw with delight that it was Maggie as expected. Justin saw she was wearing a dress with a bright floral design, which was cut low at the top and ended just above her knees. She wore no tights and her tanned slender legs were finished off by feet in white open-toed sandals showing her toe nails painted the same glossy pink colour which matched her finger nails and her lipstick. Not normally one to be stuck for words, Justin was speechless as he took in the vision before him.

“Justin, what's the matter, has the cat got your tongue?” Maggie gave an infectious giggle. “I'm not made from spun glass, you know. You are allowed to give me a hug. Why, you're even allow to kiss me."

"Sorry, Love. I don't know what has come over me," he said as he took Maggie in his arms and planted a lingering kiss on her up-turned lips. "I must say you look absolutely stunning and I love the dress. Anyway come on in and sit you down. Fancy a glass of wine as an appetiser?"

"Thank you. I'd love one." She delved into the shoulder bag she had brought with her and produced a bottle of white wine. "I've brought an offering for the evening. It's cold as I've taken it out of the fridge at home as I left."

"Should be quite an evening as I've got two more chilled to perfection," replied Justin as he led her over to an armchair with his arm around her waist. He went into the kitchen and busied himself pouring two large glasses of wine which he took back to the sitting room. For some reason he found himself feeling awkward and unable to come out with his usual chat-up line and teasing which was his way with the women in his life. He was acutely aware once more that Maggie had awoken in him feelings he had never experienced and it left him at a disadvantage as he wasn't sure how to proceed. He hope that a glass of wine would relax him and loosen his tongue.

Maggie realised that Justin was struggling and decided to get the conversation started.

"Lovely wine, Justin. Just what I need after a hard day's toil. Now, am I allowed to ask what epicurean feast you have prepared for me to-night. Or is it a secret?"

Justin pulled himself together, smiling at his uncertainty, and regained some of his cheery chat. "No secret and so I shall tell you what to expect. First I have decided on a starter of sliced avocado with prawns in a sea-food sauce which I shall prepare in just a minute. Then the creation to follow will comprise a huge fillet steak cooked how you like it with button mushrooms, cherry tomatoes and asparagus with a mountain of thick-cut chips. Then, if our groaning digestive tracts allow, we can squeeze down a sophisticated pavlova with lashings of cream. How does that grab you?"

"It grabs me greatly," said Maggie entering into the spirit of the moment, "don't want to interfere, but I'll be happy to give you a hand with the preparation if you like. Good heavens," she held up her wine glass in mock surprise, "my wine appears to have evaporated in the heat – any chance of a refill?"

The unease which possessed Justin and had made him feel like a love-struck teenager was now gone, and telling Maggie that he'd love some help they both went through to the kit-chen where they recharged their glasses and chatted happily away as they prepared the ingredients for the starter. Maggie was impressed with the way Justin dealt with the avocados. She would have peeled them, but watched Justin take a sharp knife and cut the fruit lengthways and separated the two halves. He then took the half with the stone and chopped down on it with the knife and with a twist neatly removed it, before taking a dessert spoon which he worked in between the skin and the flesh, scooping out a perfect half avocado which he proceeded to slice and arrange in a circle around the edge of the plate. The prawns, which he had washed and dried earlier, were placed in the centre and the dressing poured over them with paprika sprinkled on top. Maggie was impressed with Justin's culinary skills which, he told her, was all thanks to his Mother taking him in hand when he was a horrible spotty teenager.

They took their starter back to to the table where Justin lit the candle and turned down the main lights at the dimmer switch. With the first bottle of wine between them they started into the first course with relish. Justin found it difficult to stop looking at Maggie and he thought how lovely she looked in the soft light and with the candle flame putting a warm glow in her eyes. Despite her clandestine role, and the necessity for professionalism, Maggie couldn't help but admit that Justin was quite a dish. His lean, muscular body and skin deep tanned from his outside work topped by a handsome face and sun-bleached blond hair, all enhanced by his cheerful and out-going personality, was a package which Maggie found very attractive. With a feeling of disappointment she wished that they could have met under different circumstances, but her work meant that she was never able to develop any relationship outside of the specific tasks her department gave her. She stifled a sigh of regret and returned to her enjoyment of the moment in hand.

"Justin that was delicious. You know," she said with a satisfied smile as she put her knife and fork together on her clean plate, "I'm beginning to think that you might just make a good husband for someone." As she said it, she thought it might be a bit too suggestive and quickly tempered it. "Mind you it would depend on how good you are with the cleaning duties, washing up, dusting and so on."

Justin laughed. "I've got to admit that I do have the makings of a good house husband but I have to draw the line at changing nappies. Anyway, enough of this nonsense, time for the main. Want to come in to the kitchen and watch a genius at work and at the same time charge our glasses and talk of sweet and frivolous things."

As Justin skilfully started on his tasks they talked freely and easily as Maggie took the opportunity when it offered itself of standing close to Justin and putting her arm around him in warm companionship. She had to admit that everything was going as planned and that it was likely – indeed, almost inevitable – that she and Justin would end the evening as lovers. Her team leader had impressed upon her that the intelligence which had come to them concerning a terrorist atrocity led them to believe that it had been planned for over the Christmas period, and it was essential that she developed as quickly as a relationship with Justin where he would ask her to move in with him. She felt confident that she would achieve that goal but again had to admit to herself that there were times when it was difficult to remain dispassionate when she was manipulating someone she found attractive.

Soon the smells of chips and steak filled the kitchen as Justin and Maggie chatted and laughed as the food was prepared and eventually arranged tastefully on two large oval platters which they carried back to the table and set to with gusto. By this time it was necessary to open a second bottle of Chardonnay and with the influence of the wine, the joys of a good steak and lively conversation the meal soon passed with the crowning glory of the pavlova finishing the feast. At last they leaned back replete.

"Justin, that meal was divine, " said Maggie with a sigh of deep satisfaction, "I don't want to sound unladylike, but after that I couldn't even manage a wafer-thin mint."

"What a shame, I was just about to bring out the cheese board," teased Justin. " I'll just clear the table and we can settle down with another glass of wine as the night is yet young. I'll leave the washing up until later."

"Tell you what, Justin, I'm a dab hand at the sink – no corny male jokes about women's short feet, please. Let's do it together. It'll only take fifteen minutes and we can slurp wine at the same time. Okay?"

Maggie was pleased when Justin agreed, as it was part of her plan to generate, as far as was possible in an evening, a feeling of domesticity between them in order to bring them together as a live-in couple. The washing up and putting away was carried out with their usual high spirits and once finished they walked through to the sitting room. As they came to the settee, Maggie took Justin's arm and gently pulled him down besides her. She needed to bring matters to the point where Justin would know she was ready to be seduced and her experience told her that it was now.

Her assumption was correct as their lips met in a lingering kiss filled with the promise of what would follow. What Maggie couldn't know was that Justin's embrace was filled with a tenderness which was, for him, unusual. Although generally considerate in his relationships, he set about them with his own interests foremost in everything he did, primarily setting out to satisfy himself before the needs of his girlfriends. But this time it was different. Maggie was not to know that Justin was slowly but surely falling in love with her and that it was having a profound effect on the way he had decided to conduct this current relationship. For the first time in his life Justin was putting the desires and feelings of a woman ahead of his own and had, to his surprise, found he actually wanted to treat Maggie as an equal. He found the decision comforting and he knew from past experience that, although he intended he and Maggie would become lovers that evening, he would be treating her in a very different way from all his other conquests.

Their embrace became more passionate and, as their hands began to explore each other, Justin gently took Maggie's hand and together they slowly walked into the bedroom where, with controlled passion, they undressed each other and lay expectant with desire on the bed. Maggie knew from her research in to his past that Justin was an accomplished lover, but any doubts she may have harboured about his techniques were soon dispelled as with his hands, tongue and fingers firmly but gently exploring her body and senses, he raised her to a level of passion she had never experienced before as he took control, without ever being controlling, as she experienced climax after climax until, a simultaneous cry of ecstasy from Justin, told her their union was finally complete.

With passion spent, they lay together in a silent warm embrace as the light faded outside until Justin pulled her close to him and kissed he gently on the lips. How he felt about Maggie was a whole new experience for him and he was unsure of what to say as he struggled to assimilate these new feelings which had surfaced from deep within his inner self. He took a slow breath and waited a moment before he felt able to speak.

"Maggie, darling," he paused, again still unsure what to say. "I have never felt like this about anyone else – I mean, how I feel about you. I'm not used to talking about my emotions, but I feel like a tongue-tied teenager after his first kiss. I'm sorry Maggie if I sound daft but I really think I'm falling in love with you."

This was a development that Maggie had

not expected and, indeed, it was not one she wanted as it could create problems in the future. She had hoped for a relationship similar to the ones she knew Justin had with his girlfriends. Carefree with fun and laughter but not intense and certainly light on commitment and one from which they could both break free once the surveillance operation was over. Maggie decided that as there was nothing she could do to change his feelings for her, she would have to go along with pretence and declare feeling for him which she knew she could never achieve. She looked at him in the gloom and softly returned his kiss.

"Justin, this is a surprise and I'm flattered you think so much of me." She searched for the right things to say. "It's just that we haven't known each other for long and I want us to establish a strong relationship over time. But, dear Justin, I am very fond of you and just being with you makes me feel happy and fulfilled, but can you be patient and wait a bit longer until I feel ready to commit myself?"

Justin gave a resigned sigh before replying. "Of course. I hope I haven't come on too strong. I don't want to make you feel uncomfortable so I'll rein in my feelings until the time's right. How does that sound to you?"

Maggie thought it sounded just fine and with a feeling of relief said so. "Justin, I'm going to take a shower and then perhaps we could finish off the wine before I have to go back home?"

Justin looked up in surprise. "Go home! Maggie, please tell me you're joking. Can't you stay the night. I've got a late start tomorrow, what about you?"

"Took your time, didn't you," she teased, "of course I'd love to stay over. In fact, naughty girl that I am, I'd anticipated you'd ask and told my publisher I'm having a day off tomorrow. So no problem with a lie-in."

"Great stuff." replied Justin, giving her nose a playful tweak. "Now get showered and don't take too long as I want my turn before the midnight hour strikes and the wine turns into a pumpkin – or something like that."

Maggie giggled at Justin's mangling of a fairy tale and took herself off for a quick shower. She had just finished drying herself when Justin came into the bathroom holding a pyjama top.

"No point in getting dressed as we'll be in bed in a couple of hours. Thought you could use this. It's a bit like a baby doll nightdress so your modesty is assured. Anyway, I don't think it's seemly drinking good wine in the nude."

"Very appropriate, I'm sure, and good to know that you uphold the highest standards in these matters." Maggie buttoned up the pyjama top and turned to inspect the result in the full-length mirror on the wall. "Um, I think my modesty is only just assured but I don't mind as I know you would never take advantage of a helpless maiden."

"Not sure about the maiden bit but never mind. I'll only be a minute taking a man-shower so why don't you get the wine out of the fridge and charge a couple of glasses?"

Maggie hadn't heard of a man-shower before but imagined it was a very brief one and was proved right in her surmise as Justin was out, dried and wrapped in a dressing gown with combed hair shortly after she had put two full wine glasses down on the low table in front of the settee. There they stayed snuggled up until the last of the wine was finished and they decided to take themselves off to bed where, relaxed and at ease, they chatted until tiredness overtook them and with legs entwined they fell into a deep slumber.

The following morning they awoke around eight o'clock and after showering Justin made breakfast for them both over which they talked easily of their plans for the future. Maggie didn't want to appear too forward, so told Justin that she was going to be very busy for the rest of the week but wanted for them to meet at the Castle with Caesar and Lynn on Friday. Justin looked a bit disappointed but Maggie was determined that nothing was going to jeopardise her plan to eventually move in with him and she now felt that it was a certainty that Justin would ask her to share his hotel room at the Bromyard folk festival. Although it was imperative she move in with Justin, she reasoned that as it was only just over a week away she could afford to leave an acceptance of what she hoped would be Justin's offer until the festival. She was not to be disappointed as they had barely started on their toast when he brought up the subject of the impending Bromyard weekend and asked her if she would like to come with him and share his double room. Quietly satisfied that matters were progressing as she had planned, Maggie said she would love to join him and thanks for the kind offer. Justin said he'd phone the hotel to say that his room was going to be double occupancy and not single as he didn't want them to be chucked out for underpaying. After they had finished breakfast, Justin offered to run Maggie back to her house rather than take a taxi. Maggie thanked him but turned down lift as it was a lovely day and she fancied a stroll back to Frankwell. In truth, she didn't want Justin to be seen anywhere near her house just in case he was being tailed or tracked and so, after a warm embrace and a lingering kiss they parted at the front door with Justin waving to her as she stepped out towards the English Bridge and the town centre.

Once Maggie was back at the safe house on Drinkwater Street she carefully prepared her report for her team leader. Everything she had to tell him she committed to memory as she never allowed anything to be written down in case it fell into the wrong hands. Similarly, she had been told that she must never e-mail through her findings to him or anyone else when on missions of extreme delicacy as, even though her department had cyber experts second to none, there was still the possibility that her laptop might have been compromised. There was, of course, the real danger that her cover had been blown and the opposition had planted listening devices in her rooms and could therefore listen in on her reports by phone. To combat this threat her technical department had issued her with an advanced detector able to pick up the electronic emissions from hidden camera and listening devices of the most sophisticated designs, and Maggie would run a sweep of the entire house every time she had been out for any length of time. It was because of this specific threat that she wanted to to be resident in Justin's flat when she would be able to be on her own and conduct a detailed sweep of his rooms as it was strongly suspected that his security had been compromised.

Once she had marshalled her report in her head, Maggie ran the detector over all the rooms and, finding them all clear, keyed in a coded number into her mobile phone then, after answering all the security questions, was put through to her team leader to give her report. After some fifteen minutes she had passed on all the relevant developments and with his congratulations on achieving her goals to date she rang off and went to the kitchen to make a drink of coffee. As she switched on the kettle and put the instant grounds into a mug, she thought about her relationship with Justin with a slight pang of regret. She prided herself, with justification, on being a consummate specialist and well able to keep her work and her private life separate but she, despite the iron control she was able to keep over her emotions, had to confess to feeling attracted to Justin and felt uncomfortable with the deception as it was now obvious that he had fallen in love with her. But by the time she had finished making her drink she had suppressed all regret and had returned to what she was – a cool, dedicated and unemotional operative who had been tasked with finding a dangerous terrorist and if it meant hurting Justin, or anyone else for that matter, she would do it without regret knowing her actions were for the greater good. Life was tough, she reasoned, and sometimes a few people get hurt, or even destroyed, in order to protect the many and if Justin got screwed up over their relationship then so be it. In this manner Maggie's professional voice had managed to drown out her personal one and returned her to her normal operational efficiency.

Friday came and with it the folk club evening at the Castle. Although Maggie had said she wouldn't be able to meet up with Justin before then, she had talked on the phone over the intervening days when they chatted and joked in their usual relaxed way. She had decided that it was important that she stayed over at Justin' place more frequently before eventually moving in on a permanent basis and thought she would leave her car at home to meet at his flat and then walk over to the Castle so that she would be free to go back with him afterwards. To this end she had put her toothbrush and a clean pair of knickers in her shoulder bag in anticipation of a passionate overnight stop, then left the house and set out to walk the mile to Justin's flat. Although warm and muggy, the evening sky had a heavy overcast and she wondered whether she should go back for her umbrella in case it rained. Deciding that she would be safe she continued on her journey through town up Pride Hill, along St. Mary's Street and steeply down Wyle Cop then over the English Bridge onto the Abbey Foregate.

Arriving at Justin's flat, she found him in his usual high spirits and dressed ready to leave and after a tight embrace and many kisses later they set off on the short walk to the Castle to meet up with Caesar and Lynn. Upon entering they were met with the usual blast of folk music, loud conversation and much laughter from the tightly-packed regulars as they greeted a well-lubricated Len whose tenure behind the bar, based on past observation, was likely to be of short duration before his vast liquid intake resulted in several hours of oblivion. Justin looked over to his friends and catching their eye waggled his hand in front of his mouth in a drinking gesture to see if they were ready for a repeat order. Caesar gave a thumbs-up and shouted above the hubbub that it was about time too and get a move on. Justin and Maggie laughed at his cheek and, after paying for the round, carried them over to the table where two seats had been zealously guarded by Caesar and Lynn who, much to Justin's gratitude, always arrived early to be sure of getting a free table and enabling them to be able to sit down for the evening.

“Well, well, this is a wonderful sight for sore eyes,” boomed Caesar as Justin put the drinks on the table, “and it's nice to see you two as well."

Maggie and Justin groaned as Lynn dug Caesar in the ribs. "It's all right Lynn," said Justin with a look of mock tragedy on his face, "we all know by now that there is no cure for this behavioural problem which tragically afflicts only those with disgustingly unkempt anti-social whiskers."

After a few more blokey insults the four of them settled down and exchanged news and views as normal. Justin decided that it was a good time to tell his friends that Maggie would be coming to Bromyard next weekend.

"Got some great news for you," he said with a satisfied look on his face, "Maggie will be coming with us to Bromyard I'm happy to say."

Caesar threw up his hands in horror. "No, Maggie, You mustn't. This man is a serial cad and once he has had his way with you will discard you like an old sock. Though from what I've heard heard all his socks are so old perhaps you might stand a chance."

"Caesar, I'm unable to follow your complex logic, and I don't believe a word of what you are saying," replied Maggie with a broad grin, "Justin has been the perfect gentleman all the time I've known him. But I have realised that you two make a competition of who can insult the other the most. Am I right?"

"You most certainly are," said Lynn, determined to bring a modicum of sanity to the proceedings, "it's like having two big children in tow. Honestly, I despair that they'll ever grow into man's estate."

Caesar gave a laugh which rumbled from his huge chest. "Many a true word and all that, and I don't think Justin and I will ever grow up properly but just for you I'll make an effort. Seriously, Maggie, I'm glad you're coming with us to Bromyard. It's a great time and I know you'll have fun. Let's keep our fingers crossed that the weather is kind to us. The weather boffins tell us that this weekend, and possibly Monday, will be a washout with torrential rain and high winds."

"Great," said Justin turning to Maggie, "I was just about to suggest that we had a run out on the bike on Sunday, so that's on hold for the time being. And, Caesar, before you ask why I didn't know what the weather was going to do, it's because I never try to find out as, whatever it does, I still have to go out and work in it. So I don't bother listening to the weather forecasts and as a consequence sleep much better. Anyway the Met Office frequently get it wrong."

They all agreed on the last observation as the conversation flowed in a relaxed and easy manner with the four of them settled into enjoying the evening's entertainment in each other's company. All too soon the cry of *time , please, ladies and gentlemen* came from the bar and, as expected, it was not Len's voice saying it, as he was nowhere to be seen. They noticed it was one of his trusty regulars who had taken over after Len had taken himself off to bed to sleep off his over-indulgence. Leaving the pub the four of them walked together back onto the Abbey Foregate before saying their farewells at Justin's flat, with Caesar saying he would be in touch shortly to finalise the travel arrangement for the trip to Bromyard. With a last *goodnight* Caesar and Lynn set off the short distance to the column. Justin turned to Maggie as they stood together on the pavement.

"I forgot to ask if you'd like to stay with me tonight," he said as he put his arms around her and pulled her close. "I don't want to take anything for granted but as we've been lovers once I thought we could repeat the experience." He looked at her with a twinkle in his eye as he added, "and I've changed the sheets and pillow cases for you."

Maggie giggled as she replied, "I should think so after the last time. So you think you are up to a repeat performance, do you big boy?"

Justin assured he was more than ready as they climbed the stairs to the flat. He was glad it was late and old Mrs. Williams from the bottom flat would be safely tucked up in bed and fast asleep, otherwise she would have been out of her front door like a shot to hold him in a grip of steel until she had grilled him about his new girlfriend. Once in the flat Justin and Maggie looked at each other and wordlessly walked with their arms around each other into the bedroom. Despite her innate professionalism, Maggie possessed all the usual female impulses and this time she took the initiative and interspersed with kisses removed Justin's clothes before undressing herself and drawing him down onto the bed. Before surrendering herself to the moment, she was impressed to observe that Justin had indeed changed the bedding.

They awoke the next morning to find that the weather forecasters had finally got things right with heavy rain lashing down and strong gusting winds making the trees dance to their tune. There is something very satisfying in being warm and snug whilst the storm raged impotently outside, and they both lay in a warm embrace as the rain battered against the window and streamed relentlessly down the glass panes.

Maggie didn't want sex that morning and was pleased that Justin didn't instigate the opening moves. Sometimes, a girl just wants a cuddle, she said to herself and wondered whether Justin had been aware of this or, perhaps, even he needed a break on occasions. Whatever the reason, she decided, the relaxed cuddle was most welcome as they held each other in easy companionship until their stomachs told them needed breakfast and they decided it was time to get up and get dressed.

"Right," said Justin as he threw back the duvet, "we've been in the scratcher long enough. Time to get up, lazybones."

"Hark at him trying to be masterful." Maggie then looked bemused. "Anyway, what's a scratcher?"

Justin grinned. "It's a name for a bed I learned in the army. Although, in honesty I can't recall doing much scratching. It probably goes back to the second world war when my uncle told me as recruits they had to sleep on mattress covers which were stuffed with straw and very likely the dust and chaff which came through the cover would be highly irritable and lead to lots of scratching. Of course, it could have been outbreaks of crabs which are very itchy things."

"Crabs," said a puzzled Maggie, "what, like the ones you find at the seaside?"

"No, you goose. Body lice. They look like little black crabs and they burrow under the skin usually around the armpits or the groin area. In fact, when I was in training there was an outbreak in my barrack block."

Maggie looked at Justin with a horrified look on her face. "Eek, don't tell me you caught a dose of those crabby things! Right, all physical contact is at an end until I have closely inspected all the relevant parts of your body. But until I can get that organised, tell me, how did you get rid of these nasty little creatures?"

"Easy," replied Justin with a twinkle in his eye, "everyone who had crabs was stripped naked and lined up on the parade ground. There we were sprayed with petrol and set on fire with a flame thrower. I can tell you it worked a treat. Not a crab survived."

"Yes, and not a soldier either. Now pull the other one, you twerp." She looked up with a squeal as Justin attempted to get back into bed with the intention of another cuddle. "Get out you horrible man. You're not allowed to touch me until I've checked to see you are free of those revolting little monsters."

There then followed the inevitable scrabble around the bed as Justin tried to embrace Maggie and she, with arms and legs flailing, made strenuous efforts to escape his clutches. The phoney war continued for some minutes until they fell off the bed entangled in the duvet, with both dissolving into peals of laughter before weakly declaring a truce and staggering to the shower to freshen up before dressing and discussing whether old Mrs. Williams in the flat below had heard the noise of their lovers' mock fight.

Over breakfast Justin said that he had some work on with a grave to be filled in after a twelve o'clock burial at Cardington and would have to be on his way shortly. He asked what Maggie had lined up for the weekend. Maggie had decided that she should not be forcing the pace with their relationship and so told Justin that as the weather was so bad she had decided to visit her parents in London for the weekend and hoped he wouldn't mind if she left things until next week. She suggested that if the weather permitted she would like a run out into the country on the Norton one evening next week for a pub meal. Although slightly disappointed, Justin agreed with her suggestion and shortly after finishing their late breakfast offered to run her back home. Again, although Maggie didn't want Justin to know exactly where she lived, she could hardly refuse a lift with the rain bucketing down, so decided to accept but ask to be dropped off at the Square as she had some shopping to do.

Shortly after, Justin dropped her off at the Square and, with a kiss and a cheery promise to get in touch when she was back from her parents, drove off through the driving rain for what he knew would be a very damp couple of hours filling in the grave after the funeral was concluded. Maggie ducked into the nearby health food shop, waited until he was safely out of sight, then found a taxi for hire at a rank around the corner which took her the short distance back to her house in Frankwell. After paying off the driver, she hurried in and text her Field Manager to confirm she would be back at the MI5 headquarters at Thames House for the meeting which was scheduled for three-thirty that afternoon. She quickly put together all she needed for a two night stop and, first checking everything through the house was secure, locked the front door and ran back through the rain to her car. Once in the driver's seat she paused for a moment as she wiped her face with a tissue and took stock of her progress with her mission which was to discover the identity and whereabouts of Justin's nemesis – the man know as John.

So far she felt that everything was on track and advancing according to her brief from her Team Leader. Putting her emotions to one side, she was confident that Justin had fallen for her and that she would shortly be his live-in partner – hopefully after the Bromyard weekend. Answers were urgently needed and time was running out for finding and arresting this John character, along with his cell, and preventing a suspected terrorist outrage. Finally, satisfied that everything was in place, Maggie started the engine and, engaging first gear, set off on what she knew from past experience would be a tedious journey back to her H.Q. on the banks of the Thames at Millbank.

Justin, meanwhile, had arrived at Cardington and remained in his van with the rain drumming on the roof and streaming in relentless rivulets down his windscreen, as powerful gusts of wind buffeted and rocked the vehicle. Although he wasn't looking forward to working in these conditions, he had over the years built up a high degree of stoicism about his chosen calling and simply got on with the job in hand irrespective of how difficult were the weather and digging conditions. He had parked his van where he could see the burial ground and occasionally switched on his wipers to clear the screen and check on progress at the grave side, hoping at the same time that the downpour would ease. But it was not to be. After a dripping priest along with the last sodden mourner had departed the rain and wind increased to monsoon intensity as Justin, after struggling into his waterproof clothing in the passenger seat, left the comfort of the van and wheeled his wheelbarrow containing his tools to the grave side.

There the rain had soaked the grass matting making it a dead weight to move and fold and such had been the volume of water that the coffin was floating on the water which had filled the grave and was unable to drain away. Justin looked at the heap of soil which he had to shift. It had turned into a heavy sticky mass which stuck stubbornly to his shovel and added a thick brown addition to the soles of his boots. With the rain hammering down onto his waterproofs, he slowly brought his work to an end having taken two hours for a job which would have taken only one in dry weather and, despite wearing waterproof clothing, he was still wet through as his heavy physical labour meant the perspiration he produced was unable to escape through these non-porous layers. It was a very wet Justin who finally returned to his van with a barrow heavy with sodden matting as the rain continued to drive down relentlessly and, with great difficulty, stripped off his protective clothing inside as he prepared to drive back along the flooded roads to Shrewsbury and the welcoming thought of a hot shower and a substantial meal.

The journey back through the storm was horrendous. With his wipers on the fastest setting they could barely cleared the screen of the rain which maintained its relentless onslaught creating huge puddles of flood water which covered the main road. With passing vehicles throwing up great sheets of spray, which obstructed his vision still further, it was a very relieved Justin who finally drew up in the supermarket car park opposite his flat. Locking the van he ran with head ducked across the road and through the front door of the building and stood dripping in the entrance foyer as he unlocked his mail box to check for letters. Finding it empty, he turned as he heard the door to Mrs. William's flat being unlocked and realising he was about to be grabbed and being wet and in no mood to listen to her past experiences, quickly ran up the stairs two at a time and was round the bend of the stairs and out of sight just in time to hear a tremulous voice call out his name.

Pleased at his lucky escape, Justin entered his flat and went into the bathroom where he threw off his wet clothes and luxuriated under a hot shower until he had driven the chill from his body. Stepping out of the cubicle he towelled himself down and, once dry, walked through to the bedroom where he took out a fresh set of clothes and stood in front of the mirror to comb his blond hair down neatly on his head. He returned to the bathroom, picked up all his wet clothing and took them to the kitchen where he put them in the washing machine. He decided there wasn't enough dirty laundry to warrant putting them to wash and left them until he had a full load.

The next pressing matter was to deal with the gnawing hunger which always followed physical exertion and drove him to rifle through the food cupboard until he found a packet of cheese and broccoli pasta. He put the contents of the packet in a pan and added cold water using a measuring jug and then took from the fridge a packet of salami which he chopped up and added to the mixture. Just as it was coming to the boil his mobile rang. He turned down the gas under the pasta and saw on the screen that the call was from Grimshaws a firm of Whitchurch undertakers. Justin sighed as he pressed the receive button and knowing what was to come next walked into the sitting room to get a pen and his diary. For some reason Mr. Grimshaw would not e-mail him with details of the grave to be dug and persisted in passing all the details verbally and at great length over the phone even though he did posses an internet connection and computer which Justin had seen when he visited his office. Despite finding these calls slightly irritating, Justin found Mr. Grimshaw kindly and entertaining and just accepted that was how it was going to be as he exchanged pleasantries and took down the decease's name, coffin dimensions along with the place date and time of the funeral. Justin was able to terminate the conversation just in time to return to the stove and give his pasta a long overdue stir before it stuck to the bottom of the saucepan.

With the rain still pelting down outside, Justin sat down with his pasta and some bread and butter and, as he ate, wondered what he was going to do over the weekend whilst Maggie was away. He looked out of the window at the rain still streaming down the glass and decided that a run out on the Norton was a non-starter and going into town to do some shopping would be a very uncomfortable experience and so made up his mind to have, what he termed, a slob weekend and not do anything in particular. His decision made, Justin thought he would spend the weekend pottering around the flat doing some long overdue repairs to various things and generally cleaning and tidying. Later that evening, Lynn phoned to ask him round for Sunday lunch as she knew that he was on his own that weekend. This was an offer which Justin accepted with alacrity knowing that the invitation would extend well into the afternoon as the fridge was emptied of its store of beer and Caesar's anecdotes grew more and more outrageous and amusing. Satisfied that his weekend now sorted, Justin poured a lager into his favourite tankard and settled down to enjoy some television before taking himself off to bed with the feeling that all was well with the world.

Justin slept late the next morning and when he awoke was pleased to see that, although the skies were still overcast, the heavy downpour and strong wind had stopped, except for occasional light flurries of rain as though to remind everyone that it hadn't quite gone away, so take care. As he was due at Lynn and Caesar's at one o'clock for lunch, and he didn't want to spoil his appetite, he made do with one slice of toast with his coffee and once finished went over to the supermarket for his Sunday paper preparatory to settling down until it was time to make the ten minute walk to Highfields and what he knew would be a superb meal.

Finally, just before one o'clock Justin put on his coat and looked through the window to check on what the weather was doing. He was pleased to see it was not raining but decided in any case to take an umbrella as it was possible to get very wet in ten minutes if the clouds decided to unload their burden. Suitably attired, he left the flat he walked briskly along, Abbey Foregate past the undertakers on his left until he reached the Shirehall where he turned left into Highfields and, a few minutes later, was knocking on his friends' front door. As he expected it was opened by the stocky, bearded figure of Caesar who immediately thrust a tankard of beer into his hands whilst slapping him heartily on the back in greeting. Walking through to the lounge Justin saw Lynn through the kitchen door and shouted a greeting as she shouted one back whilst stirring a pan which steamed on the stove. As expected, the time together grew more raucous as Justin and Caesar tipped more ale down their throats and Lynn, listening to the bellowing and laughter, shook her head with a rueful smile as she wondered why men, despite never really growing up, could be so wonderful to have around. It was a mystery she didn't think she would ever really be able to resolve. But she really valued their friendship with Justin and was pleased to see the close bond he and Caesar had developed and felt lucky to have two men in her life who meant so much to her. Her reverie was interrupted when two very jolly and shouty men descended on her to offer assistance with the meal and, batting aside the sexist jokes about women and kitchens, gave them tasks to carry out which they did with the flow of jokes and laughter never ceasing as they bustled around carrying out Lynn's instructions whilst refreshing themselves with the contents of their tankards.

As was expected by all parties, the meal was

an enjoyable time and, despite the necessity of devouring great quantities of food, they managed to keep up the flow of conversation without any noticeable lessening of volume until, after reaching saturation with the cheese and biscuits, the two men offered to clear the table and do the washing up so that Lynn could put up her feet with a glass of wine as a reward for such a splendid meal. Lynn felt this was very fair and sat down in the lounge as Justin replenished her glass. He then went off to assist Caesar who had started on the dishes, and listed to the waves of laughter and the clattering of dishes and pans which issued from the kitchen as the two men got stuck in to their task. She wondered why men had to make so much noise when they washed and dried the dishes, but then thought that it didn't matter so long as everything was clean and nothing broken. She had no sooner though this when she couldn't help laughing out loud as there was a loud crash from the kitchen with a muffled curse from Caesar and a high-pitched *soreee* in unison from them both, followed by a great bellow of laughter. Men, she said out loud so they could hear, can't live with 'em, can't do without 'em, which prompted a huge raspberry from one of them and another explosion of mirth.

Eventually, with the kitchen cleared of

washing up and everything put neatly away, the three of them sat down to enjoy the next few hours in happy association. By now the two men had settled down and were able to be talked to by Lynn on a reasonably serious level and both she and Caesar were keen to see whether Justin was still troubled and whether it showed in his behaviour. But they had to admit later that he appeared to be his normal contented self.

Just after four o'clock Justin said his good-byes to his friends and, with Caesar shouting to him as he walked down their drive to take care crossing the road as cars are very dangerous things, he walked back a trifle unsteadily to his flat and, relieved that Mrs. Williams didn't grab him on the way up the stairs, he let himself in and felt that an afternoon snooze was called for. He took off his coat and kicked off his shoes as he remembered with a start that he had forgotten to pick up his umbrella when he left. Never mind, get it later, he determined, as he walked to his bed, lay down and turning on his side fell almost immediately into a deep alcohol-assisted sleep.

Around the same time, Maggie had left her final briefing with her team leader at MI5 HQ and made her way to her car parked nearby carrying the items she had been issued with to assist her in her assignment. They had been given to her after her assurances that she was now certain that Justin would invite her into his life, as he had with most of his long-term girl friends and ask her to move in to his flat, when she would be able to deploy them safely. Whilst some of her colleagues could have entered Justin's flat without any tell-tale signs of clandestine entry to thoroughly search his property, the danger lay in their not knowing whether his flat was under surveillance and whether possibly the flat itself had been compromised with the elusive terrorist cell placing bugs in there. Maggie knew that some of these devices that her department deployed were tiny, fitted with anti-detection programmes, and there was no way of knowing how well equipped the opposition were. Intelligence sources had said there was going to be a terrorist atrocity, that it would most likely be over Christmas or the New Year, that this character who called himself John was the organiser and that, at this stage, as neither his his proper name or whereabouts were known, the only way open to them was to closely observe Justin as he was currently the only person known to have actually had face-to-face contact with the suspect.

As Maggie threaded her way through the traffic of a late Sunday afternoon, she was aware of the tremendous weight of responsibility which lay across her shoulders and the possible horrific consequences should she fail. She never once doubted her ability to carry out her assignment coolly and effectively, but was powerfully aware that being unable to complete it could lead to the deaths of scores or hundreds, or conceivably, thousands of innocent men women and children. Despite her determination to succeed at all costs, she could not quite suppress a slight feeling of regret that through the necessity of her actions she was quite possibly going to destroy a man in the process. She didn't like duping Justin as she now knew him, despite his obvious flaws, to be basically an honourable and likeable man who had unfortunately fallen in love with her.

With the traffic thinning as Maggie drove along the A40 towards Uxbridge and junction one of the M40, she stifled the feeling of regret, allowing her innate professionalism to reassert itself, and acknowledging the job came first and that it was tough if someone got crushed along the way. Leaving the A40 where it joined the M40, she put her foot down on the accelerator as she commenced the long boring run north back to Shrewsbury along a motorway which had now dried out after the soaking of the weekend. Her car being a pool car had the inboard computer remapped for more power and soon Maggie had worked her way into the outside lane and stayed there with the speed display hovering between 90 and 100 mph. She had no fear of being pulled over or of receiving a speeding ticket as her car registration, along with all the other pool cars belonging to the unit, would flag up on all A.N.P.R. systems as exempt from all further action. A few miles further up the motorway she flashed past a marked police car cruising in the centre lane and smiled as she saw it accelerate into the outside lane behind her only to drop back a minute later, leaving her to continue unchecked on her journey and trying not to feel smug at this perk of the job.

With dry roads and relatively light traffic, Maggie drew up outside her house in Frankwell just before seven o'clock and decided to phone Justin to let him know she was back safely. After she let herself in through the front door she ran a visual and electronic check to see whether her security had been compromised and, finding that all appeared to be in order and deciding that she was too hungry to phone Justin first, left the house to walk the short distance to the convenience store on the Frankwell roundabout, which sold everything you could need and appeared to stay open 24/7. Inside the store she squeezed past two youths with their hoods pulled over their heads who were arguing drunkenly over which larger was the strongest and continued along the aisle to the chilled cabinets and selected a spaghetti bolognese, then a bunch of bananas from the fruit rack and, finally, a sliced white loaf from the bakery section. She remembered to pick up a container of milk and, as a treat, bought a bottle of already chilled pinot grigio from a glass-fronted cabinet, before making her way to the till where she found the two youths who had finally made their choice of a pack of super strength export lager which she could see was 7.5% proof. After much fumbling, they eventually found enough money to pay for their purchase and left the shop leaving in their wake a strong waft of beery breath mixed with cannabis fumes, and their intoxicated conversation peppered with very audible obscenities which they must have thought was acceptable civilised behaviour. Ignoring their oafishness, Maggie paid for her items and walked back to her house. First things first, she poured herself a large glass of wine and took a refreshing drink before putting the bottle in the fridge. She quickly microwaved the bolognese and within a few minutes she was tucking into a much needed pasta meal which she finished off with two of the bananas she had bought earlier.

With a second glass of wine poured to replace the one she had finished, Maggie thought she would phone Justin to make arrangements for their next meeting. He answered the call after a few rings sounding as though he had just woken up, which indeed he had.

"Justin, Hi. I'm back," said Maggie brightly, "thought I'd give you a bell to let you know all is well. Talking of all is well, you don't sound your normal cheerful self. Is everything okay?"

"Hello, Maggie," replied Justin through a dry mouth and an unpleasant headache. "Good to hear from you. Yes. Everything's just fine. Well, almost. I went to Lynn and Caesar's for lunch today and as you can imagine the hospitality was overwhelming – especially the alcoholic part of it. I think I'll survive though!"

Maggie laughed. "You are a clot, Parkes. Why don't you learn to control yourself like me?"

"Believe me, Maggie, I'm trying my hardest to rise to your level of perfection." He gave a heart rending groan for dramatic effect. "Maggs old girl. Would you mind if we didn't meet up tonight as I don't think I could be the sparkling company you crave. I'm going to be busy with work tomorrow and Tuesday, so would it be all right if we met up on Wednesday and, if the weather is kind, take a run out on the bike to a country pub for a meal. Do you mind?"

"Course I don't mind. The run out sounds a great idea. Remember, this time it's on me. Okay?" As she had to make sure that Justin didn't offer to pick her up from her house she quickly added, "I won't quite know what has been planned for me until I get proof reading commissions from the publishers tomorrow, so best that I'll meet you at Caesar's unit at, say, seven o'clock all being well."

"That's fine with me. Look forward to it. Oh, nearly forgot, Caesar and Lynn send their best wishes and say they are looking forward to our weekend together at Bromyard."

With a few more exchanges and a big kissing sound from Justin, Maggie said goodbye and, sitting down with her glass of wine, quietly assessed how her assignment was progressing. Although her team leader had praised her in his usual restrained way and had been satisfied with her performance, she knew not to give herself any pats on the back as she was well aware that complacency could soon lead to disaster. It was the unexpected which couldn't be planned for and she knew its only antidote was ceaseless vigilance and total concentration for the success of the operation. With a determined effort, Maggie put aside that part of her which harboured warm thoughts about Justin and carefully planned her moves over the Bromyard weekend so that the next part of her assignment could succeed. Nothing, she determined, nothing must stop her moving in with Justin.

Maggie yawned. Suddenly she felt tired after her long high speed journey and decided to have an early night. She finished her wine and went round the house securing all the doors and windows and, after a relaxing bath , took herself off to bed where, being able totally switch off from the worries and problems of the day, she quickly fell into a deep dreamless sleep.

Justin, meanwhile, despite his long snooze during the afternoon, had also felt the need for some restorative sleep. As is usual after heavy alcoholic consumption, he felt the desire to eat and, finding a can of macaroni cheese in the cupboard, heated the contents in the microwave and ate it with some bread and butter. He also felt the need for a hair of the dog before turning in and found that after a tankard of lager his headache improved and, although still feeling some of the effects of his earlier overindulgence, decided that a good night's rest was the only enduring cure. He took a quick shower and climbed into his bed and, like Maggie but for entirely different reasons, also fell into a deep dreamless sleep.

The next two days passed quickly for Justin as he had four graves to dig for various undertakers which were well spread out over the county and involved many miles of motoring. He had been commissioned to dig a single and had duly informed John of the details by e-mail as usual. On Tuesday evening he had phoned Maggie who suggested she could pick him up at his flat the next day to save taking two cars to the unit. But as the weather forecast was for a fine warm day on Wednesday, Justin said he'd like to walk and they confirmed the arrangement to meet there at seven o'clock.

Wednesday dawned warm with a light overcast which had burned off by the time Justin had arrived at his first job. Unseasonally, the temperature rose steadily as the day progressed making his work difficult and necessitating drinking a great deal of the bottled water which he had brought with him. He had a break whilst the funeral took place and after filling in and tidying up he set off to his second dig at Wentnor at the edge of the Long Mynd which he had to leave open for the funeral the following day. The going was tough, as he knew from past experience that he had to remove heavy boulder clay surrounding difficult bands of shale like rock, and it was with great relief when he was finally able to clean his tools and leave a finished grave for Thursday's interment before driving back to Shrewsbury.

Justin's van had no air conditioning fitted

and so the journey back was a hot and sticky one and it was with great relief when he was back in his flat and stripped off under a shower which he ran on cold for several minutes until he felt his body temperature was back to normal. He checked the time and saw that he had forty minutes until he was to meet Maggie, which gave him plenty of time to put on clean clothing, pick up the key to the unit, and take a leisurely stroll along to Caesar's unit on the industrial estate at the far end. After walking up Monkmoor Road, he approached the roundabout at the top of the road he looked idly over to his right at the police station from where Lynn worked for West Mercia Police. It was fortunate that Justin was not to know that shortly his life was to spiral catastrophically out of his control, and that he would have more than a passing acquaintance with the workings of the police station he was passing. But, having no way of knowing what the future held for him, he continued on his way filled with the happy thought of meeting with the first woman he had ever felt love for.

As the unit came into view, Justin saw that Maggie's car was parked at the front with the driver's door open. Maggie saw him approach and slid off the seat and ran over to him to give him a warm embrace. Justin grinned widely as he threw his arms around her and gave her kiss on the lips which was so prolonged that eventually Maggie drew back with a squeak of protest.

“Justin, stop. Don't you know that a girl has to breath occasionally,” she said breathlessly as she kissed him again. “mind you, what a way to go. I've missed you, big man.”

“I've missed you too. How did your visit to your folks go? Are they keeping well? How was the journey, I believe that traffic round London is horrific. Oh, dear, I so excited I'm gabbling like a love-struck teenager.”

Maggie couldn't help laughing as Justin did, indeed, sound just like one and she couldn't quite stifle a feeling that she wanted to protect his from his vulnerability. She had to admit that there was a childlike innocence about Justin which brought out the mothering instinct in her. She wondered whether he did it deliberately in order to exploit his girlfriends' emotions, but decided that it was just how he was and possibly an explanation for his insecurity.

“Justin I promise to answer all your questions but first I am absolutely starving and if I don't eat soon I may pass out from lack of nourishment. So why don't we kit up mount your trusty steed and roar off into the sunset to wherever you've decided to take me?”

Justin agreed that her suggestion was eminently sensible and very soon they had donned their motorcycling clothing, kicked the Norton into life and set off along Telford Way onto the Whitchurch Road. At the Battlefield roundabout Justin took the inside lane for the second exit onto the A49 signed for Whitchurch and pointed the powerful machine along a road which Justin knew to be one well-surfaced with wide sweeping bends and many long straights suitable for overtaking. After a fast run to the roundabout at Prees Heath he swept the Norton round to the A41 and headed south for Market Drayton and the dual carriageway where he opened up the throttle to see 80 mph on the speedometer before arriving at the Ternhill roundabout where he turned left and travelled the few miles along the A53 until they arrived at the small town of Market Drayton.

Justin has heard good reviews about the Red Lion Inn, situated at the top of Phoenix Bank and which was attached to its very own brewery. It was one of a chain of pubs owned and run by Joule's who had built their brewery over their own water supply drawn from an underground aquifer. This reservoir of clean water had given Joule's ales a unique character which had won high praise from beer connoisseurs, though Justin was frustrated that he wouldn't be able to sample freely as, responsibly, he would only have one drink if he was in charge of a motor vehicle. He pulled the bike up onto its stand against a wall in front of the main entrance and, pulling off his helmet and gloves, turned to Maggie.

“Here you are, old girl. The final destination of the Justin Parkes mystery tour. I had been told that the food is superb, the ale even better and, of course, you couldn't improve on the company you are about to enjoy.”

“Hark at him. No shrinking violet stands before me - and I don't mind girl but less of the old! Now, I'm absolutely starving – hope they've got a horse n the menu because if they have it's in deep trouble.”

“Horse sounds absolutely fine for me. How do you like yours done?”

“Quickly,” laughed Maggie, “though I feel I may have taken on more than I can chew with a horse. I'll see what's on the menu and choose accordingly.”

They went inside and up to the bar where they asked to look at the menu. They were impressed when the friendly lady behind the bar beckoned to one of her staff who took them over to a free table in a room at the front of the pub and, handing them two menus, took their drinks order. Looking around at the low beams and the worn flagstone flooring it was obvious to them that the Red Lion was a building steeped in antiquity which was confirmed when Justin picked up a leaflet from the holder on their table. He read it through and looked up with an animated look on his features.

"Well, I don't believe it, Maggie," he said, "I have a very tenuous family link with this place."

"I'm more than happy to hear about it," she replied primly, "provided you can tell me quickly and we can order from the menu before my body gives out. What is it anyway?"

"It says here that the other part of the pub is called the Brewers' Hall and its been fitted out using the panelling from a council chamber in Yorkshire. But here's the interesting bit. The firm which originally made it was owned by Robert Thompsom of Kilburn who was famous for his fine oak furnishings. Interestingly, most of his work carried his emblem which was a small crouching mouse." Justin stabbed at the leaflet. "It says here that the panelling in the Brewers' Hall has six mice carved into the woodwork and challenges all the children to find them."

"So, don't tell me, you want to go in there and find them. Do you get a prize if you do?" teased Maggie in a resigned tone.

"No, course not, be serious. But the interesting bit is that my grandfather on my mother's side was a master craftsman and was employed by Thompsons. I believe his speciality was in ecclesiastical furniture - you know, pews, pulpits, stalls and so on – and he would have carved a mouse on his work. Mind you, by all accounts he was a difficult character to work with and I'm told he was frequently getting the sack for one reason or another and, as a consequence, money was often tight with five mouths to feed. Eventually, he and Gran divorced whilst I was a nipper, so I hardly remember him. Still, he was a highly skilled joiner and usually managed to find work within the trade somewhere."

"Actually, that is interesting. As they say it's a small world. However, at the moment I have an enormous hunger which is crying out for an enormous platter of food." Maggie picked up a menu and passed it to Justin before picking up one for herself. "Now, choose, O, mighty one, and remember this is on me and no arguing. Got it, buster!"

Justin got it and was quite happy not to argue and they quickly made their choices before the waitress came back carrying their drinks and took their orders. He took Maggie's hand in his and gave it a squeeze as he looked softly into her eyes and thought that he was a lucky man to have found such a wonderful woman as her. He was just getting use to this strange feeling of love. This strange warm surging of emotion whenever he was with her and when he thought of her, but it was one he found fulfilling and one which made him want to protect and cherish the first woman in his life who had been capable of releasing these emotions. Justin felt sure that his feelings were reciprocated by Maggie and he had made up his mind to ask her to move in with him as soon as possible, but had felt it prudent to wait until they were together at the Bromyard Folk Festival before making the offer.

They chatted easily together until the waitress returned with two enormous plates of food which she placed before them with the standard exhortation to *enjoy* before leaving them to tuck into well-presented meals which were cooked to perfection. Some while later, they both leaned back with clean plates before them and their appetites satisfied, and finished off their drinks before asking for the bill. Maggie was pleased to see that, as usual, Justin had only drunk a half of Joules' bitter and she found it intriguing that someone who was so slap-happy in many respects, could be so consistently responsible in others. Perhaps, she mused, there was more to him than meets the eye and, who knows, possibly he would be able to achieve a degree of constancy and make some woman a fine and loyal partner – possibly even a husband and father. She had to admit that she did like Justin and was grateful that her task was made easier by not having to act out a loving role with someone who she found repugnant – something which had happened all too often in the past. Still, she concluded as she settled the bill and they walked out to the Norton, whoever it may or may not be who settles down with him in the future, it certainly won't be me.

Maggie enjoyed the ride back. She genuinely did like the feel of the wind on her face and the exhilaration of the feeling of power as Justin twisted the throttle and she had to lean forward against the surge of power as he overtook slower moving traffic. She was grateful that he was a safe and competent rider as she had little option but to put up with him if he was speedy and reckless. She had in the past been fearful for her life with some of the villains she had to consort with and whose driving verged on the suicidal, but fortunately had come through unscathed, despite many near misses and a few minor scrapes. Well, she thought as they eventually arrived at the unit, this job does have its pluses. A good meal, easy company with an attentive man and a safe and enjoyable ride out, so she determined to enjoy herself whilst she could for she knew that she was up against a dangerous and clever opponent and that once she was settled into Justin's flat, the hazardous task of finding this John and uncovering his terrorist cell and stopping them would take priority over everything else, even though she knew it would leave Justin emotionally scarred in the process.

She had initially decided that she would take her leave of Justin at the unit, but thought it would appear a bit offhand if she did and she didn't want to do anything which may strain her relationship with him. Anyway, unable to suppress the knowledge that she was feeling a bit frisky and that a long fulfilling session with Justin was called for, she made it plain that she wasn't going home and that he's better be up to dealing with what only he could satisfy. Unsurprisingly, this was exactly what Justin had in mind, and pleased that she had taken the initiative, they locked up the unit and set off with barely concealed impatience in Maggie's car back to the flat and to what she knew with certainty would be Justin giving her a master class in arousal techniques. She was not disappointed and as their loving was, as usual, protracted and, it being late before they lay back fulfilled and at ease, it was inevitable that she would be staying the night.

The following morning, after breakfast, the two lovers parted after making arrangements for Maggie to pick up Justin on Friday afternoon when she would drive them up to Caesar and Lynn's house where she could leave her car safely on their drive whilst they were away for the weekend at the Bromyard Folk Festival.

The weekend of the festival had dawned with a heavy dew covering the ground, but which soon succumbed to the late summer sun as it began its long slow sweep across the sky and began to warm the ground, with the promise of a fine day to come. As arranged, Maggie came for Justin in the early afternoon and together they drove the short distance to Highfields where they found Lynn and Caesar loading their estate car. The two women waited patiently whilst the two men started to quieten down after their usual testosterone fuelled sparring filled the air and, shortly after Justin had put his and Maggie's cases in the luggage bay, the four of them set off along the Wenlock Road, onto the Shrewsbury bypass and then on the long drive south along the A49 to their final destination and a weekend of enjoyment.

Bromyard, which lies on the A44 midway between Leominster and Worcester in the county of Herefordshire, is an ancient town dating back to the Norman Conquest. In the centre of the town lies St Peter's Church with parts of it dating back to Norman times, including an effigy of St. Peter with two keys, over the main south doorway, and with its original Norman font still within. It was a thriving market town for many centuries serving the surrounding countryside and villages and was very prosperous. The town managed to escape the ravages of fire which destroyed so many timber-framed buildings and happily possesses many fine 16th to 18th century buildings that survive to this day and which line the well kept streets and lanes. It has been, and still is, a centre of the hop growing industry and there are many acres growing which were picked by labourers and entire families from South Wales or the Black Country who used their two weeks hop picking as their annual holiday. Although generally a quiet and peaceful rural town, Bromyard is know as the Town of Festivals, the Folk Festival being but one of many, when the town comes alive with music, poetry, performing arts and even a Scarecrow Festival all of which fill the narrow streets with revellers intent on having a good time.

It was six o'clock as Caesar guided the big Volvo along the main road to the Royal Victoria hotel at a snail's pace as he negotiated around large groups of happy Folkies, who were so numerous the pavements were unable to contain them, and who appeared to be well into enjoying the final products which the local hop gardens had helped to produce. Having been before and knowing their way around the town, they were soon at the hotel where Caesar eased the big car through the double gates and into a parking space at the rear of the building. Taking their cases out of the back of the car, they walked through the rear entrance to be met by a smiling and cheerful middle-aged lady who turned out to be the owner and who, after booking them in, took them up to their rooms on the first floor.

Justin and Maggie's room cosy and they were pleased to find it spotlessly clean, with fresh white towels in the en-suite shower room and tea and coffee-making equipment laid out on a table next to the television. After putting their clothes away with Maggie, as expected, taking up most of the drawer and wardrobe space, they walked to Caesar and Lynn's room down the corridor to see whether they were ready for a drink before their evening meal. Agreeing it was a splendid suggestion, the four of them went down to the bar where they spent the next hour getting in the party mood before ordering their food from the excellent menu which the landlady brought to their table. As expected, the food was first class and once they had all finished, it was unanimously decided that the evening should commence and without further delay they left the Crown and Sceptre and set off on the short walk to the field at the edge of the town where the big marquees had been erected for the performers and dancers and, most importantly, where there was an enormous beer tent filled with folk followers determined to drink the pumps dry. Using Caesar as a good-natured battering ram, Justin managed to arrive at the bar without upsetting too many people or their drinks, and after ordering four pints of bitter, managed with Caesar carrying half the precious cargo, to squeeze his way through the noisy throng to where Maggie and Lynn were waiting outside.

"There you are ladies," said Justin as they were passed their drinks, "you can thank Caesar for the quick service as he did the best impersonation of a human bulldozer I have ever seen." He turned to Caesar. "Did you see that bloke who you nudged? He was about to give you a severe attack of the verbals until he saw what he was up against."

"Did actually," replied Caesar, trying to look worried, "just as well he didn't know that at the first sign of trouble I'd have legged it, probably knocking you flat in the process. Still, all part of the fun."

Lynn took a substantial drink from her pint. "Right you lot, I'm in the Abba mood."

"Abba mood," said a puzzled Maggie, "what's that?"

"Come on, you're all old enough to remember their song *'I'm in the mood for dancing'.* Well. I'm in the mood right now and I see a ceilidh in yonder tent. Ready?"

Deciding that it was time to work off the enormous meal that had recently consumed, the four of them carried their drinks over to where the ceilidh band was in full swing and waited for the reel to end and for the caller to announce the next dance. And so the evening progressed with them dancing until, hot and flushed, they agreed a sit down would be beneficial and took themselves over to an another marquee where singers and musicians were performing. There were present some familiar faces from the Shrewsbury folk club, who gave them a wave once they had caught their eye, and also a character called Humus Jack. Humus Jack was so called as he ran a business selling peat products to garden centres and retail outlets with ever diminishing degrees of success as he spiralled downwards with a powerful alcohol addiction. In fairness, it must be said that although in varying degrees of intoxication every day, his behaviour was always gentlemanly and polite despite having the tendency to fall to the ground in the evenings, even whilst sitting down, as his coordination decreased in direct proportion to the volume of beer consumed.

Humus Jack also had a party piece when he would ask the organiser of the performers tent if he could sing a sea shanty. The master of ceremonies, being of the trusting type, would give him a slot and when it was his time the audience would watch with puzzled concern as this gangly, stick-thin, bearded person wearing crumpled clothing would stagger unsteadily onto the stage and proceed to sing in a high falsetto voice about a hapless sailor who, amongst other appalling misfortunes, was shot up the bum by a hard-boiled egg which penetrated his liver. At his first appearance three years previously, the announcer was so perturbed by this ghastly caterwauling that he sent out two heavies who physically lifted Humus Jack off the stage still defiantly singing about the sailor with a terminal liver problem. However, all was not lost for Humus Jack as his act was reinstated the following year by popular demand in recognition that, not only was the folk scene a broad church, but anyway he was absolutely hilarious and, true to form, his song delivered with the utmost seriousness was concluded with loud applause by the audience once they had emerged from their initial state of disbelief.

They watched enthralled as Humus Jack,

gratified by the response allowed himself a smile and walked to the edge of the stage to take a bow where, having refreshed himself more liberally than usual, and before anyone could react fell forwards off the stage landing in a crumpled heap at the feet of the front row of the audience. Good old Humus Jack, never fails to entertain thought a grinning Justin, as the hapless singer was hauled to his feet with the roars of appreciation from the audience filling the marquee. With a serious expression on his face once upright, he looked round until he had located the beer tent and, weaving unsteadily, made his way over there to continue his drinking until later in the evening when he would be carried insensible to his tent by some of his loyal and long-suffering his friends.

Amusing though he might be when in his cups, poor Humus Jack was not destined to entertain for long. He lived alone in a tiny terraced two-up, two-down in that part of Shrewsbury called Ditherington and had no one to assist when just a few months later, unconscious after his usual daily intake, he choked on his vomit and departed the folk scene for good. His funeral was well attended for, despite his permanent intoxication, he was a gentle person who carried no harm in his soul and as a consequence was well-liked.

But this was yet to come as the four friends

stayed to listen to some of the fine performers who were on the bill for that evening such as the groups Kiss The Mistress, Ted Webb, and The Falconers with Dr Sunshine, Flos & Friends, David Swann and The Bounty Hounds to name but a few. As there were venues back in Bromyard where various singers and players were performing, they decided to walk back through the field and along the narrow lane into the high street. The evening was typical of late September with a warm calm day giving way to that slight chill as darkness fell which reminded you that summer was just about over and autumn lay around the corner. The four friends chatted away happily as they joined the throng of folkies with the same idea whilst passing streams of revellers coming from the town to the marquees. Justin and Maggie walked with their arms wrapped round each others' waists in warm embrace and for his part Justin revelled in that glow of true happiness which had eluded him for much of his adult life. He felt himself lifted up to a level of completeness which was both new and exciting, and he had made up his mind that tomorrow he would ask Maggie to move in with him. He had deliberately kept his drinking under control, despite Caesar's ribbing, as he wanted to ensure he had a clear head the following day when he would make the proposal to Maggie. He was surprised that he felt nervous about what lay ahead as he always felt himself to be the one in control where his personal relationships were concerned. But this time it was different. This time he was in love, and a very different and finer aspect to Justin's nature had made an appearance and one which was much to his credit. He had come to the realisation that he wanted to settle down with Maggie and, to his amazement, he thought he actually wanted to have children with her.

As they walked along Justin gave Maggie a squeeze and turned to plant a kiss on her cheek. She returned both the kiss and tightened her embrace as she congratulated herself that provided nothing untoward occurred she would be shortly be Justin's live-in girlfriend and come Monday would be able to send a message back to her team leader that another phase in her assignment had been completed. She knew that at some stage Justin had to discover the truth about their relationship and she was aware that, as he had fallen in love with her, it would be a shattering blow. Despite her single minded professionalism she did feel some sympathy for the predicament which Justin was in, but had to set it against the fact that if he hadn't been greedy in the first place then would not be in the dilemma in which he now found himself - being used on the one hand as a gullible stooge by a terrorist organisation and, on the other, being set up by the needs of the state to protect itself. As they all walked into the first pub on their list to listen to some of the bar performers, she let none of this show as she gave herself over to simply enjoying the evening and the rest of the weekend festival whilst she could.

Maggie was not to be disappointed, for the following morning after a substantial full English breakfast, Justin did what she had expected and asked her if she would like to move in with him. He did so with a sincerity and gentleness which, under different circumstances, she would have found warming and appealing and once again she had to stifle a pang of regret which rose up within the hard nucleus of dedication to the crucial task which lay before her. She could cope with the weight of the heavy responsibility which she had to bear, but she was keenly aware that she was playing a crucial role in the hunt for this elusive terrorist cell, which so far had managed to stay two steps ahead of the intelligence services, and that any mistakes on her part would most certainly result in an appalling carnage of some description. She had been briefed that from the findings which had been gleaned to date, a terrorist atrocity had put in place which was to eclipse even the Twin Towers attack in America and was one which was to be co-ordinated in the capital cities across the major nations of Europe and possibly in the USA and Israel.

With Justin's invitation, which she readily accepted with well-rehearsed joy, she was now sure that she would succeed in her assignment but, despite her controlled elation, she decided to wait until she was back in Shrewsbury before sending off the coded message which would inform her boss that the next phase of the operation could commence. Meanwhile the four friends enjoyed the remainder of the weekend which concluded with a lunchtime ceilidh on Sunday and once finished, tired and happy, the four of them piled into Caesar's trusty Volvo and set off back to Shrewsbury.

After an uneventful journey through the scenic South Shropshire countryside, they drew up at Highfields where they said their goodbyes and, after Justin and Maggie had loaded their car, drove the short distance back to Justin's flat.

Maggie didn't want delay matters so decided to be proactive. "Justin, how about my moving in today. My house was let fully furnished so I've only a few bit and bobs of kitchen equipment and a few ornaments and my bedding and clothes to pack. Shouldn't take me more than a couple of hours. Would that be okay with you?"

Justin turned to her with a look of surprise. "Well, yes. Of course that's just what I want, but don't you have to give a month's notice first?"

Maggie had previously though out her answer to this one. "Actually, I've got a slight confession to make. I knew that things between us were getting intense and I took a chance that you would ask me to move in with you and I gave a month's notice at the end of August." Maggie cast her eyes down in a submissive gesture. "You're not cross with little Maggie, are you?"

"No, of course not. So using your infallible feminine intuition you figured out what would happen."

"Justin, my love," said a relieved Maggie, "don't you realise that women don't figure things out - they just know."

Justin shook his head and gave a loud laugh as they turned into the car park opposite the flat. "Well, well, well, what a woman. I'd better keep my thoughts closely guarded in future or you'll be picking them up. Now, on a practical level, do you want any help with getting your stuff over here. We could dump our cases at my – sorry, our – flat and I can come back with you now."

This was not what Maggie wanted as she

was not going to compromise the safe house by allowing Justin to know where it was. "Justin, thanks for the offer, but honestly I don't have much to do and everything will fit into the Golf with the back seats down. I'll be with you around seven o'clock and I shall bring with me the contents of my extensive wine cellar – which sadly is down to two bottles! I'll give you a bell when I set off as I'll park on the pavement by your front door so we don't have to cart everything over the road."

Once she had parked up in the supermarket car park, she pulled Justin's head round and gave him a lingering kiss before he hefted their two cases from the back seat and with a cheery, *see you soon,* watched as he strode briskly across the road and onto the pavement where he gave her a wave before disappearing through the front door of the building and, hopefully, not straight into the iron grip of old Mrs. Williams.

Maggie eased her car out onto the Abbey Foregate and drove through the light Sunday traffic to Frankwell where she parked the car and went into the safe house for the last time. Once inside she first made herself a cup of coffee and then retrieved an attaché case from inside a wardrobe in her bedroom. As she sipped her drink, she unlocked it and began checking the items inside. Once satisfied that they well all present and in working order, she replaced them except for a mobile phone. She switched it on and waited until the reception bars filled on the screen. Then she carefully entered a sequence of letters, numbers and symbols into the text screen and pressed *send.* She continued to look at the screen until, without a sound, it lit up with a code which told her that her team leader was replying. Maggie knew to keep her transmissions as short as possible and so, without preamble, gave a comprehensive and concise briefing to her controller in which she confirmed that she would be moving in with the subject shortly and that she had checked her equipment which was all there and operational, but there was nothing else of any significance to report. She then listed with satisfaction as she was praised for her efforts by her controller before being informed that the safe house was going to be used by four operatives from the department, two men and two women, who would beef up the surveillance teams already in place. So she would need to return the house keys to Inspector Fischer at Monkmoor police station for them to pick up on Monday. With a brief farewell the controller rang off and Maggie turned off the mobile, replacing in the case and securely locked it with a key kept on her car key ring.

She spent the next two hours packing her

belongings into the cardboard boxes she had retained from when she moved in, with the bedding rolled up and squeezed into black plastic bin bags. She had decided to leave all the food stuff in the cupboards and in the fridge for her colleagues who were moving in the next day but, thinking it would look odd if she arrived at Justin's without any food, packed a small selection into a box. As she did this she recalled her training with MI5 where it had been repeatedly impressed upon all the recruits that impeccable attention to detail was crucial for success, and that it was sometimes the little, seemingly insignificant actions, which could result in the failure of an operation and, worse, possible lead to the injury or death of colleagues and members of the public. She vowed she would never leave anything to chance.

Once she had carefully checked over the house, she started to load the boxes into her car then, once they were securely packed, phoned Justin as arranged to say she was on her way, and returned to the house to lock the front door. Satisfied that all was secure, she started off on the short drive through town to Justin's flat after first carefully checking all round for anything which may be out of the ordinary. She steered her car to the Frankwell roundabout and as she turned left towards the

English Bridge her attention was drawn to a Ford Galaxy people carrier with blacked out rear windows in the parking area in front of Everyman's Store. As she drew slowly level she checked the driver and noted a white male, possibly thirty years of age, clean-shaven and of stocky build in the driver's seat. She quickly looked away as she realised that his appearance matched the description of the person who had been followed by one of her surveillance team members some while back and who had managed to shake off his tail. As she crossed over the Severn at the English Bridge she saw in her rear view mirror the big Ford some three cars behind her where it remained until she drove onto the pavement in front of Justin's flat. She kept her head down as she got out of the car and, without appearing to look, noted from the corner of her eye the people carrier passing her and continuing up the road towards the Column. She had a quick impression of the passenger who was balding with a full fleshy facer though perhaps in his mid-forties, but was unable to see the registration plate as another vehicle was following closely behind. Maggie felt a surge of excitement as she now knew with certainty that she and Justin were being shadowed and it was reasonable to deduce from that that this surveillance was being carried out by this man John's terrorist cell. She determined that this information would be passed to control as soon as possible.

She looked up to see Justin coming down the steps at the front of the building with a wide grin on his face. She smiled in return as she passed him a box from the back of the car.

“Hello, lover. Took your time, didn't you,” she teased.

“The cheek of it,” he replied archly, “I saw you arrive and I've only kept you waiting,” he pretended to check his watch, “ for six and a half seconds.” He looked inside the car as he took the proffered box. “Are these all your worldly possessions?”

“Not quite. I've got a fair bit at my parents, but that's another story. Justin, do I detect a small wizened face looking at us from behind the downstairs curtains?”

Justin grimaced. “You do, and you will shortly be grabbed by the vice-like grip of the ancient and wrinkled Mrs. Williams who will not let go until she has interrogated you to her satisfaction. She's not a bad old bird but she can be a pain especially if you are in a hurry.”

As they carried their boxes up the steps they saw with a sinking feeling that the person in the window had disappeared and once in the entrance hall, surprised by her turn of speed, they were confronted by the diminutive stick-like figure of Mrs. Williams and, as expected, they were unable to continue up the stairs to the flat until she had extracted the information she needed about Maggie.

Some five minutes later, with a satisfied Mrs. Williams finally releasing her hold on Maggie's arm, they carried their boxes into the flat where they dumped them on the kitchen worktops and returned to the car to continue the unloading. Once the last items were taken out Justin pointed out that she could park in the supermarket car park opposite, and waited until she had completed the manoeuvre and walked back to where he waited on the pavement. Together they carried the remaining bags into the building, past the ever-watchful gaze of Mr. Williams, and put them with the other items in the kitchen.

Maggie eyed the pile of her possessions with her hands on her hips. “Do you think, Justin, that it would be a good idea to put everything away now? For a bachelor you keep everything all shipshape and Bristol fashion, and my gear is detracting from the pristine perfection of your home.”

“Correction – our home now. But, yes, great idea. I've cleared some drawers for you in the chest in the bedroom and there's over half the wardrobe for your bits. Bedding can go in the drawers under our bed as three of them are empty. I see you've brought some kitchen items and I thought they could be left in the box and I'll make space for it in one of the cupboards. Shall I start on the bedding?"

"Okay. I'll come with you and put my clothing away. By the way, one of the boxes has got my ornaments in it, including a wall clock. I hoped I could put it up as it was a gift and means a lot to me and possible put a few things around if you don't mind."

Justin assure her that he had not the slightest objection to Maggie putting her mark on the flat and together they chattered away until everything was neatly stowed and several porcelain figurines had been tastefully placed on various surfaces around the sitting room. Finally, Maggie brought out of a box the carefully wrapped clock she had spoken of previously. After removing the wrapping, she showed Justin a finely finished, wooden case pendulum clock and together they chose a suitable position on one of the sitting room walls. Justin rummaged around in a tool box he extracted from the cupboard under the sink and, after a short time , triumphantly held aloft a small hammer and a picture hook and pin. After offering up the clock and getting Maggie's approval that it was in the correct place, he passed it to her and tapped in the pin and watched as Maggie deftly placed it on the hook, moved the hands round to the correct time and, after starting the pendulum, stood back to admire the effect.

By this time the light was fading outside and Justin went round the flat putting on the lights and closing the curtains. “Well, my love, that's a good job well done and I'm sure I speak for us both when I say a drink is in order, followed by something to eat. I've got two shepherd's pies in the fridge which can be microwaved and I'll heat up a can of peas whilst we wrap ourselves round something alcoholic. What's your fancy. I've – sorry, we've – got lager, red wine, white wine in the fridge or some delicious tap water drawn this very day from the River Severn.”

“I'll give the water a miss, thank you kindly, but a very large white wine will do the trick. I don't know about you but I pretty shattered after the physical exertions of the weekend, and with work tomorrow I'd like an early night.” Maggie looked at Justin with a twinkle in her eye, “and just with lots of lovely sleep and nothing else!”

Justin gave a rueful grin as he poured out their drinks and brought them over to the table in front of the settee. “Not a problem. In fact that was my plan B. A couple of drinks, a large plate of food, a shower followed by bed and the land of nod. Actually, I've got a busy day tomorrow and I won't be back until around six o'clock. So, quite honestly, that suits me fine."

With the microwave humming away in the background and the peas simmering on the hob, they snuggled up together on the settee as they enjoyed their drinks and chattered away as lovers do until the timer sounded to tell them their food was ready. With healthy appetites the shepherd's pie and peas were soon finished and, after Maggie had washed up the plates, the two of them settled down for a nightcap before taking themselves of for a shower and a much needed sleep. Once in bed together, Justin leaned over and with great tenderness kissed Maggie on the forehead, once on each cheek, once on the end of her nose and, finally, gently on her lips. As he looked into her eyes he told her he loved her and she, in return, told him that she loved him as well. It was an untruth which came easily to her as, within the restrictions of her assignment, she truly liked Justin and it was not such a difficult step from there to confess an imaginary love.

The following morning the view from the window was wreathed in a mist typical for October, as Maggie and Justin rose early and prepared themselves for the day ahead. After an early breakfast Justin made his sandwiches as Maggie bustled about getting dressed and putting on her make-up. It was important that Justin believed her cover that she was working as a proof reader and so it was to remain in the flat whilst she worked from her laptop. But she had to hand in the keys to the safe house, and so made an excuse that she had to go into town for some bits and pieces that she needed. Accordingly, she left the flat at eight-thirty before Justin carrying her attaché case, then drove initially into town and along Riverside and up Castle Street and down to the English Bridge. She then took the outside lane which brought her onto the Old Potts Way until she was certain she wasn't being tailed. Finally she drove up Monkmoor Road to the police station where she had arranged to meet with Inspector Fisher in order to hand over the keys ready for the new occupants to pick up who, at that moment, were driving up from London.

Finding Inspector Fischer had left a note saying he had been called away, and as she had the office to herself, she decided it was good time to inform control of her encounter with the Galaxy people carrier and the link between the driver and the previous sighting of him. Her call was answered quickly and she succinctly passed over the details which were acknowledged with a brief *well done* from her team leader before informing her that the surveillance team of four would be in place later that morning and, for security reasons, there would be no contact between them and her. Once the call was concluded, Maggie wrote an explanatory note for the Inspector and placed the house keys on top of it before picking up some car keys and attached paperwork from the Inspector's desk which had been left for her.

Walking downstairs, Maggie exited through a side door and walked the short distance to the car pool where she presented her paperwork to the mechanic who took her over to an unpretentious Ford Fiesta which was now hers to use on those occasions when it was important she couldn't be seen in her own car. Maggie needed to return to the flat to carry out some important tasks, but before doing so it was essential to ascertain whether Justin had not returned for any reason. Whilst they were away over the weekend at Bromyard one of her team's technicians had fitted a tracking device to Justin's van behind the splash panels fitted in one of the front wheel arches, which would accurately locate the vehicle within a 30 mile radius of Shrewsbury. What was interesting was that, before the unit was attached, the technician swept the vehicle for tracking devices and located two fitted, one behind the front and rear number plates but securely hidden inside the moulded bumpers. What the technician also discovered was that the devices fitted were of a highly advanced design and equal to anything his department possessed.

A tracking device sends out a signal which used a certain radio frequency but has a weakness in that it is possible for someone with the right equipment to trace the signal to the receiver. But the trackers fitted to Justin's van had the ability to change frequencies every few seconds and send the information to a receiver which was programmed through the atomic clock to change to the transmitted frequency at exactly the same time. In this way it was impossible for any listening equipment to track the signal for long enough to locate the receiver. It also was an indication of the level of expertise the intelligence agencies were up against and, more worryingly, that another country's intelligence resources were most likely backing the terrorist cell.

As yet unaware of this latest worrying development, Maggie unlocked her case and took from it a small tablet device. Switching it on she waited until a map appeared on the screen and shortly after a moving, flashing cursor which indicated the location of Justin's van. She saw that he was still travelling en route to his first dig at Wynbunbury just over the border in Cheshire but continued to check the screen to make sure he was not deviating from his path. Finally satisfied, she replaced the receiver and drove back to flat where she parked in car park opposite and, carrying her case, made her way through the traffic across the road and up to the flat, fortunately without meeting Mrs. Williams.

Once inside Maggie placed her case on the table and opened it. Firstly she removed a small curiously shaped key and, walking to the clock she had brought with her, removed it from the wall. Putting the clock face down she inserted the key into back and opened a small panel to reveal a powerful lithium-ion battery attached to a sensitive listening device. She pressed a tiny button next to the battery and a red light flashed three times before staying on which told her that the system was live and, because once a lithium-ion battery is completely discharge it is ruined, that the micro-processor was operating which would take power from the clock batteries and recharge the lithium-ion pack when necessary. She locked the back panel and returned the clock to its hook on the wall and walking into the kitchen sang a few lines of a nursery rhyme. Within a few seconds her mobile vibrated and she checked the screen to see just one word – *okay* – which told her that one of her team was listening in and that the bug was operating correctly. To cover her movements and to give the appearance of normality, she switched on Justin's DAB radio and turned it up until the flat was filled with the music and chat from Radio Shropshire.

Next, she returned to her case and removed a small silver coloured device called a hunter which she had used in the safe house to check it was free of bugs. It was a powerful detector which detects radio and micro waves and is used to locate hidden transmitters such as covert listening and camera devices. Knowing that there was a strong likelihood that Justin's flat had been bugged, Maggie switched the device to silent so that its normal electronic voice was changed to an indicator light once a pulse was detected, before slowly and carefully running a sweep over all the rooms. It was not long before she had her first success when she located a signal coming from the ceiling light in the centre of the bedroom. Although there was nothing to be seen outwardly, Maggie was aware that the bulb holder holding the transmitter must have been changed at some stage whilst Justin was out. Moving on to the sitting room she found nothing until she moved over to the desk in which Justin kept his computer and picked up a signal. There she saw that the tower was switched off but the modem had been left on. The unit she was using could be programmed to block a certain frequency, and once Maggie pressed a certain key the steady light went out and, after a short search, the display light remained unlit showing that it was unable to locate another signal.

She continued her sweep of the room until she picked up another signal which led her to the floor lamp next to the settee and the discovery of a second device in the bulb holder. Like the signal from the bedroom, the hunter gave off a flashing light. Maggie was aware that this meant that the listening devices were constantly changing their frequencies and knew with a feeling of frustration that there was nothing her department could do to pin-point the location of the recipients. However, there was one fact of which they could be sure and that was the range over which the listening devices could transmit was about twenty-five miles. This meant that the terrorist cell was located in Shropshire within that circumference or possibly, if it had access to devices which had been developed to transmit over greater distances, increased to thirty miles or so.

A sweep of the kitchen revealed it was clean and Maggie decided to make herself a coffee before starting on her next task. As she waited for the kettle to boil she mused on the sophistication of the devices she had discovered.

Although she thought the expression naff, she had to admit that what had found were state of the art surveillance equipment and not something some half-trained jihadist group would be able to equip themselves with. In the briefing before commencing this assignment, she and her other team members were told that it was suspected that a terrorist plan had been put into operation. Now she knew with certainty that what they were up against was a highly-trained, well organised and extremely dangerous cell with access to the latest technology. She was now also certain that another country had trained, equipped and was backing them.

With this alarming prospect in mind, Maggie pressed on with the last of her tasks by taking a 32 gigabyte memory stick from her case. She was relieved that a bug hadn't been placed in the computer as she would be unable to access it as it was likely the key strokes could have been picked up and the operator at the other end would have wondered why, when they could track Justin's van and knew he was away from his flat, someone else was using the computer. Satisfied that it was safe to continue, she switched on the monitor and the computer tower and waited until it had booted up and the screen showed the systems had loaded. She was relieved to note that Justin had not made access password protected and without further delay inserted the stick into one of the UBS ports on the front of the tower. There was a short delay as the stick passed on its instructions and when the box appeared for a password to be entered, Maggie carefully entered a memorised random sequence of letters, symbols and numbers before hitting the enter button and sitting back to wait for the loaded memory stick to do its work. It was some twenty minutes before the programme was finished and Maggie could remove the stick and, after shutting down the system, took the stick to her laptop which she had previously removed from her attaché case. Knowing that what she had to do next would require a lot of power, she plugged the laptop into the mains and after logging on put the memory stick into the UBS port on the side. Next she took from her case a docking cradle which she joined to her laptop with a cable, then pressed in a memorised sequence of numbers and symbols into her mobile before placing it in the dock. A few seconds later a connection had been made and she clicked on *send* in response to the command box on her laptop screen. Sipping her coffee, Maggie sat back and waited as the entire contents of Justin's computer was passed onto her technical section who, over the next few days, would analyse Justin's e-mails, every file, every keystroke, all deleted items and, of great importance, whether his system had been infiltrated by a trojan horse or spyware.

Eventually, with the transmission complete, Maggie dismantled her equipment and replaced it in the attaché case which she locked. She carefully washed her mug, dried it, and put it away and checked that she had left no clue that she had returned to the flat whilst Justin was out. Content that all was as it should be, she put on her coat and left the flat to drive back to Monkmoor police station where she would make a full report to her team leader in a secure environment. She felt, with justification, that she was achieving what she had been tasked with looked forward to briefing her boss.

As Maggie drove to the police station, Justin had just arrived at Wynbunbury and easily found St. Chad's village church which the burial ground adjoined. Although he had a hard day toil with two doubles to dig some thirty miles apart, he was looking forward to the labour which lay ahead of him. The early mist had, by now, been driven away by a sun which still retained some of the warmth of late autumn and which would soon draw up the dew which glistened like a myriad of tiny diamonds on the grass between the burial plots. Justin felt a sense of contentment.

He had just had a really enjoyable weekend

at the Bromyard folk festival, he was in love with Maggie, she had agreed to move in with him and, knowing that this time it was the real thing, he was filled with excitement about their future together. Even that ghastly John cove, he decided, wasn't going to trouble him and anyway their iffy business arrangement would soon be coming to an end when he could get on with his life. He took a deep breath of satisfaction just as heard his mobile tell him he had a text message. Opening it up he read it with a familiar knot of fear gripping his stomach as he read: *Glad you enjoyed yourself at Bromyard. Congrats on getting Maggie to move in. don't spend any time away from now on until the job's over. John.*

All the happiness, all the satisfaction that had suffused his being was driven from him in a wave of desolation as he was brought back sharply to earth and a painful awareness the dangerous situation into which he had got himself. Justin groaned inwardly as he wondered how he would ever rid himself of this bastard. He feared that John had such a strong hold over him he might never let go, and he would be in thrall to him for ever. Justin didn't think things could get any worse but he was mistaken as not only was his life going to spiral out of control but there would be tragic consequences that neither he, not anyone else, could have possibly envisaged.

CHAPTER 7

Bahadur Najafi, or John as he preferred to be known, smiled as he sent the text to Justin. He liked to keep him on his toes and, more importantly, frightened. He felt thirsty and took out a bottle of pomegranate juice from the fridge in the kitchen of the remote farmhouse which was his refuge from discovery and one which, after his meetings with Justin he never left, using his highly trained team to be his eyes and ears as he suspected that the British intelligence services might possibly have him in their sights. They were all infidels and he spat on them, but he was also aware that they were not to be underestimated as his superiors in MOIS had repeatedly stressed. John knew that one's guard must never slip for a moment, one must never let sloppy practices take hold and always remembered the lesson on the German Enigma coding machine.

He had been taught that in WW2 the German's were confident that their code was impossible to break, and so it proved until the scientists at Bletchley Park realised that some operators were being lazy and not changing to a designated code because they couldn't be bothered. Many operators commenced their transmissions with *Heil Hitler* and another with an invariable *No change here. Everything is fine.* It was these tiny, seemingly insignificant errors which enable the British, along with their ground breaking computer technology, to break all German Enigma transmissions and in so doing, assist greatly in the defeat of Hitler's war machine.

John determined he was never going to make any mistakes like that and he was impressed that his team all demonstrated a high degree of professionalism and carried out their duties without fault. He was also pleased that he had not needed to kill any who compromised the operation, not because he had a conscience about doing so, but that he would have to find a replacement with all training and security that would involve, plus having the problem of disposing of a body.

He sipped slowly the pomegranate juice he had poured. As he sipped it he remembered with disgust how the kuffirs would consume alcohol until they were driven from their senses with men and women in obscene undress vomiting and fighting in the pubs and on the pavements of their decadent cities. John would never drink alcohol, not just because his religion forbade it, but because he refused to dull his senses in any way and so be at a disadvantage in the work he was carrying out. He had seen in the actions of others how just one lapse could lead to failure, discovery and possibly death and he was determined that such a fate would never befall him. As he sipped his drink he recalled the path which had brought him to this remote spot in Shropshire.

After his meeting with the Colonel in 2001 when his career path with MOIS had been mapped out for him an unexpected turn of events occurred when John received his papers for compulsory conscription into the army. He knew that all males in Iran over the age of eighteen were liable for call-up but had assumed that his recruitment into MOIS would over-ride this requirement. But in this he was wrong. It had been decided that he would benefit from military training as it would be to his advantage in the future mission which was planned for him, with this decision coming to him in a communication from the Colonel's office in the following day's post. Although this was a disappointment for John, he didn't let it show as he told his father of this unexpected development and promised him that he would fulfil his new duties to the best of his abilities and patiently wait until he could resume his career path.

His call-up papers informed John that he was to report in one month's time to the Do Ab Training Camp in Tehran for his initial two months' basic training before being posted to another unit, yet to be disclosed, where he would complete the remainder of his twenty-one months' call-up. John hope that his service would be only twenty-one months but had been warned by his father that it was very easy for days to be added to the length of service for the most minor of misdemeanours, such as three days added if a soldier was one day late back from leave, or a day added for a minor infringement of the rules and even having days added if your superior officers decided he didn't like you. Despite hearing these horror stories, John resolved to give his military service the hundred per cent effort that he threw into everything he did and to show himself to be a dedicated and obedient recruit – one who was going to stand out above all his comrades.

All too soon the day arrived when he had to report to the guard room at the Do Ab Camp for this first day's training. He had asked his father whether he should have his hair cut short in preparation but had been warned that it wouldn't matter how short he had it cut, all recruits would go to the camp barber who would make sure he cut off as much hair as possible. So unless he wanted to look as though he had been scalped, his father advised it would be as well to let the barber have his way. So with a full head of hair and carrying his small case of personal effects, John was driven by his Father to the barrack gates and after a warm farewell the two parted with John taking a solitary walk to the gates where he showed his call-up papers to the sentry on duty and was directed to the hatch under the veranda at the guardhouse and report in. When he knocked on the hatch it was opened by a sour-faced NCO who wore a single inverted chevron on his sleeves, which John was to learn denoted the rank of Sergeant. He brusquely took the proffered papers and barked out an order to one of the guard to take this miserable specimen up to build-up. As the two of them marched up the main drive the private who had been detailed was open and friendly and explained to a puzzled John that build-up referred to the barrack block where the recruit intake platoon of some forty men was assembled over the course of a week. As he chatted away he told him they would all have it easy until the last recruit had reported in when, the following day, their training would start in earnest and life would be horrible for the next two months. John thanked him politely for this forewarning and tried to prepare himself mentally for the ordeal which lay ahead.

And so it turned out to be. The day following the arrival of the last recruit they were rudely awaken at dawn with their NCOs shouting and tipping any sleepy recruits out of their beds and on to the floor and told to put on their civilian clothing. With shouts and shoving the bleary recruits were formed up into a squad then taken for a run of five miles The pace set by the physical training sergeant was gruelling and it was a satisfied John who completed the run without any difficulty whilst many of his fellow recruits were lagging well behind, and with some of them collapsed and having to be helped back. With more shouting and manhandling the breathless men were eventually formed into the semblance of a squad and marched over to another building some distance away which turned out to be the clothing stores. There they started at one end of a long counter behind which stood some twelve soldiers and as they came to each soldier an item of clothing or equipment was slapped down on the counter with a shouted description of what it was.

John, being a controlled and self-contained person, wondered why it was necessary to shout so much but decided that he wasn't going to worry about it and would just accept it as part of the process in which he found himself. After completing his passage down the counter past the last of the bellowing quartermaster staff he found his arms full with a heap of clothing and equipment so great that he had difficulty in carrying it without dropping any of the items. Others were not so capable and the dropping of any of the items resulted in another blast of shouting from the NCOs usually delivered close to the terrified recruits face and often including a fine spray of spittle. Formed up again into a squad, the heavily burdened recruits shambled back to their barrack block where, with great relief, they were able to dump their kit onto their beds and ease the strain on their muscles. Their equipment issue had included a mug, knife, fork and spoon and, without a break, they were told to pick up these utensils, hold them in their left hands and place the hand behind their backs before being formed up once again into a squad and taken at the double across to the cook house where they were given something to eat with the added luxury of being able to sit down.

The recruits had barely time to finish their food when the shouting re-commenced and they were ordered outside and form up before being taken at the double back to the barrack block where they were instructed in the care and maintenance of their clothing and equipment. Anyone who has served in any of the armed forces, in any country, will know what these recruits had to undergo in their training. The making their bedding into a bed block every morning, the polishing, the ironing, the bulling of boots, the cleaning of their barrack room and latrines, the late nights followed by a dawn stand-to and the inability to never get enough sleep, is the lot of all military recruits the world over, and the training that John and his fellow trainees were subjected to was no different from the rigours that all recruits would all be subjected to. The next part of their ordeal involved being marched over to the camp barber where John was grateful for his father's advice when he saw that the hair cuts they were given left only a short covering of hair through which the scalp could be easily discerned. Next came the medical where they were prodded, probed, measured and given a cocktail of injections for which they were given the following day off to recover from their effects which included stiff and swollen arms and a slight fever, which fortunately most had gone by the following morning when the instructors resumed their training.

Slowly but surely this disparate collection of recruits started to take on the trapping of a disciplined and unified body. Their drill and marching improved to the point where they moved as one. They were trained in the stripping, reassembly and cleaning of their rifles before being taken to the firing range where eventually they became proficient and accurate as riflemen. By the time a month had passed, the platoon, once a grouping of undisciplined youngsters from all walks of life, had been moulded into an efficient body trained in a range of military disciplines, where each individual was able to think of himself as a soldier. There was also a change in the behaviour of their instructors who by now, having seen their charges develop into the a unified and well trained unit, began to ease back on the bullying and hectoring which was a feature of the early days of training. Now, in the last month of their basic course, the aim was to build up the recruits rather than break them down which had been a necessary part of becoming an effective soldier. John found that he was beginning to like his training and, having been something of a loner in the past, discovered the satisfaction of comradeship which is engendered when people are thrown together in difficult circumstances. But John was not by nature a team player. He liked to be part of his platoon and helping and being helped by the other members and he felt satisfaction at being as one with them, but he realised that deep down it was not how he really was or, indeed, wanted to be. He was a person who like to be operating independently and making all the decisions without having to refer to a higher authority for permission to carry them out. It was this part of his make-up which had been identified by MOIS and confirmed by when John was interviewed the Colonel some months previously and identified by him as someone with the ability to make his own decisions, who had the potential to be part of a plan being developed at the highest levels of government. John knew it was in his interests to keep his head down, obey all orders to the letter and wait until his time had come to achieve his goal. With quiet determination and his usual iron self-discipline, John completed the remainder of his two months' training, passing out at the top of his intake with his service record marking him up as having the potential for promotion.

Following the final day at their training camp, the recruits were all given a week's leave and issued with their meagre pay up to date. They were also given the details of their posting and John was told he was to report to the 3rd Army Headquarters at Shiraz in seven days time using the airline ticket and his transit instructions which he had been given by his platoon sergeant. After the passing out parade which was attended by family and relatives of the recruits, John searched for his parents and found them by a refreshment tent which had been erected at the edge of the parade ground. He embraced them fondly as they told him how proud they were of him and did what all parents do so well by embarrassing John by telling him how smart he was and how well he marched, which he realised had been overheard by his fellow platoon members when he noted their wide grins as they looked over at him. Soon, with the refreshments over along with the farewells amongst the soldiers, John was driven back to their house with the resolve that he would do absolutely nothing but relax until he had to report to Shiraz.

The historical city of Shiraz lies about 40 miles from the ancient city of Persepolis built by an ancient people know as the Darius and named after their king, Darius the Great, who ruled over a mighty empire which existed from 550BC to 486 BC. It lies at an altitude which offers a perfect climate for vineyards and grapes. It was believed that the grape of that name originated there before being taken as cuttings a millennia before to Western and Central Europe. Unfortunately, the legend proved to be false as laboratory DNA testing carried out in 1999 showed that the Shiraz/ Syrah wine as it is known today, is a product of two French native grapes and not of Persian ancestry.

According to an Iranian myth, wine was discovered by mistake by the daughter of a king who, for some unknown reason, had rejected her. So distressed was she by the cruelty of her father, she determined to commit suicide by poisoning herself with the remaining liquid residue of rotten grapes. The grapes must had fermented and this potent brew made her pass out, only to awaken the next day and report her finding on the intoxicating quality of the grape juice to the king, who rewarded her for this miraculous discovery.

Nevertheless, the mother of all hangovers, which the princess suffered after her failed suicide attempt, had not been in vain as the Shiraz became a wine-producing area for thousands of years. Before the Islamic revolution in 1979, there were up to 300 wineries in Iran. Now there are believed to be thousands, but they are illegal and understandably kept securely underground. As a whole, Iran is not a wine producing country as the Koran forbids the taking of intoxicating liquors. The once world famous vineyards ostensibly harvest their crops solely for the table but rumour has it that villagers that live around Shiraz press the grapes in secret which are then fermented and drunk in defiance of the religious ban on alcoholic consumption.

The town of Shiraz lies some 500 miles

south of Tehran as the crow flies and is served by regular passenger services from Tehran international Airport. On the day of his departure, John's father and mother drove him to the drop-off point at the airport and, after a brief farewell, he carried his kit packed into a regulation holdall over to the book-in desk for flight to Shiraz where he presented his ticket to the clerk along with his bag for weighing. With the formalities over, and after being informed that his flight would be landing at Ahvāz before taking him onwards to his destination, John made his way to the departure lounge to relax until the tannoy called him and his fellow passengers to the boarding gate for their flight.

Soon the gong chimes from the loudspeakers preceded the announcement that the flight to Ahvāz and Shiraz was departing shortly and, after showing his boarding pass to an attendant, and a short walk across the tarmac, John mounted the steps to his aircraft. He located his seat half way down the aisle which proved to be next to the window as he had hoped. Within fifteen minutes all the passengers were seated and, with their lap belts fastened, the aircraft taxied slowly to the take off point at the end of the runway and, without stopping, was cleared to take off immediately. It climbed steeply to its cruising altitude where the aircraft levelled off and with his fellow passengers visibly relaxed, John settled down to try and enjoy the experience of being flown before the pilot began the descent into Ahvāz International Airport where he made a smooth touch-down before taxiing his craft over to the terminal building for an exchange of passengers.

With surprising efficiency the exchange of passengers along with their baggage was completed in just over thirty minutes before the pilot placed his aeroplane at the end of the runway and awaited clearance from the tower. This time there was a delay of several minutes whilst an incoming freighter had taxied off the runway before the controller informed the pilot he was cleared for take off. This leg of John's journey was some two hundred miles and it was only forty-five minutes later when he touched down at Shiraz International Airport at the completion of his journey. After disembarking he went over to the luggage carousel to reclaim his holdall before locating the military reception desk which he had to report to according to his travel instructions. It was compulsory for serving soldiers to wear uniform at all times when on duty, whether in barracks or not, and as John approached the desk wearing on his uniform sleeves the single horizontal bar of an Artesh private, he noted the four horizontal bars on the sleeve of the NCO in front of him which denoted his rank as corporal. Not wanting to get off to a shaky start, John snapped to attention and informed the corporal who he was and that he was reporting for duty as instructed as the 3rd Army HQ at Shiraz.

The corporal viewed this demonstration of military keenness with an amused look as he informed Private Najafi with a smile that he wasn't in basic training now and so he could take the ramrod out of his spine and find himself a seat on the army bus parked outside but, he was informed, they would have a wait until another flight had landed with some others also to be taken to the barracks. There then followed a hot and sticky wait of an hour in a bus without air conditioning which ended when the final passengers boarded and the corporal, who had greeted John in the airport concourse, climbed aboard, checked everyone was present from a list he carried, took his place behind the wheel and set off on the short journey Shiraz.

The corporal turned out to be a person who possessed an unshakable belief in the providence and fate, and the understanding he had with his Maker manifested itself in his driving style. This involved using both sides of the road, excessive speed and an almost continuous use of the horn as he scattered other vehicles, pedestrians and livestock on the mercifully short journey to their final destination which John sincerely hoped would be the 3rd Army HQ and not a hospital. The soldiers on the bus had started the journey in high spirits, indulging in the exchanges that soldiers all over the world are so good at, but shortly after setting off had lapsed into silence as they gripped the seat in front of them to counter the violent movements of the vehicle. Even John, a controlled and calm individual, found himself wanting the journey to finish and he wondered how on earth the corporal could have passed even the relaxed expectations of the Iranian driving test – in fact, knowing how easy it is to get what you want by slipping a wad of cash into an expectant hand in his country, he wondered if he had ever passed one at all.

It was with great relief when, with a screech of brakes, the corporal brought the bus to a standstill in a cloud of dust in front of the imposing entrance gates to the HQ which was their final destination. Somewhat weak at the knees, John and his fellow soldiers were formed into a squad and marched awkwardly, carrying their baggage, to a building a short distance away where they taken inside into a lecture room and told to sit down and wait until they were detailed to report to their place of work. A few minuted later they all stood to attention as a tall officer entered the room. John noted he wore the four stars on his epaulettes of a captain. He introduced himself as the Adjutant and proceeded to read out from a list to which department each of them was to be sent. The last name called was John's and the captain told him to stay where he was as the others were taken outside by the corporal and marched off to their living quarters in their accommodation block. Once the door had closed behind them he walked over to John and sat on the chair next to him, waving him down when he started to stand up.

"Private Najafi" he explained to John, "it is necessary for me to talk with you alone as I am acting on the instructions which have been sent to our Commanding Officer from the Colonel at MOIS headquarters. He informs us that he has interviewed you and that you have been singled you out for special training and development. That is why you have been posted here to Military Intelligence." He looked keenly at John, before continuing.

"Your path has been mapped out for you. You will initially be attached to the Codes and Cyphers Section and you will, no doubt, be pleased to know that your are to be promoted to Private E2 immediately on arrival there.

You are to spend six months in that department, and once your training has been completed satisfactorily, you will be moved to the Counter Intelligence Section where you will spend the remainder of your national service. That move carries with it a promotion to private 1st class."

John was not completely surprised by the turn of events as he had anticipated that MOIS might direct his call-up to his and their advantages, he was much gratified that he had been singled out for specialist treatment and training and felt that he should express his gratitude. "May I thank you, Captain, Sir. I am deeply honoured by the kindness shown to me and I shall endeavour to repay it by the excellence of my dedication to the tasks before me."

"It's not me you should thank," replied the Captain with a slight shake of his head, "like you I obey instructions and have no discretion in this matter. Nevertheless, let me welcome you and assure you that, knowing your past record, I have no doubt that you will discharge your duties with great diligence. Now, you will report directly to the Cypher section, which is in the main building directly opposite, where you will be shown your sleeping quarters which are separate from the others for reasons of security. Have you any questions you wish to ask me?"

Not having any, John snapped to attention and saluted before marching over to the entrance to the HQ building where he was directed to his new place of work. Once there he was met by a sergeant with a cheerful demeanour who briefed him on his duties and passed John the bar of the E2 private and told him to get it sewn on. The sergeant detailed a private to take John to his room and told him that he could have the rest of the day off to get himself settled in and to report to him the following morning at eight o'clock when he would give him an induction session and introduce him to his fellow operators. John thought he was going to like it here and was pleased to have it confirmed by the friendly private who showed him to his quarters whilst telling him all about the NCOs and officers he would have to work under. John was surprised to be shown into a single room as he expected that he would be sharing with at least three others but, as his friendly guide explained, everyone in the Cypher Section was afforded special privileges owing to the top secret work they had to undertake and in recognition of the pressures they had to work under. John's companion stayed with him as he stowed his kit before taking him over to the mess hall where they joined a table at which sat some of his fellow operatives. After introductions, they shared a pleasant half hour before his friendly private left him to return to work, telling him to enjoy the rest of his day.

The following day John reported for work and as promised his section sergeant gave him a general talk on the work of the department and what he could expect in the way of training. After induction, he was taken to a room where with six others he was taken through the basics of Morse Code and told that he had to achieve a minimum level of reception and transmission before they could move on. Over the next two weeks John had no difficulty in mastering the techniques necessary to become a qualified Morse operator and was soon able to be taken on to further training in coding and cypher work. He found the training rewarding and the company of his fellow soldiers congenial. He was also pleased that although military discipline was maintained, it was not rigidly enforced with a consequent relaxed atmosphere in the workplace.

And so the months' passed until John was told that now he had completed his course to a high standard he was to be promoted, as he had been told previously, to Private 1st Class and moved into the Counter Intelligence section where was he continued with his training until he was allocated to one of the teams as a fully-fledged working operative. He found the work fulfilling and soon came to the notice of his superiors as someone who possessed exceptional powers of observation and deduction and was someone who, although invariably respectful, was not afraid to pass on his thoughts to his superiors who were often amazed at his perspicacity, grasp of difficult matters and the discovery of intelligence which had been overlooked. This could have led to resentment on the part of others, but they were all aware that John was a protégée of a MOIS Colonel and, as in Iran it was considered prudent not to challenge such people for fear of the consequences, John was able to complete the remainder of his time at Military Intelligence without any repercussions.

As he flew back to Tehran after being de-mobilised, he was grateful for the training he had been given and knew with a quiet satisfaction that it would stand him in good stead when he commenced his first year at in the intelligence faculty of the Iman Mohammad Bagher university. As John had the luxury of some months before he was to enrol for the autumn term, he spent his time bringing himself back to a high level of physical fitness and to this end spent many hours at his local gymnasium. Although not a person to form close friendships, he nevertheless did have several contemporaries whom he trusted and would meet on occasions to drink tea at one of the many cafés which lined the streets in central Tehran and talk across a wide range of subjects.

Eventually enrolment day arrived and after signing himself in as an under-graduate he, along with the rest of the student intake, were given a welcoming speech by the faculty's principal after which John started on the first day of his three year course. The Iman Mohammad Bagher university is known as a conservative centre that trains political officials of Iran's Islamic state. It is essential that all students who are accepted for a placement in one of its eight colleges have strong loyalty to the Islamic revolution and the ideals of Ayatollah Khomeini, and also have satisfactorily passed through a rigorous staging process including the ideological admissions, known as Gozinesh, and evaluation of personality, scientific and personal abilities - particularly political aptitude.

The Intelligence faculty at the university was located in the western side of the campus and separated from the other seven colleges for reasons of security. Even the name gave little indication of its true purpose as a sign above the main entrance to the block stated simply *Faculty of Communications,* though an outsider would have been surprised at the level of surveillance once they had entered the large entrance hall under the blank gaze of cameras and being channelled to a desk with two security guards before being patted down and their credentials checked before being either thrown out or allowed to continue. As an accredited student, John had easy access whenever he showed his MOIS security pass to the guards who, in time, knew he was no risk and waved him through.

John was sure that he was going to enjoy his time at university and in this he was not disappointed as he threw himself into his studies and practical sessions with the quiet and single-minded determination that characterised his approach to life. He had been issued with the syllabus for the next three years which broke down the academic years into various modules and looked forward with eager anticipation to disciplines such as intelligence gathering; cypher construction and breaking; interrogation techniques; counter intelligence; political destabilisation; control and fomenting civil unrest and many more disciplines which he would need to master if he was to fulfil his potential as a MOIS operative.

John threw himself into his work and as was expected he excelled at everything he was taught. His studies continued until, near the end of the first term, he was told to report to the office of the Head of the faculty. There he was found, not the Head, but only an overweight, perspiring middle-aged man wearing western dress who greeted him by name and who didn't introduced himself but simply said the he had been charged by Colonel Mahmoud Taqi-Pessain of MOIS to speak with John to inform him of what had been planned for him. He waved John to a seat and seated himself in a chair opposite.

"Bahadur Najafi," the stout man explained, "as I believe you are aware, you have been singled out for a special assignment which is planned for some years in the future, and one for which you are receiving specific and specialist training in order that you are fitted to carry out your part of the plan. To this end it was necessary that you spent time in England and it had been decided that you will visit the UK on a student visa for a month between every term for the duration of his time at university." The stout man paused as he mopped the sweat from his brow with a crumpled handkerchief which he took from his jacket pocket. He looked at John with eyes that blinked rapidly as he waited for him to speak.

"Thank you for coming to see me, Sir," John replied, "you are indeed correct in saying that I am aware that a great future has been mapped out for me. For this I am deeply grateful and you have my assurances that I will will never let you down of jeopardise the workings of MOIS by my actions."

The stout man relaxed and gave a small smile. "Yes, Badahur, there is no need to remind me of your loyalty. Had we not been sure, I would not have been speaking with you today. The reason for these visits is that you must be fully conversant with the British way of life. We know that your spoken English is excellent but it is essential that you understand, and can use, idiomatic spoken English so that you are able to pass yourself off as British born. You must master slang, codes of conduct, behaviour, dress and you must join in with people of your own age and copy their life styles."

"I understand, Sir," said John, "and I am prepared to do whatever is necessary to achieve this goal."

"Excellent, Badahur, I expected nothing less. I am also aware that it will be difficult for you to adopt the decadent ways of the western world which encourages obscene, drunken and promiscuous behaviour as being normal. You will have to apply a rigid discipline in order to tolerate such evil and school yourself to act normally when you witness such depravity. But let the teachings of the true Prophet be your bulwark against such evil, and the knowledge that the days of the Great Satan are numbered as it will eventually be crushed and the unbelievers converted to Islam or face death as kuffirs when they are subjected to the lash of Sharia Law."

The fat man had become excited as he expounded his vision for the Islamic domination of the world and its peoples. He took a deep breath as he collected himself, again mopping the sweat from his brow before continuing more calmly. "Now let me give you what you need for your first visit."

So saying, the stout man opened a brief case he had placed by the side of his chair and removed a clear plastic wallet. Over the next half hour he went through the contents and explained in detail each document and how it must be used. The last document which he produced was purple Iranian passport with the legend *Islamic Republic of Iran* emblazoned in gold lettering on its outer cover. John was surprised when he saw it as he had never made any application for one and wondered how his current photograph had been obtained. Possibly, he thought, from the one held at the Interior Ministry which held one for his National Identity Card and which had to be updated annually until citizens reach twenty-five years of age. Or it could be it had been obtained from the photograph taken for his military identity card. Whatever the case John, impressed at

MOIS's efficiency in making a passport application on his behalf, listened carefully to his briefing and memorised all the instructions which the stout man relayed to him over the course of their meeting. Finally, with his business concluded, the stout man shook hands with John and, wishing him well with his mission, ushered him to the door. As John politely bade the mystery man goodbye, he wondered why the fat man had not introduced himself and although, he was not to know it, he would never see him again or discovered who he was or what department he worked for, he accepted that in the organisation he was involved with it was prudent not to ask too many questions and he reasoned that if he had needed to know he would have been told.

For John, the three years that he spent at university passed quickly – as time does when one is enjoying oneself – and, as expected he excelled at all modules, becoming also an accomplished track and field athlete, who soon gained a name for himself amongst the sporting fraternity. He still maintained his prowess as a wrestler but now found that he came across other wrestlers who would give him some serious competition and, in a few instances, prove to be the better contestant. As someone used to winning John, although finding the experience distasteful, would always face his defeat with quiet dignity and politely congratulate his opponent on the victory he so richly deserves. But a part of him would burn with an inner resolve that he would never allow anyone to be in a position to inflict a defeat upon him again. He pragmatically came to the conclusion that as there would always be times when people or events would conspire to thwart his plans, he must never place himself in a position where they would be able to prevail and to achieve this, he resolved, he would either be cleverer than his enemies or eliminate them. After his latest defeat at wrestling he determined that never again would he be the loser and that all his considerable intellect and experience would be used to to manipulate events so that he could emerge the victor.

With this resolve deeply etched into his psyche John completed his time at university with a First Class pass and with quiet satisfaction was able to put MSc after his name. Pleased though he was, he was not a person to wallow in glory as he saw the completion of his studies not as an end in itself, but as a means to an end, which was to be entirely fitted to take on the role which had been planned for him in the future. He had, by the completion of his course, been to the UK some seven times and now was able to speak English without a trace of his Iranian accent and with a complete mastery of idiom and slang. He fully understood the way of life and the attitudes of the people he had been forced to mingle with and, although he found their easy morality, their drunken behaviour and their lack of manners and basic courtesy repugnant, he had to admit that the British were friendly and appeared happy with their lot. Politically, John found incomprehensible their acceptance of democracy and was unable to understand how the section of the electorate who voted for a party which lost the election could meekly accept the result and wait patiently for up to five years until they could vote again and, astoundingly, accept the result if it again went against them. He only understood the rule of the strong man. In Iran someone, usually a religious leader, would prove stronger, more able to gather around him the support of the clergy and the military and then declare that he was the leader and all Iranian citizens would do as they were told. Should anyone step out of line by criticising the leader, then they could expect to be taken away and, if they were lucky after their session of brutal and agonising interrogation, spend a long time incarcerated in the notorious prison known euphemistically as the Evin University.

But this Elvin University is no place of

higher learning. It is one of the world's most brutal and infamous prisons. Standing at the foot of the Alborz Mountains in north-western Tehran, it is home to an estimated 15,000 inmates, including killers, thieves and rapists. But the prison has also held ayatollahs, journalists, intellectuals and dissidents over the years, and few if any who have survived time in Evin could be surprised by claims of torture and abuse made by those unlucky enough to have been sent there, usually on trumped up charges or simply remanded there without any charges having been levelled against them. Those political prisoners who were considered to be especially dangerous to the State would be despatched shortly after arrival, a procedure which John had no problem accepting as a necessity if order was to be maintained.

But in England no such regime existed. As John spent his time with the young people he was associated with, and travelled round the UK in the hire car which had been arranged for him to pick up at Heathrow on each occasion he visited, he developed a deep loathing for the decadence of the Western way of life and, although he was disciplined enough to never let his true feelings show, resolved that it was his duty to bring to the infidels the teachings of the only true Prophet, the truths of the Holy

Koran and the essential strictures of Sharia Law. For those who failed to convert to Islam, there could be only one recourse, and John resolved they must be wiped from the face of the earth until only an Islamic world civilisation existed and the true word of the Prophet prevailed universally.

With this objective now implacable fixed within him, and with his graduation only a week behind him, John was not surprised to receive a letter offering him a position within MOIS and informing him that he was expected the following Monday at eight thirty in the morning when he would report to the personnel department. He was also requested to confirm by telephone that he would be attending which John did immediately after telling his mother the good news. He did consider phoning his father to tell him of his new job, but decided that he would already know owing to his senior position in the organisation, so decided to wait until he returned home at the end of his working day when they would celebrate his good fortune.

In the intervening days he spent long hours with his father discussing all aspects of what he could expect when he commenced his duties and by the time Monday morning came he felt he was already a competent member of the organisation. So it was with eager anticipation that John set off that morning with his father driving their trusty four door Paykan saloon - affectionately known by the Iranians as The Chariot. Although his father's car was eight years old, and based on an old Roots design similar to the Avenger, it had proved to be remarkably reliable once the Iranian manufacturer had improved the cooling system to manage the heat of summer and refined the air filter to cope with the dust which pervaded everything outside of the cities and towns. After their journey to the MOIS HQ building, with his father showing his pass and John's letter of acceptance at the barrier, they drove to the first free parking space and John was taken up to the personnel office where he said goodbye to his father. He knocked on the door, waited until he was told to enter, and walked in to introduce himself to an elderly man who sat behind a desk placed to the right as he entered.

After carefully checking a list in the folder in front of him, the elderly man introduced himself as the personnel officer, shook John's hand and cordially welcomed him into the family of MOIS. He explained that security was of paramount importance and he would first need to take his photograph in order to prepare a security pass which he must wear at all times when at work in the building. He would also, he was informed, be issued with a warrant which would give him as a MOIS officer the powers of arrest, detention and forced entry when necessary, but this would take several days as all warrants had to pass before Colonel Mahmoud Taqi-Pessain for his personal approval and signature.

John was then passed over to a young man who took him into an adjoining room and placed him in front of a white screen. He gave John a board with his number on it to hold under his chin, proceeded to take photographs of his left and right profile and two full face. Telling him to wait he transferred the photographs onto a computer and, after typing in John's details, printed off an identity card which he sealed in a clear plastic wallet which had a chain attached and placed it over his head, after reminding him to wear it at all times in the building. He was then returned to the Personnel Officer who gave him a contract of employment which he had to sign before leaving the office, but, he was told, he could sit at a desk for as long as he wanted until he was sure of its contents and felt reassured that they were acceptable to him. It took John only ten minutes to scan through the details and, after signing his name at the bottom of both copies, took them back to the Personnel Officer who, after solemnly stamping and signing the contract and giving John his copy, shook hands again and instructed the young man to take John to his place of work at the Office for Security Investigations on the third floor. The young man, whose name was Heydar, chatted away easily as he gave John details of the organisation which he now worked for and proudly told him that MOIS had 30,000 operatives and was the largest intelligence organisation in the world. After climbing several flights of stairs, they arrived at the John's department where Heydar introduced him to the Section Head who asked him to be seated and then spent the next hour asking all about John's past before explaining the work of the department. Once these initial procedures were over, he was taken into a large office where he was told who he would be working with and then left with a fellow officer who began the long process of easing John into the duties he would be expected to carry out.

The work was all John expected and he found it both challenging and rewarding. His father had told him that he expected he would be moved between departments and so deal with the many aspects of intelligence work as and when his superiors felt that he had thoroughly mastered the essential details of that particular discipline. The time passed quickly, as it does when one enjoys one's work, and over the period of five years John found himself moved from Security Investigations to the Office of Spying Technology. From there he went to Counter Intelligence Directorate where he was thrilled to be part of a new intelligence force called Oghab 2 which had been set up after the USA had managed to disrupt the Iranian nuclear programme after MOIS had been infiltrated by Western-friendly Kurds, and the assassination of several of the country's nuclear scientists by Israeli Mossad operatives. A year later was transferred to Signal and Cyber Intelligence where he found that his time served at Military Intelligence was of great assistance to him in mastering his new duties, and this was followed by six months in the Office for Media Control.

The next part of his training brought into stark relief the dark side of MOIS when he began his training in interrogation techniques. At first he was an onlooker as each prisoner was put through the standard methods which were used by MOIS to extract information. Without exception the hapless victim was first told to strip naked before being given a severe beating using fists or batons by the muscle men, most of whom, John noted, plainly appeared to obtain gratification from the pain they caused, and would often joke and mock the victim as he or she pleaded for them to stop. He observed that the beatings were administered in such away that the victim's senses were not disturbed and no blows to the head were given at that stage as just the body and limbs were severely beaten, before the victim was left for half an hour until all numbness had gone and the full pain of the injuries asserted themselves.

The bloodied and agonised prisoner would then be strapped into a solid wooded chair and the interrogation would commence with the torturers standing close by. John saw that some prisoners talked freely but even though they answered every question fully they were still subjected to slaps and punches until the interrogator was satisfied he had extracted all the answers he wanted. There were those who strongly resisted, and for these the methods became more sadistic and fiendishly agonising the longer they held out. But however courageous the prisoners they almost always cracked in the end as their resistance to pain was slowly and brutally reduced to the point when they finally screamed out the answers to the interrogator's questions. John was aware that he himself was under observation in order to see whether he had the stomach to handle this unpleasant side of intelligence work. His instructors were pleased to see that he appeared unmoved by what he was made to witness and John himself was able to completely detach himself from the suffering he saw before him. He saw the process of torture as a necessary part of keeping law and order and, as he frequently witnessed, the death of the prisoner not so much as a merciful release from the appalling torment carried out, but more as a necessary consequence of ensuring state security.

There were also arbitrary executions carried out in another part of the interrogation complex in the basement of the building and which resulted in an anonymous van being driven to a commercial smelting furnace which dealt with the unwanted corpses. As expected, John learned the tools of his trade thoroughly and was noted as being able to cleverly apply a combination of pain and clever psychological pressure which obtained results far more quickly than the sheer sadistic brutality used by his fellow interrogators. Whilst this part of his work gave him no pleasure, he knew that it had to be done and, if so, then it had best be done well and to the best of his ability.

Then something completely unexpected occurred. Towards the end of his fifth year with MOIS he took a call from the office of Colonel Taqi-Pessain. The colonel's secretary informed him that the following day he would be picked up after work from the reception area and taken to a secret destination for further training. He was told to pack a suitcase sufficient for a week and to tell no one of this telephone call, except his parents who must be assured that he was going away for a week on a training course. With those instructions the call was terminated, leaving John with a feeling of intrigue at this sudden turn of events.

Accordingly, the next day as arranged, a driver reported to reception shortly after five o'clock and led John to a black Mercedes pool car. With John settled comfortably in the passenger seat, he drove north out of Tehran until, some forty minutes later, they came to a small airfield situated down a dirt track and hidden from the main road by a low line of hills. Waiting on a concrete landing spot was a helicopter in desert camouflage with the pilot standing outside smoking a cigar. John's training had included aircraft recognition and he saw the craft to be an Augusta-Bell but was unable to see whether it was the 212 or the 206 as he was quickly taken into the passenger compartment along with his suitcase and the door slammed shut. He noted that as all the windows were blacked out and that there was no forward vision through the bulkhead, it was obvious that he was not going to be allowed to see where he was being taken. Whilst he waited a small hatch slid open in the bulkhead, and the pilot's face grinned through as he apologised for the secrecy but assured him it was necessary as he was taking him to a top secret research establishment. The flight, he added, will take approximately one hour. The hatch was slid shut and John heard the turbine whine as it came up to full power and, with a lurch, the pilot tilted the craft onto the dust filled air cushion and accelerated forward then upwards as he climbed to his cruising height. At the same time the pilot put the aircraft in several banking turns which John assumed were to ensure that he would be unable to work out in which direction they were ultimately headed.

Some fifty-five minutes later John felt the helicopter made a steep descent and with a slight bump landed at what he imagined would be his destination. The passenger door was opened to reveal two soldiers dressed in the black uniform of the IRG – the Iranian Revolutionary Guard – which John knew to be elite fighting and guard force formed after the Islamic Revolution. The first soldier told John to pick up his case and come with them, and no sooner had he stepped down onto the ground, the cabin door was slammed shut and the helicopter took off in a cloud of choking dust, rapidly disappeared into the twilight with its navigation lights switched off.

As the dust settled, John saw through the gloom that he was being taken towards a steep cliff face and when they came close it became clear that a false wall had been constructed to match the surrounding rock which was concealing an entrance door behind it. One of the Guard swiped the security lock and, after waiting for a green light to show, pushed the door open and led John into an underground world. Taken down a short corridor past two more IRG privates, they were faced with a commercially sized elevator which they entered and descended for some ten seconds. When they came to a stop he was taken from the lift and escorted along a well-lit corridor where he was eventually shown into an office whose glass back wall gave onto a view of a well-equipped laboratory and, behind whose desk, sat a chubby man, in his fifties with a round kindly face, a full beard and heavy dark-framed glasses with thick lenses and wearing a white laboratory coat.

It was clear to John that he was being given access to one of the top secret research establishments which were secreted in some of the most remote parts of the country, and this was confirmed when the man behind the desk greeted him and introduced himself as the Director of the establishment and apologised that he was unable to give John his name for reasons of security. However, he explained that he had been instructed to give him complete freedom to access any part of the complex and, in the four or so days he would be with them, to answer any questions he put to them and, most importantly, reveal to him the exact reason why he had been sent.

After this short and cheery introduction, the Director told John that the tour of the facilities would start the following morning and that now he would be shown to his quarters where he would find some food for his evening meal. With a twinkle in his eye, the Director reassured John that no passing traffic would disturb his sleep at the entire complex was hidden deep underground as he no doubt realised but, he added, the air conditioning was a constant background noise, though, he assured John he would soon get used to it. He pressed a bell push on his desk and instructed the man who appeared shortly after, to take their guest to his quarters and settle him in and to bring him back to this office at nine o'clock the following morning. After a long walk along the subterranean passageways, John's quarters eventually proved to be very comfortable with en-suite facilities and a tray on the low table bearing a substantial cold meal and a jug of orange juice. The air conditioning was obvious, but thankfully not intrusive, and after his guide had left John settled down to enjoy his meal with his usual hearty appetite.

The following morning, after a refreshing sleep, and after a breakfast tray of coffee, figs, dates and yoghurt had been brought to his room and he had eaten, he was taken back to the Director's office where he was dressed in a contamination suit with an emergency breathing system before commencing his instructional tour of the secret facilities. What astounded John was that the elevator into which he was taken descended a further five levels to where the Director explained the laboratories were situated in order to be safe against any form of aerial attack - even against atomic weapons. John was told that he would be spending the first four days being instructed by the relevant scientists who were developing new strains of deadly bio-agents which could be used in the defence of the nation. The last day he was to be taken to the final research laboratory in which a new agent had been developed.

Over the following four days John was taken through the departments which had developed dangerous agents into deadly weapons. In the first he was shown how the Venezuelan Equine Encephalitis virus, the blueprint of which had been provided by President Hugo Chavez three years earlier, had been altered to now make it fatal for human beings. He was taken through the work on yellow rain which had been developed with North Korean assistance and which had now been potentised so that now only a tenth of the amount initially needed to cause severe neurological damage including seizures and blindness was now sufficient. His instructions continued through the next three days and covered the scientists success in modifying the smallpox virus so that current vaccinations are useless against it. Other facilities had synthetically created virulent strains of SARS, cholera, smallpox, Ebola and the plague, also know as the Black Death which killed a third of Europe's population in the Middle Ages and millions more when it resurfaced in China and India in the nineteenth century. A further research facility demonstrated how a selective breeding programme was creating strains of insects which would act as carriers for these deadly agents. John was told that insects such as fleas, flies and mosquitoes have been long recognized as being effective carriers for the spread of deadly diseases, and that disease-bearing insects were being used by the Japanese during WW2 against China, causing the death of hundreds of thousands of civilians. By the end of the fourth day John was astounded and impressed at the lethal weapons which were now at the disposal of Iran and, he was assured, able to be delivered anywhere in the world when the time came. But his astonishment was to pale into insignificance when he was taken on the fifth day to a deeper level where he had to exercise every atom of self-control at the sights he was to witness.

Used as he was to the sight of human suffering, John soon realised that he was now entering the very nadir of man's inhumanity to man when he saw before him, not cages for animals for vivisection, but a row of some ten identical glass sided booths, all with double air lock doors and extensive filtration systems and all of them with a medical couch with attachments for leg, arm and body restraints – very similar to the gurneys which the Americans use for the execution of prisoners by lethal injection. Some of the couches had naked people, men and women, secured to them, and as he observed the writing of their tortured bodies and their open mouths, John realised the booths were sound-proofed as well. All the victims had monitoring equipment attached to various parts of their bodies and above the couch was a camera obscenely placed recording their agony.

The jovial Director, who appeared completely unmoved by the horrendous spectacle, had been watching John keenly to note his reaction and, knowing this, John had ensured that nothing had changed in his facial expression despite the blow that even he had felt upon seeing the agonies of these tortured souls. He now had an understanding where some of the detainees he had dealt with had ended up, and he also understood what the metal rails were for in the passenger compartment of the helicopter which brought him to this place of horrors – they were to attach the manacles which restrained the hapless prisoners who were to be experimented on. Seeing that John was fully in control of himself, the Director cheerfully explained in a matter-of-fact way that MOIS supplied the prisoners for the testing of new strains of deadly agents and, owing to the virulent nature of the compounds with which they were given, very few survived the experience, and those that did were of no further use as they would have built up some degree of resistance to the agent and it was not possible to make further test on them.

John, feeling that there was little point in asking what became any survivors as he knew that all victims who entered here could never be allowed to return to the outside world, kept his thought to himself as he was led past the booths to a door which turned out to be a triple air lock leading into another laboratory with some six scientists all busy with the various items of equipment before them. The Director explained that this was the most highly sensitive section of his research complex and it was in here that top secret and hazardous research was carried out. He led John over to a position where a scientist was operating robotic arms inside a sealed chamber and made a point of saying that it was the results from this virus which would be of special interest to him as it had been genetically modified in ways that not only make it more contagious, infectious and lethal, but also gave it the ability to defy existing vaccine countermeasures. It was, the Director assured him, the most dangerous biological weapon agent in existence in the world. He went on to explain how it worked, its actions on the human body and how the virus would need to be distributed in order to have the greatest effect. Walking John back to the end booth, the Director explained that they were now going to show him the effects this newly developed agent had on a human being.

The Director with a smile nodded his head at a white-suited man who stood expectantly at the side of the booth where there was a small control panel. Without a word being spoken he pressed a button which allowed a small jet of liquid to be ejected onto the floor of the booth. John looked on dispassionately as the helpless young woman strapped to the gurney turned her head to look at him with a look of terror on her features. Within thirty seconds her body stiffened and was shortly followed by uncontrollable twitching and severe and painful muscular spasms. With her mouth wide open in a silenced scream she convulsed her entire body, straining against the restraints until blood ran from under the straps as they chafed through her skin. John watched enthralled as mucus began to pour from her nostrils and blood started to seep from her eye sockets and ears as her tortured body flailed impotently against the ravages of her ordeal. The final indignity inflicted upon her came as she lost control of her bowels and bladder just before death put a merciful end to her suffering.

It had taken just four minutes to despatch her. Now John had a better understanding of what was being planned and how it made sense to him of the special training he had received over the years with MOIS, and it was with a thrill of excitement that he suspected that it would not be long before his role would be explained.

With his tour over, the genial Director walked John back past the writhing mutilated forms in the booths without a glance, into the lift and back to his office where he gave John a letter addressed to Colonel Mahmoud Taqi-Pessain and asked him to deliver it personally where, he was assured, he would be told more about this deadly agent. After a warm farewell and an aide bringing his suitcase into the office, John was taken back outside into the darkness to a waiting helicopter with its rotor blades turning and within an hour was back at the airfield where a car and driver was waiting to take him back to his parents' house.

The following morning his father drove him to the MOIS building whilst making a point of not asking his son where he had been or what he had been doing over the last week. They both knew that it was a wise course of action not to make any enquiries outside one's sphere of responsibilities as the internal surveillance within MOIS would soon be alerted and a difficult time would be sure to follow as they were investigated for any subversive tendencies. Arriving at the headquarters building, they showed their passes at the security desk in reception where the guard , after scrutinising a clip board, informed Bahadur Najafi that he was to report immediately to the office of Colonel Taqi-Pessain. John acknowledged the instruction and, saying farewell to his father, ignored the elevator in favour of taking the stairs two at a time all the way to the top floor where he arrived shortly after barely out of breath. Walking into the ante-room he was immediately recognised by the Colonel's secretary and after a friendly exchange was shown in to the office where the Colonel sat behind his big desk with another man sitting in an armchair against the wall.

The Colonel rose from his desk and came round to warmly shake John's hand. “My dear Bahadur, it is good to see you again. How are you, keeping well I trust and not too tired after your trip last week?”

John was surprised at the unexpectedly informal behaviour but let nothing show as he politely returned the Colonel's greetings. “Thank you, Sir. I can assure you that I am well rested and I should like to take this opportunity to thank you for taking such an interest in my development and training, and for giving me the benefit of last week's instructions.”

“Be assured that you have, by your own efforts and dedication, earned all that has been placed before you,” replied the Colonel with a thin smile,” and it is owing to these attributes that you have been selected for a clandestine operation. But first let me introduce you to our esteemed guest” The Colonel extended his arm towards the small, thin nondescript man in the armchair. He was dressed in the traditional way with the shalvar and jameh combination topped with the ornately arranged headdress know as a sarband. “Sir, I should like to introduce you to one of our leading officers, Bahadur Najafi. Bahadur I have great pleasure in introducing Ali Reysahria who is the Minister for Intelligence and Security Affairs.”

Turning to the Minister, John gave a small bow and offered a formal greeting to the important person which was returned with a slight nod of the head as his small beady eyes examined the young man before him. He gestured John to a chair placed in front of the desk and spoke directly to him in a quiet, precise voice.

“I will be brief as my time is important. You along with others officers of MOIS have been selected for an operation which is of the highest national importance and one which will alter the political and religious balance of the depraved obscenity of the Western world. The precise details will be revealed to you by Colonel Taqi-Pessain once I have departed, but before this can happen I have to impress upon you that although we would normally order you to carry out any operation deemed necessary, in this case we will allow you to volunteer. The reason for this is that you will be operating abroad and, in the unlikely event that you are captured, you cannot be in any way linked to this country and, therefore, the Iranian government will strenuously deny any association with you or responsibility for any actions which you might have carried out. Also, for obvious reasons of security, once you have been appraised of the details of this operation, you cannot remain living at your parents' house and will be put into accommodation here in this building."

He licked his thin lips before continuing. "You will have no contact with them until you return to Iran at the completion of your task" Minister Reysahria paused as his dark hooded eyes looked directly into John's. "So, I must now ask you for your answer"

John returned the Minister's gaze with confidence as he replied. "Minister, may I assure you that I have fully understood what is expected of me and would like to confirm that I accept with pride the honour of the assignment. I affirm I am confident that, whatever difficulties I may face, it will carried it out successfully."

The Minister's thin dry lips twitched in what passed as a smile. "Excellent" he said as he picked up a brown leather briefcase from the side of his chair, stood up, and turned to the Colonel. "Now, Colonel, my work is done here and I now leave the matter in your hands. You will keep me fully informed of all developments."

Escorting the Minister to the door, the Colonel instructed his secretary to take the Minister to his car and, after thanking him for his time, bade him goodbye before returning to where John waited, after respectfully standing when the Minister departed. The colonel and waved him back into his chair.

"Now, Bahadur, we shall be spending some time together as I tell you what has been planned, what has already been put into place and just what your part is to be in this operation. You will understand, that for reasons of security, nothing I am to impart can be written down and you will have to use your considerable powers of memory only. But at all times I will be available to you should you need clarification on anything which is now to be discussed."

The colonel paused and gently drummed his fingers on the desk before continuing. "As you are aware from your studies of history, the balance of power between nations changes over time. Empires arise and at some time later collapse. Nations which once exercised great power become impotent, lose their way and young nations find high purpose and themselves rise up to dominance over weaker nations. It is generally believed that the next dominant power will be China, but we do not believe this will be so as it has been decided that the world will be controlled next by the unstoppable rise of Islam and that there will be one dominant power which will control this conversion across the whole face of the planet. That country will be our country Iran. Our nation will be the lead power in a Middle Eastern coalition which will eventually rule the entire planet and all the people on it." The colonel broke off as he waited for John's response.

"Colonel, Sir, perhaps I should say that what you say has come as a surprise to me, but I have to confess that I had been thinking along these lines for some time now. Am I to understand that the moment for action will soon be upon us?"

The Colonel nodded his head with an approving look. "You are indeed correct in what you say, Bahadur and you and others have been selected after special training to take the great revolution forward. You have just returned from a week at our chemical, biological and genetic research centre where you have been given an insight into the powerful weapons which we can unleash on our enemies. Its work has been greatly advanced by the addition of two scientists who have defected to us. One came from the American research facility at Plum Island, the other from the British Defence Centre at Winterbourne Gunner, and so important were they to their respective governments that a press embargo was applied once their disappearance had been confirmed." He gave a short laugh. "The Great Satans may not know where they are, but we most certainly do."

The Colonel paused as he opened a drawer in his desk and placed a matt black object on his desk. John looked with interest at the container which was approximately the size and shape of a thick paperback book. The Colonel unfastened a clasp and opened the lid to reveal a glass vial which fitted snugly into its felt-lined container.

"This is what you will be dealing with," he said, passing it over the desk to John, "You note the glass vial is completely sealed and, I am relieved to tell you is only a demonstrator and void of any toxic substances. However, when you are operational you will receive six of these and they will be filled with a deadly agent which is to be released simply by removing it from its protective container and broken open by stamping on it."

"Am I allowed to know what these vials contain, Sir?" John asked.

The Colonel gave a wry smile, "After your trip to the research establishment last week, I imagine you have a fair idea. However, I can say that they contain an unstoppable and deadly anthrax agent the likes of which the world has never before experienced, and the results of which you have been able to observe when you were shown the effects on that female at our research centre recently. Note that the outer protective container is made from carbon fibre, which as you know is stronger than steel, and coated with a substance we have developed which makes it invisible to ground penetrating radar. Observe also that there are no metal parts so it will not be picked up by a metal detector"

He closed the container and placed a fibre security pin through the catch. Again he drummed his fingers lightly on the desk before continuing. "It will be your task to ensure that upon receipt of these six containers you will keep them securely hidden until the moment you put this operation into action. Where you hide them will be your decision alone, but should you decide to secrete them you must remember that their special characteristics will render them invisible to detect. Now, it will come as no surprise to you in light of the time you were told to spend in the UK, that you will be operating from there. Our overseas department has made all the arrangements for you to be admitted to the country on a twelve months' mature student's visa which covers a course which runs from September this year to May next year. This will give you time to make all the preparations you require to carry out your task up to zero hour which is to coincide with their Christian celebrations of December 25th. As the Minister has stated, you will be on your own and cannot rely on any assistance from us at any time whilst you are in the UK, nor can there be any direct help to bring you back to Iran, though your escape, evasion and survival training should prove more than adequate to ensure you return to a hero's welcome."

"Can you tell me, Sir," asked John with great interest, "just what arrangements have been put in place in the UK for me. Once I know what they are, then I can start to formulate a plan of action."

"Certainly, Badahur. We have made the following arrangements for you. To begin with you have already in place a team of six operatives. Obviously, with the heightened tension in the West due to the attacks that have been mounted against them, security levels are high and so we have sourced white British males who have converted to Islam. As you know, we attract many who are suffering from mental instability or whose abilities and intellect are dangerously impaired by the use of narcotics and, as you are well aware from your time in the UK, over-indulgence with alcohol. Out of the original thirty or so we screened we have selected the six who will form the cell you will control. All of them have been told to wear normal western dress at all times, to shave off all facial hair and have been given dispensation by the Mullahs to be excused from formal religious observance in order to keep their true allegiance hidden from the authorities. Of course, you also have been given such dispensation. You find the arrangements satisfactory so far?"

"Yes, Sir, I do," said John thoughtfully, "But I would be grateful if you could tell me what training these men have received which will enable them to carry out this plan?"

"You can be assured that they have received a high level of training in the same escape and evasion techniques which you have been trained in. They all are experts in carrying out surveillance and, equally importantly, how to evade hostile surveillance. They are all in peak physical fitness and trained in unarmed combat and, although they have received weapons training, no firearms of any kind will be carried to ensure that there are no shooting accidents. Your team has a leader who is a trained locksmith and includes an electronics expert who deals with the bugging and tracking devices. Another specialises in IT and cyber disciplines.

There is a retired anti-terrorist police officer along with a trained vehicle mechanic with a useful skill in obtaining cloned car registration plates. The last, who is ex-commando and a martial arts, explosives and survival expert, can be used to support any of the others in their duties."

"What you have told me so far is reassuring." John looked questioningly at the Colonel. "Naturally we will all require a safe house. Can I assume that this has been taken care of?"

"This operation has been a long time in the planning," the Colonel continued, "and about a year ago it was arranged for one of your team to locate a suitable building which would fulfil the requirements with which he was furnished. The man chose well and funds were made available to him to make an outright purchase of a farmhouse in a remote location in a county called Shropshire close to the county town of Shrewsbury." The Colonel grinned at John as he added, "I have been told to inform you that Shrewsbury can be pronounced in two ways – either as *Shrewsbury or Shrowsbury.* It is, perhaps, a trifling point but one which you should know should a different pronunciation catch you out. But back to your safe house. It is what is called there a smallholding and comprises a fairly large farmhouse with five bedrooms and what is important buildings which are large enough for your vehicles and can be secured against prying eyes. You will find it is reached by a long private track and hidden from the road by a large stretch of woodland and by a similar wooded area on its far side and with no other habitation within sight around it. Your team have been living there since its purchase so that any coming and goings are seen to be normal movements for a lived in dwelling."

"Sir, may I know why Shropshire was chosen for my base. I have to confess that in my travels around the UK during my many visits, I never went to that part of the country."

"We looked very carefully into where your safe house should be located," replied the Colonel. He walked over to where a map of the British Isles hung from the wall. "Firstly, it is important that your base is centrally placed to the sphere of your operation and to this end we looked at the West Midlands counties and, after careful consideration, it was decided that Shropshire was suitable as it was close to the motorway network. Secondly, we looked at the county which has both a low crime rate and the absence of what the British call terrorist attacks, and found Shropshire to be the best in that respect. The outcome of this is that the police in the county are more relaxed and as a consequence less observant."

"That all sounds most satisfactory," said John, "but there is the matter of the vehicles which you implied had already been purchased. What I still don't know is how these vehicles are to be employed as I am still in the dark as to just what I am expected to carry out once in the UK." He looked apologetically at the Colonel. "I'm sorry, Sir, I'm jumping the gun as the British say. I'm sure you were just about to tell me."

The Colonel gave a rare laugh. "Bahadur, don't apologise. You must feel free to ask anything you want and I'll make sure you have the answers. Now, the vehicles," he went on. "There are six in total and they are of different types from a three year old people carrier, I believe it is called, various common saloons and a small van which is used for the shopping and, as the farmhouse has no mains gas, to purchase the gas cylinders you need from an agricultural supplier. All the vehicles are kept in first class condition by your mechanic who also ensures that they meet all legal requirements. He also has had made, through his shadier contacts in the motor trade, four sets of alternative number plates for each vehicle which have been copied from another vehicle of the same year, make, model and paint colour. Now, Badahur, I must now give you the final details of your assignment."

The Colonel again drummed his fingers on his desk as he collected his thoughts. “As you are aware your operation is part of a greater plan which will have world-wide consequences. For obvious reasons I am unable to tell you more than I am about to relate to you, not because I don't trust you, but because even I am not party to everything that has been planned. Even I am subject to the need to know principle.”

Picking up the metal capsule and holding it up before John, the Colonel explained. “The vial in this container contains, or I should say, will contain the anthrax virus.” He glanced at a sheet of paper on his desk. “You may already know that the British contaminated Gruinard island off the Scottish coast in 1942 using a virulent strain of anthrax they called Vollum 14578 which rendered the island uninhabitable for nearly fifty years. That strain, however, could be neutralised by spraying affected areas with a sea water and formaldehyde mixture. The strain which you were shown at the research facility, and which has satisfactorily fulfilled its human effects requirements, has been genetically altered so that will subject the victim to an agonising death shortly afterwards. Within forty-eight hours an area approximately two hundred kilometres in radius will be contaminated. Our strain as you know will remain in the ground and on clothing and, unlike the British Vollum strain which could not be passed on by physical contact, ours can, until neutralised by the antidote which we alone hold."

John had listened carefully to the Colonel's chilling revelations and waited until he had paused before speaking. "There is something which has come to me about the manner in which the virus will be released. Are you able to give me more precise details about what has been planned?"

"What you are to arrange once in the UK is this." The Colonel leaned forward as he spoke. "Using our embassy's diplomatic bag, six of these containers are to be brought into the UK and will be posted singly to you using a box number registered at the Post Office Sorting Office in Shrewsbury. It will be your responsibility to securely hide them as they must not be kept in the safe house. How you do this will be left entirely up to you. At the given hour you will designate three of your team to drive to London, Birmingham and Manchester using your pool cars. There they will break the vials and so release the spores. To make allowance for any unforeseen mishaps, we have ensured that your team contains three back-up drivers and three spare vehicles which can be used to deliver any of the remaining three capsules if necessary. I hope we have covered everything but any fine tuning will be your responsibility when you take over control of the operation. Have you any questions?"

"Yes, Sir, I have. You have told me of the speed with which the spores spread. If our operatives are to break the glass vials themselves, how are they to escape the effects? Will they have the antidote?"

"No, Bahadur. Only you will have the antidote." The Colonel picked up a keyring with two keys from his desk and passed it to John. "Keep these with you at all times. Your men are guarding a strong box which can be opened only with these two keys. Inside you will find 100,000 British pounds in used notes which you can use at your discretion. You will also find a 9mm Browning automatic and silencer, with fifty rounds of ammunition and spare clips. Also the antidote to the anthrax agent which carries with it directions for its application. We have also added two pairs of night vision goggles which you may find useful."

The colonel, leaned across his desk to emphasise his next words. "You have correctly surmised the fate of the three who release the anthrax spores. You will appreciate the necessity of ensuring there are as few people as possible who could be made to talk if captured. You will ensure that the other three cannot."

"Yes, Sir, you can be assured that your instructions will be carried out in all respects. Once these steps have been taken to stop tongues wagging, do I have your assurances that my tongue will not be included?"

The Colonel threw back his head and gave another rare burst of laughter. "Bahadur, you sly dog, I was waiting for you to ask that. You have my word that there are no such plans for you. It has been decided at a level far above mine, and with my full support, that you are too valuable to lose and that all clandestine efforts will be made to have you safely returned to Iran. Documents have been prepared for your extraction upon the completion of your assignment which you'll find in the strong box. You will find a driving licence and passport in the name of Patrick Rowlands and a short history of his past which should hold up under routine examination. There are also various travel tickets which can be used once your mission is completed. Be assured we want you back here but, I must stress this again, you are on your own as the state will deny all knowledge of you should you be captured."

John smiled back. "Thank you, Sir, I'm aware of the nature of this assignment and I'm greatly reassured by the measures which you have put in place. Now all that remains is to be told when I depart for the UK."

"We have your tickets and visa ready for you to fly out in two days' time. There is a car and driver outside who will take you back home where you can pack what you will need for your stay in the UK. When you take your leave of your mother, just tell her that you are being sent on an extended mountain survival course. You will be brought back here to stay in our accommodation for final briefings and to ensure that you are fully conversant with the requirements of your assignment until it is time to be taken to the airport. You will be able to to say goodbye to your father once you return from your home."

As he spoke the Colonel walked from behind his desk and, as John rose to stand before him, took his hand in both of his. "Bahadur, you have been given a difficult and dangerous task but I have no doubt that you are more than capable of success. To you has been given the opportunity to help change the course of world history and to create the first and final universal Islamic Caliphate. May the protection of Allah be with you at all times."

After thanking the colonel for his valued guidance, John left the office and descended to the foyer where his driver was waiting to take him back home. His driver was friendly soul who tried without success to engage John in conversation, but soon gave up as it was obvious that his passenger was deep in thought. John was bending his mind to the practicalities of his task, not least as to how he would hide the anthrax containers until they were needed, when the journey took him past the huge Behest-e Zahra cemetery in the south of the city. With a twinge of sorrow he recalled the sad time when he had attended the funeral of his much loved grandmother when he was thirteen. As in his mind's eye he recalled with painful clarity the cloth-draped wooded coffin being lowered into the ground and the clean cut sides of the grave, a germ of an idea came to him. He worked silently on the idea and by the time his driver drew up outside his parents' home he had already formulated a plan.

Telling his driver to wait, John went in to what he knew would be a tearful time with his mother as she fussed around putting things into his case which he knew he would never need but which he hadn't the heart to remove. Within half an hour his clothing, toiletries and passport were packed and, with one last tearful hug from his mother, was taken back to MOIS headquarters and shown to his room which was to be his for the short stay before he flew out to the UK. After settling in, John went to his father's office to take his farewell of him, and then back to his room where later a he answered a knock on the door to find a clerk from the travel section who brought all the documentation he needed along with an envelope containing twenty British ten pound notes for emergencies. As John signed for the money the clerk told him that arrangements had been made for him to be collected at Birmingham airport where his flight was due to land, but the cash is a safety net in case the flight was diverted to another airport. Wishing him good luck, the clerk shook John's hand and left quietly closing the door behind him.

For some reason, John's stay at MOIS headquarters was only overnight and the following morning after breakfast he was taken to the Iman Khomeini International Airport to the south-west of Tehran where he boarded his Iran Air flight to the UK. As there were no direct flights to Birmingham, John had first to land London Heathrow and then take a connecting flight to Birmingham International Airport where he would be met by one of his team.

Eventually, as his flight departed and John relaxed into his seat, he began the meticulous planning which he knew would be essential if his mission was to be successful. As the huge air liner arrowed through the air high above the clouds and his arrival in the UK became closer, so also did the moment when the paths of John and Justin would intertwine with terrible and unexpected consequences.

Meanwhile the flight to the UK was, as John expected, long, boring and cramped and it was with relief that he felt the aircraft touch down with a thud of the undercarriage on the runway and, with a roar of the turbines in reverse thrust bringing the huge craft to taxiing speed, John felt a sense of relief at having completed the first part of his assignment. Although he wouldn't admit it to anyone, he did not like flying as he was not in control of events and, although that was something he had vowed in the past would never happen again, he had to accept that with flying he would have to trust to the skill of the pilot. Finally , the airliner docked and with the engines now silent and the doors opened, John took his place in the slow line of fellow passengers as they shuffled out onto the walkway and towards the customs and immigration controls. As a foreign national, John followed the signs to the immigration desks where a bored-looking officer checked the documents which he had been passed and, after a few brief questions relating to the educational course on which he was enrolled, he was waved through with the officer wishing him a pleasant stay. It was just as he had been told by the colonel. The stupid British had immigration procedures which were so slack as to be a joke, and John wondered what was wrong with them as it looked like they actually wanted the country to be flooded with foreigners. Well, he thought, it suits our purposes but once we are in control, then the British will have a shock as their complacency is shattered by the imposition of Sharia law.

With these thoughts in mind, he walked over to the baggage carousel, retrieved his suitcases from the slow-moving conveyor belt and carried them the short distance to the entrance to the main concourse. John had been briefed to look out for a man holding a sign on which was written SANDFORD COLLEGE and, as expected, he soon located his contact who turned out to be a stocky man of Caucasian appearance who looked to be in his mid-thirties. As John walked over to him their eyes met and his contact gave a smile and a nod of recognition. He found reassuring to know that this team member had been well briefed as to his appearance. Taking one of his suitcases, and with a brief greeting, the man led John out of the arrivals hall, into the darkness of a summer evening, and a short distance to the parking place where his cases were put into the boot of a 5 Series BMW. Only when they were settled in their seats and the powerful car was headed towards the motorway did he speak to John.

"Sorry about the strong silent treatment, but I felt it better not to say anything that might be overheard." He turned his head briefly to look at John. "Hope you don't mind, but could you put your seatbelt on. It's against the law for a front seat passenger not to be strapped in." He turned back to the wheel. " I'm Junead Hussain, but I'm told you'll want us to revert to the names we had before we converted to Islam, so I'm Charlie, though I'm sure you knew that before you flew over. May I welcome you to the UK. Sir."

"Thank you Charlie, and you can drop the Sir. Like you I'm to be known by an English name which is to be John. May I add I approve of your caution which gives me reassurance that your training has been thorough. As you say, I have been well briefed about my team and I know you to be the team leader, that is now, my second in command. I'm sure we will work well together. I've already formulated the necessary actions for first part of our assignment and I want you to call everyone together after breakfast tomorrow to be allocated their duties. Will you see to that."

Charlie grinned. "Yes, Sir, sorry, John. I'll have them on parade for you first thing. I told 'em we'd be getting cracking once you arrived, and they'll be pleased as we've been hanging around a lot of the time once we had everything in place waiting for you. Mind, I expect after your long flight you'd like me to shut up whilst you catch up on your sleep."

John had been checking on Charlie's driving and was pleased to see the speedometer rarely displaying over seventy miles per hour and that he kept a safe distance from the vehicle in front. He was just about to praise him for his driving, but decided against it until he had seen the rest of the team, and assessed their skills and capabilities over the next week after he had set them their new tasks. There was little point in dishing out praise to begin with, then having to row back if they were not up to scratch. Better, he decided, to wait and see how they shaped up,

"Thank you. I would like to catch up on some sleep. I find it very difficult to get some shut-eye whilst flying." John found it easy to slip back into the vernacular of his second language and suiting action to words, reclined his seat and, within the silent luxury of the big limousine, soon fell asleep as the powerful car drove through the darkness and towards the commencement of his given task.

Some while later he was woken as the car slowed and looked up to see they had left the motorway and were pulling out from a country lane onto a main road. John put his seat upright as Charlie glanced at him.

"You've had a good sleep. About an hour, I think" he said. "We've just come on to the Cressage road. Won't be long now."

John nodded and yawned as he looked down the beams of the powerful headlights probing the darkness as Charlie signalled to turn left and pointed the car down the A458 towards Cressage. After about three miles he slowed down and turned the car into a gateway which had a dilapidated sign on a post with the words *MANOR FARM* barely discernible as the headlights washed over them. The track was in a poor state of repair and John noted that there had been some heavy rain recently as the ruts were filled with water. The big car bounced and lurched as it progressed slowly for a quarter of a mile, until it passed through a wooded area where it took a sharp turn to the left, to reveal a farmhouse with an outside security light illuminating the sprawl of out-buildings around it. Charlie drove the BMW across the yard towards a barn where he pulled up and stepped out to open the big double doors. He then got back in and carefully manoeuvred the BMW alongside a small saloon. Inside the barn John could see in the headlights several other vehicles neatly lined up.

"Here we are, John," said Charlie as he switched off the engine and went round to the boot to retrieve John's two suitcases which he carried outside before putting them down and turning back to the barn. "Just bear with me, I've got to shut the doors. Security, y'know."

As he swung the big doors closed he spoke to John. "Although it's late, I told the lads to stay up until you arrived. But if you want to leave it until tomorrow I'll dismiss them. What do you want to do?"

John didn't need to give it much thought. "I think tomorrow will be fine. Pack them off to bed now and, as I'm feeling hungry, I hope you can find me something to eat before I turn in."

Walking carefully across the uneven cobbles of the yard, Charlie took them to a low door which he opened to reveal a large farmhouse kitchen with a long scrubbed pine table with hard-backed chairs arranged around it and, in an alcove to the right of the door, a large double oven cast iron Rayburn. Next to it was a conventional gas cooker which John imagined would be the one which needed bottled gas. He was pleased to note that at the far end of the room was a washing machine and a tumble dryer. An old-fashioned Belfast sink and drainer and a large dresser with cups and plates on it completed the austere appearance of what must have been the centre of a working farm.

"If you want to wait here," said Charlie waving towards the chairs as he put the suitcases down. "I'll tell the lads you'll be seeing them in the morning so they can take themselves off to bed. Then I'll get you some grub."

John seated himself at the big table as Charlie disappeared through a door which led to the rest of the house and listened to the muted voices which came to him as his team members were spoken to followed by the clatter of feet upon the uncarpeted stairs as they made their way to their rooms. A moment later Charlie bustled back into the kitchen when he offered to make John scrambled eggs on toast. He chatted away cheerfully as he broke the eggs into a bowl and whisked them up with some milk, salt and pepper before putting two slices of bread into the toaster. John listen carefully to his appraisal of the other team members and the set up at the farm as he gratefully ate the plate of food eventually put before him with a steaming cup of tea to go with it. He was impressed with Charlie's concise summing up and listened carefully to all the details which he passed on, as his agile mind assessed how he would use his team according to their individual abilities.

With his keen appetite John soon finished his plate of scrambled eggs and asked to be shown to his room. Picking up his cases, Charlie took him out of the kitchen along a dimly lit corridor to the stairs which he ascended to a large landing at the top. He pointed out the bathroom before opening a door to a surprisingly spacious room with a double bed with a small locker at one side, a large wardrobe and a table with a chair set against one wall. He was told that the best bedroom had been reserved for him and was pleased to see that it had the luxury of a wash-hand basin plumbed in alongside the window and a large oil-filled electric radiator against the other wall. Also in the room, placed neatly at the foot of the bed, was the large metal strong box he had been told to expect. John thanked Charlie, telling him that he would be down for breakfast at eight o'clock and would be addressing the men once they had all eaten, before bidding him goodnight.

As soon as the door had closed behind him, John took his toilet bag and towel out of one of his cases and went to the basin, where he first cleaned his teeth, then washed his hands and face before drying himself with the towel. Opening the other case, he took from it a small roll of heavy cloth. Once opened, he picked up the small compass which had been placed inside and, studying the needle's direction, placed the mat on the bare boards facing towards Mecca to began the ritual of prayer which was an essential part of a true believer's sacred duties. Only when he had made his peace with the Prophet did he undress and climb into his bed. He was pleasantly surprised to find that the bedding was clean and smelled fresh and was much reassured that his team were able to give attention to even small details. He felt satisfied that they had been well chosen and, all being well, would be up to the high standards which he knew would be essential if his mission was to succeed. He switched off the light and lay on his back, and as his eyes adjusted to the pale light of the half moon as it shone through the threadbare curtains covering the window, ran through in his mind what had to be done at the morning briefing. So far, he decided as he turned onto his side to sleep, everything was going to plan.

The following morning, John awoke after a refreshing night's rest to find the rain of yesterday had returned. He looked out of the low window in his room to see dark clouds being driven by a gusting wind which shook and twisted the boughs of the trees which surrounded the farmhouse. As he washed he heard the sound of voices and the tread of feet descending the stairs as his men took themselves down for breakfast making sure they were in place before their new leader appeared. John sniffed the air as welcome smell of coffee wafted up from the kitchen. After washing and dressing he went to the bathroom to relieve himself before making his way to the kitchen, and a keenly anticipated cooked breakfast, where he entered to a chatter of voices. He seated himself at the long kitchen table all talk stopped as he took stock of his team members. They, in turn, examined their new boss.

"Right," said John with a smile, "I haven't just come down from Mars, and I don't eat children for breakfast, so you can all relax. And, by the way, the name's John"

The men laughed as the tension eased with his words and, as the one team member who had been allocated coking duties carried on with putting food on to plates and dishing them to the each person in turn, Charlie made the introductions around the table as they ate their breakfasts.

"I'd better tell you who's who, John." Charlie put his hand on the shoulder of the man to his left. "This frivolous looking man with the horrible coloured hair is Ginger and he's our electronics expert. He deals with bugging and tracking devices, and I can assure you there is none better."

He gestured at a thin, studious man with protruding ears wearing round glasses which gave him an owlish look. "Next in line is Woody who deals with all IT matters. He can insert Trojan Horses, worms and generally take over anyone's computer and take out and put in what we want."

Charlie waved his hand at the next person who was older than the others, possibly in his mid-forties, of stocky build, with a receding hairline and a strong determined jawline. "This is Bill, so named because he's a retired anti-terrorist police officer and we've no one better at surveillance, tracking and counter-intelligence." Bill gave a tight smile as he nodded in acknowledgement.

"Now on to Chalky," continued Charlie, indicating a wiry man in his late twenties wearing a pair of blue overalls. "He's our resident vehicle mechanic and what he doesn't know about vehicles isn't worth knowing. Despite his unkempt appearance, he keeps all our fleet in first class order and, very importantly, he ensures that they are all properly insured, taxed and have an MOT. We don't want this operation compromised by being pulled in for minor traffic violations. Plus Chalky has some friends in the trade who have supplied him with different sets of registration plates for each vehicle which have been cloned from a vehicle similar in every respect." As Charlie gave a cheery wave of the hand holding a fork loaded with food, John saw with distaste that evidence of his last job was present under his finger nails.

Charlie gestured toward a large, thick set

man who, even sitting down, towered above the others. He was wearing just a sweat shirt which exposed a thick neck and powerful arms. "Lastly, but by no means least," he continued, "we have Mike, ex-Royal Marine Commando and a martial arts, explosives and survival expert. His primary responsibility is security but he assists any of the others when necessary. He is also very strong so I'm always polite to him. Then, of course, there is me, a time-served locksmith. That, John, is your team. All specially selected, highly trained and ready to carry out your instructions. We hope you approve."

John did approve of the skills and abilities of his team. What a shame, he thought, that all of them have only a few months to live.

With the formal introductions over, John told them that he would be setting out their duties once breakfast was finished and was assured by Charlie they would all be in the sitting room for their briefing once they had finished eating. They all chatted away informally until breakfast was finished, when John stood up and said he would shortly be explaining to them his plan for dealing with the containers and he wanted to see what equipment he had been issued with and what he might need in the future. Returning to his room, he went over to the strongbox which had been placed against the end of his bed and, using the keys given to him by the Colonel, operated the high security lock and opened the lid.

Inside he saw that the interior had been neatly divided into compartments which were sized to fit the various items which it contained. In one compartment he saw the browning 9mm automatic with the silencer, spare clips and ammunition. In another larger compartment he found what he was looking for. Two Swedish Armasite M-16 infra-red, night vision goggles with the head straps which enabled them to be used hands-free and next to them six spare lithium-ion battery packs with their charger unit. With just a few minutes to spare before he had to address his team, John quickly opened another compartment in which he saw his new passport in the name of Patrick Rowlands and a Stena Line ticket dated the 24th December to take a car and one passenger from Fishguard to Rosslare in the Irish Republic departing 0230 hours and arriving 0630hrs. The next document was a an Etihad Airways ticket also for the 24th December departing Dublin at 1615 hours for Abu Dhabi. John was unsure of distances in the Republic but was soon able to calculate his driving time from Rosslare to Dublin when he found his MOIS quartermaster had included road maps of the UK and Ireland in the compartment. Unfolding the map, he quickly measured the distance he had to drive and was reassured that he had been given plenty of time to cover the distance which separated the two places.

There were other items in the strong box but, wanting to start his team briefing as soon as possible, John replaced everything tidily, locked the box and, removing one of the two keys, went over to the curtains at the window and pushed it into the hem at the bottom of one of them before making his way downstairs to the sitting room where his team members were waiting seated around the room in a variety of sofas and arm chairs, none of which matched. A large flat screen television stood on a low table in one corner and, set against another wall was a small table, strewn with magazines and paperback books, with three hard-backed chairs around it. There was a fire alight in the grate on which were piled several logs which crackled as they threw their heat out into the room, with the entire wall either side of the fireplace lined with logs stacked up to knee height. John had noticed that, despite the warmth of late summer outside, the house had a cold and damp atmosphere which even the blazing fire did little to dispel. The room fell silent as John entered and the men started to rise to their feet. He waved his hand at them down.

"Gentlemen, please be seated. I'm going to get cracking and explain the reason why we are all here," he said without preamble. "Before I flew into the UK I'd been briefed on my team members and the skills each one of you possesses, and the fact that you have been specially selected because it was felt that you alone would be able to help me carry out the assignment with which I have been charged." Despite his ruthless nature, John knew that a line of subtle praise was a prerequisite for getting the best out of the men under his command.

"In the short time I have been here I've been impressed with your professionalism and this gives me encouragement that together we will succeed. I am not empowered to give you full details of this crucially important mission and, indeed, I also am not privy to all the details. But this much I can say, that it is absolutely crucial that we triumph and that whole of the Islamic world is waiting for us to signal that we have carried out our sacred duties."

He turned to Charlie. "Charlie, have you got a spade, a shovel and a garden trowel here?"

Charlie didn't appear fazed by the strange request. "I know we have a shovel in the barn, but no spade or trowel. But there's no problem with that as I'll can send Chalky out to the garden centre at Meole Brace to get them. He should be there and back in thirty minutes."

Charlie turned to Chalky and gave him a credit card with the instructions to purchase the two items, before turning back to John. "Is there anything else you might need?"

"Just one more thing. I noticed you have some paperback books. I'll need a fairly thick one like that Wilbur Smith novel I saw as I came in. Now, I'd like you to send Chalky off now whilst we continue with the next phase."

Chalky stood up and left the room as John continued. "As you know a Post Office Box with a collection facility has been set up by you and it will soon be used to send us specialist containers over the next few months which have to be securely hidden. I've been instructed that under no circumstances can they be kept here at the farmhouse and therefore it fell to me to devise a secure way of securely concealing them and, more importantly, being able to find them again when they are required. As you no doubt are well aware, it is one thing hiding an item, but quite another making sure it can be both safe from prying eyes and able to be easily retrieved."

"Now, Charlie," John continued, "this is your next task. I want you to find me someone who digs graves. Not someone who works in a municipal cemetery, but a self-employed person who digs graves at small and remote burial grounds. Do you think you can find such a person?"

Charlie's brow furrowed as he thought about the request. "Well, I never thought I'd be faced with that one. Let me see. I do know there's an itinerant grave digger in Shrewsbury because I saw him when I went to a friend's funeral who was buried at Dorrington. Tall bloke, fair hair, in his late thirties or so."

"Can you track him down," asked John. "I'll want his full contact details, phone number, e-mail, address and the vehicle he drives if possible."

"Shouldn't be too difficult. I'll phone Percivals first as they're the busiest undertakers around here. Should be able to get the information you want."

"Excellent, but leave it for the time being as we have another training exercise to carry out once Chalky returns from his shopping trip. As I said earlier, when something is to be hidden it must not be able to be found and also be able to be retrieved without difficulty. I have given much thought to this problem and have come up with the ideal solution. If you want to hide something where people are unlikely to be digging around can you think of a better place than a cemetery. And when the time comes to recover it, its location can be precisely established as the name of the deceased will be on the headstone. Have you any questions so far?"

"Yes, I have," Bill spoke with a puzzled expression on his face, "I follow your reasoning but there appears to be a great difficulty as I see it. If you are suggesting hiding something in the bottom of a grave before the burial, then I can't see how you are going to get it out afterwards. I'm no expert on burials but having to open a grave, shift a small mountain of earth and then lift out a coffin doesn't seem feasible. Unless I've missed something."

John smiled as he replied, "You're quite correct, Bill. Such an arrangement would not be feasible, so we are going to use the facility of the grave but utilise a practical method for concealment and retrieval." John continued to talk to his men about other matters as he waited for Chalky to return.

After twenty minutes he paused as he heard the sound of a vehicle outside. "Ah, that should be Chalky back with the tools we shall be needing. Now gentlemen we are going to have a practical demonstration of how we can achieve the secure concealment needed. Follow me, please."

He addressed Charlie directly as they filed out of the room. "I want you to get that shovel I asked for earlier. Also a large knife, a sheath knife or a large carving knife, which we will also need. Then we'll have to find a place where the soil will give us easy digging and, most importantly, where there is turf."

"You're lucky with that one," replied a clearly intrigued Charlie, "the entire area is a light sandy soil and if we go to the side of the barn where the cars are stored we've got the conditions you want. Must say, can't wait to find out what's going on, especially as the rain has stopped."

Charlie led John and his men outside and across the cobbled yard to the side of the barn where he pointed out a suitable area. "This okay, John?" he asked.

"Just fine. Now I want a hole dug to replicate a grave. It doesn't have to be the length of a coffin but it has to be about this width." He extended his hands to indicate the distance he wanted.

Taking the spade, Mike drove it into the turf and took it round the shape he was to dig out then, with powerful strokes, began the task he had been set. "How deep do you want it," he asked without breaking his rhythm, as he rapidly moved the earth onto a spoil heap by the side of the hole.

"If you take it down to waist level that should do it." John replied, impressed with the speed with which the hole was being excavated in the loose sandy soil.

Within fifteen minutes the hole was ready. John told Mike to get out and he then took his place in the hole and asked for the knife, trowel and book to be passed to him.

"Right, men, watch carefully." He held up the book. "This represents the item which has to be hidden and, in fact, is just about the correct size. I told you, it would be pointless burying it in the bottom of a grave as it couldn't realistically be recovered. However, I have devised a practical method of concealment which will be secure and enable easy recovery."

John stood at the end of the hole and, taking the hunting knife carefully cut the turf for an arm's length as a continuation of both sides of the end of the hole. Taking the spade he drove it in below the level of the grass roots and across until he had a thick piece of turf which he then carefully folded back to expose the soil beneath. With the trowel he scooped a neat depression in the centre of the exposed area deep enough to take the paperback and, throwing the extracted soil onto the spoil heap at his side, inserted the book into its cut-out and relaid the flap of turf. He then carefully brushed the grass over the two cuts until it was impossible to see that there had been any disturbance around the hole.

"There you are," said John, looking up at the faces around him. "Look closely. Can you see anything untoward? Remember that the grave digger we find will not be told that something has been secreted in any grave he digs, so what we have just done has to be invisible to him. I think you'll agree this method of concealment will do the trick and, what is more important, we will know exactly where to make the recovery when the time comes to move."

The men looked carefully at John's work and nodded in agreement as Charlie spoke. "Yes, first class job with nothing to arouse suspicions. Actually, I recall at my friend's funeral the grave had this green coloured matting draped over all the sides of the grave, so our work will be hidden from view from everyone. It'll only be uncovered when the grave digger starts his work filling in."

John placed his hands at the side of the hole and, with a powerful leap, sprang out. "Right, now we have the method of concealment we have to look at the practicalities of carrying out the concealment. In the strong box in my room there are two sets of night vision goggles. When we have a suitable grave, two of you go out at night to effect the concealment. The location of the grave will be provided by this grave digger we have yet to locate. Charlie, can you get on with that now. Find us someone who digs graves in out of the way places. The rest of you fill in this hole."

A short while later, back in the house, Charlie, with Woody in tow, approached John with a smile on his face.

"Got what you want, John, no problem at all. I phoned Percivals and they gave me a name straight away. It's a bloke called Justin Parkes who's been digging their graves in burial grounds all over Shropshire for a couple of years, or so. In fact, he digs for many undertakers some in Cheshire and across the border into Wales. He's reliable, I'm told, and I have his mobile number and e-mail address, but they don't know where he lives except that it's in Shrewsbury."

"Good work, Charlie. Now I think that it is time we knew what Mr. Parkes is about." He turned to Woody, "I take it Woody that you're quite capable of hacking into his computer."

"Not a problem." Woody's face was alert with expectation at finally having the opportunity to put his talents to good use. "It's unlikely he's got a sophisticated firewall in place and even if he has, I can get round it. I've got a brute force cracking programme which will find his password quickly. But it's quite likely he hasn't bothered to use one. I'll try and get his home address whilst I'm in there. Have to say though, I can't do anything until he's not using his system."

John nodded in approval, "I understand. Let me know when you've something to report." He turned back to Charlie. "I want you to show me where everything is round here. Let's go, shall we."

Charlie led John out through the kitchen and across the cobbled yard to the big barn where he showed John the six vehicles they had at their disposal. Along the left hand wall was a workbench with a vice and a pillar drill attached to it. An open tool box was sitting at the end of the bench with a neat stacks of vehicle registration plates along side. Walking over to the back of the building, he showed John another door.

"This one is important," he explained as he lifted the locking bar out of its rests and swung open the door. "You can see there's a short track to the gate opposite. If you go through it and drive over two fields you'll come to a lane. Turn right and you'll come to Acton Burnell. There you can turn north to Shrewsbury, or carry on south west onto the A41. I've checked out the two fields and they are both pasture land and well-drained so we shouldn't get bogged down in the wet if we have to make a hasty exit."

John looked carefully round and noted with satisfaction that the farmhouse was completely surrounded by woodland and totally invisible from the main road and so far back that it was impossible to hear traffic noise. He was much reassured with the level of planning his team had put in place.

Charlie carried on with his tour, showing John the outbuildings which were filled with a lot of rubbish and discarded broken farming implements left by the last occupants, and a loose box which was stacked high with split logs. Charlie walked him round the farmhouse to the other side where he took him in through what would have been in better times, the front door with its decrepit porch covered with an overgrown dog rose. Once through the door there was a gloomy hallway which led to the stairs and, placed one either side of the front entrance, there were two small rooms . The first was plainly used as a fitness room as it contained a bench with weights on a rack and an electric tread mill. The other was being used to store canned and dried food along with a stacks of shrink-wrapped bottled water and, what appeared to be, bottles of UHT milk A large catering sized chest freezer stood against the far wall which John opened to discover was filled a variety of foodstuff which included ready meals, a variety of meats and a stack of wrapped sliced bread.

“There's enough food here and in the kitchen to last us a week, no problem, just in case we can't get out for any reason. Nearly forgot to tell you, hot water comes from the Rayburn in the kitchen which is kept alight all the time, and the cold water comes from a well which is pumped up to a holding tank in the roof space, so we're not reliant on a mains supply. And, can I reassure you," said Charlie as he patted the now closed freezer, "there is not a pork product in there or anywhere in the house and all meat is halal."

"Excellent, but just as I expected. You have prepared us for every eventuality and I'm pleased. Now I want to see where Woody has his electronic equipment."

Taking John through the sitting room to a door at the far end, they walked into a small room with a window which looked out into the yard. They found Woody at his desk seated in front of a monitor screen, surrounded by an array of electronic equipment, busily typing instructions into a keyboard.

Woody turned slightly to see who it was. "Oh, hello. Just bear with me, can you, I'm nearly there and can't break off without compromising the programme." Without waiting for an answer he turned back to his task until, a minute later, he gave a low cry of triumph.

"Got it! Easier than I hoped. This Parkes hasn't used a password protected e-mail system and, what's more, he has put his postal address on his e-mails." Woody passed John a piece of paper. "That's where he lives, Flat 2, 11 Abbey Foregate in Shrewsbury. Don't know where that is as I'm not from round here, but Chalky will as he's a born and bred Shrewsbury man. And, what's more, I've planted a trojan horse in his operating system which will give us access, and total control, at any time we choose."

"Well done, Woody." John turned and pointed at a small blank screen of a monitor next to which was yellow and black striped box with a protective spring loaded cover over a red button. "What does that do?"

"That's how we cover the entrance," explained Charlie with his usual enthusiasm. "We don't want anyone coming up the drive so we've put a mail box at the entrance so the postman doesn't have to drive to the farmhouse. Woody's put a motion sensor at the side of one of the gate posts. When the beam's broken, it activates an infra-red camera mounted on a tree a little way up the track. The camera's in sleep mode in order to save the batteries and only wakes when someone breaks the beam." He tapped the monitor. "Then the image comes up on this screen. That's why we have a permanent watch in here at all times. Mind you, we do have the problem of badgers and foxes setting it off but we've discovered they do tend to keep to fairly regular times."

"Very good," said a clearly impressed John, "you have a first class system in place. But what is this yellow and black box for?"

Mike pushed forward and patted the unit. "This is my baby. If we find we're under attack that button must be activated immediately. There are two conifers halfway up the track which I've rigged with Semtex cutting charges so they come down and cause a complete blockage. Press the button and they'll be down in seconds. That should give us just enough time to get into our vehicles and out by the rear escape route."

"Well done, all of you." said John, clearly impressed by their level of expertise. He pointed to another set of electronic equipment which had been placed on another table to Woody's right. "And this one, what does that do?"

"That's our monitoring equipment. This one here is for any listening devices, you know, bugs, which we may want to place. The unit next to it is the receiver for a tracker. It can cope with six separate tracking devices at any one time and what is more the signals they put out cannot be tracked back to here as their signals are routed via a server whose location is unknown even to me. All I know is it isn't in this country."

"All very well done," John responded, "but, tell me, how accurate are these tracking devices?"

"About this accurate." Woody spread his arms wide. "The tracking nodes are linked to the latest GPS satellite technology and are up to military grade. Mind you, we had a hell of a job getting a decent signal because of all the trees round here. In the end Mike climbed the tall fir at the front of the house and lashed a pole at the top for the satellite dish. Once we bought enough cable, it works just fine."

John thought quickly and spoke to Charlie. "I want you to organise a tracker on this Parkes' vehicle, which I would imagine is a van, and parked up at his home address. You'll have to wait until after dark. Shame we don't have any way of knowing when he'll be back."

"Can help you there," said Woody as he scrolled down his screen. "I've got an e-mail here from an undertaker giving him all the details of a job. See," he jabbed his finger at the screen, "coffin size, location, time, date and the name of the stiff. Looking at the date, which is today, and time it's likely he's out on a job now, but once Ginger has tagged his vehicle we'll know for sure where he is at any one time."

The other team members had followed them into Woody's room and Chalky spoke. “I'm a born and bred local boy, so I know roughly which 11 Abbey Foregate is. It'll be in a terrace of big houses, most of them converted into flats, close to the Abbey. I'm sure they don't have any parking there. But there is a supermarket opposite and I imagine this guy could park his car or van there.”

“Good thinking,” said John, “now, Charlie, I want you to take Ginger with you when you go. Take everything you need to fix the van and to bug the flat. I realise the flat might be a problem as we don't know when Parkes will be out but don't worry if you can't manage it tonight as we can work out when he'll be out on a job now we have intercepted his e-mails, and you can do it then.”

“Just one thing I'd like to mention, if I may,” said a puzzled Charlie, “isn't this a bit premature. After all, we don't know if this Parkes cove is suitable and, even if he is, we don't know he'll play ball.”

“I understand your concern, Charlie, but let me assure you that, as our timetable is tight, we have to move boldly. True, Parkes might not be suitable, though at this stage he appears to fit the bill admirably, but we have to put monitoring in place just in case, even if he eventually he proves to be unsuitable and we have to look elsewhere. But I can assure you that the incentives I am able to offer will make it very likely he will play ball, as you put it. Right, get yourself organised with Ginger for tonight and better take Chalky with you as he knows the area. Woody, I want you to print off all e-mails from the undertakers giving Parkes work." He indicated an empty filing tray. "Just leave them in here where I can find them."

John paused as he looked round to find Bill. "Right, Bill, at this stage I have no suspicions that we are under surveillance, but I want you to take another vehicle and put yourself in place close to this Abbey Foregate to look out for any suspicious activity. Can you find your way there?"

Bill, a taciturn man of few words, nodded. "Yes, no problem. I know how to get to the Abbey . Number eleven is close by so I should be able to sus it from there." He turned and spoke to Charlie, "I'll need to be fifteen minutes ahead of you so I can get in place."

John addressed his men. "Right, that's all sorted. You know what to do. Mike, that just leaves you. I want you to do a clearance patrol after lunch and tonight I'll give you the night vision goggles and you can do one after dark. Charlie, what security have you organised?"

"I haven't put out foot patrols, though we thoroughly checked our patch when we came here, but we do have someone on watch at all times day and night monitoring the surveillance screen. They're on a duty roster of two hours on, eight off. Not too bad as it means that everyone can get a proper break for sleep. Of course, your good self is exempt from this mundane chore."

To his surprise John shook his head. "From now on the roster will be seven strong. Include me as from tonight." He smiled as he added, "but I do draw the line at cooking, so don't put me on that duty list. Anyway, I'm always hungry. So whoever it is, get cracking." There was laughter as the men left the computer room to carry on with their duties and prepare the equipment needed for later.

At eleven o'clock that evening the men departed for the short drive into Shrewsbury leaving John waiting patiently for their return. It was just after midnight when he heard the two cars drive into the yard, with the slam of the barn doors telling him that they had been secured for the night. Shortly after the outer door opened and shut as the four men entered the kitchen where John waited for them. He looked quizzically at Charlie and waited for him to make his report.

"Not too bad, John," he said with quiet satisfaction. "We found what appeared to be his vehicle. There was a red Vauxhall panel van parked in the supermarket car park which had two scaffolding planks on the roof fastened to ladder racks. There was no sign writing on the sides but when we looked in we saw digging equipment and rolls of green matting, so we're sure it belongs to this Parkes fellow. Ginger did his work and put two trackers where they won't be found."

"What about the flat itself," asked John, "would you have any problems getting in?"

"Well, as Chalky said, there's no parking at the house but there is a sort of archway between numbers nine and eleven, with a shared passage under the ground floor level leading to the gardens at the back. I did a quick recce once the coast was clear and found there was a back door with a three lever lever mortice lock which won't be any trouble to open. So we can gain entry that way once we know Parkes is away on a job and fit the bugs. Once Woody has confirmation that he's digging away we can be in and out within thirty minutes. Reckon that's long enough, Ginger?"

Ginger thought for a moment, then nodded. "Yep, should be long enough for me to do my work. But there is something that troubles me, John. It's that the big bay window at the front, which presumably belongs to the lower flat, has a clear view of the entrance to the house and the archway to the back of the property.

We have no idea who is in it. It could be someone who goes out to work and it's empty during the day, but it could be a retired person or possibly a shift worker and if they were looking out would wonder what two blokes were doing creeping round the back."

"That's a good point, agreed John. " Any ideas, Charlie?"

"Let me see." Charlie scratched his head as he thought. "There is another way, although it would mean we would be clearly seen, and that's to pose as, say, British Telecom engineers and just go in through the front door. Woody, can you make two authentic-looking identity cards for me and Ginger?"

"No problem. When you know where to look on line its easy to print them off. I'll need you both to have a mug shot taken and I'll put them on the cards. I haven't got any of the holders which let you put the ID on a chain round your necks but I can laminate them which should make them look official enough if you're challenged. If you drop into the IT room after breakfast tomorrow I'll take your photos there as it's got white painted walls. I'll have them for you ready shortly after."

Having dealt with the business in hand and it being late, John dismissed the men after thanking them for their efforts. He took himself off to bed feeling satisfied that everything was going to plan, but with the pressing knowledge that his first delivery would be made at the end of the following week and would have to be concealed that night. All that remained at this stage was to make sure this Justin Parkes was brought into line. He didn't like showing his face unnecessarily for obvious reasons of security, but knew it was essential he had to personally make contact with him as he was unable to trust the others to work on Parkes with an offer which he would find too tempting to reject. He prepared himself for bed and, after observing his requirements of prayer, reminded himself to take £1000 out of the strong box ready for his meeting, all being well, with Justin Parkes the following day. Satisfied that nothing had been overlooked, John climbed into bed and within minutes had fallen into a deep uninterrupted sleep, with the knowledge that he was not rostered to be on watch that night.

The following morning, after his ablutions and prayers, he remembered to take the money he needed from the strong box with the hope that somewhere in the farmhouse there was a suitably sized envelope in which he could put it. Downstairs in the kitchen he found breakfast was under way with, this morning, a very competent Mike dishing out the eggs, mushrooms, fried bread, beans and tomatoes as the duty cook for the day. After they all had finished eating, Charlie and Ginger went off to have their photographs taken with John following them into the IT room to have a look at Justin Parkes' e-mails which had been printed off and put in a neat pile in the tray as requested. Scanning through them revealed that Parkes had been commissioned to re-open a grave at Church Stretton for a ten o'clock burial for the following day. John, thought carefully. It was unlikely, he calculated, that there would be enough time to do the work in the morning, so he must be digging it out today. But when.

He tapped Woody on the shoulder. "I want to know where Parkes' van is now. What's the tracker showing?"

Nothing at the moment," replied Woody as he pointed to the screen. "The tracker has a motion sensor fitted and switches off completely when the vehicle has been stationary for forty-five minutes, though I can change that if you want. It only activates when it's moving so as to save the battery. So I would say he hasn't left the flat at this point. But I looked at his e-mails and I think he'll be setting off at some time today to dig out a grave at Church Stretton."

"Just what I thought. Let me know as soon as he's mobile." He looked round for Chalky.

"Right there you are. I intend to go to this place called Church Stretton today. I noticed a sat-nav in the BMW and I want you to put in the post code for the church there. Meanwhile, Charlie, as soon as you've got your identification sorted out with Woody, get going with Ginger and get that flat bugged. Don't forget to carry a bag of tools and, if you haven't got any here, go somewhere and get yourselves a pair of overalls apiece. Right, gentlemen, it's the waiting game until Mr Parkes decided to get going. By the way, is there a large envelope here I can have?"

After a suitable envelope had been found for him, John had not long to wait until a call came from Woody to say their target was mobile. Swiftly, John, instructed Charlie to get moving and not to forget the overalls, whilst he went outside to the BMW which was parked by the back door ready for his departure. Punching *start* into the satnav, John drove slowly down the rutted track to the main road where he turned left towards Shrewsbury. Once on the A5 bypass which loops to the south of the town, he drove the short distance in light traffic until the voice of the satnav told him to take the next left onto the A49, when it informed him that it was thirteen miles to his destination. After an uneventful journey, John drove into the sleepy village, where he saw almost immediately the church on his left with its burial ground alongside. At the far end of the boundary wall was a small track into which John reversed his car. A little further down the track he saw a red van parked by the lytch-gate which he assumed belonged to the man he wanted to talk with.

John was about to step out of his car when a man appeared from out of the gate which led into the church yard and went to the parked van. John watched in his interior mirror as the man opened the rear doors and took out a crowbar and a shovel and, closing the doors after him, carried them back the way he had come. Satisfied he had the right man and it was Justin Parkes, John left his car and walked slowly up the track to the gate. Before going through it he saw a small hatchback drive into the lane which looked like a Volkswagen Golf or Polo. As he walked through the gate and into the burial ground a young woman entered the graveyard, walked to a headstone behind him and, bending over tidied up what looked like plastic flowers which straggled out of a small urn placed in front of it. Looking over to the other side of the cemetery he saw that Justin had put down his tools by the side of a partly opened grave and had jumped down into it before picking up the pickaxe and, with an easy but powerful action, started to break up the compacted soil at the bottom of the grave.

Before approaching the grave, John looked carefully around the area but could see only the young lady with her back to him tending the grave. As nothing aroused his suspicions, he walked over to the man in the grave and spoke to the top of his head.

Good Morning." He waited until the man had straightened up and returned his greeting. ""Justin, it's nice to talk at last."

CHAPTER 8

Tonight Justin was determined to have a good time. It was his forty-third birthday and he knew he would have an evening to remember with Maggie, and his two friends Caesar and Lynn, as they celebrated at the Mytton and Mermaid over many drinks and high dining. The Mytton and Mermaid Hotel is situated on the banks of the River Severn at Atcham a few miles east of Shrewsbury and opposite the imposing gated entrance to the grand pile of Attingham Hall. Justin had chosen this venue for the excellence of its reviews as a high quality dining experience and in this he was not to be disappointed.

They all travelled together in Caesar's Volvo, and once settled with their first drinks, and knowing Caesar's unique sense of humour, Justin was ready for the presents he would receive from him and which, as usual each year, became more outrageous.

Seated comfortably in the lounge, Caesar handed over two packages to Justin. "There you are, me old stallion. I realise the passing of time has not been kind to you so I scoured the bazaars of the world to find what a fading soul like yourself needs. Go on. Open them."

Justin shook his head and gave a resigned smile. "My dear Caesar, I can't wait to see what mysteries lie inside." He stripped the wrapping off the first one to reveal a bottle of Wincarnis Tonic Wine. "My, just what I need. I'll leave it for now as it's before nine o'clock and I still have some strength left"

Exactly," boomed Caesar, "I knew you'd eventually appreciate its necessity. I've been concerned that you have been looking a tad peaky of late, so I know you'll like the next present."

Gingerly, Justin removed the wrapping from a box and extracted a box which was a spoof on the product Philostan which made the claim that it *fortified the over forties*. Only this was labelled Philostand which claimed it provided a powerful aid to a flagging sex life.

"Charming, you old dog," he said shaking his head sadly, "I should have known it would be you who drags the evening down to raw procreation. Anyway," he added, "I most certainly don't need any assistance in that department."

Lynn rolled her eyes at Maggie. "Too much

detail! I had hoped that by now our man-boys would have grown up, but it seems I'm mistaken. Now, Justin, here's a real present for you."

She handed over a neatly wrapped package which Justin opened to find a photo in an ornate frame showing the four of them enjoying themselves during the ceilidh at the Bromyard Folk Festival.

Justin was delighted. "Well I never did," he said in astonishment, "how did you get this taken? I don't remember being set up for a photograph."

Caesar laughed. "You wouldn't. I asked Ken from the folk club to take my digital camera and take lots of snaps whenever he could. He snapped away mightily all evening and Lynn chose the best out of some very iffy attempts. I can see you like it."

"Yes I certainly do, and quite a surprise as well. Thanks." He turned as Maggie passed him her gift and took from her a long narrow package. "Ta, Maggie. Now what have we got here."

Justin carefully removed the fancy wrapping paper and opened the box inside to discover a bracelet watch. "Just what I need. The watch I've got has been losing time even with a new battery, and I keep meaning to buy another but never got round to it." He leaned over and gave Maggie a kiss as he took off the watch he was wearing. "Thanks love, I'm going to put it on now."

"Glad you like it," said Maggie, "I remember you told me your watch had run out of time, so to speak. You can wear this one for work as it's waterproof, shockproof and even alpha-male proof," she grinned. Just then a waitress came over to tell them their table was ready and, as they made their way into the dining room.

Justin laughed as Maggie whispered in his ear, "and make sure you take plenty of that Philostand when we get back home tonight!"

The rest of the evening was filled with delicious food, fine wine and much laughter as the four friends chattered away until the coffee was brought to the table. Lynn announced that she was going to visit her parents over the weekend and couldn't make the Castle on Friday, but Caesar would be there as he had a backlog of work to clear before Monday and couldn't go with her, but teased she was sure they would manage without her.

Later, Maggie insisted she'd settle the bill as the evening was on her. After much good-natured arguing from Caesar, it was finally decided that he and Maggie would split the bill so it was a joint treat for Justin on his birthday. With this resolved, and in high spirits, they all clambered into the Volvo for the short journey back to Shrewsbury where Justin and Maggie were dropped off at their flat, and with loud *good nights* the four friends took leave of each other with Caesar, as he drove off, reminding Justin to take his tonic wine before retiring.

The following morning, with both she and Justin nursing a hangover, Maggie realised that she had missed a text the previous evening. She saw it was from her section head telling her to attend a security meeting in London at nine o'clock that Saturday. Knowing this meant she would have to travel down the night before, Maggie made the excuse to Justin over breakfast that she wouldn't be able to make the usual Friday meeting at the Castle, claiming she had to visit her parents as she'd received a text from her sister to tell her that her father had fallen and damaged his leg. Obviously she wanted to be sure that her mother could cope looking after him, and she hoped he wouldn't mind if she set off on Friday afternoon, but would be back on Sunday evening if all was well. Justin assured it was no problem at all and asked her to pass on to her father his best wishes for a speedy recovery and teased he was sure that he would be able to cope without her. Maggie quickly packed an overnight case and, giving Justin a kiss and a long embrace, set off for her meeting in London. Justin meanwhile had some time on his hands as his first job was to fill in after an eleven o'clock interment at Montford Bridge.

Later, during the drive to Montford Bridge, Justin pondered on his predicament. He knew that he was in thrall to a ruthless man and possibly an equally ruthless organisation and he found the strain of keeping his knowledge secret an overwhelming strain. All he wanted to do was to share his problems with someone else in the hope that a way could be found to extricate himself from this mess he had got himself into. Finally, after much agonising, he decided that despite John's threats he would talk to Caesar and ask for his advice. He trusted him as, despite all the insults they threw at each other, they had a warm friendship. He knew that Caesar's heart was in the right place and he possessed a sound common sense and could be serious when it was necessary.

Justin resolved to phone Caesar and suggest that as the girls were both away on Friday, that he dropped round at the flat as he wanted to discuss an important matter. As soon as he drew to a halt at the churchyard, Justin put a call through to Caesar who readily agreed to meeting at the flat for a change and assured Justin that he would come well supplied with cans of the falling-down liquid as he called them, but it would be some time after eight as he was up to his eyeball in work which he had to finish before he could enjoy himself.

Greatly relieved after his conversation with his friend, Justin completed his work on the grave and drove back buoyed up with the hope that his friend would be able to offer him a way out of his nightmare.

Parking his van at the supermarket, he went in to buy some groceries and a six pack of lager before returning to his flat where he was relieved to find no welcome from old Mrs. Williams whom, he imagined with relief, was probably having her lunch. Feeling hungry, and as he couldn't be bothered to cook anything, Justin made himself a ham and lettuce sandwich which he washed down a can of lager. Despite the relief of knowing that he would be able to unburden himself to Caesar, he felt the hollow void of fear as he was once again forced to face the reality of the terrible dilemma in which he found himself. However hard he tried, he was unable for any length of time to forget that he was caught up in something which he was unable to control or comprehend and which he wondered, if at the end of this arrangement with this John character, he would be allowed to remain alive as a witness to these strange and worrying events.

Suddenly, possibly after the relief of knowing that Caesar would be round later and he could unload his problems, Justin felt very tired and going into the bedroom, he pulled the duvet over him without undressing and very quickly fell into a troubled sleep where his recurring nightmare came back to torment him. Again, as he tried to run as through through treacle, John his pursuer was able to sprint after him. As usual, just before the horror of being caught, he awoke sweating in the darkened bedroom with his heart racing and filling with a feeling of horrible dread. Switching on the light, he looked at his watch and saw with surprise that it was seven o'clock and that he had slept for five hours of unrefreshing slumber.

Rising from the bed, Justin stripped off his work clothes and walked to the bathroom where he stood under the hot shower jet until he had washed the sleep from his eyes and he felt he was awake and ready to open up his soul to his friend. Once he had dried himself and dressed in clean casual clothes, he went to the kitchen and prepared a large plate of different cheeses with rye biscuits with a jar of ploughman's pickle, which he placed on the coffee table in the sitting room ready for the time when the beer consumption had reached the level when a raging hunger would overtake them later in the evening. He had only just finished setting everything up, when there came the sound of a heavy tread coming up the stairs followed by a thunderous knocking on the door. Good old Caesar, thought Justin, everyone else can use the bell push but not him. He was reminded of Brain Blessed, the actor who conducted himself on a decibel level which most people found damaging to their thought processes, to whom Caesar bore a striking resemblance and who closely copied his approach to life that that if something is worth doing, it's worth doing loudly!

Justin grinned as he opened the door to reveal the barrel-chested shape of his friend who waved two four packs of lager in the air.

“Greetings, dear friend,” he boomed through his thick beard, “I've brought a small offering to help the conversation along. Although, I know it's not strictly necessary as we usually can't stop yacking.” Justin took the proffered cans as Caesar rubbed his hands together and blew on them. “Blimey, it's as cold as a politician's heart out there. Nice and warm in here though.”

Taking Caesar's coat Justin hung it on one of the hooks which lined the wall by the front door. “And a warm welcome to you, me old mucker. First things first though, I'll open up some cans of this nectar just to get the ball rolling.”

After pouring two of the cans into tankards and putting the remaining cans in the fridge, Justin took the drinks through to the sitting room where Caesar had made himself comfortable in one of the armchairs. He passed a drink to his friend and felt a great sense of relief course through his body with the knowledge that he would at last be able to unload some of the burden he carried onto Caesar's broad shoulders. Despite his invariable ribbing, Justin knew that he was a person who possessed a great deal of sound common sense and that, when occasion demanded, he would shed his jokey front and be deadly serious.

Caesar, on the other hand, knew better than to force things and waited patiently as they exchanged small talk until Justin felt ready to unburden himself. Once the tankards had been filled a second time, and they had helped themselves to cheese and biscuits, Justin leaned forward in his seat and took a deep breath.

"Caesar, I've got to talk to you. I don't quite know how to put it but I think I'm in deep trouble and I can't find a way out. I really need your advice."

"I'm glad you've decided to open up, Justin," said Caesar with concern in his voice. He looked sympathetically at his friend. "For some time now Lynn and I have been very worried about you. We knew something was troubling you, but when we asked if everything was okay you said all was well with you. We suspected that it wasn't but we couldn't press you, even as friends, as it really wasn't our business to pry into your private affairs. Anyway, take your time. I'm all ears." He stopped and waited patiently for Justin to continue.

"Well it started like this. A little while back I was digging a grave at Church Stretton when this well-dressed bloke approached me and said he had a business proposition he wanted to put to me. To put it in a nutshell, he wanted to tell him when and where I had dug either a single or re-opened double grave which had to be left open overnight. All I had to do was tell him by e-mail all the details once an undertaker had given them to me, and every time I passed on this information and had dug the grave, he would send me five hundred pounds in used notes. Before he left he bunged me a cool grand in notes as an inducement."

"Ah, now I see" interjected Caesar, "that explains why you were flashing the cash and treating us all to a weekend at Bromyard. Not to mention all the expensive motorbike gear you bought. Have to say though, I can't get a handle on why anyone would want to give you so much money for what appears to be useless information. What do you think this character, what's his name, is up to?"

"He called himself John, that's all. I thought initially he was another undertaker but I couldn't see how the information he wanted could possible assist him in gaining any advantage over any other undertaker. But to my shame, although I thought the whole affair a bit iffy, I let my greed take over at the though of this easy money and eventually agreed to do as John had asked me." Justin shrugged apologetically. "Well, I didn't see any harm in giving him what appeared to be useless information. I mean, it wasn't going to hurt anyone, was it?"

Caesar looked at him with concern as he noted Justin's face had taken on a drawn look. He said nothing as he let Justin continue.

"But then I did something stupid. This John had told me not to interfere in any way. Just carry on digging the graves, giving him the information he wanted and then fill in afterwards. All I had to do was make sure I didn't get nosey until the agreement ceased around the end of December and all would be well. But like an idiot I didn't listen. One night I went out to a single I had dug just to see if there was anything untoward. I had a good look round and, as far as I could see, there was nothing amiss. But what happened next scared me. Once I was back here in the flat, I got a call from this John who told me in no uncertain terms that if I ever stepped out of line again I would be dealt with. He also told me that my computer had been taken over by him and it now has downloads purporting to show me as a pervert with sick child porn on my computer and if I ever disobeyed him again the police will be informed. I've checked my files, and it is there."

"Bloody hell, he does mean business." Caesar though carefully before asking, "tell me, did you notice whether you were followed when you checked out that grave you mentioned."

"No I didn't. Although in truth I didn't think I would be followed, so I wasn't looking out for anything untoward. But it did occur to me after John phoned to give me a warning that perhaps my van had a tracking device fitted. The following day I checked the entire vehicle from end to end and found nothing. In fact, I did wonder if the flat had been bugged but after I went through the entire place with a fine toothed comb, I found nothing here either."

Caesar listened patiently and let Justin pour out his troubles. Once he had finished, spoke in a serious tone. "Justin, my friend, to say what you have told me is outside my experience is a monumental understatement. But for sure you're mixed up in something which has plainly has a criminal element to it. What it is, I don't know and just what you must do is something I need to think about. Tell me, have you tried to trace the sender of your e-mails and texts?"

Justin nodded his head. "I do have an e-mail address which I use to send the details he wants but although he, or one of his cronies, acknowledges receipt I'm blocked from finding the return path. And on the occasions I get a text or a phone call nothing comes up on the screen and again I'm blocked from replying. He must have some very sophisticated communication systems in place."

"Yes, I'm inclined to agree with you. It's plain you are up against a very sinister and dangerous organisation – not just this John bloke - and I agree with you that you are in deep trouble. But what to do?"

Caesar was silent for some moments as he pondered on his friend's dilemma. "Justin, it's clear that something has to be done, but at this time I'm not sure what's the best way forward. Look, let me sleep on it and tomorrow we can get together and I'll put my ideas to you. You can be sure of one thing though, we're in this together and I'll be with you until it's resolved."

At his friend's words, Justin felt the prickle of tears of relief welling up in his eyes, but just managed to contain them as he thanked Caesar for his unstinting support. "Caesar, thank, mate. I knew I could rely on you and I'm sorry to load my problems on you. But I do feel better just talking about them. It's true, isn't it, a problem shared is a problem halved."

"Yes, course it's true. And don't worry about me, alpha male through to me bone marrow. I like sorting out problems and we'll find a resolution for the pickle you've got yourself into. Give me until tomorrow and I'll come up with something. At the moment I'm up to my eyeballs, as you know, with a huge backlog of work. I've loads of deliveries to make, but what I'll do is send you a text some time in the afternoon when I back at the workshop and we can thrash things out then. How does that sound?"

Justin assured him that it was just what he hoped and he'd wait until he heard from him tomorrow. Caesar drained his tankard but shook his head when Justin offered him a refill, telling him that he wanted a clear head and a sound night's sleep in order to come up with a solution by the time they met up. It was with a tremendous sense of relief that Justin bade his friend goodnight and deciding to take himself off to bed shortly afterwards, fell into a deep sleep which this time was untroubled by his recurring nightmare.

But Justin's worst nightmare was yet to come, and this time it would not be in his dreams. Barely ten miles away in his farmhouse base, John had been eavesdropping on the conversation relayed by the listening devices which Justin had failed to find in his flat. John did not waste time on letting his emotions take control, but was filled with an icy determination to act when he heard Justin reveal his part in the operation to his friend Caesar. He knew he had made it plain that if he opened his mouth Justin would suffer the terrible consequences which he had promised. Once he had heard enough, John quietly decided on what steps had to be taken and, after some thought, summoned two of his team to instruct on what he wanted them to do the following day. He made them repeat everything back to him until he was satisfied they understood, before retiring to his bed where he quickly fell into an untroubled sleep satisfied that shortly he would have the situation under control once again.

With the damp late autumn cold of the previous day a distant memory, Saturday dawned to reveal a warm Atlantic front driving before it low clouds, strong winds and heavy rain showers, which sent the weekend shoppers in Shrewsbury scurrying along the crowded pavements with heads down, struggling with their umbrellas as they dodged in and out of the shelter of the shops. Caesar had risen early and was in his workshop by eight o'clock and working hard to clear the backlog of work which had built up over the last few weeks. As he he applied his craft to the task in hand, a part of his thinking was given over to finding a resolution for the disturbing mess Justin had got himself into.

At the same time, Justin had just woken feeling lighter in spirits than he had for a long time. As he lay snugly under his duvet, he heard the thermostatic timer click and the boiler firing up. He decided to afford himself the luxury of waiting in bed until the radiators had warmed the flat, before getting up to shower and make his breakfast. From what Caesar had said, he imagined it would be in the afternoon before he heard from him, so decided to try and dodge the showers and go into town to buy himself a new pair of work boots to replace the ones which were falling apart.

Half an hour later, with the flat now warmed up nicely, he took himself off for a shower and to his surprise he found he was singing a folk song. He wondered how long it was since he had felt relaxed enough to sing and thought that it was far too long. He realised that it was the relief of having Caesar take on the role of the big brother Justin had never had and try to come up with an answer to his problems. Yes, thought Justin, I like this happy feeling.

At precisely fourteen minutes past two that afternoon an emergency switchboard operator took a 999 emergency call. Responding to her prompt, the caller had asked for the police and so she quickly made the connection to the West Mercia control centre, located in a modern building on the Battlefields Business Park on the northern edge of Shrewsbury, where it was picked up by the first available operator.

It was a difficult conversation as the caller insisted on giving the information his way and would not comply with the structured questioning which the call handler was trained to use. Despite repeated requests, the caller refused to give his name or any other details but kept repeating that a serious crime had taken place then terminated the call. With the details logged the call handler called over the Dispatcher for advice on how to action the call and, after a short appraisal of the information, was instructed to pass all the details to the Inspector who was the current Force Duty Officer (FDO) for his decision on the appropriate course of action.

Earlier, Justin, had decided to drive up to

Harlescott to look for a pair of work boots at Charlies Store on Brixton Way. Some months previously he'd bought his work trousers from there and, finding them to be hard wearing and good value for money, was sure he could find suitable footwear there. After arriving at the store and looking over their wide range of working boots, he chose a pair of brown, calf-length boots with a heavy sole which he paid for on his debit card. Feeling hungry he decided to treat himself to an all day breakfast at the Diner by the traffic lights on the Whitchurch Road, before he returned to the flat to relax until he heard from Caesar that afternoon.

Driving back through the lashing rain and driving wind and parking at the supermarket, he remembered his newspaper and some items of groceries which he needed and hurried through the downpour into the welcome shelter and warmth of the store where he quickly selected the items he needed. He then cursed quietly as he realised he had forgotten to bring a shopping bag with him for his purchases. Knowing that he had more than he could carry, he gritted his teeth as the cashier added the cost for the carrier bag to his total, and leaving the store carried his shopping through the wind and rain and across the busy road to his front door. Once inside he checked his mail box and found, amongst the flyers and other junk mail, a familiar envelope with which he put into his inside coat pocket. Then, with a terrible inevitability, the door to old Mrs. William's was flung open and the diminutive figure scuttled over to grab Justin's sleeve and with her little beady eyes boring into his, started to tell him how strange people were coming into the building and they had gone up the stairs to his flat, and she didn't know what they were doing there. Having, heard all this before, and having discounted it as the febrile ramblings of an ancient mind, Justin listen politely and made all the right soothing responses until she had got the problem off her chest and released her grip to allow him to continue up the stairs into the warmth and quiet of his flat. Inside he made himself a mug of tea and settled down with the Daily Express which he had bought whilst he waited expectantly for the call from Caesar. He checked the time on his watch and saw it was 1.55 p.m. just as his mobile rang to tell him he had a text. Opening it up he saw on the screen it was from Caesar and read: *Justin. Free now. Can you come?* Very pleased that things were moving, Justin texted back: *On my way. See you in 10,* before taking his coat of the hook by the front door and making his way with head down against the wind and rain back across Abbey Foregate to his parked van before driving up Monkmoor

Road to Caesar's workshop.

At the same time at Monkmoor Police Station, the FDO had carefully assessed the information which had been passed to him from the Control Centre and made the decision that it warranted an armed response. He put an urgent call through with all the necessary information to the Bronze Commander who logged the call at 2.20p.m., before picking up the direct line to the armed response team who were on permanent standby at Monkmoor police station and instructing the team leader to arm up and wait in their vehicle for further orders. Within fifteen minutes the four firearms officers kitted up, and were sitting waiting in their unmarked SUV in the garage at the side of the station from where they radioed their Bronze Commander to inform him they were ready to move. After a careful appraisal of the information he had been given and a study of the location of the reported crime, the FDO had decided on the tactics to use and passed on his instructions to the Bronze commander who then conveyed them to the armed response team. He briefed them that a call had been received reporting that an armed man had entered unit 24 on the Monkmoor Industrial Estate and shot the proprietor and that the armed man was still on the premises. The name of the gunman had been given as Justin

Parkes along with his van registration, before the caller rang off.

With his wipers on fast speed barely clearing the wind-driven rain that lashed the windscreen, Justin drove carefully up Monkmoor road with his headlights on dipped beam, past the police station and ahead over the roundabout into the industrial estate where Caesar had his unit. At the entrance to the estate Justin didn't give a second glance at a Toyota saloon parked at the roadside with two men inside who watched him park up and draw up along side Caesar's Volvo at the front. Running through the pouring rain to the side door, Justin stepped into the welcome shelter of the workshop. As he did so the saloon with the two men inside, following the instructions which John had given them, turned round in the road and drove the short distance to a row of shops in the adjacent housing estate where one of them went into the public phone box next to the newsagents and dialled the emergency number. The time was exactly fourteen minutes past two.

Closing the door behind him with difficulty against the pressure of the wind, and looking round the workshop, Justin was puzzled to see no sign of Caesar. He called his name over the noise of the storm outside but with no response. He wondered if he had been called away suddenly and had forgotten to tell him, then realised he couldn't have been as his car was parked outside. As he pondered, he walked around the large workbench and with a sudden shock saw a pair of legs protruding from the end. He ran forward to see the body of Caesar lying on his back where he had been hidden from view. Justin's first thought was that his friend had knocked himself out or perhaps he was ill and fainted, but as he bent over his inert body he saw with horror that a large hunting knife with blood around the blade had been placed on his chest. Under it, over his heart, was a dark red stain which had spread over his dust coat.

In shock, Justin hesitated as he wondered what he should do next. Then he remembered having seen on television chest compressions being carried out on an episode of Casualty and knelt down by Caesar's side. He first felt for a pulse on his wrist but couldn't find one and then put his cheek next to Caesar's nose to see if he could detect any breathing. Finding nothing there, he realised that he should first call for an ambulance but realised with horror that he had left his mobile in the van. Then, deciding that he couldn't delay any longer, he picked up the knife and dropped it to one side before locking his fingers together and, placing the heel of his hand on Caesar's breastbone, commencing the chest compressions hoping that, once his heart was restarted, he could make a dash for his phone. As he pressed up and down on Caesar's barrel chest he thought he heard some shouting over the battering of the storm outside but ignored it as he continued the task of trying to revive his friend. But had Justin not been in a state of shock he would have realised that, when he tried for a pulse, Caesar's skin was icy cold and the blood on his coat was congealed and dark after being exposed to the air for some time. In fact Caesar had been killed on John's orders early that morning with the assassins locking the unit until it was time to send the text Justin was expecting. Then unlocking it once he had replied to say he was on his way. All of Justin's efforts were in vain. Caesar had been dead for a long time and that big heart of his would never beat again.

Whilst Justin tried in vain to revive his friend inside, the Bronze commander arrived at the unit with his armed team and employing the tactics given to him by the FDO immediately sent two of his men to cover the rear of the unit who were each armed with highly effective Heckler and Koch 5.56mm carbine with a thirty round magazine. The firearms unit usually made every effort not to use their two-tone horns and flashing blue lights – known to them as *blues and twos,* if at all possible

- so that they could arrive without alerting any villains to their presence. In fact the drive from the Police station to Caesar's unit was so short that they never got beyond third gear. With his two men confirming on their personal radios that they were in place, the Bronze commander checked that the approach road had been blocked at both ends by marked patrol cars and waited until a uniformed constable had confirmed he had told everyone in the adjacent units to stay inside away from the windows. He then nodded to his sergeant and constable, who had drawn their Glock 9mm pistols, and crouched down behind the SUV which had been parked across the front of the unit. By this time the rain had stopped except for brief flurries, but the wind had increased in strength until it rocked the cars on their suspension and howled around the buildings. The commander, deciding that his voice wouldn't carry over the wind noise and through the closed door, with difficulty opened the passenger door of his unmarked car and took out a loud hailer. Switching it on he checked the battery level readout and put it to his mouth.

"Justin Parkes, we know you are in there." The Commander's amplified voice boomed out above the howling of the wind and bounced back from the unit's façade. " We know you are in there. We want you to come to the door with your hands up. Do you understand?"

With the noise of the wind buffeting the building and rattling the cladding on the unit, Justin had difficulty in hearing what was being said but, despite still in a state of shock, he knew that he must get help and decided that he had to get to his van in order to retrieve his mobile and call for an ambulance. He opened the door, which slammed against the front of the building as it was ripped out of his hands with the force of the wind, to be confronted by a bright searchlight probing through the gloom beyond which he could vaguely make out the outline of two vehicles, one of them with police markings. Before he could go any further a tinny voice boomed out.

"Armed police. Put your hands above your head. Do not make any sudden movements. Do not move until you are told to." Without taking his eyes off Justin, the commander then shouted above the roar of the wind. "All officers on aim."

Justin stood in open mouthed bewilderment and shouted back. "There's a wounded man in there. He needs an ambulance."

His plea was ignored as the loud speaker blared. "Walk slowly towards me. Do it now until I tell you to stop. Keep walking. Now stop. Kneel down. Now lie face down with your arms out."

Justin, in a state of disbelief, had no option but to do as instructed and lay down on the wet ground with arms outspread as constable walked over and swiftly pulled his arms behind him before clicked a pair of manacles round his wrists. He pressed the lock buttons to secure them before pulling Justin roughly to his feet and expertly patted him down for any hidden weapons as the sergeant and Commander walked over to their detainee. Whilst this was going on the two officers who were covering the rear had been recalled and told to check the building. Within a few minutes they came out and with a shake of the head one of them reported to the Bronze commander that there was one deceased male inside but no sign of a firearm, only a knife. The Commander looked directly at Justin, raising his voice over the howl of the wind.

"I'm arresting you on suspicion of murder. You do not have to say anything but it may harm your defence if you do not mention when questioned something which you may later rely on in court. Do you understand?"

Without waiting for Justin to reply the commander waved over the two uniformed constables from the patrol car and told him to get the prisoner booked into custody. Justin felt his arms gripped as he was led, buffeted by the storm, and put into the back of the car for the short drive to the custody suite at Monkmoor police station. In the back of the car his vision started to swim and he thought he was going to vomit as the shock and horror of his situation started to sink in. Just managing to hold on, he was aware that a minute later, the driver turned into the station entrance, drove to the rear of the building before pulling up in front of a tall roller shutter door. Lowering his window he pressed a button on an intercom box fixed to a post and, after a short exchange, the shutter began to raise letting the vehicle drive into a brightly-lit enclosed bay. The two officers waited until the shutter had rolled down before taking Justin from the back of the patrol car and leading him up a sloping ramp to the outer door of the custody suite, where one of them pressed a button which allowed them into a holding room. Once the outer door had closed the inner door opened and Justin was led up to the counter behind which a female sergeant sat waiting to begin the booking-in process. Justin stood mutely wondering whether he would have the strength to remain upright with his legs trembled weakly as the full horror and hopelessness of his situation hit him like a hammer blow.

A short after Justin's arrest, the two men in the Toyota saloon parked by the telephone box watched the unfolding drama until they had seen Justin being put into the back of the police car. They then waited patiently until the police re-opened the road and, satisfied that they had carried out their task to the letter, headed back to the safe house to report to John that his plan had worked and Justin had been arrested.

CHAPTER 9

The female custody sergeant, who faced Justin from across the chest high desk which separated them, was a slim officer in her mid-thirties with her blonde hair drawn tightly back in a pony tail, exhibiting a brisk, no-nonsense manner. She introduced herself then asked one of the constables who had brought him in to explain the reasons for his arrest. On the keyboard in front of her she efficiently typed in his response, before looking at Justin and asking him if he understood the reasons why he had been arrested.

Even in his bemused state, he realised that this was not the time to start protesting his innocence, and so nodded dumbly and said he did. She asked the constable if he had been any trouble when arrested and, when told that he had been fully compliant, told him to remove the handcuffs. With his arms now free, Justin was told to take off his coat and remove his trouser belt and shoes, empty his pockets and put everything on the counter where it was checked. The sergeant turned to a detention officer who stood behind her and told him to carry out a body search whilst she logged Justin's personal belongings. The detention officer walked round to the front, told Justin to put his hands on the counter as he asked whether he had any sharps on him, or anything which may harm him and, upon being told no, commenced a thorough body search which even included his hair, inside of his mouth and the soles of his feet. The search was concluded with a hand-held metal detector called a wand which was run over his entire body to discover if there were any metal items secreted about his person. Apart from it sounding when passed over his trouser zip, the scan was clear and the detention officer told the sergeant that he was clean.

With this procedure completed, the sergeant ran through a further fifteen minutes of questions prompted by the booking-in system before she told Justin that he had the right to legal representation. He could use the duty solicitor, a lawyer of his choice or, if he wished, he could leave the decision until later. Justin felt that he would like his confused thinking to regain a better level of clarity before making a decision and told her that he would leave it until he had made up his mind. The sergeant logged his response into the system before telling the officers to take him to cell 12 and give him a blanket and pillow. She then gave him the unwelcome information that as it was a weekend he would be held in custody until Monday before he could be interviewed and put before a court.

Justin was taken from the reception counter a short distance along a corridor and told to go into the cell indicated by the detention officer. Inside, he stood mutely until the cell door shut behind him with a heavy thud and, with one last glance at his charge, the detention officer slid shut the inspection hatch in the door, leaving Justin to slump onto the mattress on the sleeping platform with a regulation issue of a rip-proof blanket and pillow by his side where he sat still in a state of shock until he started to feel more in control of himself.

Now feeling slightly more focused, Justin thought he might as well explore his new quarters. He measured the cell and found it to be three and a half paces long and two and a half paces wide, with a partitioned lavatory in the corner by the door and with a small wash basin set into the partition with a timer button which, he discovered, controlled the water flow. He noted that the walls were coloured a light blue with a speckled finish, with the only natural light coming from a window set high up on the outside wall which was made up from small thick frosted panes. But, with the heavy storm clouds outside and the onset of winter darkness, the ceiling light high above was switched on to dispel the gloom and illuminate every corner of his cell.

He sat down again, looking bleakly round his new accommodation and trying to take in all that had happened to him since waking up with a light heart that morning. With a sick sensation, his thoughts turned to the death of his dear friend and a shudder ran through his body as the picture seared into his soul of the shocking image of Caesar's bloody dead body and his vain attempts to try to bring life back into what he knew to be a corpse. Now, arrested for a murder of which he was totally innocent, he had lost not only the only true friend and confidant he had ever had, but he now had lost his liberty and was going to be put in front of a judge and jury at some stage to be tried for something he hadn't done. Justin's vivid imagination took him on a nightmare journey where he recalled the instances of miscarriages of justice, where innocent people had been framed for crimes committed by others, and spent decades in prison before, like the Birmingham Six, being cleared and released. With a sudden shock he recalled how he had pulled the knife from Caesar's chest and which now had his fingerprints on the handle. He now understood the feeling of helplessness which incarceration produced, and the impotence which it generated knowing that he was powerless to change anything whilst the judicial system exercised its slow and inexorable control over him.

Justin put his head in his hands and groaned as he remembered he hadn't thought to ask if he could tell Maggie of his plight. Although she wasn't due back until Sunday evening, he felt she should be told what had happen to him and wondered what he should do. As he thought of banging on the cell door for attention, he noticed that there was what looked like an intercom system let into the wall by the cell door. Just as he stood up and walked over to it, the hatch dropped down and one of the detention officers asked whether Justin would like an evening meal. To his astonishment he was given a choice of three microwaved meals and a choice to drink of tea, coffee, hot chocolate or water, although the kindly detention officer informed that the tea was undrinkable, the coffee only slightly better but the chocolate was very nice. The chatty officer told him that usually the meals would come from the staff canteen upstairs but as it closed Friday afternoons for the weekend the detention officers used the ready-made meals instead. Despite his depressed spirits, Justin found the officer's cheerful demeanour gave him some relief from the circumstances which oppressed him and told him he would have the shepherds pie and a chocolate drink. He asked if he could make a phone call to his partner but was told that nothing could be done at present as the meal routine was a priority, but although his request would be put to the sergeant later Justin had to remember that it was a Friday night and they would likely be very busy from now, as they knew from past experience, until the early hours of the morning. Still, he promised, he would do what he could but told Justin not to hold his breath as the drunks were already being brought into custody.

Some twenty minutes later the hatch dropped to reveal the face of another detention officer who passed through the polystyrene box containing Justin's meal along with a plastic eating implement combining a spoon and fork with a cutting edge, which he informed Justin was called a spork, with the added surprise of a chocolate bar and, with a cheery *enjoy,* slid the hatch closed leaving him to explore his first meal in custody. Although the nauseous feeling persisted in his stomach and he didn't feel particularly hungry, Justin felt he should keep up his strength. He determinedly worked his way through his shepherds pie consisting of a thin covering of greyish mashed potato over some small pieces of meat swimming weakly in a thin gravy. It being a small helping he managed to finish it all before drinking his hot chocolate, which he found to be very good, and finally savouring his unexpected chocolate bar. As he was eating his meal, he noticed that the cover over the small spy-hole in the cell door was slid to one side and an eye appeared which looked around the cell before the spy-hole cover was swung back. His watch having been taken from him when he was booked in he was not to know that low risk detainees had to be checked on every hour and that this procedure had to be followed by law, day and night, with the observations recorded on the computer programme of custody records.

Once he had finished his unappetising meal, and as the shock and adrenalin levels subsided in him, Justin feeling sleepy decided he would lie down when hopefully his over-active mind would quieten down and allow him to get some much needed sleep. He pulled the blanket over him and tried to find a comfortable way of using the unyielding pillow with its thick plastic cover. Eventually, he managed to cover it with some of the blanket so that he didn't have to put his face on the sweaty plastic and, after some moments found his eyes becoming heavy as he began to drift off. But his repose was short-lived as, before he could fall asleep, the hatch dropped down with a clang and he was asked by one of the detention officers to hand over the used meal containers, who then informed him that his next call would be for breakfast so he might as well get his head down until then. Before the hatch slammed shut, Justin reminded him that he had been promised a phone call, only to be told that they were too busy booking people in to be able to bring him out to make it, but things usually quietened down at about three in the morning and if he was awake they would see to it then.

As it happened Justin was not able to make his phone call as the entire night in custody was a cacophony of shouting and cursing from drunks locked in their cells, screams and howls from the detainees who were overdosed on drugs and out of their minds, the constant slamming of cell doors, and the ringing of the telephones which served as a constant reminder of the call he was unable to make. Sleep was also made more difficult by the fact that the cell light, although switched to a low level, remained on throughout the night so that the detention officers who carried out the cell checks were able to see whether or not their charges were giving cause for concern.

Eventually, although he was unsure of the time, the custody block did achieve some sort of peace, in what Justin believed to be the early hours of the morning, and allowed him to fall into a fitful sleep until he awoke a few hours later to find a thin grey light coming in through the rain-spattered window panes. He judged the time to be around seven o'clock but couldn't be sure. Now he desperately needed to use the toilet but found there was no toilet paper to be seen. He was not to know that toilet paper was never left in the cells after a disturbed and vulnerable detainee had been found on the brink of death with a large wad of toilet tissue stuffed down her throat after a failed suicide attempt. Justin pressed the intercom button and, after a short delay, a voice asked what he wanted. He explained his pressing need and was told that someone would be with him straight away. Within a minute the hatch dropped as several sheets of toilet paper were passed to him by a new female detention officer, who Justin thought would probably be from the morning shift. She asked if he wanted breakfast which was a choice of cereals and the usual drinks. Needing to get rid of her with some urgency, Justin quickly chose cornflakes and hot chocolate as the detention officer closed the hatch leaving him to deal with more pressing matters.

Shortly after, as he waited for his food, Justin washed his hands and face at the little basin and, in the absence of a towel, used a corner of his blanket until they were dry. Feeling more like his normal self, he sat on the mattress as he attempted to take stock of his situation. Although his booking in was a bit of a blur, he did recall that the custody sergeant who dealt with him had said that it would not be until Monday that he'd be interviewed. This being so, he reasoned, he was in for a long boring time as the hours drifted by in his solitary confinement. He wondered whether it was possible to ask for some reading material and, more importantly, be allowed to make his call to Maggie, but decided he would wait until his breakfast came before asking the detention officer. When eventually the hatch dropped another new face from the morning shift, this time male, appeared in the aperture and with a friendly *Good Morning* passed Justin another polystyrene box containing corn flakes slopping around in milk, a small sachet of sugar, a spork and a cup of hot chocolate. Thanking him, Justin asked about his phone call and could he have some reading material as well. With a cheery smile, the detention officer promised he'd drop off some magazines later and would ask the sergeant if he could make his call, but Justin had to remember that they were processing as many of the detainees they could to get them out of custody quickly so the cells could be cleaned ready for the next batch of wrongdoers.

It was not long after finishing his cereal that the cell door was opened, and the detention officer who had brought his breakfast informed him that it was his turn to be finger printed and his mug shot taken. Justin was walked in his stockinged feet the short distance back to reception and into a small open side room where he was seated in a corner opposite a camera mounted on an arm fixed to the wall. The detention officer wrote on a white board which Justin saw displayed his name, date of birth and a reference number before he was told to hold it across his chest whilst his photograph was taken. Next the officer pulled on a pair of latex gloves and taking a small screw-topped container extracted a cotton swab on a stick. He explained that it was a legal requirement that Justin provided a DNA sample and that he needed Justin to open his mouth whilst he wiped the swab inside his cheeks. Once he had carefully run the swab round his mouth, the detention officer replaced it in its container and sealed it in a large envelope on which were written Justin's details. Next the officer went over to a computer and opening up a page, started to ask Justin a comprehensive range of questions to which his answers were all carefully entered before he signed off. Justin was then told to follow him into an adjoining side room which contained a large machine with a display screen fixed to the top. It was then explained to him that this was called a Livescan and it took fingerprints electronically so that there was no need to use the wet print system where each finger was inked and the print transferred onto a card. Despite his predicament, Justin was intrigued as the officer, with an ease born of familiarity with the process, took each of Justin's fingers in turn and rolled then over a small glass plate set into the top of the unit and watched as his print came up on the large screen fixed to the top. Once the officer was satisfied, he pressed his foot on the accept button on the floor and continued onto the next finger until, with all prints taken, he finished by pressing both palms down onto the plate to complete the process.

With a *that's it chum,* the officer told Justin that he would be taken back to his cell and that he hadn't forgotten his magazines and would drop them off shortly. He said he also hadn't forgotten his telephone call but pointed out that both custody sergeants were busy trying to clear as many detainees as possible and he couldn't ask now as the phone was on the desk where the other detainees were being processed. Doubting that he would ever be able to tell Maggie of his plight, Justin was taken back to his cell and the door slammed shut with a thud that he found unsettling. However, the detention officer was true to his word and just a few minutes later the hatch opened and, much to Justin's gratification, two magazines were passed through to him. His keen anticipation of some interesting reading soon evaporated when he saw that he had been given a year old copy of the Farmers Weekly and Golf News which, dated March, was at least relatively current. Well, Justin said ruefully to himself, at least it's something to read and who knows, I might actually learn something. He made himself comfortable on the mattress and propped himself upright by placing the pillow he had been given against the wall, before settling down to read the farming magazine, which to his surprise he found interesting as he had never given much thought as to how the food on his plate was produced. As he read the poor night's sleep started to catch up with him and before long his eyes grew heavy, his head fell forward and he fell into a deep sleep.

He was woken with a start as his name was called out and, with difficulty, opened his eyes to see the cell door open and a detention officer outlined in the aperture.

“Mr. Parkes, you're for interview now.” He

thrust a pair of grey canvas slip-on pumps at Justin. “Here, you'd better put these on. They should fit as I got your the size from your shoes you came in with.”

As Justin put them on he looked up puzzled. “I thought the Sergeant told me I wasn't going to be interviewed until Monday?”

The detention officer shook his head. “Don't know about that, I wasn't on that shift. I've been told to take you for interview. I'm sure it'll all be explained to you when you get there.”

So saying, he led Justin past the cells in his corridor, some now with their doors open after the detainees they contained had been released, to another door which led into a long carpeted corridor lined both sides with doors above each of which was a large unlit red globe. Once the door to the custody reception had closed behind them, all the noise and bustle from there was magically silenced as Justin and his escort walked to a door above which was an illuminated sign saying *Interview in Progress*. The detention officer knocked briefly on the door and pushing it open beckoned him forward announced as he announced to the occupants that he had brought Mr. Justin Parkes for interview.

As Justin walked in he saw a small desk behind which a large man with a florid face sitting in a chair. He was just able to see over the edge of the desk he was wearing dark blue trousers, with a matching jacket which hung over the back of his chair, revealing a somewhat overweight person, wearing a white shirt with and striped tie. His rounded face wore an expression which was neither friendly nor unfriendly as he looked keenly at the worried looking detainee before him. As Justin took in his new surroundings, he became aware that there was another person in the room who had been initially hidden behind the door when he entered. As the big man started to stand up, Justin turned to look at the other person and as he did so his mouth opened in total surprise, coupled with enormous relief. It was Maggie.

"Maggie," Justin stuttered once he had collected his senses, "I thought you were in London. How did you find out? I tried to phone you but they wouldn't let me. Maggie I'm in deep trouble, and I don't know what's going on." He took a pace towards her and held her in his arms whilst she returned the embrace. Before she could answer the large man interrupted with a smile.

"Right, I'm going to have to call this meeting to order." He extended his hand towards Justin. "May I introduce myself. I'm Marcus Baxendale and I'm a commander in the Metropolitan

Police Anti-terrorist unit and Maggie is part of my team. By the way, please call me Marcus."

Justin tentatively shook the proffered hand and sat in the chair on his side of the desk which the Commander had indicated. If he found his predicament puzzling before, he was now utterly bewildered at this turn of events,

"But I don't get it," he said switching his gaze between them, "What do you mean, Maggie's in your team? He turned to Maggie in bewilderment. "You told me you were a self-employed proof reader. What the bloody hell's going on here, Maggie!"

Before Maggie could answer the commander quickly took control. "Justin, I can understand your confusion and frustration but nothing will be achieved if you get excited. If you'll calm down I'll explain everything to you. But you must be patient as there's a lot to cover and I have to deal with matters which are both complex and of the highest security level. You ask what's going on, and I'll tell you. You have, in short, been unwittingly been caught up in a national, and possibly an international terrorist operation. We have been aware for some time that a terrorist cell is operating in the UK and that you have innocently been used to further their aims."

He paused and gestured over towards Maggie before continuing. “Maggie is an undercover surveillance officer with the UK Security Services – more precisely MI5 - and she has been detailed to try to discover more of what was being planned by entering the organisation through the only opening we were able to discover.” The commander looked directly at Justin. “That was you, Justin.”

At the Commander words a terrible feeling started to creep over Justin as he was made aware of the implications of what he was hearing. It wasn't the terrorist implications which troubled him most. It was that he could barely believe that the one person in his life to whom he had opened his heart, and with whom he had found a genuine love, was capable of playing a game with him. He felt as though a band had tightened around his chest as he turned to Maggie.

“Am I hearing right. You were just doing your job. You mean that everything that you said about loving me was just a sham. But, but...” he struggled to find the right words, “when I said I'd fallen in love with you you said you loved me as well. You're telling me you were lying all along?”

Maggie had seen the terrible hurt etched on Justin's face at the realisation that he had been used by her. Though a professional through and through, she was not without feelings and felt she had to explain herself.

She turned to the commander. “Sir, may I try to explain things to Justin?” With his nod of assent, she turned back to him. “Justin, love, I'm sorry, truly sorry, that I had to deceive you but there wasn't any other way. I don't take any pleasure in playing a role which I know usually ends in someone being hurt but you were the only lead we had. I had been tasked with locating this person known as John and the only possible opening we had was through you. Do you remember the first time you met John when you were digging a grave at Church Stretton? And do you recall seeing a young woman tidying the flowers on a grave nearby?”

She waited as Justin nodded in numbed silence. “Well, that young woman was me and that was the only time I have seen this John. I had a choice to make, follow him with the possibility he would realise he was under observation, or follow you. I decided that you would be the softer target and tailed you back to your flat. But although I had this John's registration details it led nowhere. After that we lost track of him and we decided that it was only through you that we could find his whereabouts.”

“That's quite correct,” interposed the Commander, “there was a marker put on him shortly after he entered the country, ostensibly as a mature student, because we had information that he was a member of MOIS." He saw Justin's blank look and explained, "MOIS is the name of the Iranian Secret Intelligence Service, but by the time our inefficient Immigration Service had flagged him up to us he was long gone. We trawled the cctv footage from the arrivals cameras at Birmingham airport and saw him and the person who met him, getting into a dark blue BMW 5 series. But the registration had been cloned from another similar vehicle and so we were no further forward.

The commander leaned forward to emphasise his next words. "We tracked the vehicle using the ANPR cameras along the M6 motorway until it left at junction 13 onto the A449. But they were one step ahead of us as the car turned off onto minor roads in Staffordshire where there are no cameras and we lost it. Then we thought we had a trace on him when Maggie brought back his car registration after he'd approached you at the graveyard. But no surprises there. It was also cloned and belonged to a respectable business man with a similar vehicle in Chester." He paused to allow Justin to take in what he was saying before asking, "are you with us so far?"

Justin took a deep breath to try and ease the frustration that we welling up in him. "Yes, as you put it, I'm with you so far. But just putting aside the fact that Maggie and your plan has bloody well broken my heart and destroyed my trust in women, there's the small matter of Caesar's murder. It might have escaped your notice that I'm banged up here charged with his murder – a murder which I can tell you I had no part in. So how much use am I to you now. Tell me that?"

Commander Baxendale leaned back in his chair and spoke in a reassuring tone. "Justin, can I assure you that we know you didn't kill your friend Vincent, or Caesar as you know him, and that you had no part in his death. We know that when he was killed you were just leaving your flat and we tracked you to Charlies Store at Harlescott. We still don't know who killed Caesar but we are sure this John ordered it and we think we know why."

"Let me get this straight," said a perplexed Justin his voice hoarse with strain, "you tracked me, you say. How? Did you follow me, did you have me tailed?"

"No. there was no need as we have put a tracking transmitter in your van which pinpointed its location. I can now tell you that we also planted a voice transmitter in you flat. Remember the clock Maggie put in a prominent position on the wall? It's in there."

Justin started to feel the anger rising in him at the commander's revelation. "Nice one Maggie. So not content with destroying me you bugged my sodding flat." A sudden thought struck Justin. "I've often wondered how this John was able to know where I was, and where I'd been, and how he knew what I had been saying. I checked my flat for any listening devices and just about took my van apart to see if anything had been planted there. But found nothing. How do you explain that?"

"You have to be aware that we are not dealing with lucky amateurs here. This John, whose real name I can reveal is Bahadur Najafi, is an experienced operative and has behind him, we believe, the sophisticated resources of the Iranian state. Believe me, we had difficulty in uncovering these tracking and listening devices but managed to locate two on your van hidden behind the front and rear registration plates, but right inside the bumper assemblies. There were two in your flat - in your bedroom and the sitting room. I won't tell you where they are as they have to remain in place. If they were removed it would give notice that we were onto then. Let me show you this, Justin."

The commander picked up a mobile phone from the desk, which Justin recognised as his, and quickly brought up a text which he held up so that Justin could read the message on the screen. With a lurch in the pit of his stomach, he saw the words – *I told you to keep your mouth shut. Next time it will be you.*

"I think," he said deliberately, "that we can assume that text came from your John. Once he had overheard, as we did, that you'd told Caesar all about the mess you were in we knew this John would be set on revenge. I may add that we have been unable to trace the caller or his location."

"Hang on Baxendale," interrupted Justin as a sickening realisation crept up on him. "You're telling me that you had listened in when I talked with Caesar and you knew that this John was listening in also." The anger which had started to slowly subside now rose up in him with a volcanic intensity as his voice rose "Are you telling me, you murdering bastard, that you knew Caesar was going to be killed and did nothing about it?" Justin's face contorted with rage as he clenched his fists. "That you let a man worth ten of you be slaughtered deliberately. You bloody, shitting scumbag!"

Before the commander could respond Justin, consumed with a berserker rage which made him impervious to pain and reason, launched himself violently across the desk with his fists making heavy contact with the commander's cheek and mouth. Maggie had been closely observing Justin and knew from her police experience that he was about to explode. She had noticed his face becoming flushed, his head lowering into his shoulders, the clenched fists and his fixed stare directed on the commander. The commander had also seen an impending danger but being older than Maggie his reactions were slower and he was unable to avoid the blows from Justin's fists. As soon as Justin launched himself across the desk with a roar of rage, Maggie slapped her hand onto the panic alarm button and, as the deafening wail of the emergency siren screamed around the custody suite and duty sergeant's office in the main building, threw herself across Justin's back attempting to pinion his arms. The interview rooms had been designed, from past experience, to limit the damage an out of control detainee could inflict on his interrogator, and to this end the desk was bolted to the floor and the detainees chair not only immovably fixed but placed close to the desk. These precautions had meant that Justin found it impossible to fully cross the desk but allowed the Commander time to push his chair back to avoid some, but not all, of the punches which Justin threw.

Once the panic alarm had been activated and the siren triggered, the internal doors between custody and the duty room in the body of the police station, automatically opened and latched back to allow all the police officers in there to run to the assistance the custody staff. But before they ran in, the two custody sergeants and one of the detention officers had sprinted round from behind the reception desk and seeing the flashing red light above the door of the interview room, burst in. Very quickly, and with a calm efficiency, the female sergeant pulled Maggie away whilst the male sergeant grabbed the arms of a violently resisting Justin and pulled him through the door, which the detention officer was holding open, and into the corridor. Shouting at him to stop struggling, they kicked his feet from under him and dropped him heavily onto the floor with a force which drove the breath out of his lungs, as all three proceeded to put the violently struggling Justin into a control position with his arms taken into his side and then pulled forward past this head with his hands bent palms facing up. At the same time the Detention officer placed one of Justin's ankles in the crook of the opposite knee and bent the extended leg over it until the his legs were painfully immobilised. Justin struggled impotently until, suddenly he felt the fighting madness drain from him to be replaced by the pain of the holds he was being subjected to. Finally he lay still groaning with the discomfort of the restraint position he was in.

"We'll put him back in his cell until he's calmed down." the female sergeant shouted above the wail of the siren. "Do you want him charged with assault, Sir?"

The commander had walked into the corridor after Justin had been dragged out and stood quietly dabbing at a thin stream of blood which came from a rapidly thickening upper lip. He shook his head as he replied.

"Just hold him there for a minute, Sergeant. I want to have a word with him. Take the pressure off a bit, will you." He looked down at Justin. "Justin, you dope, if you'd given me a minute I could have explained everything, because it's not what you think. If I tell these officer to let you up will you promise to behave yourself." He turned to the officers who had responded to the alarm from the duty room, and had been looking on with interest at the unfolding drama. "I'm taking full control of Mr. Parkes now. We won't be needing you. Thanks for your assistance."

As the officers turned to leave, and he turned back to the prone contorted figure of Justin, the siren suddenly stopped its banshee howl as one of the Detention Officer reset the alarm system. When he heard Justin mumble weakly that he was all right now, the commander told the sergeants to release him and sit him down in the interview room, but could someone bring them some cups tea with sugar in - but not the custody brand. As they waited for the tea, the Commander took stock of the situation. Across the desk sat the subdued figure of Justin who appeared to him to be unmarked, although he knew that the holds he had been subjected to would give him painful joints for a few days. Maggie had her head banged against the desk as she struggled to restrain him, whilst he had come off worst from Justin's flailing fists with an upper lip which had been pierced by a canine tooth and a numb feeling around his right eye socket, which he knew from past experience was the precursor of an impressive shiner. The three of them sat silently for a while as they waited for their breathing to return to normal.

There was a knock on the door and one of the detention officers came in with three mugs on a tray. "Thought you'd need these quickly, Sir, and we've found some biscuits for you" he said casting a wary eye towards Justin. "Is there anything else you need?"

"No, nothing more, and thanks for all your help." He looked at Maggie as the officer left, closing the door silently behind him. "And how's the head?"

"Nothing I haven't had before, thanks, Sir." She probed in her hair. "Bit of a lump forming but nothing serious."

The Commander turned back to Justin who sat with shoulders bowed. “And what about you, Justin. Any damage done?”

Apart from two painful shoulders and an aching right knee, Justin had scraped his shins when he flew across the desk but, looking at the commander's fat lip and a rapidly forming swelling around his eye, didn't feel that this was the right time to list his problems.

“No, no, I'm fine thanks, Marcus. I'm sorry I lost it and I'm truly sorry I hurt you both. It's just that I've been through so much lately.” He took a shuddering breath and released it in a long sigh before continuing. “I'm not a violent man, in fact I try my hardest to avoid confrontation, but when I heard that you had let Caesar be killed I just saw a red mist and, I'm ashamed to say, I actually wanted to kill you. I don't know what came over me. I've never attacked anyone in my life. I really am sorry for the damage I caused.”

“Don't worry, Justin,” the Commander tried to smile but stopped when he realised his fat lip made it too painful. “We've got bigger things to worry about. Drink your tea and I'll tell you what I was going to explain before you decided to teach me the basics of bare knuckle fighting.

The Commander dabbed at his swollen lip with a blood-speckled handkerchief. “I was going to tell you of the dilemma we faced when we heard your conversation with Vincent, that is Caesar, on Friday night. We knew that you were in danger by divulging this information but we got one thing wrong. Catastrophically wrong. We thought that this John would have you eliminated, not Caesar, and so we put you under covert surveillance and had you watched by some of our team from a vantage point close by, ready to step in when needed. Not for one minute did we think that Caesar would be the victim, so we left him to his own devices. I'm sorry, but in trying to save your life we lost Caesar's."

Justin took a deep breath. "All right, I can just about accept that," he said reluctantly, "but what I don't understand is why, with all the resources and experts at your disposal you couldn't trace these phone calls and texts and find out the recipient of the e-mails I send off with details of the graves this John wants. Surely, it can't be that difficult?"

"You're right, in one surmise, Justin," said the commander as he carefully took a sip of his tea. "We do have experts and some of the most sophisticated equipment in the world, and there was a time when the criminals could stay one step ahead of the law by routing all their internet traffic through the dark web. You know the one I'm talking about?"

Justin shook his head. "I've heard of it, but I don't know anything about it."

The Commander looked over to Maggie. "Right, as Maggie's the expert in this field I'll let her explain."

Maggie collected her thoughts. "No disrespect to you, Justin," she began, "but it is a difficult subject so I'll try to simplify matters. The Dark Web is a term that refers to a collection of websites that are publicly visible, but hide the identities of the servers that run them. So any web user can visited them, but it is very difficult to find the return path and discover who is behind the sites. And you cannot find these sites using conventional search engines. Almost all sites on the so-called Dark Web hide their identity using, what is know as, the Tor encryption tool which hides the end-user identities and spoofs the users location. Are you with me so far?"

Justin nodded cautiously. "Yes, just about so far. Is there more to it?"

"Yes, lots, but I'll keep it simple. In short using this Tor system means that the end user's IP is batted through several layers of encryption which make it look like another IP address and thus keeps the end user's identity, or return path, secret. However, over the years we have managed to crack the Tor encryption code and have had great success in uncovering criminals who thought they were safe from the detection. But, as you are well aware, the villains always manage to keep one step ahead of us so that we are always doing catch-up – though, in fairness we often catch up quickly."

"Let me take over from you, Maggie," the Commander interposed. "In short, Justin, just as we have cracked the dark net the lawless are able to use another more secure level of secrecy. It's known as the deep web, or deep net. In short, this is as benign as the dark web is sinister but the difficulty we have is it sheer size and the immense difficulty in finding what we need to know, especially as these criminals and subversive groups have learned how to run their dark web encrypted communications through the deep web where they effectively disappear and can only be recovered by those who hold the encryption key. So, to answer your question, that's why we can't find where these texts come from and where your e-mails go to."

Justin looked at the Commander with a furrowed brow. "Right, I can understand that you have a problem there, but what about these tracking and transmitting devices which have been planted in the flat and on my van. Can't you find out where the information they transmit is being sent to?"

Maggie again took over. "I can answer that,

Justin. I can't stress enough the levels of sophistication we are dealing with. We are looking for a terrorist cell, which appears to have the full technical resources of the Iranian state behind it. Both the devices which you refer to have one thing in common. They have the ability to change their transmission frequencies and band widths in milliseconds, so quickly, in fact that we don't have the monitoring equipment sensitive enough to follow them. And, no surprises here, the signals are run through a remote server, which we suspect is in MOIS headquarters in Tehran, using the Tor encryption and via the deep web."

"We also have another problem," added the Commander, "as it is possible for our tracking to be discovered we have to exercise extreme caution with surveillance, both electronic and physical, as we can't afford to let this John character know he has been rumbled. So now you know why Maggie had to subject you to this deception of being your girlfriend. We've completely lost track of this John and his cell, and it was only through you that we could have any chance of finding him. Please don't feel bitter, Justin, we are dealing with what we think is a very serious attempt on the well-being of our nation. In short, our intelligence leads us to believe that a terrorist outrage is being planned way beyond anything this country, and indeed the world has ever seen. Because of the enmity the Islamic religion has toward Christianity, we strongly believe that their actions will coincide with the Christmas festivities. So you can appreciate why, with Christmas fast approaching and time running short, we have to use all legitimate means at our disposal to find this man. In short, Justin, we believe you could be the key to unlocking our problem"

Justin had perked up after drinking his tea. "Well, I'm as patriotic as next man so I'll do what I can to help. Although you'll allow that I'm somewhat constrained by virtue of being banged up here. But fire away."

Justin watched as Maggie fiddled with a small recording device and placed it on the table between the them. "Hope you don't mind, Justin," said the Commander with a smile made lop-sided with his damaged lip, "but it's easier that writing everything down. Right, let's start with the graves you dug that this John wanted you pass the details on to him."

He looked at Justin apologetically. "Actually we do have a complete record of the graves you dug and the details which you passed on to John as Maggie copied everything on your computer for our boys to analyse. We know that this Bahadur Najafi, or John, only wanted the details of single or reopened graves which were left open overnight. Why do you think that was?"

Justin scratched his head before replying. "Well, like you, I don't know for certain as John wouldn't tell me when I asked. But I've had some thoughts on the matter. With both a reopen and a single he would know that they would never be opened again, except, of course, in the unlikely event of a Home Office exhumation order, so he'd be confident they would remain untouched. So I can only assume that whatever was to be hidden there would be safe until it was wanted. But for the life of me, Marcus, I just can't think of any item that could be hidden in a grave and yet be available when it was needed. The work involved in opening up and reinstating the grave would be time consuming and, as it would be unlikely to be done during the day, virtually impossible at night-time. I did think that he was some sort of hit man who wanted to hide the bodies of his victims, but that can be discounted as it's too difficult and, anyway, you couldn't do it in a reopen as there isn't enough room without removing the original coffin. A single would also be problematic as the amount of spoil would be a dead give away. No, it couldn't be bodies he wanted to dispose of."

"Justin," asked Maggie, "we overheard you

tell Caesar you went back to one of your graves to check on it. Did you see anything untoward?"

"No nothing at all. In fact I went out that night to a single I'd dug at Ceredigion to have a poke around. Although it was in the dark, I had a good look all round with my torch and found nothing untoward. I suppose you know that I got a threatening call from John when I got back. That's when I realised that I had been tracked and when I started to get frightened I was into something I couldn't control."

A thought suddenly came to him. "Mind you, I can see several advantages to hiding something in a grave. You know exactly where to find what has been hidden as a grave with a headstone with a known name is a first class locator. In case there is no headstone in place, I had to pass on to this John the headstone details of the graves, or grave, either side. Also you know no one is going to start digging by accident and when you have to dig up whatever it is that's been hidden, you can be reasonably sure of not being disturbed."

The Commander listened intently to Justin's thoughts. "I agree with you there, and we know all about the control John had over you," he confirmed. "As an aside you ought to know that West Mercia Police have received a detailed file on the actions of a child porn pervert called Justin Parkes. Everything is there on your computer as we well know after Maggie downloaded the entire contents of your system."

Justin looked stunned. "You mean I'm going to have this added to my charge of murder. Bloody hell, you can't be serious."

The commander gave a short laugh. "Well, I'm serious that the information has been sent to the local police, but you can stop worrying on two counts. Firstly, the charges would never hold up under scrutiny as there is no viewing history and, secondly, and more importantly, we have taken your charge sheet from West Mercia and will deal with it directly ourselves. You can be assured that it will be filed NFA – no further action. But let's get back to these graves."

The Commander looked at his watch and shook his head. "Look at that, it's half past one already. I imagine that you would like some lunch." He turned to the telephone mounted on the wall by his chair and, pushing the button for reception, asked for sandwiches and drinks for three to be brought to the interview room. "Hope you don't mind if we press on, Justin, as we have a lot to get through and time isn't on our side. We can tell you that we sent two of our people to give a clandestine check on one of the graves you told John about but, just like you, we couldn't find any thing amiss. We even ran GPR, that's ground penetrating radar equipment, inside the hole and round the outside and found nothing. But one of the problems is that its penetration is limited in moist or clay soils which unfortunately abound in many parts of Shropshire - especially on the Welsh side - and, also the ongoing problem we have in acting in secret so we don't arouse anyone's suspicions."

Justin pondered for a moment. "Just a thought. Do you think that I've been set up as part of a deception plan. You know, the authorities are led to believe that these graves are key to the success of John's plan and waste a lot of time up a blind alley?"

"We have considered that possibility, Justin, but as I've said we're in possession of some high quality intelligence which lead us to believe, with increasing certainty, that a large scale terrorist atrocity has been planned to take place around Christmas and which will coincide with similar attacks in France, Germany, Israel and the USA. I am constrained for reasons of security from telling you more but can tell you that you are central to this operation in the UK. To be quite frank, Justin, despite all the resources we have at our disposal, and to our intense embarrassment, we've completely lost track of this John, even though we believe him to be based somewhere in Shropshire. At every turn he stays one step ahead and we're playing catch-up all the time. We have to locate him and his cell before they can carry out their plan and you, Justin, are the key to all this."

Before Justin could respond, there was a knock on the door, and at the Commander's summons, a detention officer brought in a tray piled high with a variety of sandwiches packed in their individual plastic containers and three mugs of tea. Once they had all chosen the fillings of their choice, Justin rubbed his hand over his forehead in puzzlement before taking a large bite of his sandwich.

"You say that I'm key to finding this John, but I would have thought that I'm of no use to him now I've been arrested. I don't see how he could use me again even if I were released."

Marcus took a sip of his tea and winced as the hot liquid touched his painful lip, before answering . "Let me explain it this way. If we discount the low grade, brainless villains whom the police catch and the courts convict with nauseating regularity, there are basically two types of criminals who give us a lot of trouble. Firstly, there are the one-off offenders. These are people without any criminal record who commit just one crime, which can be serious like robbery, murder, abduction or rape for example, but who never re-offend and are, therefore, never added to the police databases to be referenced at a later date. Sadly, these are the crimes which the police on many occasions are never able never solve. The other group of criminals which give the police enormous problems are the persistent offenders who possess a high level of intelligence, cunning and organisational ability and who commit back to back crimes with seeming impunity and, sad to admit, are able to evade arrest. But clever thought they are, they invariably have one fatal flaw – hubris, you know arrogance. The more they escape arrest the more they think they are untouchable and this leads them to believe that they can get away with anything. In short, they become over confident and that's when they start to make mistakes."

"Are you telling me, Marcus," said a surprised Justin, "that this John bloke has made a mistake?"

"I certainly am," he replied with satisfaction. "We expected that John would have you killed for talking to your friend Caesar. But he decided to punish you instead. In short, he made his first mistake by setting out on a journey of revenge and allowing his emotions to over-rule his professionalism. By deciding to punish you for disobeying him by killing your best friend, he has by default allowed you to remain as the one catalyst which can draw him out of hiding."

"Call me dim , Marcus, but just how am I able to draw anyone out of hiding whilst I'm in the nick. And even if I were free why would I be the irresistible attraction which will make him break cover."

The Commander paused for effect before answering. "Because, Justin, he will kill you. No ifs or buts, once you are free one of his men will eliminate you."

"Well call me old fashioned, Commander Baxendale my old chum," expostulated Justin, his eyes wide with horror, "but I have a definite aversion to being killed. So I'm going to suggest I stay in custody for a long time, and in the meantime you can find another sacrificial lamb to assist you in finding this John. If you really think I'm bloody well going to walk the streets waiting for the assassin's bullet, you can think again, buster. I'm not playing. So get round that one."

The Commander and Maggie exchanged looks. "Justin, we understand that this comes as a shock but I can tell you that you will be released from custody and you will be given bail when you appear at the magistrates court on Monday. Before you ask, you have my word that bail will definitely be granted, as we have arranged for the police to make no objection and you will, therefore, be released. Once this John knows you are free and a threat, he will have you eliminated very quickly. Don't you see, Justin, there is no one else we can turn to. We have to find and neutralise this cell and it's only you who can help to flush him out of his bolt hole, a bolt hole we suspect is somewhere close to here. We are hampered by the fact that Shropshire is a big county and also that we are unable to brief the local constabulary as this operation is classified as top secret and there is a limit as to how much information we are able to release."

"If that's supposed to fill me with confidence, Marcus," rejoined Justin with heavy irony, "you've fallen at the first hurdle. But let us imagine I'm free, and knowing that I have a deep-seated aversion to being killed, just how do you propose to keep me alive."

"I'm glad you asked that." The Commander spoke reassuringly. "What we've done is take an upstairs room in the cottage next to the supermarket where we can keep your flat under twenty-four hour surveillance. There is also another specialist team based close by on immediate standby, who will be deployed as and when necessary. But is is essential that we can keep track of you at all times without actually visually following you around. To this end, Maggie has put a GPS transmitter in the lining of the parka you were wearing when arrested. You must always wear that coat and no other. How do you feel about things so far?"

Justin looked bleakly at the commander as he slowly shook his head. "If you're referring to my impending doom, decidedly unenthusiastic. But now you tell me that I won't be held in custody, I can't see any way out other that putting my faith in your ability to keep me alive. What happens now, Marcus?"

"We've made the following arrangements. You'll remain in custody until Monday morning when you'll be taken to Shrewsbury Magistrates Court where you will meet with the solicitor we've arranged for you. She will request that you are released on bail. A police officer will act for the constabulary to say that they have no objection to bail, provided your passport is surrendered and you report to the bail office here every week. Once the court proceedings are finished, the police will drive round to your flat to pick up your passport and then you'll be brought back here to the bail office where your conditions will be arranged. After that, you will be free to return home."

The commander looked seriously at Justin. "You are no doubt aware that, once you are free, this John will realise that something is amiss, as someone charged with first degree murder and child pornography offences is unlikely to be released on bail. He'll have to move quickly in order to neutralise the threat that you pose to him and that will be the moment when we make sure we thwart the hit team, who then can be tailed to their hideout when, hopefully, we can arrest this John character along with his cell. Maggie has been detailed to be in the public gallery when you're in court and to keep an eye on your welfare. Don't worry, Justin, you will be under constant covert observation at all times by our operatives. You'll be just fine, trust me."

Justin gave a hollow laugh. "If I didn't think that you would need me as a witness later on, I would have my doubts about you assurances. But I don't want to sound ungrateful, so thanks for everything. There is something else though." He turned his head to look at Maggie. "Does Lynn know. About Caesar's death I mean?"

"Yes, Justin, she does know. She didn't get back from visiting her parents until late Saturday. The police Family Liaison officer wasn't able to contact her earlier on the mobile number I gave her as she must have forgotten to take it with her, or she'd turned it off. I spoke with the officer earlier this morning and she told me Lynn's trying to be brave but, as you would expect, it's a losing battle. I'm going to visit her tomorrow after your court appearance. I pass on your concerns."

"Thanks, Maggie. I'd appreciate that." Justin stopped as a sudden thought came to him. "Bloody hell, I almost forgot. I've got a grave to dig, and fill in, tomorrow for Thompsons at Chirbury and I won't be able to do it as I'll be in court."

Maggie gave a reassuring grin. "We're ahead of you on that one. I had access to your diary and after you were arrested yesterday I contacted Thompsons and told them you had had an emergency appointment with your dentist for a very painful abscess. Mr. Thompson was understanding and assured me that he, like all competent undertakers, had someone he could call on at short notice. He sends his best wishes. I didn't make any other arrangements as we knew you'd be back in harness for Tuesday's bookings. Oh, I nearly forgot, your van has been returned to your usual parking place at the supermarket. The keys are with your possessions here in custody."

Justin raised his hand as another problem came to him. "Hang on a second. You talk of me being back in harness but have you considered that when all this hits the papers I'll be dropped by all undertakers like a hot brick. No one will want to employ a murderer to dig their graves. I won't have any job to go back to. How am I going to get round that one?"

"We had talked about that, Justin," admitted the Commander, "and at one stage did contemplate asking the Home Secretary for a D Notice to be applied – you know, where the Press cannot report on a matter where they could compromise an investigation – but realised that it was not a good course of action. Had we done so, this John would have immediately realised that something was not right as there is no reason why a murder shouldn't be reported in the papers. We reluctantly had to allow due reporting process to take place and, I'm sorry to relate, your name and the charges against you are now common knowledge."

"Bloody nice one, Marcus," said Justin, slapping his hand down on the desk, "not content with having me charged with murder and child porn, and then making me a moving target for a bunch of deadly assassins, you now tell me that my business is finished. Mind you, if you don't stop the hit squad doing its job, then it won't make much difference in the short term. Come on, got a clever answer to that one as well, have you?"

The Commander held up his hands apologetically. "Justin, I can understand you anger but it won't help if you get upset. Look, we believe that this John will make his move against you very soon. Immediately we have him and his cell members under arrest the police will drop all charges against you. We have instructed the Chief Constable that, once that happens, he has to issue a clearly worded press release that you are cleared of all charges. You will then be able to contact all your undertakers and put the record straight, hopefully without too much damage being done to your reputation. I'm sorry, Justin, if that's cold comfort for you, but it's the best we could do under these difficult circumstances. I hope you understand."

Justin did realise that the Commander was doing his best for him and, his temper having cooled, thanked him for his efforts, before the Commander spoke into the telephone next to him to tell the custody staff that he had finished with Mr. Parkes and could they take him back to his cell.

He turned back to Justin with a satisfied look on his face which was now sporting a well-developed black eye. "Well, that seems to have wrapped things up for the time being, Justin. You'll now be taken back to your cell and legal process will take place tomorrow with your court appearance. Just two things before we part. Don't do anything out of character, keep to your normal routines, and remember to wear your coat with the tracker in it at all times when you are out and about. Is there anything you're not sure about?"

Justin assured the Commander that he was clear on everything that was expected of him, though added he felt that it was the unexpected things which were the most worrying, as he stood up and shook his proffered hand. Despite the bitterness which he felt towards Maggie for her betrayal, Justin decided that it would be churlish to ignore the hand she held open for him, and took hold of it for a brief clasp before letting go as a knock on the door of the interview room announced the arrival of a detention officer. After being taken back to his cell, Justin lay back on the bunk with head whirling with troubled thoughts as he contemplated all that had befallen him over the months since his first fateful decision to to agree to John's proposals and, latterly, charged with murder. And if that were not enough, with the unpalatable knowledge that he was shortly to be on a terrorist hit list.

He moved his arms around gently as he tried to ease the discomfort in his shoulder joints after his painful constraint at the hands of the custody staff, and though back to the good times before this sinister John had entered his life. He realised that the carefree Justin of old was no longer available to him and that he had to find that part of him which was capable of facing life as it actually was, not how he wanted it to be. It was as well that he had found a new resolve as, mercifully unbeknown to him, he was to endure a trial greater than anything he had encountered to date.

CHAPTER 10

As Justin waited impatiently in his cell until he was to appear in court the following day, John, secure in his safe house, had called his team members around him to brief them on their next tasks. He felt satisfied that he had punished Justin enough with the killing of his friend and his arrest for his murder. He was close to the culmination of his task, and the horrific climax which he was to inflict on the British people, and he couldn't afford to make any mistakes at this crucial stage. With this in mind, he instructed Bill, the ex-police officer, to drive to the court on Monday morning, find out when Justin's hearing was listed, find a seat in the public gallery and report back on the magistrate's decision. John felt confident that he had everything under control, but had no way of knowing that in the morning he would have some very disturbing news from Bill after he had observed the court proceedings.

As Justin waited in his cell for his court

appearance the following day, he hoped that Sunday night would be quieter than Saturday. But in this he was to be disappointed as there appeared to be just as many revellers who had exceeded their abilities to control themselves whilst in drink and drugs as the night before. It was, he estimated, in the early hours before the noise levels in the cell block dropped to a level where he could fall into an uneasy sleep, and it felt like only minutes before his hatch dropped down, his cereal and a drink thrust through the opening, as he was told get himself ready for the transport which would be taking him to court in half an hour. Justin was intrigued to find the detention officer had brought a small plastic tube which, on examination, he found unscrewed to reveal a toothbrush which had some sort of dental powder on the bristles. By the time he had eaten his cereal, cleaned his teeth and washed the stubble on his face using his blanket to dry himself, he started to feel more like his old self, although somewhat short of sleep and still painfully stiff around the shoulders and one knee after being restrained the day before.

A short while later, the cell door was pulled open and a detention officer took him round to the booking in desk where a custody sergeant went through the release and hand-over procedures before discharging him into the custody of the security officers who would take him and his sealed plastic bag of belongings the short distance to the courthouse. After his shoes had been returned to him and he had put them on, he was given a pat down by one of his escorts and then handcuffed before being taken out through the security doors through which he had entered two days' before and into the covered yard where his transport waited. Climbing up the steps into the prisoner transport vehicle he saw that there were rows of individual box-like cells with basic seating and a small darkened glass window to the outside. After being told to sit down in one, the door slammed shut followed shortly after by the engine starting up and the vehicle pulling out into the half-light of a cold, misty December morning. Without his parka it was cold in his little cell, and Justin shivered as the transport drove from custody down Monkmoor Road to the traffic lights at the end, when it turned left along Abbey Foregate, past the imposing figure of Lord Hill atop his lofty column, the short distance to the magistrates court which was situated behind Shropshire County council offices at the Shirehall.

Eventually the vehicle crawled to a stop in a covered bay, similar to the one at the police station, and Justin, along with his fellow travellers, were led out one by one to be checked in against a list held by the court reception officer. After taking custody of Justin's bag of personal possessions, his escorts were told they could take off his handcuffs, then to take him to interview room one where he was to meet his solicitor.

Once ushered in, and with an unexpected *good luck* from his escort, Justin found himself facing his legal representative for the first time. He shook the proffered hand as she introduced herself and, asking him to sit down, explained her role and what would happen once they were called into court. She added that it was unusual for a solicitor to be introduced to a client at this late stage but had been assured by Commander Baxendale that all she had to do was to request that bail be granted, and that the representative from the police would not object subject to certain conditions being imposed. All Justin had to do, she assured him, was confirm his name and address when asked by the clerk of the court and plead not guilty after the charges have been read out. She would then deal with the remainder of the proceedings.

Feeling reassured that he was in safe hands, Justin tried to relax in the small room after his solicitor had left him. He had a long wait, as it was half past ten before the door was unlocked and the court officer told him he was due next in court. He was escorted down a long corridor to a door which the officer opened to reveal some steps which led up into the dock, where he was told to sit down until the magistrate entered. Justin looked down into the court and spied his solicitor sitting at one tables with her papers neatly arranged in front of her. Catching Justin's eye she gave him a reassuring smile which he acknowledged with a slight wave of his hand. At the other table in front of the Magistrate's raised bench he saw a smartly dressed police constable seated at a table next to his solicitor. Looking idly around at the public gallery, Justin saw Maggie along with some eight other men and women who had attended hoping to hear some sordid details about a gruesome murder. On the press bench and two bored looking hacks doodled aimlessly on their pads as they waited for what they hoped would be some exciting copy.

Shortly after the Clerk entered from a door behind the bench and told the court to be upstanding as the Magistrate and her wing members took their seats. The Clerk addressed Justin asking him to confirm his name and address before reading out the charges against him and, as instructed, Justin pleaded not guilty. With this stage of the proceedings over, his solicitor made her representations to the bench asking for her client to be allowed bail whilst he waited for his case to be heard at the Crown Court in due course. At the completion of her address she sat down as the police constable was asked by the Magistrate whether the police had any objections to the granting of bail. He identified himself before stating that the police had no objections to bail subject to the conditions that Mr. Parkes' passport was surrendered and that he should sign at Monkmoor police station bail office every Monday and Friday at a time to be arranged. He also assured the Magistrate that as Mr. Parkes was in the custody of West Mercia police he would personally accompany him back to his home address to pick up the passport, then take him back to the bail office for his bail conditions to be arranged.

Justin waited as the Magistrate conferred briefly with the Clerk of the Court then with the two other members on the bench, was told to stand and heard, with great relief, that the court was agreeable to these conditions and that he was being released into police custody until such time as bail arrangements had been finalised and the case could be heard at the Crown court at a date to be arranged.

Once the Magistrate and the other bench members had retired to his rooms, the constable walked over to the dock. "Right, Mr. Parkes," he said in a business-like manner, "you're to come with me. First we'll get your belongings back, then go to your flat and pick up your passport. After that I'll take you to the bail office where we can sort out your signing on."

Thanking the officer, Justin stepped down from the dock and followed him towards the exit. He stopped briefly to thank his solicitor for her efforts before the two of them walked through the entrance foyer to the court officer's room where Justin signed for his belongings which had been brought from custody. Then it was out into the chill wind of the December day and across the Shirehall car park where the constable had parked his marked police car on double yellow lines.

As Justin as he settled himself into the passenger seat, the rear passenger door opened and Maggie slid in behind Justin's seat.

"Oh, hello," he said with some surprise. "Don't tell me you've come to arrest this nice police constable for parking on double yellow lines. But I suppose parking restrictions don't apply to coppers."

"No, not when they are dealing with hardened villains." She smiled apologetically at the officer as she went on. "Nice to see a bit of the old cheeky chappie returning, Justin. Now, it's been arranged that I'm to accompany you to the flat as I'm not allowed to let you out of my sight. Remember, you're still under arrest until your bail conditions are arranged. By the way, I'll have to pick up my things from the flat. Can I come round tomorrow when I've got some free time? I'll post the key in your letter box if you're not there."

"No problem," said Justin, then added, "but give me a bell first so that I can be there to help."

Maggie nodded. Perhaps it was a bit much, she thought, saying she would let herself into the flat when Justin was out. "Yes, of course. Here, you'd better have it back now." She fumbled with her keyring and eventually, after a short struggle, handed Justin her door key as the constable started the engine, told them to put on their seat belts, and started on the short drive to Justin's flat.

Unbeknown to them the proceedings in court had been observed by an interested member in the public gallery. The previous evening John had detailed Bill to find out when Justin's case was listed, attend court as a member of the public, and report back to him with his findings. As the public gallery started to fill, his attention was drawn towards Maggie. He already knew that she was Justin's girl but had never had the opportunity to observe her closely. As he carefully looked again, a tiny warning bell started to sound in the distant recesses of his mind. Not wanting to draw attention to himself, Bill made a point of not looking at her again and, once the proceedings were concluded, remained seated until Maggie had left the Magistrate's court as the realisation of the danger she posed became a certainty. Walking swiftly to his car, which he had parked on Highfields Road, he drove quickly back to the farmhouse to report in to John with his disturbing news. He had a bombshell to deliver and he couldn't wait to see John's face when he delivered it.

As Bill drove back to the farmhouse, Maggie and Justin were driven round the roundabout at the Column, then past the side of the Abbey, taking the right turn at the front, looped all round the Abbey, and back onto the Foregate, where the constable bumped over the kerb to park the car on the wide pavement in front of the door of number eleven. Together the three of them walked up the steps at the front of the building into the entrance hall where, unsurprisingly, old Mrs. Williams was waiting goggle eyed to find out why a police officer was bringing Justin and his girlfriend into the building. But Justin needn't have worried about being trapped by her as the constable immediately saw the danger and with a brusque, *police work, can't stop now,* took Justin's arm and propelled him up the stairs to his flat. After a short search, Justin found his passport and handed it over to the constable who put it in his uniform pocket. Leaving the flat they went down to the hallway where they could see old Mrs. Williams had retired to her flat and was peering out through the slightly opened door determined not to miss anything.

Back in the car they travelled in silence as they were driven the short distance up Monkmoor Road to the police station where they parked up in one of the staff parking bays. As the constable picked up his paperwork from where he had had put on the rear seats, Maggie spoke to Justin.

"The constable will take you to the bail office and hand you over to the sergeant in charge, who'll take over. I'll hang on here until you come out so I can give you a lift back to the flat. My car's here so it's no problem. And also, Justin, it's really important that I talk to you."

Although Justin didn't feel a chat with Maggie was what he wanted, he also felt that it would be childish not to let her have her say.

"All right," he agreed reluctantly, " I go along with that and I'll take up your offer of a lift. See you in a bit."

Escorted by a plainly intrigued constable who had heard their exchange, they walked the short distance to the door of the bail office which was situated at the side of the custody block. Once there, the officer punched the intercom button and identified himself to the voice which crackled out of the speaker and pushed open the door when instructed. Inside, to their right was a line of hard-backed chairs, whilst to their left was a glass partition which ran the length of the wall. As they waited, a panel was slid open and the constable passed the papers over to a very tall police sergeant who scrutinised them carefully before he said he would take over. After a formal farewell from the constable, the sergeant operated the remote release allowing the officer to leave the bail office, as the bail sergeant put Justin's details onto the computer system. There was a short delay before he printed off a letter which stated the signing on requirements at the bail office and the date of Justin's appearance at Shrewsbury Crown Court in January the following year. With the letter in his hand the door was opened for Justin and he was free to leave and make his way to where Maggie was waiting besides her Golf.

As they both slid into their seats, Maggie switched on the engine and fiddled with the heating controls. "Bit cold for sitting around," she explained. "it'll heat up quickly as I've put the heater on full to warm us up whilst we talk."

She paused for a moment as Justin looked at her wondering what it was all about. "There's something I've got to get off my chest and it concerns us."

His feelings were still raw. "*Us*! What do you mean *us*?" Justin burst out, "there's no *us*, you made bloody sure of that. You stole my heart then you stabbed it to death. Don't you know you were the only woman I've ever fallen in love with, and the only woman who brought out the best in me. Can't you understand I love you."

Maggie felt her throat tighten and she fought hard to stop the tears which threatened to fill he eyes. "Justin, please hear me out. Please don't make this any more difficult for me but I want to try and clear things up between us."

She waited as Justin stared at her then, with a resigned sigh, slumped back in his seat. "Okay, go on then. I'll listen."

Relieved, Maggie took a deep breath as she looked at him intently before continuing. "Thanks, love. There are two things I want to make you aware of, both of them equally important to me. You now know that I work undercover. It's something I'm trained to do, and do to the best of my ability. It's work which can be, and often is, of vital importance for the maintenance of law and order and the security and safety of the public."

She saw she was beginning to loose Justin's interest and quickly continued. "Just bear with me, Justin, it's crucial you understand. My work is difficult and sometimes dangerous. I have to mix with and befriend all sorts of unsavoury characters. Some are sadistic, psychopathic, drugged, drunkards. Some are dirty in their physical habits and often in their warped minds, but I have a job to do and I put up with the human dross I have to pretend to like for the greater good. Believe me, sometimes it takes all I've got not to run back to my boss and hand in my notice."

Maggie turned in her seat to look directly at Justin. She put her hand on his and her voice softened. "But with you it was so different. You are nothing like the people I usually deal with. Of course, you're not a law breaker, just an innocent caught up in something which eventually was beyond your ability to influence. Yes, I had to deceive you. Yes, I had to steal your heart because it was essential that we took control of the dangerous situation which you were trapped in, and for that I make no apologies. It was my job."

Justin returned her gaze as she turned down the heater fan before continuing. "But this is the other thing I want you to understand. You were so different from all the others I had to come into contact with. They were bad people doing bad things, but you are nothing like that. You're a good person unwittingly caught up in wrongdoing. You looked after me. You treated me with kindness and consideration. You're amusing, fun to be with, in short the problem I had was not falling in love with you, that would have been easy, the difficult bit was stopping myself falling in love."

She took his hand in both of hers as Justin blinked as his eyes misted. He was not a person to bear grudges and he was moved more than he thought possible with Maggie's words.

"So we were nearly there, then?" he said with a catch in his voice. "Perhaps, a different time, a different place and we would still be together."

Maggie saw Justin's obvious tears, and the ones she had managed to hold back now flowed unchecked down her cheeks. "Yes," she whispered. She leaned across and he tasted the salt of her tears as she kissed him gently on the lips, "yes, we could have been."

Still holding hands, they sat in silence until they had regained control over their emotions. Maggie was grateful that Justin had listened to explanations and Justin, for his part, felt a great burden lifted from his shoulders as the dreadful hurt of what he saw as a betrayal of his love was in large part assuaged. He was able to forgive Maggie for using him, but that it was clear that there would never be the possibility that they could rekindle their relationship. She hadn't said it directly, but it was obvious that her job came first.

"Actually, Maggie," Justin said after a pause, "when I realised in custody that you were not who you said you were and the initial anger had left me, I tried to hate you for what you'd done to me. But I found I couldn't. I discovered that true love can't turn to hatred, only possessive love can do that, and my love could never be possessive as I'm not that type of person and there's no place within me for it. I want you to know that I do understand that what you had to do was necessary, and I do now know how you feel about me. It has helped to hear what you had to say and I want you to know that there are no hard feelings." He gave Maggie a cheeky smile as he said, "and I hope your next victim is as nice as me."

Maggie laughed as she dabbed her eyes with a tissue she took from her handbag. "At last the real Justin Parkes has surfaced. Seriously, it means a lot to me that we can part friends. Thanks, Justin."

"Right, secret agent Challinor," said Justin

with a grin as he recovered himself, "I'll tell you what happens now. Hope you don't mind, but I'm going to turn down your kind offer of a lift back as I want to stretch my legs and breath in some of the cold clear air of freedom."

"No problem," Maggie smiled back as Justin opened his door. "I'll be in touch once you've settled in and make arrangements to pick up my stuff from the flat. Bye, love. Take care."

Justin set off on his short walk back home into a typical mid-December day. The morning's chill wind had now died away, and already a light mist was forming in defiance of the low, weak sun which tried and failed to send out any warming rays. He was glad of the walk as it helped to clear his head. He'd been through a lot over a short space of time and he found it difficult to take in how his life had irrevocably changed within the space of three days. The list was horrific. His best friend murdered, the love of his life gone forever, arrested and that wasn't the end of it. He recalled the words of Commander Baxendale when they had their unforgettable meeting in custody, who had made it plain that the only lead they had to this elusive John character was through Justin himself. He suddenly remembered that he'd been told that Maggie had placed a tracking device in his parka and he felt around the hem until he located something about the size of a thick fifty pence piece. As he zipped up the coat to under his chin, he felt some reassurance from this discovery and determined to make sure he always wore that coat whenever he was out and about.

After turning right onto Abbey Foregate, he remembered that he would need bread and milk and dodging the traffic, crossed the road to the supermarket opposite his flat. There he bought milk, his usual granary loaf and a copy of the Daily Express before paying at the checkout and making his way back over the road to his flat. He was relieved to find that old Mrs. Williams was nowhere to be seen and, after taking a solitary letter from his post box, made his way upstairs and into his flat. He took of his coat which he hung on a peg behind the front door and turned the central heating control up to 22° C. He felt his stomach rumble and realised he hadn't eaten anything since his early breakfast in custody that morning. He rummaged in the cupboard and found a tin of beans which he poured into a bowl and put in the microwave. Whilst they heated he put two slices of bread in the toaster and put the kettle to boil whilst he waited for his meal. Within a few minutes he was sitting down with a large plate of beans on toast and a tea bag stewing in a mug ready for when he had finished.

After finishing his meal, Justin took his mug

of tea over to his computer and, opened up his e-mails. He saw that he had nothing booked for the rest of the week with any of the undertakers which used his services, just one from Grimshaws of Whitchurch for an afternoon interment for the following Monday. Justin wasn't surprised as he knew from his own experience as a grave digger and when he worked for Percivals, that there was a quiet time in December as fewer people died, but he was surprised that Mr. Grimshaws had booked him. Perhaps he didn't read the local papers , he surmised. Whatever the reason, he was glad that he had some days of rest in front of him whilst he tried to get his life back on track and, not least, until his painfully damaged shoulder muscles had repaired themselves.

He switched off his computer and took his tea over to his favourite armchair where he sipped the hot brew with relish. The central heating was beginning to to do its work and as the flat warmed up Justin suddenly thought of Lynn. So much had happened to him that he had hardly had time to think about her. He realised, with a feeling of guilt, that her pain must be far greater than his. With Caesar's murder he had lost a dear friend, but Lynn had lost her dearly loved husband, and he knew that he had to make contact with her at some stage. The problem he had was that he felt in large part responsible for Caesar's death. If only he hadn't told him about the dubious arrangement he had with this John, Caesar would still be alive. Justin groaned inwardly with the knowledge that his actions had effectively signed his friend's death warrant and Lynn by now would be aware of this. How on earth, he anguished, could he approach her.

As he wrestled with this problem, he suddenly remembered his mobile was had been turned off when he was taken into custody and he went to where his coat was hanging up inside the front door to retrieve it from one of the breast pockets. Turning it on he was surprised to see he had a text and was even more surprised to see it was from Lynn and had been sent on Sunday. Fearing the worst, he opened it up and read: *Sorry you arrested. Maggie said you out Monday. Must talk. Please get in touch asap. Love Lynn.*

Having been through so much lately, Justin's emotions were all over the place and, as he read Lynn's words, he felt the tears again fill his eyes, now with relief that he hadn't got to face what he feared would be a fraught meeting with her. Then it all became too much for him to contain. The pain, the shock, the despair, the guilt all came together in one overwhelming surge and, sitting down heavily in his armchair, he leaned forward, put his head in his hands as his body was racked with deep painful sobs whilst, helplessly, he allowed their cathartic release to wash away the traumas of the preceding days.

Justin wasn't sure for how long he had succumbed to his grief, but eventually he regained control of himself and, feeling he needed to clean himself after his incarceration he undressed in the bedroom before taking a long hot shower. Afterwards, he dried himself then pulled a change of clothing before deciding that he shouldn't put off phoning Lynn any longer. He pressed her speed dial number and after a couple of rings a connection was made and he heard Lynn's voice.

"Oh, Justin, I so happy to hear your voice." Unsurprisingly there was a tremor in her voice. "I've been so worried about you. It's so important I talk with you. Can you come round to the house now? My parents are here but we can talk privately in the dining room."

Justin was staggered to know that, despite all her shock and grief at Caesar's death, she could find time to worry about him. "Yes, yes, of course, Lynn," he replied, " I'll be with you in ten minutes."

Picking up his van keys from the table, Justin took his coat from its peg and shrugged into it as he walked down the stairs and back into the chilly air, and crossed the road to where his van had been parked by the police. His old but dependable van started at the first turn of the key and, easing himself out onto the main road, he turned right towards Highfields where, a few minutes later, he parked on the road in front of Lynn's house as the driveway was full with the big Volvo and a Honda saloon, which he imagined belonged to her parents. As Justin stepped out, he saw that Lynn had seen him arrive and was already standing at the front door waiting for him. He walked up to her and, before he could say a word, she had thrown her arms around him in a powerful embrace and burying her head in his chest burst into a flood of tears. It was all Justin could do not to let go again and give way to a grief which had not yet healed, but he managed to contain himself as he comforted Lynn whilst he led her inside. Quickly, she managed to suppress her tears and, dabbing her eyes dry with a tissue she had clutched in her hand. She turned up her face to Justin and, with a strained smile, gave him a kiss on the cheek.

"Sorry about that," she said finally, swallowing hard. "Everything is still pretty painful and just when I think I'm on top of it, back it all comes and the waterworks begin all over again. Still I suppose its part of the healing process. How are you, love?"

The situation in which Justin found himself

was one completely outside his experience. Even the death of this mother couldn't prepare him for the emotion turmoil which Caesar's death and Lynn's grief had created within himself. His life to date had been directed towards avoiding problems and emotional entanglements, as he airily floated around them without accepting any personal responsibility. Now everything had changed. Now he had been brought down to earth with a bang and he found himself ill prepared to deal with Lynn's distress. He struggled to find the right words.

"How am I," he stuttered, "Well, I mean, how are you getting on. Oh, gosh. I'm sorry but I feel so inadequate." He pulled himself together. "Lynn, I want to say how sorry I am at your loss. I... I don't know how to say this but I feel responsible for Caesar's death and I didn't think you would want to talk to me ever again."

"No, Justin, I don't blame you for anything," she said as she took his arm and walked him into the dining room when she shut the door after them. "My folks are in the sitting room but I told them I had to talk with you in private. You can say hello once we've finished."

"Justin, I have a confession to make." She took a deep breath before continuing. "I find this very difficult to say, but I was partly responsible for Caesar's death."

Justin stared at her, his eyes wide with surprise as he responded. “What, you? How on earth can you say that. I also find this difficult to say but it was me, not you. If I hadn't told Caesar about the arrangement I had with this dubious person I've got involved with, after being told by him to keep my big mouth shut, nothing would have happened. I only found out later, after I'd been arrested, that my flat had been bugged and this evil bastard John had heard every word I said. I can't tell you how sorry I am for the grief I've caused you. I want to turn the clock back, but it's impossible. I'm so, so sorry, Lynn. I take it you know that I didn't kill Caesar?”

“Of course I know you didn't, Justin. I knew as soon as I heard you'd been arrested. I knew without any doubt they had the wrong person. But there's something I have to tell you. It's obvious that you haven't been told or you wouldn't be taking all the blame yourself.”

She looked at him squarely as she went on. “You ought to know I was working with Maggie. Or, more accurately, she approached me to play a part in getting you and her together as an item.”

Justin sat with a bemused look on his face. “Are you telling me that you and Caesar were in on the plot?”

Lynn shook her head. “No, just me. That's

what makes it so hard. I wasn't forced to join in this deception, but it was impressed upon me that a grave danger to the nation existed and it would help if I'd go along with it, so I made the decision to take part. You're probably aware that I am bound by the Official Secrets Act and I was ordered not to tell anyone what was going on, including Caesar." She put her head in her hands as she said in a muffled voice, "God, what a mess." She raised her head to look at Justin with eyes red-rimmed with grief. "So you see, I played a part in his death."

With a sudden surge of compassion, Justin moved his chair so that he was sitting close to her. He put his arms around Lynn as tears coursed silently down her cheeks. "I'm sorry. I didn't know. But we both have to move on." He took a handkerchief from his pocket and gently dabbed at her tears. "At least you have the consolation that you acted out of a desire to serve the public. You can hold your head up there."

Lynn sniffed as she took Justin's handkerchief and wiped her eyes. She gave a wan smile. "Now look, I've got your hankie sodden. I'll wash it and get it back to you."

"That's all right, Lynn, don't bother," he replied with a smile. "I think I've got another one. Seriously though, what happens now?"

"There has to be a post mortem carried out

over the next few days, and then Caesar's body can be released to the undertakers. Once they have have him, then they'll get in touch with all the arrangements they've made. I've asked for Caesar to be cremated so we'll be at the crematorium on London Road some time next week. I'll talk to Len when I feel up to it, and get him to put on a spread in his back room at the Castle for all the folkies. You'll be there won't you?"

"Yes, of course, love. If you want any help with anything, just ask. I suppose your folks are staying with you until after the funeral?"

"Yes, they are. And thanks for your offer. There's nothing at the moment as Mum and Dad are seeing to everything. But I want you to phone me, or call round when you can. I'm still a bit fragile and I might need your broad shoulders, but I'll try not to cry on them next time."

Justin laughed as he gave her a squeeze before letting go and standing up. "Don't you worry about that. My shoulders were designed for crying on." He put the chair back neatly under the table. "Well, I'll leave you now, but I'll just say hello to your folks before I go. I promise to keep in touch."

Lynn drew in her breath as a sudden realisation came to her. "Oh, Justin. I almost forgot. You can leave your motorbike at the unit for the time being. Caesar paid a quarter's rental up front so it's mine until the end of February. When everything has settled down and I feel up to it, I'll try to sell the business or, at least, the lease but it won't be for some time yet."

With all that had happened in his life, Justin had completely forgotten about his Norton. He was touched that Lynn could think of him despite the pressure she was under. "Thanks, Lynn. I'll find somewhere else for it as soon as I can. So don't worry about it. I'll just go through to the lounge now and say hello to your folks."

In the lounge Justin spent a few minutes speaking with Lynn's parents before excusing himself. At the front door he gave Lynn one last embrace prior to climbing into his van for the short journey back home. As he drove through Highfields, now somewhat relieved after his talk with Lynn, he saw all the windows were alight with festive decorations. Windows with small illuminated Christmas trees, nodding Santa's, flashing lights draped over bushes and in the trees, and he realised with a start that he had been so caught up in his troubles that he had quite forgotten that there were only six days left before Christmas day and he hadn't bought any presents.

Justin, like most men, found present buying a really difficult task, putting it off until the last minute when he would dash out and buy anything, however unsuitable. Thinking that there is no time like the present, he drove with his headlights on, past his flat into town through the late afternoon gloom and into the multi- storey car park in Raven Meadows. It was packed with cars of the Christmas shoppers and he had to drive up the ramps almost to the top level before he could find a parking space. Ignoring the lift, he ran down the stairs to the entry level of the Darwin shopping centre and walked through the automatic doors into a concourse teeming with people.

For an hour he wandering indecisively past the shop window displays in the various levels of the mall, dodging the hordes of grimly determined shoppers, all of whom seemed to know exactly what they were looking for, before finally decided that he'd look to see what Marks and Spencer had to offer. Although he had only to buy one present for Lynn, a part of him wished that he had to find presents for Maggie and Caesar - however difficult the task might be. He thought warmly of the watch which Maggie had given him for his birthday, and which he wore all the time, and some of the suggestive presents that Caesar had managed to find to give him. He'd really miss them both and it was difficult to believe that he would never see either of them again.

But Justin's nature was not to dwell on past misfortunes and, shaking off his nostalgia, he went upstairs to the M&S ladies section where, after some deliberation, he selected a pair of fleece-lined mittens, a brightly coloured ski hat with a huge knitted pendant bobble and a matching scarf with tassels at both ends. Pleased with himself, he went to the checkout where he paid using some of the money which he had received from John. He had meant to bring a carrier bag from the van but, having forgotten it, was forced to pay for a shop one much to his annoyance. Leaving the store, on the way back to the multi-storey, he smelled the irresistible smell of fast food and decided that he couldn't be bothered to cook anything for his evening meal, turned into the café where he sat down and ordered a large americano and a cheese burger and chips. As he sipped his coffee and waited for his food to be served he thought of his meeting with Lynn, and how afterwards he felt lighter in spirits than he had for some time.

As he ate the food which the waitress had put in front of him, he wondered how good was the surveillance that Commander Baxendale had promised he'd organised to keep him safe. Justin looked surreptitiously around but was unable to see anything out of the ordinary. It was of some consolation that he'd been assured that highly trained operatives had him under twenty- four hour observation, but he also knew that this John was also very clever. After all, he'd managed to evade the finest of our security services and remain at large whilst planning a terrorist atrocity and carrying out a murder.

Justin wondered with a shiver of fear just how good Commander Baxendale's men would be at protecting him from John's retribution. Had he known that John was shortly to be informed of a dangerous development by Bill he would, with justification, have been very worried indeed. But Justin didn't know and, after finishing his burger and chips, he returned to the van with his purchases. He drove slowly back through the darkness and the rush hour traffic to his usual parking place at the supermarket, before dodging through the crawling lines of traffic on Abbey Foregate into the calm of the house and the warm security of his flat.

CHAPTER 11

After observing Justin and Maggie at the magistrates' court, Bill walked to his parked car and drove the fifteen minute journey back to the farmhouse. He parked up in the yard and hurried inside in to find John and report his worrying news. He found John in the sitting room watching Mike teach the others some self-defence techniques when he burst in. They all stopped what they were doing and looked up as he spoke with urgency in his voice.

"Have I got some news for you," he began as they looked at him expectantly. "Three things. First, Parkes has been bailed, would you believe it. He had to surrender his passport and has got to sign on as his bail conditions, but incredibly he's been allowed out."

John sat up at this revelation but spoke calmly. "You say he has been bailed. Is this usual when someone has been arrested for murder?"

"Not usual, John. In my twenty-two years'

service in the force I have known it on only a few occasions. From my experience I've found it to be when the police and the Crown Prosecution Service don't think their evidence is particularly strong, so they don't oppose a bail request. Actually, from what I know about how we've framed Parkes, there is very little actual hard and fast evidence which would incriminate him. Funnily enough, I think the child porn frame is the best as he could have a problem worming his way out of that one. But for some reason that never came up in court, just the murder."

John thought carefully. "Okay, that's a surprise but you mentioned there was more."

"Is there more? There certainly is and I've saved the best for last," said Bill. "The second thing I saw was that Parkes' fancy piece, Maggie. She was in the public gallery just in front of me. No surprise in seeing her there as she's his bint, but there was something which troubled me about her. I just couldn't put my finger on it at the time. As I walked out into the car park afterwards, I saw her get into the police car which was taking Parkes back to his flat for his passport and then the police station. It was then I remembered."

Bill paused for dramatic effect as his audience listened attentively. "But that brings me to number three which is the icing on the cake," he continued emphasising each word, "I'm convinced she's with the Met. Anti-terrorist unit."

The assembled men looked at Bill in stunned silence. John, as always fully in control of his emotions, but shaken nevertheless, spoke quietly. "This could be a very significant development. Bill, you say you think she is an undercover anti-terrorist officer. How sure are you?"

"About ninety-nine percent certain. About three months before I retired from that unit there was an intake of a dozen or so new personnel. I sometimes fall down on remembering names, but I never, ever forget a face, and I'm convinced that this Maggie bird was one of the new intake. We were on different teams, but we all used to come together on occasions for briefings and training sessions, and I know she was there. In fact, John, I'm one hundred percent certain it was her."

There was a clamour of noise from the assembled men as they shot questions at Bill. John held up his hand and the room fell quiet.

"Gentlemen, please. Nothing will be gained by this unseemly excitement. We are all highly trained professionals in our respective fields and it now falls on us to take the appropriate steps to ensure the success of our mission." He paused to gather his thoughts whilst the others waited respectfully to hear what he had to say.

"Right, let's look at this objectively." he went on. "I think we can be assured that Bill is right about Maggie and that she is working undercover. What we can't be sure about is that Parkes knew that she was a police officer when she became his live-in girl friend, but it is very likely that he does now. Indeed, it could just be possible that our Mr. Parkes is himself working for one of the security agencies. If this is, the case this makes him dangerous as he obviously is part of the operation to find us. We can also be sure that if the police infiltrated one of their officers into Parkes' life, they must have some knowledge of my arrival in this country and possibly who I am."

"Yes, that makes sense," interposed Charlie, "but I think I'm right in saying that they can't have a clue where we are because they would have busted us before now. I think they've lost track of you, John, and logically we are still free to carry out our mission."

Chalky looked at John with a quizzical look on his features. "Well, John, you're the boss. What do we do now?"

John thought before replying. He was not a man to make knee-jerk decisions but, also, he was someone who had been selected for his mission because he remains calm under pressure and could take swift action when an emergency arose.

“Right, gentlemen, let's look at things calmly.” John stood up and faced his men the better to emphasise his words. “We can be reasonably certain that the authorities know who I am and that I am in the country. We can be sure also that they know we are using the services of Parkes and, by logical deduction, it must be known that there is some association with the graves he digs. It is almost certain, knowing the technical expertise of the intelligence services, that they are aware that we have bugged Parkes' flat and also can track his vehicle movements. As we can still monitor his conversations and follow his movements, it means that our devices are still in place. This clearly indicates one thing only. They don't want us to know we are being hunted and from this, I am certain they are not aware that we know this.”

“I agree with everything you've said so far,” said Bill with a troubled expression, “but what we don't know is whether the capsules we've hidden have been discovered. Have you thought of that, John, because if they've gone our operation is over.”

John had, indeed, thought about that possibility. “Yes. I have and I'm confident that they are still where we have left them. Firstly, five capsules have been hidden out of the twenty-five to thirty suitable graves that Parkes has dug over the months he has worked for us. Secondly, even if it were suspected that we were using graves for concealment, the authorities would be reluctant to reveal their hand by digging them up. They don't want us to know we are being hunted and the last thing they would do is try to find what we've hidden in case it was fitted with a tracking device or, more seriously for them, with an anti-lift explosive charge. No, gentlemen, we are far from compromised and our opposition is clearly floundering. Nothing has changed. Our mission will be completed at midnight on the twenty-fourth of December as planned."

There was an audible sigh of relief in the room as the men talked excitedly amongst themselves whilst John gave serious thought to his position. The knowledge that British security had him tagged was most unwelcome, but this was offset by the fact that he and his team were still at liberty which meant that they were still safe at the farmhouse despite being under the noses of those hunting him. So far his plan had worked out as he wanted. It was now the nineteenth of the month. Five of the capsules had been hidden as soon as they had been picked up from the Post Office box. The last one should be available for collection tomorrow, though he wondered whether the dispatcher had made allowance for the build-up of mail in the weeks before the twenty-fifth. He quickly calculated and decided that it wouldn't make any difference if it was a few days' late, and, anyway, he couldn't do anything about it now even if he wanted to. He knew exactly what had to be done now.

He held up his hand for silence. “Right, this is our plan of action. Ginger and Woody, I've got a job for you both. I have to be sure that the capsules are in place.” John took a piece of paper out of his top pocket, unfolded it, and gave it to Ginger. “This is a list of where the capsules are hidden, the location, name on the headstones either side of the grave that Parkes dug. Decide which two graves you'll visit, remember the details and give the list back to me. Get one of the night vision goggles and a spare battery from the table in my room. I want you set off once it's dark and check on those two locations. I don't think they'll be under observation as it would be impossible for all the thirty or so sites to be kept under constant surveillance. Of course, if the capsules have been discovered, it is possible that the five sites could be. Make sure, then, that you park a long way from the graveyards and approach across fields where possible. Take your time, don't rush, and use the night vision kit to make sure no one is there before you check the grave. And take a thin rod with you to probe the ground. That way you'll leave no visible sign you've been there and you can be in and out quickly."

After Ginger returned with the night vision goggles, he turned to beckon Charlie, Mike and Bill to gather round him. He spoke urgently as he gave them precise instruction for their next task. After ensuring that they knew exactly what they had to do, he told them to make all the necessary preparations and be prepared to move when he gave the word. As the three men left the room, John went into the computer room and carefully checked the screen which displayed the whereabouts of Justin's van. Satisfied he called Charlie back to him and told him to get his men together and leave immediately.

He needed information, he needed it quickly and he was going to make sure he got it. Nothing, or nobody, he determined with icy resolve, would get in his way or stop him carrying out the mission he had been tasked with. Confident that he had done all that was necessary, he waited patiently for the return of his men.

After Justin had finished his burger, he relaxed, sipping his coffee, and watching the

Christmas shoppers bustling about the mall laden with bags and packages. He noted how few of them looked happy or at ease. Instead, nearly everyone had a strained and impatient expression as they swerved and dodged through the crowded walkways. Justin smiled inwardly as he leaned back in his chair with the pleasing knowledge that his Christmas shopping was over and, as an added bonus, he had the rest of the week off with no work in hand. Despite all the shocks of the past few days, along with some physical discomfort, much of his innate cheerfulness started to return and, with something of a spring in his step, he walked slowly back to the ticket machine to pay his parking charge before returning to his van and zig-zagging down the exit ramps to the barrier where he inserted his parking ticket before the barrier lifted allowing him to ease out into the line of cars on Raven Meadows.

The traffic was dense as he expected and it was a crawl up Castle Street and left along St. Mary's Street before he was able to pick up some speed down Wyle Cop and across the English Bridge back to the supermarket where, with some difficulty, eventually found a free parking bay. Justin never ceased to be amazed at how early people started to do their food shopping before bank holidays.

He recalled a job he had some years previously, driving for a mushroom farmer at Hinstock. He took lorry loads to supermarket distribution depots in Chepstow and Filton near Bristol and the first time he saw how much food was being delivered for Easter, he was utterly amazed. He asked the goods-in supervisor if this was normal, only to be assured that it was, and that he also was at a loss to understand why more food was necessary. After all, the supervisor reasoned, if you entertain obviously you will need more food, but then, as a direct consequence, the people being entertained would need less. So therefore, he told Justin, it should balance out. He shrugged his shoulders as he waved his hand across the bays where an extra fifty percent of his usual deliveries was piled high, then at the extra mushrooms in Justin's load, as he added how he couldn't understand why anyone would buy mushrooms eight days before Christmas knowing they would be useless by the time they were needed. Justin smiled ruefully at the recollection as he made the decision that he deserved a drink after all his travails. With difficulty he made his way through the crowded aisles of the supermarket to buy some of his favourite lager from the chiller cabinet.

By the time he left the store it was quite

dark and the evening mist was filled with the headlight beams of the slow moving traffic. He dodged between cars to reach the other side and ran up the steps into the entrance hall of his building and quickly up the stair to his flat. This was done deliberately as he had found out that if he moved quickly enough when he came in, he was able to beat old Mrs. Williams to her front door and thus escape the iron grip of her enforced conversations. He heard her door open and her querulous voice urgently call his name, but by this time he was round the turn of the stairs and out of sight. He felt a bit mean as she wasn't a bad old stick but today he didn't feel like talking with anyone. He just wanted to shower away all the problems of the past, change into clean clothes and have a few beers in front of the television.

At the top of the stairs he slowed down and took the door key out of his coat pocket before letting himself into the safe haven of his flat. He had left the central heating on and a welcome waft of warmth met him as he eased out of his parka, juggling the cans of lager from hand to hand as he did so, and then hanging his coat on a peg behind the front door. Walking into the kitchen he switched on the light and put his purchases down on the kitchen worktop. Just as he did so, he caught a movement out of the corner of his eye. Before he could turn to fully face the threat he received a tremendous blow to his solar plexus. Not for nothing is it called the abdominal brain as, just like a blow to the head, a blow to the solar plexus can render the victim unconscious or, at the very least, incapable of movement. So it was with Justin, as a pain he had never before experienced doubled him up, followed by it radiating outwards through his entire body until his legs ceased to do what his brain told them and he collapsed, helpless, on the floor of the kitchen. Through pain misted eyes he was vaguely aware of two pairs of legs approaching him as he was roughly yanked upwards by his arms as he heard one of his assailants speak unbeknown to him into his mobile phone.

"Okay, Bill, we've got him. Bring it round to the front." He gave Justin arm a powerful shake. "Now, Justin, me lad, someone want a word with you and we're the kind people who are going to give you a lift to where he is." He gave another violent shake to Justin's arm. "We're going to pretend you are drunk and as your concerned friends we are giving you a lift. Nod your head if you've got that."

Despite still being in crippling pain and still finding it difficult to breath, Justin managed to nod that he understood as he was carried down the stairs by Charlie and Mike and out of the front door where their Ford people carrier was stopped with Bill behind the wheel holding up the traffic. The pavement was busy with people who, in the main, kept their heads down at the sight of someone being helped by two burly men into a waiting vehicle. To allay any suspicions the two men kept up their pretence of helping an inebriated friend telling him he shouldn't have drunk so much and laughing and joking as they manhandled him across the pavement and through the open passenger door and into the waiting vehicle.

As the door slammed shut and the vehicle drove forward Justin, still bent over and in considerable pain, was suddenly pulled forward and forced into the foot well between the seats. His arms were wrenched behind his back and he was aware that a tight ligature was put round his two wrists with a clicking noise. Even in his bemused state, he knew that a cable tie had been used to pinion him and he winced as the thin plastic strap dug into his flesh and grunted as two pairs of heavy feet stamped down onto his legs and back forcing his face into the dusty carpet.

"There you are, old son," said a voice, "all nice and comfy down there, we hope."

Justin heard the mocking laughter from the three men and wondered whether he was going to throw up. He swallowed hard as he feared he would get a beating if he vomited in their car, and was relieved when the feeling passed. The men were silent as the car picked up speed once it reached Wenlock Road and the traffic thinned. Justin tried to work out where they were heading but soon gave up as the effort made him feel sick again. After about a quarter of an hour, by his estimation, the vehicle slowed, turned right bumping along a roughly surfaced track and, after a short uncomfortable time, drew to a stop when the driver switched off the engine. Justin's head was pulled back and a cloth bag was put over his head, before he was dragged along the floor and onto his feet in the cold darkness when, with unsteady feet, he was marched with his arms painfully gripped, a few paces before tripping over what turned out to be the threshold of the door he had been taken through.

Once inside he was walked unsteadily further into the building where his escorts stopped and pulled the bag off his head. Justin looked at the person standing in front of him. With a sick feeling he saw it was John and, as he looked into those dark soulless eyes, the sinking feeling hit him like a physical blow in the pit of his stomach and turned into one of will-sapping terror. Justin knew he was in deep trouble but the one thought that buoyed him up was the knowledge that Commander Baxendale's men would be aware that he had been taken and would find him with the tracker Maggie had put in his coat.

Then, with a feeling of utter horror which hit him like a hammer blow, followed by an all consuming hopelessness, he remembered that he wasn't wearing his coat. He'd taken it off when he entered the flat and it was still on the peg where he put it. Still sending out a signal that he was safely there. His despair must have shown on his face as John stepped closer to him.

"Ah, I see that you have realised what a difficult situation you are in, Justin." His voice took on a sinister chill. "I want some answers from you and you can be sure that I will get them and that you will give them. But it is up to you whether you whether the truth is extracted painfully or not. Do you understand?"

Before Justin could reply, John had delivered a vicious straight fingered blow to his solar plexus. This time the pain was so great that he lost consciousness and would have fallen senseless to the floor if he hadn't been held by Charlie and Mike. At what seemed an age later, Justin slowly dragged himself out of the darkness as a bucket or water was thrown in his face and he slowly regained his vision from the floor where he had been dropped, to see a ring of laughing faces looking down at him. But he could see that John wasn't laughing and, as those cold black eyes drilled into him, Justin realised that he had a choice to make. He could do what he had done all his life, go for the easy way out and tell John everything he wanted to know. On the other hand, he could hold out for as long as possible, though he wondered for how long he could resist without giving away anything.

Looking into those soulless eyes, Justin wasn't sure he could hold out forever and, if he could, he came to the horrific conclusion that he would probably die under torture as John would have no further use for him once he had got what he wanted. Then, despite the pain he was in clouding his thinking, he came to the ghastly realisation that, even if he told John everything he wanted to know, he would still have no further use for him and he would be killed. His despair plunged even lower at the realisation of the ghastly plight he found himself in. If only, he thought, if only I'd just kept my coat on when I entered the flat I'd have been rescued by now. Then the low sinister tones of John's voice broke through into his thoughts.

"Justin, my boy, I want some answers. If you co-operate with me, then you'll live to a ripe old age. If you don't, then you won't leave here alive. Understand?" He continued as Justin nodded with pain clouded eyes. "I want you to tell me who you are working for. Then you will tell me what your organisation knows about me. Right, now start talking."

Justin understood all too well. He understood that he hadn't a cat in hell's chance of getting out of there alive, and he again reminded himself with chilling clarity that with his tracker in the flat there was no possibility of being rescued. Just as he felt he had reached the very nadir of despair, a feeling of defiance rose up from within him. It was something which he had never experienced before and as this sensation of moral courage diffused itself throughout his being, he determined that whatever John could throw at him he would resist until his body could take no more. He raised his head and looked directly at John.

"Now, Justin," John continued quietly, "I also want to know more about this girlfriend of yours, Maggie. I know that she's in the Metropolitan Police Ant-Terrorist unit. Did you know all along that she was working undercover?"

"No, I didn't." Justin took a deep breath as he met directly John's unwavering eyes. "In fact, I don't believe she is. With a sudden surge of courage, Justin spat out. "But more to the point, you murdering little shit, why did you kill Caesar?"

Justin's head snapped to one side as John slapped his face hard, and then snapped back again as his hand delivered a powerful back-hander across the other side of his face. Justin's head rang with the force of the blows, and his senses swam as trickle of blood ran down from the corner of his mouth and down his chin where it dripped slowly onto the wooden floor.

Dear me, Justin," John said in his flat emotionless monotone, "you have to learn that I ask the questions and you give the answers I want to hear. Now, you can stop pretending. This Maggie was recognised by one of my men as being a member of the Anti-Terrorist unit. I want to know whether you have been working with them all along. And I want to know just what information you have been feeding them. I want answers, Justin, or pain will make you speak."

A surge of defiant anger coursed through Justin as he thrust his head forward. "When I look at you I see a carbuncle on a pig's backside and a brain the size of an ant. Ask all you want, you little twat. You'll get nothing out of me."

John smiled thinly at the insults. He had been through all this before during the interrogation and torture sessions with MOIS. He had seen the courage of some of his victims and had listened to the defiant insults a few had thrown at him, but in the end the most brave had eventually been broken by the relentless scourge of the fiendish torments inflicted on them, as John had listened with satisfaction to their incoherent pleas for mercy. Justin, he knew would be no different.

Turning to Chalky, John quietly gave him instructions, before turning back to face Justin. Suddenly his mobile vibrated in his pocket. With no change in his expression, John turned away and looked at the screen to read the terse message in capital letters: *ABORT.* Without showing any sign of alarm or urgency he led the way out of the sitting room and up the stairs to the bathroom with Justin being manhandled after him. Telling the three men to wait he went swiftly to his bedroom where he had his case already packed with the cash, pistol and travel documents. He left the case out of sight just inside the door to his room and returned to the bathroom.

There Justin had watched as the deep old-fashioned bath in the centre of the room was slowly being filled with water. His stomach gave a lurch as he knew with certainty what he would have to endure.

"Ah, I see you know what is in store for you." John has been closely observing Justin and had noted that flash of horror when he had seen the bath. "This is your last chance, Justin. I want to know everything about your association with Maggie and the anti-terrorist police."

Justin knew that it wouldn't matter what he told John, he was going to be tortured until John was sure that there was nothing left he could tell him. He didn't see any point in delaying the inevitable and so said nothing. John waited for a few seconds and, when it was evident that Justin was not going to speak, turned to his men.

"Right, Charlie," he said in his normal controlled voice. "I'm going downstairs to the computer room. Once there's enough water to drown our friend, you can start on him. Give me a shout when he's ready to talk."

As Charlie nodded with a grin on his face, John walked out of the bathroom and, out of sight, picked up his suitcase and a set of night vision goggles from his bedroom. Walking quickly but silently down the stairs and along the inner hall to the kitchen, he walked out into the cold darkness of the December night. Swiftly crossing the yard he paused briefly at the barn doors whilst he put the night vision goggles on before letting himself into the barn where threw his case into a small Ford hatchback which was parked in front of the rear exit.

John had anticipated all that could go wrong in this operation and had resolved that he would never be caught. To this end he had put everything in place to ensure his survival and freedom. He allowed himself a feeling of satisfaction as he opened the barn doors and returned to his car. He fired the engine and, with the engine barely above tick over, started to drive carefully away across the fields along the escape route which Charlie had shown him when he arrived at the farmhouse. There had been flurries of snow from the heavy overcast but it had now changed to a steady downpour which the wipers cleared as John peered into the darkness through his night-vision goggles.

Back in the bathroom, Justin and watched with a sick feeling in his stomach as the bath was filled nearly to the brim. With a nod from Charlie, Justin was dragged to the end of the bath and pushed backwards into the icy cold water. He felt his legs being held as Charlie and Bill pushed his body down until the water had closed over his face and he saw their grinning faces indistinctly through the water that covered him. Even in his desperate predicament, Justin realised that he wasn't going to be killed immediately as John wanted him to talk, but he was aware that he was going to be drowned and resuscitated repeatedly until he gave him what he wanted. He held his breath for as long as he could until, with lungs bursting, released the air in one explosive burst. Despite his desperate struggles, he was held down until he had to breath in. The pain as the cold water filled his lungs was indescribable and as his breathing reflex continued to pump the water in and out he felt a remote feeling overtake him and, with his struggles weakening, he slid eventually beyond pain into a deep blackness.

How long he was released from his suffering, Justin didn't know, but he slowly regained awareness bent forward over the end of the bath as a searing pain followed the emptying of water from his tortured lungs onto the bare boards beneath his head. Coughing and retching he painfully dragged in the life-saving air he desperately craved then, just as he regained full consciousness, he was pulled face-up and pushed back into the horror of the unforgiving water where again he went through the increased agonies of suffocation by drowning. Before he slid down once again into the dark tunnel of oblivion, Justin wondered how long he could hold out and came to the agonising realisation that he hadn't the bodily strength to take any more. Once he had been revived, he knew he would tell John all he wanted.

Justin came to again bent double over the end of the bath and through pain clouded vision saw the pool of water spreading outwards on the floor as the water from his agonised lungs once again poured out of his mouth and nose. He tried to speak to tell John that he'd talk now, but only a strangulated hoarse noise came out of his mouth. Through the fog of pain he became aware of raised voices in the distance, followed by feet thundering up the stairs and before anyone could react, the bathroom door opened and Justin dimly saw two round black objects thrown in and the door slammed shut as they bounced as though in slow motion across the floor. Within seconds there was bright flash which seared his eyeballs and destroyed what vision he had left, followed by a deafening succession of cracks as two concussion grenades exploded. Justin's ravaged body, already at the limit of his endurance, could take no more and, with merciful speed, he slid back down the dark tunnel of oblivion far from the pain which coursed through him.

Justin had no idea for how long he had been unconscious. With eyes which had difficulty focussing, he saw orange flames flickering in front of him and wondered if the house was on fire and he was going to be burned to death. Slowly, as his vision started to return, he became aware that he was lying on his side in the recovery position in front of a blazing fire piled high with logs. Someone had put a duvet around him, which had become soaked from his wet clothing, and was steaming from the heat of the fire. Though he felt relief that he was still alive, it was somewhat overshadowed by the pain which started its relentless coursing through his body. He slowly focused on someone kneeling by his head, and eventually realised it was the familiar figure of Commander Baxendale which peered down at him with a concerned expression on his face which sported a magnificent black eye and a swollen lip.

"Welcome back, Justin," said the Commander gently, putting a reassuring hand on his shoulder, "you had us worried for a while. Don't try to speak, now. Two of my men are going to take you to hospital for a check-up and hopefully a good night's sleep. I've work to do here but I'll see you tomorrow when you're feeling better."

Justin couldn't have spoken if he wanted to as his voice was nothing more than a hoarse whisper from the shock of drowning. He nodded mutely as the Commander detailed a sergeant and a constable from his team to take Justin out to a waiting Land Rover Discovery, and was grateful for the reassurance of their strong arms which part carried, part walked, him out of the house and helped him into the vehicle parked outside. He was even more grateful when the driver put the heating on full when he noticed Justin shivering uncontrollably from shock. Justin was surprised when the driver took them over a field and onto the main road through a farm gate and, as he accelerated up the road, vaguely heard him explain that the track to the house had been blocked by some fallen trees and he had to use the field to leave. Despite slipping in and out of consciousness, Justin was aware of the blaring of the two tone horns and the blue flashing lights of the police vehicle reflecting off the passing traffic as they entered the outskirts of Shrewsbury. Expecting to be taken to the Royal Shrewsbury Hospital, Justin was taken aback some five minutes later when the Discovery drew up at the entrance to the Nuffield private hospital onRacecourse Lane.

He was helped from the car by the Sergeant as a nurse and doctor hurried out to meet them at the main entrance. Vaguely, Justin heard the doctor tell the Sergeant that he'd had an urgent call to say they were to receive a VIP by the name of Justin Parkes for check-up and any necessary treatment, and, also that he was to have a twenty-four hour police guard on the door to his room. Once in the foyer Justin was put into a wheelchair and taken in the lift along with the constable who had brought him in, up to the first floor, down a short corridor, and into a large en-suite room.

By this time he was on the point of collapse but had to force himself to stay awake whilst the nurse and the doctor stripped off his wet clothes, dried him with a towel and put him into a pair of pyjamas after which the doctor examined and questioned him. After what seemed an eternity, the doctor was finished, when he was helped into the bliss of a warm bed with crisp white sheets. He vaguely remembered the nurse telling him he wouldn't be disturbed and to get some rest and, despite his aches and pains, he just managed to whisper a thank you to her as his eyes closed and he slipped almost immediately into a deep sleep secure in the knowledge that he was now safe, and there was a police officer outside his door to make sure he stayed that way.

The following morning, Justin slowly surfaced from his slumber to see a weak winter's sun was struggling through the curtains of his room. The events of yesterday seemed like a bad dream, until, by now fully awake, he stretched and discovered that it was all too real as the pain of his damaged body told him. Carefully he tested his limbs and found that the various aches and pains were now just tolerable and that he now felt hungry, which was a good indication of recovery. He decided he would freshen up before his breakfast and very carefully he levered himself up before swinging his legs over the edge of the bed. His head swam and he had to wait for it to clear until he felt confident he could make it to the en-suite. He walked slowly to the wash hand basin after deciding he wouldn't have a shower as he didn't feel he had the strength be able to dry himself, and there washed his face and carefully brushed his teeth trying to avoid the lacerations on the inside of his cheek. He looked at himself in the mirror and saw a haggard face with dark rings round his eyes, and a right cheek which was still puffy after John's vicious backhander from the day before.

Feeling somewhat better after his ablutions, Justin carefully walked to his bed and, after painfully getting back in, pressed the buzzer for attention. Within a minute a smiling nurse entered his room and, after taking his pulse and temperature tidied the bed around him as she told him that the doctor would be along shortly. She laughed when Justin asked if he could have some breakfast informing him he had been asleep for some eighteen hours but, as the next meal would be lunch in an hour, she promised would get someone to bring him a cup of tea shortly. Justin was impressed when an orderly arrived ten minutes later with a tray bearing a pot of tea with milk, sugar and a plate of biscuits, and even more impressed when she poured him out a cup.

He was on his second cup, when there was a knock on the door and a doctor entered accompanied by a nursing sister. After some pleasantries, Justin was given a thorough examination after which the doctor pronounced him fit for discharge later that afternoon if he felt up to it. He also informed Justin that he had been asked to phone Commander Baxendale once he was willing to receive visitors. Justin assured the doctor that he would welcome a visit by the Commander, and at this he was left alone until his lunch arrived an hour later when he set to with a keen appetite and in a short while had cleared his plate of breaded haddock, new potatoes and garden peas, along with the syrup sponge pudding and custard. When he had finished, Justin leaned back in his bed, gave a restrained burp of satisfaction as he started to feel slightly more human and wondered what Commander Baxendale would have to say to him when he arrived.

He hadn't long to wait as, shortly after an orderly had cleared away his lunch tray, there was another rap on the door and the familiar face of Commander Baxendale appeared in the doorway.

"Good afternoon, Justin," he said cheerfully, "My, you are looking well. Amazing what a good night's rest can do. Seriously thought, how are you feeling?"

Justin blew a long slow raspberry at the

commander's words. “How am I feeling, I hear you ask?" He wheezed. "Well, let me see. The inside of my cheek is shredded with the bonus of two loose molars. I have a dinner plate sized bruise on my midriff where I have been viciously bashed twice. My lungs and rib-cage hurt like crazy and my voice is hoarse and weak after being drowned twice, plus my wrists have cuts on them where my friendly abductors used a cable tie to restrain me. Oh, and I nearly forgot, both my shoulders and one knee are hurting where your gorillas in custody tried to dislocate them. Apart from all that, Marcus, I've never felt better.”

The Commander threw back his head and roared with laughter as he pulled up a chair to the side of the bed and sat down. “Good old Justin. You've certainly got some grit. Maggie told me that you would always bounce back quickly after a setback. It's good to see you still have a sense of humour after all you've been through.”

Justin gave a wry smile as he answered with a hoarse whisper. “Marcus, let me assure you that my reserves of humour have just run dry. Now, there are a lot of unanswered questions concerning this mess I've got myself into and I'm looking to you to supply them, and this is the first - did you expect to see me alive again?”

The Commander's face grew serious, and he

pursed his lips before answering. "I've been honest with you from the start, Justin, and I'm not going to change now. We knew there was a distinct possibility that this John could have killed you just as he had your friend Caesar killed. At the same time we did everything possible to keep you from harm. We had you under constant surveillance but we were always hampered by the necessity to ensure that this terrorist cell was unaware that we were on their trail. You remember the court hearing?"

Justin nodded as he listened with interest. "Well, it's unlikely you looked closely at everyone in the public gallery, but we did and we clocked someone on the cctv system who made us suspicious. We watched as he left afterwards and made a phone call on his mobile before driving off, but we couldn't follow him without him being aware that he had a tail. Of course, we could have pulled him in, but by the time we had got the information out of him we wanted, the rest of the cell would have been long gone."

"Let me get this right," Justin said with a furrowed brow as he tried to make sense of what he had been told. "If I was being observed all the time, it must have been obvious that I had been abducted from my flat yesterday when I was dragged out and bundled into that people carrier." A thought suddenly came to him. "In fact, you must have seen the goons who grabbed me go into the building at some stage."

"Yes, we did. It was cleverly done. There were three of them and my men observed them parking their vehicle at the back of the Abbey, before they walked round to your number eleven. Two of them held back as the third went on and climbed the steps up to the front door. It was obvious that they knew the old lady in the downstairs flat sits in her bay window and goes into the hall once she sees someone come in. As soon as she left her vantage point the man at the door turned round and went back to the vehicle which was parked at the back of the Abbey, whilst the other two quickly dashed down the tunnel to the back of the house where they must have managed to open the door to the cellar. Then they must have waited behind the door at the top of the cellar steps until the old lady had gone back inside, and quietly climbed the stairs and let themselves into your flat."

Justin had learned nothing new as he had already worked that scenario out for himself, but there was something which he couldn't work out. He swallowed painfully before asking. "One thing puzzles me greatly, Marcus, how on earth did you manage to find out where I'd been taken. Just before I was grabbed I'd taken off the coat with the tracker in it. You tell me you couldn't follow the vehicle I was in for operational reasons but you managed to rescue me. How?"

"For that, dear boy, you have to thank Maggie." Justin looked in bewilderment as the commander continued with a smile. "I thought that would surprise you but it's the truth. You remember the watch she gave you for your birthday, well it had a dormant tracker in it. Owing to the size constraints, it has a limited range and sleeps until activated as its battery capacity is limited. Once you had been abducted and it was obvious that the tracker in you coat was stationary, we then woke up the one in your watch. We just hoped and prayed that you hadn't taken that off as well."

Justin looked impressed. "So you and your posse of hand-picked hard men thundered off into the sunset to rescue me then."

The Commander shook his head. "No, not us. The danger this cell posed meant that this operation was controlled at the highest governmental level and they had on stand by an eight man SAS hostage rescue team. Obviously we couldn't give you details about that side of the operation, but I can tell you now that they were on instant readiness in two four wheel drive vehicles waiting on the Abbey council car park. I was at the debrief this morning and it would appear that they followed your tracker using GPS mapping. Once they'd confirmed the building you'd been taken to, they drove across the fields using their night vision equipment and split into two sticks of four. One went in through the front door, the other through the back into the kitchen and they had the place secured within minutes. You might find this hard to believe, but both doors were unlocked and didn't have to be blown to gain entry."

"Tell me Marcus," Justin asked, "just before those grenade things were thrown in to the bathroom, I thought I heard some popping noises. Was it gunfire?"

"Yes, it was. Surprisingly, no one in the building was armed. But one of the terrorists downstairs was in front of a monitor when the room with the computer equipment was entered. He was told to lie down but decided to reach across and trigger a switch at the end of the table. He was shot dead but not before he had set off some explosive charges which brought down two trees effectively blocking the track to the farmhouse."

"Ah, now I understand," said Justin as realisation dawned on him, "what the driver said to me as he took me to hospital. I wasn't with it, as you know, but he mentioned trees down and we had to leave through a field. What about the others, especially this John."

The Commander looked pleased as he replied. "Apart from the demolition man who was shot, we captured three others relatively uninjured. A sweep of the farmhouse revealed that there were seven beds, all of which had been slept in. We deduce from this that there are two others who had been sent on a mission of some sort, so the SAS put in a stop group by the fallen trees on the track. They weren't disappointed, as a van turned up at about one in the morning and two very surprised men were arrested. But these six were just the foot soldiers. We were especially interested in this John character and, after putting his image through our facial recognition programme, our suspicions were confirmed. Your John, as he like to be called, is in fact Bahadur Najafi and we have had him flagged for some years as a MOIS operative. He's clever, resourceful and very dangerous officer in the Iranian secret intelligence services, and had been deployed here as the leader of this cell, and as we now know, part of a bigger international operation."

Justin let out a long slow whistle as he took in this revelation. "So without realising I've been a part of an international terrorist plot and, what is more, have managed to survive the experience thanks to the experts who had been sent to protect me. I owe you all a big thank you."

But just as he spoke, Justin held up his hand and looked at the Commander with a confused expression. "Hold on a minute Marcus. Maths isn't my strong point but something doesn't add up here." Justin started to count on his fingers. "One shot dead and three more captured in the farmhouse makes four." He bent two more fingers down into his palm. "Then you say two more were picked up in the track to the farmhouse in the early hours, which makes six. Lastly, you say that there were seven beds slept in. Marcus, old fruit, you have been suspiciously quiet about number seven. There's something else you are going to tell me, aren't you?"

Commander Baxendale looked grimly at Justin. He slowly let out his breath before replying. "Yes, there is, but you've beaten me to it. This John character managed to get away. We searched the farmhouse from top to bottom – in fact, we pulled it apart in case there was a concealed space built in - but found nothing. We did the same with all the out buildings. Again, nothing."

Justin felt anger welling up inside him. "God all bloody mighty, Marcus," he wheezed, "this is the bastard who wants to kill me, and the entire resources of the intelligence services and the police have let him escape. What the sodding hell are you lot up to."

Realising that Justin was still in a fragile state after his ordeal, the Commander spoke gently. "Justin, I'm sorry to be the bearer of bad news. But try and see our side of things. You're aware of the importance of ensuring that this terrorist cell didn't know they were under surveillance, so we had to hold back until they moved. Once we saw you being abducted we put the rescue plan into operation and it worked well. But we couldn't put in armed stop groups as we didn't know the location of where you were being taken until the last minute. Remember, even though the farmhouse was only fifteen minutes away it was impossible to mobilise in time to stop Bahadur Najafi escaping."

Justin scratched his head. "Still confused, Marcus. If this John escaped he must have had warning of the raid. If that's correct, why didn't the others take off as well?"

"That's simple, Justin. We know he must have had a warning from someone – just who, we don't yet know – but knowing how this John works, we are certain that the six members of his cell were not going to be allowed to live to tell tales. Fortunately for them he had to take off so quickly he wasn't able to eliminate them." The Commander felt he ought to shift the conversation onto safer ground. "But coming back to you and your actions, Justin, it's we who owe you a big thank you. It is quite likely that without your decision to help us, and putting your life at risk in the process, we may never have discovered this Najafi and his cell in time to prevent a national catastrophe. Don't worry, Justin, he'll soon be rounded up and I'll let you know once he's safely behind bars."

"Thanks, Marcus. Sorry I blew my top. I'm still a bit on edge." There was something which had baffled Justin for some time. "Marcus, tell me, do you know why John wanted to know about some of the single and reopen graves I'd dug? I racked my brains but haven't a clue how the information was of use to him. Did you ever find out?"

"We did, indeed. Before I continue you must understand that there is a high degree of security around this whole operation and the full details are only available to a few who need to know, so I am constrained in what I can reveal to you. But if you give me your word that you will not repeat a word of what I say to another living person, I'll go off message and tell you what your actions have helped us to avert."

Justin met the Commander's eyes and nodded and replied hoarsely. "You have my word,

Marcus. Go on, I'm all ears"

The Commander hesitated, considering carefully just how much he could reveal to Justin. "You'll be aware that we went through the farmhouse with a detailed search team and were not surprised to find very little of an incriminating nature. There were no arms and ammunition or anything of a subversive nature - apart from the explosive charges on the trees along the approach track to the farm. But we did find paperwork for a Post Office Box number at the Shrewsbury sorting office. We immediately sent two officers there and they were able to bring back a small package. It was felt be prudent not to open it as it could quite possibly be booby trapped and, having planned for all eventualities, we had an Army Air Corps Gazelle on instant readiness at RAF Shawbury which took the package to Porton Down in a high security chest. You know the place, it's the chemical and biological testing establishment in Wiltshire, and it was taken immediately to their Super Toxic department."

Justin was intrigued. "And just what was in that package, are you allowed to tell me?"

"Sorry, Justin, I can't. But this much I can to say. When the chest was opened under highly controlled conditions it was found to contain a black plastic container about the size of a thick paperback novel. What was interesting was there were no metal parts which could be picked up by a metal detector and, even more intriguing, it was coated with a highly sophisticated substance which made it impervious to radar detection. It's like the coating, only a great deal more advanced, put onto stealth fighter aircraft which absorbs radar beams, and this would have made it invisible to any ground penetrating radar equipment."

The Commander lowered his voice and leaned towards Justin. "But it was what was found inside which was chilling. I can't tell you exactly what was discovered when the contents of the glass container which fitted inside underwent initial analysis, but this much I can say. Even at this early testing stage it was clear that the substance inside was a biological agent of such appalling virulence that, had it been deployed, it would have led to the deaths of hundreds of thousands, and quite possible, millions of innocent civilian. We calculate from the information we have that this atrocity was planned to take place on Christmas Eve or Christmas Day. You may draw your own conclusions from the timing."

Justin's face had turned pale at the Commander's revelation. "But where do my graves fit in all this," he asked, his voice strained and weak with shock of what he had heard.

"I see this has hit you hard, Justin. I'm sorry. But there is some good news. When we searched the computer room we discovered a piece of paper with details of five of the graves which you had passed on to him. We sent men out to them and discovered five more of these containers. You told me you had gone out to check on one grave to see where, if at all, something had been hidden. Although nothing was hidden in the grave you checked, you would have found nothing even if one had been, as the containers had been cleverly secreted under the turf at the foot of each grave. There was nothing to be seen by the naked eye. Nothing to show up with any electronic detection equipment. In short, Najafi had found a method of concealment, and retrieval, which was as close to foolproof as any."

"So you've found six containers," said Justin as the colour slowly returned to his cheeks, "but how do you know there are no more?"

"We don't for sure. But we're fairly certain there are only six. We have the details on all the graves you've dug since Najafi made contact and, as we speak, they are all being checked out. As there are some thirty or so it is obviously going to take some time"

Justin pondered for a moment. "From what you've told me, it would appear that John, Najafi or whatever, was working directly under orders from the Iranian government. Is that a reasonable assumption?"

The Commander gave a snort. "Well, let me put it this way. Our government has approached the Iranian Ministry for Foreign Affairs over this serious matter directly concerning one of their nationals, and they responded with almost indecent alacrity. They've assured us that they have no knowledge of this Bahadur Najafi and that he must be a rogue element from whom the Iranian government completely disassociates itself. Ignoring the contradiction in their statement, it is exactly the response we expected."

Justin took a deep breath as he remained silent whilst the full import of the Commander's words sunk in. The planned outrage was a scenario which chilled him to the core, as had the unwelcome news that this John was still at large, but following that there welled up within him a feeling of deep gratitude at his deliverance from the evil in which he had been unwittingly involved. Then a stab of conscience made him painfully aware that none of this would have happened if he had not succumbed to greed. He tried to remember the seven deadly sins he had been taught in Sunday school. What number was greed – three, four? He couldn't recall, but felt it didn't really matter as, with a new and steely determination, he resolved that that part of his nature was banished for ever. He woke from his reverie as there was a knock on the door and a nurse entered the room.

"Sorry to interrupt," she said with a smile, as she placed a stack of neatly folded clothes on the armchair in the corner of the room. "Here are your clothes all nice and dry. What on earth were you up to yesterday. Did you go for a swim in the Severn?"

Justin gave a short laugh. "Yes, sort of, but not by choice I can assure you," he joked back.

"Doctor said you are fit to leave when you want but there is no hurry if you need to stay longer," the nurse informed him as she left the room closing the door quietly behind her.

By now Justin had recovered much of his cheery nature and looked at the Commander with a twinkle in his eye. "Y'know, Marcus, there was a time when I didn't like you one bit. But for some inexplicable reason I'm beginning to take a shine to you. In fact, I can now see that you are actually human."

"That's a huge relief," he said with a laugh, replying in the same vein. "I couldn't bear the thought of going through the rest of my life knowing you didn't like me. Now, if we can be serious, what do you want to do now?"

"I just want to be back in my flat, licking my

wounds and downing a well-earned lager. You any good for a lift?"

"Of course. I'll run you back and see you safely into your lair. I have to keep a close eye on you as you appear to have a habit of getting into scrapes. Oh, by the way, nearly forgot. My boys have gone through your flat and removed all the bugs and cleaned your computer. They found the hard drive so corrupted that they had to replace it. The good news is that they managed to save just about all your files, e-mails and your address book. Also, your van is now clean with all the trackers removed."

"That's a relief," said Justin, "but there is one more thing. What about the men you arrested. What's happened to them?"

"By now they should be safely behind bars in Paddington Green police station. The interrogators down there are leaning on the six men of his team and don't expect they'll have too much trouble getting them to talk. However, as Najafi's foot soldiers, we strongly suspect that they know very little of the operation they were involved in and we won't get anything of value from them. Anyway, you're safe now, and, what's more your stay here is on us. We thought it was the least we could do to put you up in five star accommodation after all you've been through. Also, it was easier for us to keep you under guard."

“Thanks, Marcus. So all that is left is to relax and get better.”

“Not quite all.” The Commander pushed his chair back and stood up. “There's the small matter of Maggie's belongings. She came in with the men who debugged your flat, but as you'd made it plain you didn't want her to collect anything unless you were there, she left all her things where they were. She asks, can she come round tomorrow, about ten o'clock if that's all right with you?”

“Yes, tell her that'll be fine. Better still I'll text her when I'm back home. If you'll excuse me now I'll get freshened up and into my togs. Won't be long.”

The Commander left saying he would wait in the reception foyer, whilst Justin went into the en-suite to wash and comb his hair. He looked at himself in the mirror to see a face still furrowed with all he had been through staring back at him. His cheek was puffy where John had back-handed him and the dark rings under his eyes appeared to be getting darker. He tried to work out what day it was and eventually calculated it was Thursday. Only Thursday, he thought as he shook his head in disbelief. Since the previous Saturday he had discovered the murdered body of his friend, been arrested for murder, realised the love of his life had deceived him and appeared in court and bailed. Then, as if that that wasn't enough, he had been abducted and tortured within an inch of his life. Bloody hell, he thought, all that in only five days. Well, he decided, there is one thing for certain which has come out of all this. The old Justin is gone for ever, and a new, stronger and better Justin has taken his place.

Buoyed with this encouraging inner revelation, Justin patted his face dry and after dressing went down to reception where he found the Commander reading a magazine. Justin asked him to wait a moment longer whilst he thanked the staff who had looked after him. Once the farewells were over, he settled himself into the Commander's Jaguar at the front of the building and, within ten minutes driving through light traffic, they drew up in the supermarket car park opposite his flat. Unsurprisingly, as they approached the steps up the front door, Justin saw old Mrs. Williams rise from her window seat and knew with certainty he would encounter her in the hallway. Sure enough, she was there and as she looked at Justin's face she realised that all was not well with him. Instead of talking about herself as usual, an unexpected softer maternal side to her nature showed itself, and Justin was touched when she asked how he was and said that if he wanted anything he only had to ask her. To Mrs. William's total surprise, as Justin thanked her, he bent down and gave her a kiss on the cheek - an act which rendered her incapable of speech and movement as she looked on wide eyed as Justin and the Commander carried on up the stairs.

Once inside, the Commander walked round the entire flat to check everything was in order before taking his leave. Justin thanked him for all his support and warmly shook his hand as they parted. Once Justin had closed the front door behind him, he went back into the kitchen to open the can of lager he had promised himself. The ones he had placed on the worktop before his abduction were still there, but as the central heating had been left on he decided they would be too warm and went to the fridge to get a cold can. As he was about to open the fridge, he saw, on the worktop a carrier bag which he was sure hadn't been left by him. Looking inside he saw it contained a granary loaf, a carton of milk, half a dozen eggs, a spaghetti bolognese ready meal and a four pack of his usual lager. Intrigued, he saw at the bottom of the bag a folded piece of paper which he opened to read; *Justin, I didn't think you would be up to shopping once you got back home. Just a few things to keep you going. Love, Maggie. XX.*

As he read the words, Justin realised with a jolt that although in his head he thought he had got over Maggie and had put their relationship behind him, he knew in his heart that it was not so. His heart told him he still loved her and now knew with certainty that it was a love which would endure for all time, however unrequited it was on her part. He groaned inwardly at the thought that he would see her tomorrow, when a part of him really didn't want her to come and remind him of what could have been, whilst another part of him desperately wanted her to stay. So this is love, he thought.

He recalled that someone had said that if love didn't hurt occasionally, it wasn't true love. He had to agree, as he felt he was being ripped apart by this unresolved affair of the heart. Realising that nothing he could do would alter the fact that Maggie was going to call round tomorrow, he shrugged his shoulders in acceptance, went to the fridge to liberate a can of lager, and toast his first drink of freedom, but not before he had sent her a text saying that ten o'clock tomorrow was fine by him.

The following morning Justin woke to a thin grey light which struggled to penetrate his bedroom curtains and, despite the aches and pains from his ill-treatment the day before, felt much more like his old self and ready to face the day. He levered himself carefully out of bed just as the central heating timer clicked on, and pulled back the curtains to reveal a gloomy scene with dark louring clouds and a fine drizzle relentlessly falling on the few scurrying pedestrians who had to ventured out. He walked gingerly into the shower where he let the hot jet wash over his body for a long time, until his muscles loosened and he felt he had washed away some of the mental and physical pain from the past.

As his spirits rose he began to sing one of his favourite folk songs, but soon stopped when he realised that his voice was still hoarse and painful from his drowning at the hands of John's men. Despite the physical trauma, Justin felt he was on the mend. True, his midriff was still stiff and painful if he twisted his torso, as were his neck muscles from when his head had been snapped from side to side with John's blows. He checked the inside of his mouth and found the painful swelling had gone down, although the two pre-molars were still loose. His chest was sore from inhaling the cold water of his immersions but, like his voice, all the symptoms were starting to ease. Even his strained shoulders were almost better and for all this he was grateful as he had to look ahead to his next commission to dig a grave, then realised with a start that he hadn't checked his e-mails to see if anything had come in from an undertaker. First things first, he decided, as he slowly and carefully dressed before going into the kitchen, where he turned up the central heating before sitting down to enjoy his toast and coffee.

Once finished, and with the washing up done and dried, he checked his watch and saw that it a quarter to ten. He considered whether he should pile all Maggie's belongings together before she arrived, then decided that it might look a bit unfeeling on his part if she saw everything stacked as though he couldn't wait to get her out of the flat as quickly as possible. Having made up his mind, Justin settled back in his armchair to wait.

Just after ten o'clock he heard Maggie's familiar footsteps on the landing, followed by the trill of the door bell being rung. As he went to open the door, Justin struggled with the ludicrous dilemma of how he ought to greet her. Should he give her a brief peck on the cheek, or would it be better if he formally shook hands. His indecision was resolved when upon opening the door Maggie took the initiative by warmly embracing him with a kiss on the cheek. Without needing to think about it, Justin had returned the embrace and the kiss as the most natural thing to do. Maggie spoke first.

“Hello, Justin, good to see you again.” she said, releasing her arms from around Justin who stood mute and unmoving in front of her. She giggled with her hand over her mouth. “Well, are you going to ask me in or do I have to conduct my business from here? This is becoming a habit, you know!”

Justin recovered himself and apologetically stood back to let Maggie enter. He had been overwhelmed at the powerful response her presence had produced in him, but not altogether surprised as he was well aware that his love for her existed unabated. He picked up the two large cases that she had put down when they embraced.

“Sorry, I was dreaming. Can I take your coat. Let me take the suitcases. You'll be stopping for a coffee. Won't you?” Realising he was once again gabbling away like a lovestruck teenager, Justin pulled himself together and led Maggie into the sitting room where they sat down in separate armchairs.

“Commander Baxendale told me what you'd been through,” said Maggie with genuine concern in her voice. “How are you feeling now, Justin?”

“Thanks for asking, Maggie. In fact, loosely speaking, I'm feeling surprisingly well. Obviously, you know what was done to me and it was pretty grim, but being relatively young and fit, not to mention stunningly good looking, I consider I've come through everything without any lasting damage. Good of your boss to put me up in a private hospital, though."

"I can see you've picked up," she replied with a warm smile. She hesitated as she hunted around for the right words. "Justin, love, I know I've hurt you and I think I can understand how you feel, but I want you to know that I'm terribly fond of you and have never wanted to see you in any danger. I'm truly relieved that you have come through everything in reasonably good condition, if I can put it that way."

"Yes, I know, Maggie." At that moment Justin wanted to tell her of his love for her and ask if their relationship could be rekindled, but something made him hold back. He knew it wasn't the right time, if, indeed, there ever would be a right time. "You know my feelings for you, and they haven't changed one bit. Let me put you mind at rest and tell you that I bear you no ill-will whatsoever. Does that help?"

"Yes it does, Justin." She found herself unexpectedly moved by his words and pretended to look for something in her handbag for a moment to hide her face before recovering.

"I went to see Lynn earlier this morning. She said you'd been in touch a few days ago, so I brought her up to date and told her about your abduction and subsequent ill treatment.

She sends her best wishes for a speedy recovery and says to get in touch when you feel well enough. She told me that Caesar's post mortem will be carried out shortly and then the undertaker can take over with all the arrangements. She asked if I would be at the funeral, and I told her I would without fail."

"Lynn did talk about it when I saw her last." said Justin. "I'm glad you are going to be at the funeral. I suppose you can make the wake as well. It'll be at the Castle she said and, with any luck, Len will be able to remember it," he joked.

The initial awkwardness now gone, they chatted in a relaxed fashion as Justin made Maggie the coffee he had offered and, once finished, set about packing her belongings into the two suitcases and the large plastic carrier bags which she had inside them. It didn't take long for her to pack up all her things and, once done, she and Justin carried the suitcases and bags out of the building, into the cold drizzle and over the road to where she had parked her car. There she dropped the back seat of the hatchback and allowed Justin to pack everything neatly on the exposed deck. Closing the tailgate, she turned to Justin and, under the beady gaze of old Mrs. Williams seated in her usual place in her window opposite the car park, they warmly embraced each other.

Maggie gave Justin a hesitant kiss on the lips which, after a second he returned before they stood back from each other and said their goodbyes. Justin waited, oblivious to the rain, until he gave one last wave as she drove out onto Abbey Foregate and out of sight. Walking back across the road the rain had turned to sleet and he was glad of his parka he had put on before leaving the flat. A sudden thought came to him. Was the tracking device which Maggie had secreted behind the lining was still there. Feeling round the hem he found it still in place and realised that she must have forgotten to retrieve it, and the crew who came to clear the flat must have missed it as well. Well, not to worry, he determined, I can give it to her when I see her at Caesar's funeral.

Caesar's funeral on the third of January had managed to coincide with one of those rare winter days when the sun, although still lacking warmth, shone out of a cloudless pale blue sky. There was not a breath of wind to be felt and together the conditions managed to bring some measure of cheer to the sombre gathering at the Shrewsbury crematorium. Justin had determined that he didn't want to arrive at the crematorium in a works van and so had arranged a lift with some of the folk club regulars. As he, along with many from the folk scene and Inspector Fischer and colleagues from Lynn's department, waited outside in the cold still air for the funeral cortège to arrive they exchanged small talk in muted tones as the tall leafless trees in the grounds stood motionless in the still clear air.

Justin kept looking round for Maggie's car and was relieved when eventually he saw her drive in. She parked in a free bay at the far end of the visitors' parking area, and walked over to him to greet him with a kiss and an apology for being late owing to an accident on the M54 which reduced the motorway to one lane. Then they stood silently next to each other and waited. Justin looked back at the long line of mourners and saw the rotund figure of Len from the Castle. He was wearing a black suit which appeared to been made when he possessed a slim figure as the jacket buttons strained to contain his ample stomach and his trousers, encircled by a black leather belt, finished at ankle length. Good old Len, Justin thought, but at least he's managed to turn up, and he looks sober.

Finally, and timed to the minute, the dark procession of the cortège swept in from the London Road and slowly drew to a halt under the portico at the front of the crematorium. The funeral director, who was Mr. Percival himself, levered his portly presence out of the front passenger seat of the funeral car and walked round to the back of the hearse where the bearers had already taken Caesar's coffin off the deck and placed it on a wheeled bier. The coffin, Justin noticed, was made from a light coloured wood, with bright brass handles. On top, just below the engraved plaque, was just a single wreath. Lynn had asked that, instead of flowers, donations be made to the Police Widows Fund, for which a collecting box had been placed in the foyer of the crematorium.

When he was satisfied that all was in order, the Mr. Percival walked to the stretch Jaguar and helped out Lynn and her and Caesar's parents, before escorting them to stand behind the waiting coffin. Justin tried to catch Lynn's eye to give her a reassuring smile, but she kept her head down as she stood behind the coffin supported on either side by her mother and father. He could see that she was crying silently, occasionally dabbing her cheeks and eyes with a large white handkerchief.

Slowly the coffin was wheeled inside preceded by a priest whom Justin hadn't noticed before as he was standing inside the entrance foyer just out of sight. With the priest intoning the words of the committal, everyone filed in to the chapel after the coffin and, with Maggie following Justin, they took their places on the hard benches. Justin was somewhat surprised that Lynn had asked a priest to officiate as she and Caesar had never given him any inkling that they had any religious beliefs, but personally he was glad, as he found the positive words of the service gave him comfort. He hoped that they gave Lynn comfort also and the strength to bear up under the sorrow she so plainly felt.

Eventually, the priest concluded the committal service and nodded to the Crematorium Manager who operated buttons on a panel to draw the curtains around the coffin on the catafalque. As solemn music played through the speaker system, the now concealed coffin was propelled along rollers and out of sight. Allowing a respectful pause, Mr. Percival motioned the family towards the exit door where the priest waited to meet all the mourners. Once outside, under a covered walkway, Justin saw Lynn and both sets of parents waiting to greet everyone. Lynn had, by this time collected herself which was not unusual, for once the actual funeral service was over, most bereaved felt a great sense of relief following the completion of possibly one of the most difficult parts of dealing with the death of a loved when they are finally laid to rest.

It was some while before Justin and Maggie along with all the other mourners had filed past Lynn and expressed their condolences and, as everyone talked in small groups in the cold fresh air, they waited until Lynn and the parents had been ushered into the funeral car and driven slowly away. Justin was pleased when Maggie asked him if he wanted a lift with her to the Castle, and he readily agreed, pleased to be close to her for as long as possible. They didn't say much as Maggie drove the short distance to Coleham Head, but the silences were comfortable ones.

At the Castle they found that Len had put on a fine spread which he had laid out on two cloth-covered trestle tables in the spacious function room. Soon he was back in his usual place behind the bar dispensing drinks and cheerful back chat. Justin saw he had removed the restriction of his under-sized jacket to reveal his fine publican's paunch which strained mightily against the restriction of his shirt buttons. Justin wondered how long it would be before he would retire in his cups to a corner seat for one of his regular snoozes, for he had been behind the bar for only five minutes and was already on his second large whisky.

Justin and Maggie went over to sit with Lynn and her parents. As so often happens with the bereaved, once the difficulties of the funeral are over, there comes a time of great relief. And so it was with Lynn as she put her grief behind her for the time being and was talking happily with all around her. Justin asked them what they wanted to drink and, after fighting his way to the bar, brought a tray of drinks back without spilling too much. He passed the drinks around and sat down opposite Maggie.

Something made him look up at her. He found her gazing at him with eyes that radiated that honey-soft glow that only love can bring into being. Their eyes locked for what seemed an eternity as the noise of the room faded into the background and it was then that Justin knew. Knew with certainty, that she loved him in return. Now, he told himself with a feeling of elation coursing through his entire being, everything was going to be all right.

But Justin was wrong. Very wrong. Still on the run his nemesis, Bahadur Najafi known to him as John, was waiting for the moment to wreak revenge. Justin had got the better of him and, he promised himself, would pay for that with his life.

Read how Justin's life is threatened by Bahadur Najafi in the second of the Justin Parkes thrillers entitled:

FIRST DIG TWO GRAVES, available Autumn 2019

THE END

CHARACTERS

MAIN CHARACTERS

Justin Parkes - Main character and gravedigger.

John - Born Bahadur Najafi in Iran. Mastermind of a terrorist plot.

Parents - Father Daichi Najafi in MOIS intelligence and internal security. Mother Nasrin Najafi.

The Colonel - Mahmoud Taqi-Pessain Head of international counter-intelligence MOIS

Lynn Hall - Wife of Caesar. Ex-police officer now civilian crime scene investigator.

Caesar Hall - Real name Vincent. Husband of Lynn. Self-employed joiner.

Maggie Challinor - Sergeant Undercover anti-terrorist metropolitan police officer.

Marcus Baxendale - Commander Met. Anti-terrorist unit and Maggie's superior.

TERRORIST CELL

Charlie aka Junead Hussain - Second in command to John. A trained locksmith.

Ginger - Electronics expert deals with bugging and tracking devices.

Woody - IT expert. Trojan Horses, worms.

Bill - Retired police officer. Specialises in tracking, surveillance & counter-intelligence.

Chalky - Vehicle mechanic.

Mike - Martial arts, survival and explosives expert.

MINOR CHARACTERS

Ali Reysahria - Minister for Intelligence and Security Affairs.

Len - Landlord of The Castle public house.

William Percival - Proprietor of Percival's Undertakers.

Tom Gollins - Embalmer at Percivals.

W.C. Fischer – Inspector i/c crime scene investigation dept. Lynn's boss.

Mrs Williams – Old lady who lives in downstairs flat below Justin.

17468586R00300

Printed in Great Britain
by Amazon